"Kardon, you ever wanted something so bad, it never left you alone?

"It's like when I hear a new tune once in a while, it sits in my head. I work on the harp until I nail it, get it right. This camp is the same. I want to get it out of my head, make it real. When the camp really happens, I'll feel like I've done something."

"Whatever you need, we'll work on it," Jenny said.

"Gonna get after 'em with some hard-core legal mumbo-jumbo?"

Jenny smiled. "Bet your ass," she said.

I shook Jerome's hand and Jenny gave him a short hug. We walked to my SUV in the parking lot carrying the files Jerome had given us. As we got back to the car, there was a new sound, neither the chirping of birds nor the buzz of a machine. Jerome stood silhouetted against a descending sun, surveying his empty eighteenth hole, his harp to his lips. He played a slow, mournful blues dirge, the notes fading slowly in the still air. I'd heard a lot of music over the years, but this was the first time I'd heard an instrument cry.

Other Books by
Jamie Katz

DEAD LOW TIDE

A Summer for Dying

JAMIE KATZ

AVON BOOKS
An Imprint of HarperCollinsPublishers

AVON BOOKS
An Imprint of HarperCollins*Publishers*
10 East 53rd Street
New York, New York 10022-5299

Copyright © 2000 by Jamie Katz
ISBN: 0-06-109712-8
www.avonbooks.com

First Avon Books paperback printing: August 2000

Avon Trademark Reg. U.S. Pat. Off. and in Other Countries, Marca Registrada, Hecho en U.S.A.
HarperCollins® is a trademark of HarperCollins Publishers Inc.

Printed in the U.S.A.

WCD   10   9   8   7   6   5   4   3   2   1

For Cynthia,
who believed from the start

ACKNOWLEDGMENTS

As before, I had considerable help. My thanks to the experts: Jack Escher, Suzanne Fowle, Harvey Katz, Jack Lash, Bob Ritchie, Jim Sperling, and Jack Wofford—all gave me valuable assistance and the mistakes are mine, not theirs. Julie Rold once again did a great job casting a critical eye on my manuscript. Others helped the book as well, particularly my father, Arthur Katz, a born-again writer, who waded through the worst of it, as well as Dan Hammond and Jane Tewksbury. My colleagues at the Attorney General's Office—particularly Judy Yogman and John Hitt—gave me considerable support. A wonderful group of Katz and Piltch family members provided great assistance—a special note of thanks to my mother, Gladys, a librarian who has nurtured a passion for books in so many students, children and grandchildren. My editors, Jennifer Sawyer Fisher and Jessica Lichtenstein, were delightful to work with and improved this book. Ed Breslin is a terrific agent and just as good a friend. And thanks to Lee, who leaves joy and laughter in her wake and allows me occasional leave to write.

Some of the legal processes and procedures described in this book have been deliberately altered for dramatic purposes.

ACKNOWLEDGMENTS

CHAPTER——

ONE

The spotlight glinted off rivulets of sweat running down the smooth, ebony half dome. From the same place came a high-pitched wail, halfway between the squeal of a bagpipe and the keening of a coyote. The sounds came from an immense, bald, black man standing on the small stage in the corner of the bar along with the other members of a band.

He stood at least six feet eight or nine inches tall and wore black jeans and a navy shirt. A gold stud gleamed in his ear and he had a harmonica on his lips. The other five musicians in the band were white, wearing blue jeans or khakis, and stood no more than six feet tall. According to a flyer I noticed on the way in, the band was called Whose Muddy Shoes, a name I guessed they took from an old Elmore James blues tune.

I stood at the back of the bar, watching and listening as the band played a slow ballad. The harmonica player moved rhythmically and gracefully, bending and twisting to the beat. His hands, big enough to palm a newborn baby, instead held the smallest instrument on the stage.

When the song ended, the other musicians talked among themselves but said little to the harmonica player before they started into an old New Orleans standard, "St. James Infirmary." I looked around for Jenny Crane,

1

who had asked me to join her at the bar, but didn't see her so I listened some more. At the end of that tune, the leader, who sang and played electric guitar, announced a break after the next song. He introduced the other members of the band. When he got to the harmonica player, all he said was, "And sitting in with us is Jerome Mann." That got my attention since Mann was the other person I'd come to meet.

The bandleader conferred with Mann for a minute until they nodded to each another. The group started in on "Bad Moon Rising," a Creedence Clearwater Revival chestnut. Within a few bars, the musicians found a new energy. The lead singer filled the microphone with a growling emotion not heard in earlier tunes. The harmonies on the chorus became tighter, more spirited, and the musicians bounced higher on the stage. Then the harp player finally stepped up.

The notes bent around and blurred, soared and stuttered, as Mann alternately caressed and abused his harmonica. He played without acknowledging the crowd, bobbing and weaving with his eyes closed. He danced in and around the melody, then veered into something like the wail of a foghorn. Sweat poured off his face and he played the song as if it was his own personal anthem. Gradually, the other musicians joined in and the band ended with a big finish and generous applause from the audience. The other members gave high-fives to the harmonica player. He gestured to the bar, said something I couldn't hear, and they all laughed. The bandleader announced they'd return later.

Mann pulled a red handkerchief out of his back pocket and dried off his scalp, still glistening. He stepped down and walked through a slalom course of full tables, stopping to chat at two or three of them, then stopped at a booth tucked away in the far corner.

From inside the booth, Jenny rose and gave Mann a hug. She laughed at something he said, he laughed at something she said, and she put a hand on his arm. I started fiddling with the keys in my pocket.

Jenny had called my house at the end of the day and left a message to meet her and Mann here, but I had no idea why. Seeing them greet one another left me no clearer about why Jenny had called but I waded through the room to where she and Jerome sat.

Jenny had come directly from a flight that arrived at Logan Airport in Boston. I'd walked over from my house near Coolidge Corner in Brookline to the bar on Beacon Street, called Mann's Best Hope. Jerome Mann owned the place along with his younger cousin, Daryl Mann, high-priced star of the Boston Shamrocks.

Jenny and I first met the previous September. At the time, she was an out-of-work lawyer. She had just quit a firm where the managing partner prized her body more than her brain. She began work for me in my solo law firm in Boston doing both secretarial and legal work. When Jenny walked in my office door, my enthusiasm for the practice of the law had reached an all-time low. But by the end of a particularly difficult case involving a murder I reluctantly took on, things changed for the better.

Jenny had done good work in the office and quickly graduated from secretary to lawyer. Soon after we met, though, her father suffered a serious stroke. Since then, Jenny had made regular visits to her parents' home in Johnson City, Tennessee. This trip, she stayed there about two weeks.

Jenny gave me a hug and a quick kiss when I arrived.

I tried to reciprocate but couldn't muster much of a smile. Mann stood up and extended his hand. Mine disappeared into his like a pebble down a mineshaft. I'm six feet, three inches tall. Mann towered over me.

"Dan Kardon," I said.

"Thanks for coming," he said. "A beer, some munchies?" he asked, motioning a waitress over.

"Sure."

Jerome gave the waitress an order of food and drinks, then turned back to us.

"You play a mean harp," I said. "Kind of a lost art, these days."

"Thanks. Been fooling around on these for years. Got hooked on an old Little Walter tape when I was a kid. Feels good, having the harp to pull out and blow whenever I want."

"You play with a group?"

"Nah, don't need to. One of the perks of owning this place is, I tell a band I want to sit in, they don't argue. I play with everybody—rock, folk, jazz. Even have some Irish bands come through here—but blues is what I get off on most. Some bands don't want me, but what the hell, I have a good time. These guys," he pointed to the stage, "they're pretty good. We finally got a groove going."

"You always had a good time," Jenny said.

"Yeah," Jerome said and gave out a big laugh. "Got me there."

Jerome and Jenny talked for a while about old friends and a couple of the cases Jenny was handling. Listening to them, I became annoyed, first with them and then with myself at the discomfort of a jealous itch. Jenny, shoulder-length blond hair, long-legged and about five feet, seven inches, sat smiling at everything Jerome said.

Her hazel eyes filled with laughter. Some of it was the beer, some of it was me sitting next to her, and some of it was returning from Johnson City. But a part of it was her obvious comfort and intimacy with Jerome.

In the end, the bond between them was so strong and the respect for each other so palpable that it was impossible not to smile when Jenny laughed gleefully at something Jerome said. I started to relax and opened a second beer. Then, under the table, Jenny placed her hand on my thigh. I immediately put down the beer. I'd had plenty of beers while Jenny'd been gone and would have more when she left again. While she was around, I had a lot of reasons to stay sharp. It was also almost impossible not to look to the door as Jenny's fingers danced from the top of my thigh to the inside of it.

Jerome must have picked up on my drifting thoughts.

"Sorry, didn't mean for you to sit through all that. Thanks for coming and meeting with me—I know it's short notice, but I'm getting really antsy and wanted to move fast. Jenny, you have a chance to give Dan any background on the case?"

"No, but I'm sure we're interested. Dan and I agree on everything," she said and looked at me with an exaggerated smile.

"I already told her, she's a big girl," I said. "She's been doing a fine job navigating our so-called system of justice. She wants to take on a new case, that's fine."

"This one can't be just mine," Jenny said, "it's for both of us."

"Yeah, it's messier than most," Jerome said. "Let me tell you about it—may take a while, but I told the band to take a long break and gave 'em beer, so we got a little time. Basically, I got legal problems with a couple of real estate projects I got going out in Meadowbrook and I need your help."

"I'm not a real estate attorney, neither's Jenny. You hire us, you're likely to end up selling instead of buying."

"I know, your firm does civil litigation, some criminal, other stuff. But Jenny's doing fine with the smaller things I've given her. Plus I checked you out. I hear you take something, you work it like a hungry dog with a new bone. Word is, you're stubborn. I need that."

"Well, could be, but still, if it's a deal with all sorts of deeds, covenants, transactional documents that you want me to do, it may be out of our league."

"We get to the point that documents are a problem, we'll deal with it. I need somebody to figure out how bad things are and then fix 'em. Has to be somebody I can rely on—not like the lawyer I've been using, Chuck Wells. I'm afraid things might be coming apart."

"It'll take us a little time, and you a little money, to get us up to speed on what you're doing, how things're supposed to go," I said.

"Hey, so long as you keep me informed, and you feel like you can handle it, it'll be cool."

"Do you mind if we consult with a real estate attorney if we need to?" Jenny asked.

"Nope. If it'll get the job done, you can consult with Mickey Mouse or Donald Duck. You need help, hire him. Or her," Mann said to a pointed look from Jenny. "I want this thing done, fast as possible."

"Tell us about the projects," Jenny said.

"You've probably heard of my cousin, Daryl Mann."

"Who hasn't?" I said. Daryl Mann was an All-Star power forward for the Boston Shamrocks. He signed a huge contract four years before. For three years before that, he'd been an up and coming NBA star.

"Yeah, well, I own some buildings and he and I also own a couple properties together. Like this bar. You probably know he signed a nice contract a while back."

I laughed. "Anybody gave me a contract for eighty-four million bucks, I'd call it something better than nice."

"Brought me a wiseass," he said to Jenny and then looked back to me. "The contract gave us some real cash to play with. All of a sudden bankers want to talk to us. I've done okay so far on some properties, but this Meadowbrook project is much bigger than anything else I've put Daryl into. He's no dummy—he'll go with it awhile, but he doesn't like losing money."

"Afraid he'll back out?" Jenny asked.

"Things don't turn around soon, yeah."

"What's the project?" I asked.

"Partly a golf course, part of it's a summer camp for kids."

"First one sounds good. Golf courses are doing well around here," I said.

"Yeah, and once it gets underway, we'll get some nice publicity. We'll be the first minority-owned golf course in New England."

"The camp, that's a tougher call," I said. "A lot of camps have folded in the last few years. People make more money using land for other things and camps aren't as popular for kids."

"Yeah, I know, but as long as we do well on the golf course, we can handle the camp. And we can get some funding from some other places, we do it right. The camp's going to be for inner-city kids."

"So what're your problems?"

"Other than goddamn endangered turtles closing the

golf course, a lawyer who won't call me back, and a bunch of white racists who don't want black kids messing around their town, nothing."

"Turtles?" Jenny and I spoke as a chorus.

"You got it. Blue spotted turtles, in a pond on the course. The state says they're endangered, they want us to close the areas around the pond."

"And what about the town not wanting black kids around?" Jenny asked.

"Zoning laws didn't allow us to put in a golf course or a camp out there. Town gave us a special permit for the golf course, no problem. But they've delayed giving us the special permit for the camp, even though they had a Boy Scout camp out there for years."

"So what do you want from us?" I said, taking another drink of beer.

"Take over the cases, deal with the town and the state. We need to work around the damned turtles and get the golf course running. It's already May—the course has to open soon or we'll get killed financially. Then do whatever it takes to help me get the camp renovated and running. I want to open the camp for at least a week or two at the end of the summer for a few kids, show people what we can do."

"Jerome, you said the town was racist. What's gone on besides the delay in the permit?" Jenny asked.

Jerome motioned a waiter over and had him bring a large envelope from the kitchen. From the envelope, Jerome pulled out a newspaper. "Take a look," he said, pointing to an article on the front page of a paper called the *Meadowbrook Chronicle*, dated the day before.

A headline read "Local Camp for Inner City Kids." The article described the sale of old farmland to Jerome's group and the plan to rehabilitate the camp and operate it. The description of the plans was straightforward. Chuck Wells, Jerome's lawyer, was reported as having no comment. The quotes from town residents were less restrained.

"Over my dead body," one Meadowbrook citizen remarked. "Put kids like that near the pond and the bike path, they'll cause trouble for people all around," said another.

A couple of town officials stated they'd never been informed that the camp was intended for inner-city kids and that they would review the situation closely. The implication, of course, was that town officials had been deceived.

"What's this about?" I asked. "What had you told town officials about the camp?"

"Shit, I told people all along I'd be doing the golf course and rehabbing the camp. Nobody bothered to ask me a damn thing about the camp, including what kind of kids would be out there." I made a mental note to contact the reporter—I wondered who had leaked plans for the camp to her.

"What about Wells?"

"We talked about it a few times. He didn't pay much attention until a few weeks ago."

"What did he say then?"

"Said some people might not like it, but he thought it would go okay. He told me not to talk to anybody about it, he'd take care of it. He said the hearing before the zoning board of appeals would be no big deal. He knew the players in town, so I went along." Jerome finished his beer and grabbed another. I took a handful of pretzels instead.

The band went back onstage and started noodling on

their instruments. A couple of them looked over their play lists, talking about the second set.

"How you want to handle Wells? Bring us in to work with him?"

"No. If you guys are willing to take the case, I'll just fire his ass. I'd hoped hiring a local guy would help me, but it's turning ugly and I can't figure why. Last few weeks, faxes, phone calls, e-mails, it doesn't matter, I can't get through to the guy. When I do, there're no real answers."

"Firing him will complicate things," I said. "He'll be pissed, may not cooperate. If we can't get his files quickly, we'll need to sit down with you, take whatever you got, go from there. Let's hope he sent you everything important."

"Okay, I'll dig things out for you."

"Did he tell you what was supposed to happen next with the town?" Jenny asked.

"Said the zoning board of appeals would hold a hearing, we'd have to make a presentation."

"When's the hearing?" I asked.

"Wells told me a while ago it would be in the next week or two, but who knows what he's done or what's up with the town?"

"We'd better talk to Wells and the town officials right away," Jenny said to me.

"Yeah. And meet with Jerome, maybe at the site to see how things look," I said.

"How about tomorrow?" Jerome asked.

I looked at Jenny. It was a Friday night and we hadn't seen each other for a while. Most times, Jenny wouldn't go for it, but it was her client, her call to make.

"No," she said. "Maybe Sunday. Can we call you tomorrow?"

"Yeah. Why don't you come out to the club, I'll show you around the course, the camp, then we can talk. And I'll bring some files and phone numbers for you."

"We'll talk, then call you to confirm." Jenny put her hand on Jerome's. "I'm sorry you're going through all this," she said.

Jerome sighed. "You know, I love that damn golf course, the camp, but this latest stuff is a bear."

"You think Wells is deliberately creating problems?" I asked.

"No, the turtles are real, we gotta deal with 'em. But I'll be damned if I know what he's doing. He should be persuading people that nothing's going on that should have 'em riled up. But instead, getting the golf course and camp going just keeps getting harder."

"Look, we can't promise miracles," I said, "but we'll talk with Wells, town officials, the state agencies, and find out about the hearing."

"Damnit, Jerome, all the things you've toughed out before, you can handle this," Jenny said.

"Thanks," said Jerome. "Okay, time to play the blues instead of singing them to you two." He stood up to leave. "Nice to meet you," he said, "and sorry to lay things on you like this, give you some of it, then go."

"It's okay, we'll need to know a lot more later," I said. "You want us to stay so we can talk at the next break?"

"From what I can see, that little girl doesn't want a lot more talk, she needs some loving."

Jenny smiled and said, "I'd agree with that."

Jerome took a look over at the stage. Unconsciously, his hand went to his pocket and pulled out his harmonica. He held it in his hands, lightly rubbing it.

He turned to Jenny. "You play golf yet?"

"No," she said.

"How about you?" he said to me.

"Not well."

"Good, my kind of golfer. We'll play the course on Sunday and I'll tell you whatever you need to know. I'll see if I can get my lazy-ass cousin to come out too. You'll be the cutest caddie ever lived," he said to Jenny.

"I thought you said the course was closed," I said.

"Can't run a commercial operation yet and we've cut back on staff so the fairways and greens aren't too great, but it's still playable. No way I'm staying off it."

Jerome and Jenny hugged and my hand again disappeared into his. As soon as the band started playing, we got up and left. The band was back in form again. Jerome gyrated with his harmonica, playing a Wilson Pickett oldie, "Mustang Sally."

Jenny and I walked back to the house, my hands full of her luggage. The air was unusually warm and heavy with moisture. We saw occasional arcs of lightning in the distance and the rumble of thunder grew louder as we walked.

"I've never talked with you much about Jerome," I said. "I know you two went to college together and he's given you some work. How'd you two get connected?"

"Basketball—we met hanging around the gym. He'd been a great high school player in Boston, but he blew out a knee his senior year. He was supposed to go to Duke on a basketball scholarship, but instead came to ETSU. He had a lot of family in the area—his grandmother, some aunts, uncles, and cousins, like Daryl."

ETSU stood for East Tennessee State University, where Jenny played on the women's basketball team.

"Looks like you guys are still pretty close," I said.

Jenny gave me a sideways look, shook her head, and gave a little laugh. "I wondered why you were so uptight back there. If you're asking whether we have, or had, a romance, the answer is no. Just really good friends, then and now. On campus, some people thought we were a couple. A few neanderthals didn't like what they saw, gave us a hard time, and spread some nasty rumors, but we got through it. We didn't see much of each other for a long time, but when I came to Boston, we reconnected. That make you happier?"

The answer was yes, though I didn't say it. "You talk with him about wanting to work as an agent?" Besides playing basketball and other sports as a kid, Jenny knew professional baseball players. Her father, an English professor and baseball nut, took her to minor league games in Johnson City. Jenny wanted to find a way to tie together her legal training and her sports background.

"Not yet. I was happy about the work he gave us and I'm excited he's interested in us for this case. I don't want to push it. I know he represents Daryl and maybe he's thinking about expanding, representing other players. I don't want him thinking I'm trying to horn in on. But . . ." Her voice trailed off.

"But what?"

"Well, if we do a good job on this case, I hope we'll do more with him, including sports projects. He's got a lot of contacts and energy, so it'd be a great opportunity."

"Your first big case. Congratulations."

She smiled. "Thanks. I'm sorry about working Sunday."

"It's all right, meeting Jerome at the course makes sense. Plus I get to play golf and tell you where to drive the cart, a great two-fer."

She gave a little laugh. "What do you think about Jerome?" she asked.

"Interesting guy. Unusual combination of talents. Tough project, though."

"I know, but when he puts his mind to something, he sticks with it."

"How'd he get into golf as a kid? Pretty unusual for the Roxbury kids I've known," I asked.

Jenny shook her head. "That was about the only thing he picked up from his dad. His father played semi-pro and minor league baseball, hurt a leg, so he took up golf. He'd travel around the country, playing golf, giving lessons. Lots of gambling going on, I guess. Stayed with different women along the way. According to Jerome, there were enough black golfers playing on municipal courses so his father could support himself."

"But not his family."

"Right. Jerome never had much to do with his father."

"Why'd he say his cousin is lazy? I hear Daryl works hard as hell. Pretty much came out of nowhere by practicing and playing hard."

"Daryl does work at his game and Jerome's the first to tell you that. It's weird, I don't know what it's about, but Jerome's always been tough on Daryl. He's proud of him, always talking about him, but there's a way in which somehow he wants Daryl to be different, do something else, maybe do more outside basketball."

"I thought Daryl grew up poor in Tennessee with plenty of hard times. That'd prepare him pretty well for anything that goes along with a contract with lots of zeroes."

"I don't know what it's about. That's all I can tell you about the Manns. They're still competitive as hell, they fight, but they're close in their own, weird way."

"You mean, they're close in the weird ways that guys are close."

"You said it, not me. Maybe there's some jealousy, I don't know," Jenny said. "That article that Jerome showed us—boy, it made the town look bad."

"Yeah, but it's been a long time since I put a lot of faith in a newspaper story. The paper's just looking for a story, trying to get things stirred up. I'm sure most people out there don't care about the camp. I'm not ready to buy Jerome's charge of racism just yet."

"I'm not surprised."

"What do you mean?"

"I haven't met anybody whose opinion you bought the first time. Especially mine."

"Yeah, well, I knew you had lousy taste in men back then."

"That so? You know, now that you mention it, I can't remember how you taste. Come here."

We kissed in the middle of Stetson Street under a streetlight in front of my house. I finally let her go, mostly because I had to handle her suitcase and pick up my briefcase that I'd left in my car.

Jenny went ahead of me and left the door open leading to the stairs up to the second floor unit of the two family house I own. I made it inside just as lightning flashed, thunder clapped, and the rain came down hard. Just inside the door, I found Jenny's jacket. I picked it up and walked to the bottom of the stairs, where I found her pants. Two steps up lay her blouse, and, a step or two above that, her bra, then her underwear. I looked up at the top of the stairs just in time to see her cute butt swivel behind the door. I dropped the bags and ran upstairs after her.

CHAPTER

TWO

      Saturday morning, I woke up earlier than Jenny. I ran for a couple miles on Commonwealth Avenue towards Cleveland Circle. On the way home, I picked up coffee and muffins at a coffee shop Jenny liked. When I walked in the kitchen, Jenny was sitting at the table with the sports section of the *Boston Globe* spread in front of her. She looked up and smiled when she saw the coffee and bag of muffins in my hand.

"Nice to see you're educable," she said.

I leaned over and gave her a kiss. "Yeah," I said, "but some things you and I need to practice over and over."

"Don't make promises you can't keep, buddy," she said and reached for the coffee and muffins.

I drank from a large orange juice and scanned the front section of the paper. From the bedroom, I heard a radio and a couple of sentences of news caught my attention.

"Be right back," I said.

By the time I got to the bedroom, the brief top-of-the-hour news report had ended. I turned on the television and switched to a local all news cable station. A reporter was relating that police were beginning an investigation into the overnight murder of Charles Wells, a lawyer in Meadowbrook. The solemn young woman in a gray suit

17

reported from outside a nondescript building. Wells had
been assaulted in his office and died sometime overnight. The report ended and the news anchor moved on
to a report about another bank merger in the region,
news only because there were so few banks left to
merge.

I walked back to the kitchen. Jenny looked up at me
and said, "What's wrong? You look like you've seen a
ghost."

"Pretty damn close," I said.

I told her what I'd heard. Her mouth and eyes went
wide.

"Oh, my God," she said. "I can't believe it. I wonder
if Jerome knows?"

"Better call him," I said. All the endorphins that my
run had released seemed to dissipate instantly. A wise
man I had often turned to in the past, William Shakespeare, once wrote, "First thing we do, let's kill all the
lawyers." In fact, killing lawyers didn't happen all that
often. When it did, there was usually an aggrieved party
in a divorce or a family dispute who went over the edge.
I didn't know enough about Wells or his practice to
hazard a guess about what happened there. But the cold,
hard knot in my stomach made me hope fervently that
it had nothing to do with Jerome.

Jenny couldn't track down Jerome, so she left him
messages at a couple of numbers. We went out for a
long walk along the Charles River. Walking past the
dam in Watertown Square, we saw a large white heron
stalking the river's edge for fish. The sunshine and light
breeze should have enlivened our moods as the day
warmed. But try as we did to talk about other subjects,
we kept coming back to Wells.

When we arrived back home mid-afternoon, Jerome

had called and left a message. Jenny phoned back, talked to Jerome briefly, then motioned to me to pick up a second phone.

"The police wouldn't tell me anything," Jerome said, "but I got hold of a couple of people. One guy talked to a cop who'd been there—no question it happened late last night, maybe early this morning. They're not giving any details yet."

"Hey, Jerome, it's Dan. Any idea what happened to him?"

"Whacked in the head pretty bad, I gather."

"Police name any suspects?" I asked.

"No, not yet."

"They talking about any weapons or other evidence at the scene?" Jenny asked.

"Not that I heard about."

"Any motives so far?" I asked.

"I guess the place was ransacked, files a mess, and maybe things missing, so it could have been robbery. But Meadowbrook's full of rumors that the murder's linked to gambling, drugs, maybe a woman. Turns out Mr. Wells had a reputation for dabbling in all three. Some of the women were married. Great American, my lawyer was."

"That doesn't mean he deserved to be shot," Jenny said. From across the room, she stared at me, shaking her head.

"Yeah, I shouldn't be so sarcastic about the poor bastard. I feel bad for him. Shit like this happened when I was a kid in Roxbury—guys shot in gang bangs, knifed over their basketball shoes, beat up over gold chains, whatever. You'd wake up one morning, some guy you knew from the streets, from school, gone for good. Glad to say they've cleaned things up in Boston, but hearing about Wells brings it all back."

"Also means we'll never get his take on what's going on in town," I said.

"Does he have a secretary or office manager, somebody who might help us out?" Jenny asked.

"Gloria Duchesne," Jerome said. "She's good, but she's out of town. Talked to her a few days ago. She told me she'd be out of the office for a couple weeks, a big anniversary trip to Europe. No help there. The whole thing's a nightmare."

We were quiet for a moment, waiting for Jerome.

"Anyway," he continued, "it means it's even more important I get you guys on board. You on for tomorrow?" We assured Jerome we'd meet him and then said goodbye.

That night, Jenny and I made love again. It took longer for both of us to get there and it had a darker, more urgent edge to it. For a short time, we escaped into caresses, strokes, hard kisses, and the rhythms of moving hips and low moans.

When it was over, we were both tired but still too jazzed to sleep. I went to restore my strength and subdue the buzz with some chocolate chip ice cream. When Jenny didn't join me and stayed quiet as we got ready for bed, I sensed something had changed.

"You want to tell me what's going on?" I asked.

She moved over and put her head on my chest. "Don't really know," I heard from a muffled voice.

"Did I do something wrong?"

"No."

"Give me a clue—animal, vegetable, or mineral?"

"Wells getting killed. It makes me worried about Jerome."

"We could try to talk him out of it, or pull out ourselves."

"No, he's committed to it. And he wants us, so we should help. He's been a good friend. But I'm still nervous."

"Jerome's in a property dispute, that's all. The murder probably isn't even connected to what Jerome's doing. You think about it, it's a fluke we care about Wells. If the guy had been killed a couple of weeks earlier or later, we wouldn't have even paid attention, just like we don't pay attention to most of the people murdered around here."

"I know you're right. But still, I'm nervous about Jerome."

"Hey, it's your case, you make the decisions on what we do."

"Thanks." She pulled herself further up on my chest. "What about you? Do you ever feel nervous or afraid?" she asked.

Yes, I thought, but words to talk about it wouldn't come.

She stirred against my side. "I feel so safe here," she murmured, then said nothing more.

I held her and stroked her hair as she slept. Nobody had ever said she felt safe in my arms. It felt like a heavy load to bear but one I could carry with a light heart.

We stepped into my Chevy Blazer at nine A.M., Sunday, and made a beeline for Dunkin' Donuts. Well-fortified with a large black coffee, orange juice, one plain and one cream-filled donut, and a banana nut muffin for me along with a coffee and a bran muffin for Jenny, we headed off to Meadowbrook. From the Mass Pike, we took I-495 north for a bit, before driving on Route 25 into Meadowbrook and then turning onto a smaller road to get to the golf course.

The flood of mega-stores, warehouses, fast food restaurants, franchise stores, and national retail stores that had enveloped much of eastern Massachusetts had not yet reached most of Meadowbrook. Route 25, the only major road, veered through the southern tip of town and most of the industries and businesses in town were located there. Elsewhere, Meadowbrook still looked much like it had fifty years ago.

We took a quick detour through the center of town to check out where Wells had his office. The town had a small oval common in the center with blinking yellow traffic lights at each end. Around it were a few local businesses, most of them in buildings that looked more like homes than businesses. The center held a diner, a pizza place, a printing shop, a dentist's office, an old hardware store that looked like it might close any minute, and a couple of assorted convenience stores. Two stately churches faced the oval from opposite sides, one a brick Congregational church and the other a wooden Catholic church. Both churches had seen more prosperous days.

Wells had an office in a single-story brick building. It looked just as it had on the television news the day before. Even up close, there was nothing distinctive about the building besides the yellow police tape across the entrance. We took a quick look around then headed out, not saying much.

"Damn, it's a good day to be playing golf," Jerome said.

"Yeah, but we stopped by Wells's office. Sort of

funky to go from there right to a golf game," I said.

"That's part of why it's good to be here. The golf ball doesn't care what you're thinking. Cleans your mind. You think about anything else besides the ball, you can't play this game." Jerome turned to look at Jenny. "You all right? You're awful quiet."

"I'm fine," she said and took a sip from another coffee she'd picked up.

"Racing around in the cart in the fresh air'll be good for you, get rid of that pasty lawyer's face you been wearing," Jerome said. Jenny gave a little laugh and flashed a small smile at Jerome. It was her first since we'd left Wells's office.

Jerome stepped up on the tee. After a couple of practice swings, he took a graceful swing and the ball took off with a sharp crack, headed straight out from the tee for a moment. Then it veered way right into a stand of oaks. Jerome Mann looked around at the clear blue sky and deep green fairway that bent slightly left and smiled.

"Course," he said, "sometimes, even when you got your mind right, things don't work out."

"I'm impressed," I said. "Guys I play with, they slice it out of bounds on the first tee, they get a little annoyed."

"Kardon, you got the reputation of being a smart guy. Don't prove your lovely cart driver wrong."

"That ball's not out of bounds, all the way over there?"

"Hey, man, you forget, I own the damn course, I set the boundaries. Anywhere I'm likely to hit ain't out of bounds on this course."

"We could have an interesting philosophical discussion about whether that prepares you well for the game of golf."

"No, we couldn't. I've wanted a course like this for a hell of a long time and I couldn't care less about how a fancy-ass course designer would set things up. Walking along, hitting at the flags, knowing any of the guys I hang with can come here without looking over their shoulders, it feels pretty damn good."

Just then, a cart skidded to a sharp stop behind us. A black man about Jerome's size stepped out of the cart. He wore a blue polo shirt, khaki pants, wraparound sunglasses, and a blue baseball hat with a gold M on the front of it.

"Well, look who's going to join us," Jerome said. "The wizard of the parquet, the big black leprechaun of the Boston Shamrocks, Mr. Daryl Mann."

"Jerome, I didn't come all the way out here to listen to you flap your jaw all day now, did I? Golf's supposed to be a nice quiet game, dignified and all that crap," the newcomer said.

"Nobody ever called your golf game dignified, Daryl."

"Hey, man, I can play this game. I'm just a little inconsistent."

"No," Jerome said, "you can be inconsistent in basketball. Some nights the ball just won't drop, the legs don't move. But golf's different. Any asshole can par two or three holes, still shoot a high score, and claim he's inconsistent—if he played enough, he'd par every hole. But you're inconsistent in golf, it means you suck. Golf's all about steadiness, consistency, making the right shots under different conditions, under pressure, day in, day out."

"Did I come to the wrong place? This some kind of 'golf is life' spiritual retreat?" Daryl asked. "I sure as hell ain't paying for it."

"Boys, boys," I said.

He'd been ignoring us but now Daryl gave Jenny and me a long look.

"Well, lookie here," he finally said. "Barbie and Ken go golfing. Jerome, who the fuck are these people?"

"Come on, Daryl, no need for that," Jerome said. "This is Jenny Crane and Dan Kardon, the new attorneys I told you about. They're going to come to our rescue, get some paying bodies on this golf course."

Jenny and I each extended hands to Daryl. He just nodded at us.

"Excuse my little cousin," Jerome said. "Somebody gives him a big contract and he thinks he's different than the rest of us."

"Hey, I agree with him, he is different. Rude maybe, but different," I said.

"Huh," Daryl said, " 'cept he's a lawyer, I might get to like him."

"Man, you party with all the wrong crowd," Jerome said. "Only lawyers you know kiss your butt then charge you four hundred and fifty an hour for the smooching. This guy's different. He'd rather kick your ass than kiss it."

"Which is what I'll do to you, you don't shut up and let me hit," Daryl said.

"I'll give you a stroke every other hole," Jerome said.

"Every hole," Daryl responded.

"You're a wimp, but okay," Jerome responded.

"I thought you had a shoulder injury," Jenny said to Daryl. The papers had reported in late March that Mann had a bad shoulder injury that would keep him out for the season.

"Yeah," he laughed, a low rumble. "I had a shoulder injury. Should have kept me out of the lineup for five days, a week max. But the team sucked and the brains up top figured hell, we're not going to make the play-offs, so we'll go down further, aim for the lottery. Only thing I'm not allowed to do with my shoulder is tear Jerome's head off."

He stepped up to the first tee and took a few practice swings with an enormous driver. He swung, connected with a loud crack, and the ball took off like a bullet, straight and gorgeous. Jerome chuckled. "Got him just where I want him," he said. "When the going gets tough, Daryl, just remember what my daddy always said. Any day on the golf course is a good day because you're on the right side of the grass."

"Only time your daddy said anything right, he was talking in his sleep. Let's just play some golf here!"

Jerome waved Jenny into his cart and they took off down the right side of the fairway. Daryl and I took a cart down the middle, each of us silent. He dropped me at my ball and then went to his, about forty yards further toward the hole.

From his ball's position in the trees, Jerome couldn't get to the green with his second shot. But after superb second and third shots, his ball lay within a few feet of the hole. Meanwhile, I'd taken three more shots and my ball still lay thirty feet from the cup. Daryl had taken only two shots, with his ball resting at the back edge of the green twenty feet from the pin.

I putted first and came within about three feet of the hole. Daryl then putted. The moment he stroked the ball, I understood Jerome's comment. I'd seen guys with jackhammers with better control. The ball took off like a scalded rabbit and passed the hole by ten feet. His next putt went four feet past the hole back the other way. Daryl hit his third putt hard enough so that the ball went over the hole, hit the far edge, and gave a little jump straight in the air before it settled in the hole with a loud click.

"Soft touch," Jerome said. Daryl glared back. Despite Jerome's tee shot into the woods, with the stroke he gave Daryl, Jerome had halved the hole with him. We left the hole with the cousins going at it about who owed who money for the previous round of golf they'd played.

By then, I'd had a chance to look at the two more closely. From a distance, they looked similar, both large, black, and bald. Jerome had a more wiry build, a thin mustache, and a perpetual half smile, as if bemused by a thought. Daryl, maybe an inch taller, also had thicker legs, a broader torso, and shoulders that resembled boulders. His face carried a stern expression, with high, chiseled cheekbones and an impassivity that gave away nothing. His few comments to Jenny and me were no more communicative.

As we went around the course, I asked Jerome about himself and the project. I started with who he was and how he ended up in the position he was in.

Jerome said he'd learned to play golf when he was a kid, but he didn't tell me anything about his father. Jerome played the game more seriously after his basketball career ended. Following college, he came back to Boston for business school. Afterward, it took him a while, but he did well in real estate. In addition, Jerome gave basketball clinics and short summer camps for school kids throughout eastern Massachusetts. He'd hooked up with the Shamrocks and some of their players, along with other coaches and players he roped in, who participated in the clinics and camps.

Once he built up his properties, he decided that operating the first minority-owned golf course in New England would give him a kick. Golf was booming and blacks were playing as never before. He didn't do much about it for a couple of years but when Daryl came to the Shamrocks, new financial doors opened.

At about the same time, a kid from Meadowbrook showed up at a basketball camp Jerome was running at a local college. Andy Dennison was a white kid with slow feet and not much hop in his legs, but he had an appetite for hard work and loved to run. By the end of camp, Andy Dennison had new moves, a better shot, and an award as the most improved player in the camp. He attended a second camp with Jerome and improved even further.

That fall, Andy invited Jerome out to his home. The whole Dennison family gathered and Jerome brought Daryl. While the rest of the family pressed Daryl for stories, Andy's grandfather, Arthur Dennison, talked to Jerome. Arthur got Jerome to talk about his camps, how he ran them, who they were for, and what he wanted to do in the future, including the golf course. Finally, Arthur Dennison stood up and told Jerome to come with him.

Dennison drove Jerome out to a small hill looking out over a dam and a good-sized pond. The leaves were just beginning to turn to bright oranges and reds. On the right, there was an open field and some forest. On the left, down near the water, Jerome saw some small cabins and buildings.

According to Jerome, Arthur Dennison pointed to the buildings and said, "That's an old Boy Scout camp. Operated for about thirty years, but stopped maybe fifteen years ago. And that's some open land over there, used to be part of a farm."

"Awful pretty view from here. You own some of it?"

"Just about all of it."

"Nice piece of property."

"Yup, Echo Pond there makes it special. Pretty much every nice weekend, I get real estate people out here hassling me, trying to get me to sell. I got plenty of money and never wanted to see it carved up."

"I can understand that."

Arthur turned to Jerome. "You got ideas that fit this place. Can't say I'm big on golf, but damn, I'd hate to see this turned into cardboard cutout condos or fancy-ass executive houses where they got more bathrooms than people. Too many people in this town already sold out for the highest dollar. What you did for my grandson, if you can do that for others, I'd be proud to have your camp on this land."

Jerome said it took a minute for him to figure out what Arthur was saying, but they shook hands on the sale of the land that day. It took some time to put it all together, but Arthur Dennison's word was good.

Jerome took some of his own money, a large chunk of his cousin's, added a few more investors, and got a loan to buy the properties and build the golf course, a driving range, and a camp. They bought the land at a reasonable price over the squawking of many in Meadowbrook who would have gladly paid more. Altogether, everything had been budgeted at about $12 million.

Jerome, it turned out, had gotten lucky. "A few months after we bought the property, a large software company took over a big office building nearby that had been mostly vacant. Company also announced they were putting up another building next door. Meant lots of new folks to buy houses within about three miles of the property. With the good economy right now, the property's worth at least thirty percent, maybe more, since we bought it."

"So people are lined up, hoping the deal dies and you decide to sell off the land," I said.

"Bingo."

"I went to a couple of camps when I was a kid," I said. "This one have everything you need to get started?"

"Yup. Some of the cabins and other buildings are in rough shape, take some money to put it all back right, but it'll be a damn sight cheaper than starting from scratch."

We talked in between shots. As much as Jerome pointed out features of the golf course that he wanted me to see, he also kept coming back to the camp and how he wanted that to operate.

The golf course itself was empty of people and in reasonably good shape, given the cutbacks in personnel and its recent creation. There was plenty to be done in trimming a few fairways and fixing some of the greens. In other places, the fairways and greens needed more time for the grass to fill in consistently, much like any new course.

Echo Pond, into which Daryl knocked a ball, bordered the tenth and eleventh holes. In addition, the small pond that harbored the infamous turtles came into play on both fourteen and sixteen. And since you could only get to fifteen by walking through fourteen, closing fourteen would close fifteen as well.

When we arrived at sixteen, the turtle pond stretched from about two hundred yards down the fairway to a point close to the green, which was about four hundred yards away, on the right side. All three of us hit safely left of the pond, Jerome and Daryl well beyond me as usual. I hit my second shot just short of the green and

Daryl hit his over the green into deep rough. We walked up to where Jerome stood. Instead of facing the green, he had turned to the pond and was dropping about a half-dozen balls on the fairway. Daryl dropped a couple there for him as well.

"Got any crappy balls?" Jerome asked me.

I reached into my bag and pulled out four or five old ones that I'd cut or beat up badly.

"Here," I said. "What are you doing?"

"About what we did to Yugoslavia," Jerome said and then started firing away. With great precision, he hit wedge shots high into the air and into the middle of the pond. The first two came quite close to a small branch floating at the water's edge.

"I'll bet the sons of bitches like to lie on that log in the sun," he said. After that, he sprayed them around.

When he was finished, he and Daryl exchanged a high-five. Then Jerome hit his one good ball from where it lay to about fifteen feet short of the pin on the green.

He turned to me. "I know I can't kill the damn things with golf balls, but I keep hoping I'll at least force 'em to move out."

"I don't know," I said. "They might think those dimpled golf balls are pretty cute and start mating with 'em. That'd start a whole new endangered species of mutant dimpled golf ball turtles."

"Don't even joke like that," Jerome said, and Daryl laughed.

When we finished, Jerome totaled the scores and reported that he had shot an eighty-eight and that Daryl and I had each shot ninety-threes. If he'd taken eight off his and added five to each of ours, he might have been close.

Daryl ignored my hand and Jenny's again, said a simple "good game," and spun out of the parking lot in a black Range Rover. Jerome, Jenny, and I went inside the still-empty clubhouse.

It had a kitchen and bar, an informal but graceful eating area and porch overlooking the first tee and eighteenth hole, lockers and changing areas, a nice pro shop attached, nobody in it and nothing on the walls. Somebody had stocked one of the refrigerators with beers and sodas and had brought in a couple of cases of chips, pretzels, and cookies. The only thing missing was golfers.

We sat down and looked at the fairway on eighteen, watching the green deepen as shadows began to fall over it in the late afternoon sun. A pair of squirrels played on the lawn in front of me and somewhere I could hear a truck going, but there were no other people in sight.

"You've got a great golf course here," I said. "You guys didn't cut any corners."

"Nope. Taken us nearly three years so far. Could have cut back on moving dirt around, used lousy topsoil, skip the bunkers, stuff like that. But then you have a boring course and more maintenance problems down the road."

"Pretty nice to look at. Must have had a pretty good piece of land to start with."

"Yeah, we lucked out."

"But even with a skeleton crew, it has to cost you a fortune to keep it going," Jenny said.

"Yeah, we got to pay for water, fertilizer and pesticides, electricity, some personnel. Tough nut every month, on top of the financing costs."

"So what are all the hassles you're having?" Jenny asked.

"You saw the pond on the course where the goddamn blue spotted turtles supposedly live. I've never seen the bastards, but they're supposedly endangered, can't be disturbed. I got a notice, sent it on to Wells. He dealt with it. But this goes on much longer, I'll go and catch 'em myself, make soup to sell at the club."

From my days as an Assistant Attorney General and from doing some environmental work, I knew that the state Division of Fisheries and Wildlife had authority to declare a species endangered. There were strict rules about protecting wildlife and also wetlands. But I also knew that strict as the laws were, there were not enough people to enforce them.

"You negotiate with the agency?" I asked. "I know sometimes they talk with people before taking action."

"Wells was supposed to deal with it. According to him, there wasn't much to discuss. The state closed the two holes that border on the pond and they want a buffer zone around the area, too. Means we can't operate the course as we planned," Jerome said. He looked out the window to his course for a moment.

"What about Wells," Jenny said. "Why did you hire him initially?"

"When we bought the property, I hired a real estate broker who knew Meadowbrook, David Granger, as a consultant to help me figure out the price and work out some parts of the deal. A Boston lawyer did most of the transaction. But we figured a local guy would be better for handling the Meadowbrook permits. Granger recommended Wells. I kept pushing Wells to get it done. Granger tried to light a fire under him too, but nothing happened."

"We should contact Granger," Jenny said. "He can fill us in on people in town. I'll try him tonight so we can get started tomorrow."

"Don't bother. Far as I can tell, he's off to Foxwoods

or Atlantic City most weekends, gambling. Wait until later tomorrow."

"The hassles you're getting from the town," I asked. "People know Daryl's involved? I'd think that would help your reception out here."

"Yeah, but that hasn't meant squat. He's just an investor. He doesn't have time to get involved, or much interest, so I'm carrying the ball. Did everything I could. Met with the local business folks, town officials. Even put some of my money in the Meadowbrook Savings Bank and gave it a little piece of the loan when I didn't have to. Now, town officials just blow me off whenever I try to get anything out of 'em."

"What are your options?" I asked, opening a second Rolling Rock.

"Well, if the damned turtles stay there and the state won't open up fourteen, fifteen, and sixteen, we could cut back to a nine-hole golf course but that'd be a financial disaster. I guess we could cut those three holes out and add three holes somewhere else. But that'll be expensive, set us back a year, probably more. Might also mean we can't put in a driving range we have planned, or maybe take land from the camp. Any of that happens, some of the investors, maybe Daryl, will want to sell off the whole thing. With the way land prices have gone up out here recently, we'd take a loss but we could probably get back a fair bit. If we're going to get whacked, though, the investors will want to do it quickly, while prices are strong."

"Not real attractive options," Jenny said.

"No shit, Sherlock. That's why I need your help."

"It depends a hell of a lot more on those turtles than it does on us," I said.

"Yeah, I know, but we've got to do something about that, as well as get the camp going."

"I hear you. I'd like to see the rest of the property, the old camp area. That okay?"

"Sure, I'll give you a guided tour in one of our customized tour vehicles."

"Another golf cart tour, oh boy," Jenny said.

"Hey, beats working."

"You forget," I said, "we are working. Though given your description of the lawyers who hang around Daryl, our hourly charges just doubled."

"You get the golf course back and my camp on schedule, we'll talk about raising those rates. Till then, don't press your luck, boy." Jerome smiled, but his eyes told me that he'd give away dollars in his business about as readily as he'd given up hoops to the other teams on the basketball court.

We climbed into a couple of golf carts and drove out past the sixteenth hole and the turtle pond. Jerome drove by the pond and hollered just to harass the turtles.

Adjacent to the seventeenth hole, the golf course ended with white stakes marking the boundaries and a metal fence. Jerome unlocked a gate in the fence and we drove down a path through a meadow. Straight ahead about one-quarter mile was a collection of old wooden buildings, most small and some sagging. To our right, the meadow sloped slightly downhill to Echo Pond.

"This is where I want to put the driving range, fence it off from the camp," Jerome said.

We drove further to the buildings and stopped in front of a large one-story wooden building with a flagpole in front of it. The building had one wing with large windows and one with smaller windows. It looked out over an expense of unkempt lawn that went down to the shore.

"I think this is the main cabin," Jerome said.

"No, probably not," I said. "It's probably a cafeteria. In my day, we called it a mess hall. At night you could push the tables aside, have movies, Ping-Pong, stuff like that. Probably a kitchen at the back and offices to the side."

"You went to camp?" Jenny asked.

"I went to a couple and they're pretty much alike. They usually put the big buildings somewhere central, near the water so it looks great in brochures and stuff. Funny how they never put pictures of the food they serve in the brochures."

Jerome laughed. "Come on, I'll show you the rest of this place."

We walked past about twenty cabins. Most had six bunk beds. Some still had one metal single bed up front, where the counselor would have slept. I hadn't seen a camp cabin in years or thought about my days as a camper and then a counselor.

Back down at Echo Pond, we walked the water's edge until we reached a boathouse that had seen better days. It had no windows, only a couple of doors that swung wide open to reveal a single large room. There were no boats inside, but there were oars, some pieces of hardware, old wooden masts and booms from small sailboats, and some tools, along with evidence that animals had made the place their home. The floorboards groaned as we walked.

"Gonna have to replace this one," I said.

"Not just this one. We get this camp going, we'll build some new cabins and bath facilities, fix everything up, set up a new dock. Kids that are coming here see too many beat-up houses and buildings where they live. This place has to be different."

"You really have a vision, don't you?" Jenny asked.

"Yeah. Had an itch to do something like this for a long time. Sometime after I started the clinics, I started thinking about something bigger, something the kids just can't get otherwise. Spent too much time and money on the golf course to start planning the camp until last year, but we're ready now, soon as we get the permit. We'll have hoops, but I want the kids to learn the same stuff you white middle class kids did—archery, softball, tennis, arts and crafts, swimming, sailing, all that stuff."

I laughed. "Wait'll they find out how boring we white folks are. You're really building a training ground for black activists, right?"

"Damn, Jenny, you were right about this guy being smart."

Our brief tour of the camp finished, we headed back in the golf carts to the clubhouse. The light was fading to the west, just over one of the hills. The trees cast long shadows and the only things moving out on the fairways we passed were some squirrels and one red fox that trotted alongside a fairway before disappearing into the woods. The crisp, clean air carried a tincture of evergreen and mown grass. Birds chirped and our electric cart made no noise as we went along. I could sense Jerome brooding as we drove, looking at an empty golf course. I enjoyed the silence but based on all I'd heard, feared it might last too long.

CHAPTER

THREE

Back at the clubhouse, Jenny and I each declined another beer. Jerome went ahead and opened one for himself and we sat down outside, watching the sun set.

"Daryl's a man of few words," I said.

"Great player, good guy," Jerome said. "Doesn't have to say much."

"Seems wound pretty tight. Does he ever relax?"

"On the basketball court, a little at home. And he loves playing paintball out in the woods."

"Paintball? You mean running around firing guns with paint pellets at people?" Jenny asked.

"Yeah. When we were kids, I'd spend a lot of the summers with his family in Tennessee. Daryl had a twenty-two rifle, loved to shoot squirrels, groundhogs. Now he goes home in the summer, plays paintball with his buddies. Better than cocaine, whiskey, or pissing his money away on a lot of other stuff."

"I agree, I'm just surprised. I don't know many paintball players."

"Daryl surprises a lot of people."

"You know he could make it easier for other people if he wanted to," I said.

Jerome looked at me. "From what I hear, so could you."

"Point well taken."

"Daryl does what he has to do."

"Does he work with the kids and the basketball clinics with you?"

"Nope."

"What's he do besides basketball?"

"Kardon, let's get one thing straight. What I see of you, I like, but you're my lawyer, that's it. You don't need to know any more about my cousin than any fool buying the sports page. You ever walk in the man's sneakers, than you talk to me about him."

"Fair enough. I'll stick with lawyering."

"You do that, we'll get along just fine."

He pulled a briefcase out from behind his chair. "Here," he said, "these are the papers Wells sent me, along with some other stuff. You two need anything else after you've gone through these, let me know."

"Who've you dealt with in Meadowbrook besides Wells?" Jenny asked.

"Talked with the Selectmen, some of the other officials, the building inspector, public works guys."

"How about businesspeople?"

"I talked to a small group at the Rotary Club once about the golf course."

"You said the local bank has a piece of the loan," I said.

"Smaller banks around here have had a tough time. Big banks come in, steal their business. Local companies who are their clients get sold, the new companies taking over use out-of-town banks for payroll, operating accounts, stuff like that. I figured it would help the bank and me, so I gave the Meadowbrook Savings Bank a little business."

"Who's your contact there?"

"Roger Vaneck, the bank president. Good guy to deal with. He's helped me out on a couple things."

"You catch any flak before that article came out from nearby residents, other people who live on Echo Pond, about the camp?" Jenny asked.

"No, but I never went out of my way to talk to them. Used to be a camp there, so putting one back in shouldn't be a big deal."

"What else is near the camp or on the pond?" I asked.

"Well, on the other side of the camp is a dam."

"Who owns the dam?"

"I do. Came with the Dennison property. Used to be a small mill near where the camp is, according to Dennison. Mill was destroyed by a fire. The dam's still there. We got to maintain it, unless I give it to the town."

"What about the other side of the dam?" Jenny asked.

"Let's see. There's an old, enormous Victorian mansion, used to be a spa for people coming out from Boston. What I understand, it stayed in one family for a long time. Last year or so, it's been renovated into townhouses. Just starting to sell them. Then there's an area with a bunch of small homes, cottages. One new development with about fifteen sites on it—just starting to put homes in there. Beyond that, a town beach."

"So the shore's all developed."

"Except for our property, yeah."

"The article you showed us at the club, what did it mean about a bike path?" I asked.

"An abandoned rail line goes out to the mansion from Meadowbrook center. Story I heard is that the guy who owned the spa also owned the Boston and Montreal Rail

Road years ago. He put a private line in to the spa from the main line. Tracks are out now, but the rail bed is still there."

"You mean, like a paved bike path?" Jenny asked.

"Nah, it's grass mostly, some dirt. Runs around most of the other side of the pond."

"So people think gangs from your camp will mount their mountain bikes and descend on them, sort of junior Hell's Angels," I said.

"Guess so. It never even occurred to me. Jesus, these people got active imaginations."

"Yeah," I said, "but Jerome, you see the same reaction whenever a town wants to convert old railroads into paved bike paths. Businessmen love it, it brings people in to buy snacks, drinks, all sorts of stuff. But nearby residents always scream about crime going up, littering, loss of privacy, you name it."

We sat quietly for a moment. Jenny and I watched Jerome. He looked out over the golf course, then back at us. The usual half smile on his face was gone. "All right, guys, let's get going," he said. "Anything you want me to do, I'll do it. I'll be real unhappy with a lot of people if the camp doesn't work."

We walked outside and both stood for a minute, just looking around. Jerome surveyed the course and the clubhouse, then looked back at us.

"You think I'm nuts to keep going?"

Jenny shook her head. "No."

Jerome turned to me. "Kardon?"

"Not yet. I'll tell you if I do. But success may not come easy or cheap. Be prepared for a fight on your hands. Maybe more than one fight. Or maybe we'll need to make a deal."

Jerome nodded. "Yeah, I hear you." He turned back

and looked out over the course. "Kardon, you ever wanted something so bad, it never left you alone?"

I knew exactly what he meant. There were a couple of people I'd missed for too damn long. Easy to feel it, but hard to talk about it, so I just shook my head.

"It's like when I hear a new tune once in a while, it sits in my head. I work on the harp until I nail it, get it right. This camp is the same. I want to get it out of my head, make it real. When the camp really happens, I'll feel like I've done something."

"Whatever you need, we'll work on it," Jenny said.

"Gonna get after 'em with some hard-core legal mumbo-jumbo?"

Jenny smiled. "Bet your ass," she said.

I shook Jerome's hand and Jenny gave him a short hug. We walked to my SUV in the parking lot carrying the files Jerome had given us. As we got back to the car, there was a new sound, neither the chirping of birds nor the buzz of a machine. Jerome stood silhouetted against a descending sun, surveying his empty eighteenth hole, his harp to his lips. He played a slow, mournful blues dirge, the notes fading slowly in the still air. I'd heard a lot of music over the years, but this was the first time I'd heard an instrument cry.

CHAPTER————————

FOUR

Late Monday morning, we checked in with Jerome. He'd called a couple of town officials and found that a hearing on the permit had been set up for the next Monday night. The officials had been completely noncommittal about their position. One called some of the comments quoted in the Meadowbrook paper "unfortunate," but said that if the article represented the real sentiment of the town, he couldn't ignore it. Jerome wanted us doing damage control as soon as possible.

Jerome had given us the number for David Granger, the broker who had worked with Jerome, so Jenny put a call in to him. Granger said he was still recovering from a long weekend at Foxwoods, the gambling resort in Connecticut, so he didn't want to meet us that day. But he agreed on dinner the next night.

Out of curiosity, I called the police in Meadowbrook and learned they had no suspects in the Wells killing. All they would say was that there was an ongoing investigation with a number of leads. Meaning, I surmised, they were looking into any of the husbands he might have enraged, women he might have betrayed, clients he might have embezzled from, drug dealers he could have ripped off, or bookies he stiffed.

I had nothing but instinct to go on, but I wondered

why Wells had been murdered just as the news about Jerome's camp broke. Certainly drugs, gambling, and women could all provide some pretty good reasons for visiting harm on him. But what I didn't like was that, based on what Jerome reported, either Wells had a pretty cavalier attitude about the board and its willingness to grant a permit or he was confident he could deliver the board despite public opinion. Did his confidence rest on a greedy town official who promised to grease the permit? If so, maybe the official reneged when the town opposition became apparent. In any event, I resolved to check out Wells's background more closely, if necessary, after the hearing.

Tuesday afternoon, before our meeting with Granger, we stopped at the Meadowbrook town clerk's office. The office, along with all of the other town offices, was in a large brick building that fronted Common Street in the center of Meadowbrook, just down from the town green and not far from where Wells had died. Two columns stood astride the main door, each sporting peeling paint and streaks of grime that made them look tired from holding up the building for the last 150 years or so. On the first floor, we passed a large gymnasium with a battered and scarred wooden floor that apparently doubled as a meeting hall for the town. A brown, wooden sign with badly faded black lettering directed us to the basement to find the town clerk's offices.

In the basement, none of the rooms had windows. To brighten the place, somebody had once painted the rooms bright yellow. The paint's glow had faded long ago and now the yellow had become a sickly tan.

A woman in the clerk's office sent us further down the hall to the small office where the clerk of the zoning board of appeals worked. The board members were all citizens serving voluntarily who voted on requests for permits and variances while the clerk handled correspondence and administrative matters.

We walked in, identified ourselves, and Jenny asked for the file on Jerome Mann's request for a permit for the camp. The clerk looked startled and then started to fidget.

"I'm sorry," the clerk said. "It's with the chairman of the zoning board." Her eyes shifted and looked through the door we'd just come in.

"I assume he has an office down here," Jenny said. "Could you see if the file is available for just a few minutes? We've come out from Boston and we'd like to take a look at it now, rather than having to make another trip back."

"I don't know if—"

"Angie, is there a problem?" A stocky, balding man with a moustache walked in.

"No, George, these are lawyers from Boston. They just asked for the file on that camp that the Manns are trying to build, and Ed Brown told me—"

"It's okay, Angie, just go tell Ed Brown that I told you to give me the file. I'll handle it." Angie walked around her counter and scurried out the door, taking a nervous look at me as she left.

"I'm George Sheehan," the man in charge said, holding out his hand and speaking to me.

Jenny spoke up and extended her hand. "Jenny Crane."

"Dan Kardon. Are you on the zoning board of appeals?"

"No, I'm the chairman of the board of selectmen. May I ask why you're here?"

"We're attorneys for Jerome Mann, just here to check out the file on his camp property. Dan and I know the hearing is next Monday and we understand that there's some opposition to the camp. We're hoping to work out any problems with the zoning board quickly so Jerome can get moving on the construction, before we lose the summer."

"You're replacing Chuck Wells. Terrible thing, his murder. The town's still in shock over it. I knew Chuck for a long time. He was well-liked in this town." At least by the women, I thought.

"Yeah, I can imagine," I said. "I didn't know him, but Jerome's pretty upset about it. Still, we want to get moving, so we're here trying to figure out what the beef is over the camp."

"You want to reschedule the hearing, take it off the agenda for next Monday?"

Jenny gave me a little look and hesitated, so I spoke up. "For the moment, no. We're planning to be ready. If we need time, we'll let the board know."

Sheehan looked us over for a minute. "Well, we'll be happy to show you the file. Last few days, a number of people have complained about the camp, the construction the Manns are planning, and the environmental impact of the building they'll do, so the town has to be concerned."

"But there was a camp there for years," Jenny said.

He smiled and shrugged. "Times change, Ms. Crane, as does the town's population and what people want for the town. Can't stop progress and there's no question that camps are not nearly as attractive as they used to be."

"The folks quoted in the article we read weren't talking about progress," I said. "They were talking about not wanting black and Hispanic kids coming to the town."

The smile left Sheehan's face. "You're reading only what was written and what may, or may not, have been said by a few people. And if anybody did say anything like that, they're not typical. We have good people in this town, people with a sincere interest in building a strong, cohesive community. With the tremendous growth going on around here, we have to look carefully at our open spaces, make sure land gets used for the right purposes. Don't just read the papers, Mr. Kardon. The unhappiness in this town isn't about kids from Boston—it's about the fear that some of the last, best open space in town will be forever destroyed."

The guy should be spinning stories for somebody in Washington. But I also recognized the echo of some of the same things I'd been saying and didn't like the feeling.

"Will you be meeting with the board on this case?" I asked.

"Oh, I just like to know what's going on in town," he said, and smiled again, but only with his mouth. "Anything I can do to help, just let me know." Angie gave him a file and slipped away without saying a word.

"Well, after we take a look at the file, we'll talk things over with Jerome and then give the town's attorney a call. As we said, we'd like to try to work things out."

"That's fine. Here's the folder," Sheehan said, "and Angie here will help you with copies. See you Monday night."

"Thanks for your help," Jenny said. She opened up the file on the counter.

Sheehan walked out the door. Angie found a file drawer she had to look into.

The file didn't tell us much. The only encouraging note was that it contained only three letters filed at the end of the previous week complaining about the camp reopening. Two came from individuals named Tom Jordan and Linda Redmond, both of whom said they lived on the pond. The third letter was from a woman named Stephanie Williams, on behalf of her environmental group, the Wild Woods Warriors. That letter described the endangered turtles on the golf course and explained that the group was also concerned about leaching from the camp's septic system into the pond. Finally, the letter stated that the Wild Woods Warriors did not want the last open space on the pond developed and the town had an obligation to protect the land.

The file also included a letter from Wells dated almost two months back requesting a hearing as well as a copy of a notice that had gone from the zoning board of appeals to Wells placing the hearing on the board's agenda. I pried Angie away from her file drawer and asked her to make copies of everything. As we walked down the hall and out to my car, people in a couple of offices turned and stared, then whispered to one another. Next time we come back, the voice in my head said, you'll have even more to whisper about.

After leaving the Meadowbrook town hall, we headed over to the golf club. Jerome wasn't there, but the golf course superintendent tracked him down and let us into Jerome's office to talk to him on the phone. We told him about Sheehan and what we'd found in the file.

"We've got to talk about the hearing," I said. "We'll meet Granger tonight, and get a better understanding of who's who out there, but I'm betting the good Mr. Sheehan is a player in this game. And I'm also betting he's against us."

"What happens if we don't show up Monday night, just tell 'em we need more time?" Jerome asked.

"Sheehan all but suggested we postpone it, so I'm sure we can get time if we need it," Jenny said.

"What do you guys think?" Jenny nodded to me to go ahead.

"We postpone it, we might be able to meet with the town, see if we can work things out. But the other side is, the longer we wait, the better the chance the bad publicity will snowball. We'll have more rumors and bullshit to deal with. We're the ones with a problem here—it's easy for the board to say no to us. We've got to persuade them to give the permit. The more town opinion is against us, the tougher it'll be. So the question is whether we'll get more or less support from the townspeople if we put it off."

Jerome was silent for a moment, then sighed. "Sorry to speak ill of the dead, but that asshole Wells said this was no big deal."

"Yeah, I know," I said, "I've been trying to figure out what he knew that we don't. Maybe he didn't focus on what kind of camp it would be or he thought having Daryl involved would make everybody happy. Or maybe he had pictures of the chair of the board in bed with all of the members of Meadowbrook's Brownie troop. Anyway, Wells can't tell us a damn thing now, so we've got to make our best judgments and go with 'em."

"Shit, that town had a camp full of white boys there for twenty, thirty years. Now they squawk when somebody else wants to play in their neighborhood. This kind of crap gets old. I should go out there, whack Sheehan and the whole damn board upside the head. Call 'em what they really are." I heard Jerome sighing again. "But I know what you'll tell me. The last thing I need is to piss off the town while I'm still hassling with the state."

"That's right," Jenny said. "If the town wants to send the health inspector to the camp or have the building inspector out there every day just to harass you, you'll have more trouble than you can imagine."

Jerome's voice grew louder over the phone. "Believe me, I've thought about it. Some night, a bunch of yahoos in pickup trucks might take a midnight drive over a few of our greens, wipe 'em out. Or the town tries to raise our taxes an exorbitant amount." We heard Jerome breathing heavily for a moment. "I don't know, I'm busting my ass to build a camp we'll use ten or twelve weeks a summer. The kids there are going to be so scared of grizzly bears in the woods they'll be afraid to go outside to pee at night, let alone sneak out of camp to go into town. This is such a crock, but all right, I'll be a good boy, at least for now. So can you guys be ready for Monday night?"

I nodded to Jenny. "Yes," she said. "But, Jerome, we don't know whether the board's going to be hostile or friendly. We ought to think about the best way to do this."

"What do you mean?" I motioned to Jenny to mute the phone since I wanted to talk to her before we made decisions with Jerome. But she waved me off and stared intently at the speakerphone as she spoke.

"Well, I'm thinking we should go in strong. Dan and I can talk about the merits of the camp, how important it is for the kids, what you're trying to accomplish. We can talk about things we can offer the town if they let us go forward. Then we'd raise the discrimination and civil rights claims we'll bring if they rule against the camp. Kind of a carrot and stick thing."

There was silence for a moment. Jenny sat on the edge of her chair, turned from the phone, and peered at me. I didn't say anything.

"Sounds okay. Kardon, what do you think?" I hesitated for a minute.

"Jerome, you mind if Jenny and I take some time—"

"Dan," Jenny said, "we don't have time. We need to decide things quickly."

I gave an inward sigh. "Okay, there's nothing wrong with that approach, but there's another way to do the hearing. Remember, this isn't really a legal decision for the town, it's mostly political and social—do they or don't they want to give a permit? Question is, will a Boston lawyer have more or less clout with the board than Jerome will? Instead of Jenny and me, Jerome could do the presentation. You can use the same kind of format, though personally I hate to threaten lawsuits to a crowd. Get a bunch of people together, they get a lot braver and a lot dumber all at the same time."

More silence. Jenny sat back in her chair, crossed her arms, and directed a small frown my way.

"Interesting—I'll think about it. I sure as hell stop listening anytime a lawyer starts in," Jerome said.

"I'm just giving you an alternative—it's your call. You know the town, the officials better than we do. We'll play it however you want. We can talk later in the week, no need to decide now," I said.

"Where's the hearing held and what kind of crowd will be there?" I glanced at Jenny and she motioned that I should keep talking.

"Should be in town hall. Most places, no more than ten, twenty people would be in the audience, plus the five members of the board and some other officials. Might have more people attending because of the publicity, but generally these aren't big deals."

"What do you think about bringing Daryl?"

"You think he'd come?" I asked.

"Don't know—not his usual kind of gig. But he's getting a little bored just working out. And a chunk of his change is on the line, so I'll ask him. Might give the crowd a thrill, make 'em feel better about the project."

Jerome paused and then spoke with new intensity. "I gotta get this deal done for the camp soon. Daryl and some of the others, don't know how long I can hold them in line. This hearing goes badly, they may want to bail."

"How about you?" Jenny said.

"The damn turtles, I know they can really screw things up with the state, so they've got me nervous. But the town—nah, we can work out something. We'll give 'em a piece of land, build a playground, give some town kids scholarships to the camp, do something to make people happy. Sheehan and his buddies may think they know how to play the game. But hell, I pulled my sorry black ass up from way down in the crapper doing deals with Boston Brahmins and Irish pols from South Boston. Nothing in Meadowbrook comes close to what I've already been through."

"You got quite a jones for the course and the camp," I said.

His voice softened. "Yeah, maybe, but in the end I'm a businessman too. I want to get it done. But I know you can't do every deal. If we can't get this one done right, I'll start over somewhere else."

"All right," I said, "it's gonna take some work, but

let's see what we can do with the town. Then we can go talk to the state about the turtles."

Jenny spoke up. "I'll talk to you later in the week to report on anything we learn and to discuss how we're going to handle things."

Jerome just grunted in response. Jenny started to tell him one last thing, but he'd already banged down the phone.

I looked at Jenny. "Go for a walk?" I asked.

She just nodded.

We started down the first fairway, both of us still in our suits. Jenny had her arms folded across her chest and her head down for the first few minutes. Neither of us said anything.

"You wanta tell me why you're so pissed?" I asked.

"I can't believe you don't know," she said.

"You weren't happy when I didn't agree with your plan for the hearing."

"Didn't agree? You didn't just disagree—you basically told Jerome the plan sucked. I can't believe you'd do that to me in front of a client, particularly my client on a big case."

"You thinking I'm trying to steal the client?"

She paused. "I'm so mad, I don't know what I'm thinking. Except I think you can be a shithead when you're being a lawyer."

"Not just when I'm being a lawyer," I said and laughed. Her face became closed and hard. She turned around and started walking away.

"Hey," I said, "how come you're always telling me to talk about things, and when I start a conversation, you walk away?" It didn't stop her, but it slowed her down so I could catch up with her. I thought about putting an arm on her shoulder but figured that would only wind her up tighter.

"Look, I'm sorry," I said. "I wasn't laughing at you, I was laughing at the thought of stealing Jerome as a client. Besides me, the guy's your biggest fan. He listens to you, wants to hear what you have to say. He doesn't know me at all, except he's heard that I can be a pain in the ass. And he thinks he needs that, so that's all I am to him, a tough shyster. You, you're special."

She didn't say anything for a minute but finally stopped walking. She turned and looked right at me. "Maybe, but I'm still not happy about you contradicting me in front of Jerome."

"Two things," I said. "First, I motioned to you to stop talking, remember? I wanted us to talk together so we had a strategy before we talked to Jerome about it. And you went ahead, right over me."

She thought, then nodded her head a couple of times, just slightly.

"Second," I said, "I just gave him the option. You've got to do that, you want to serve the client well. Some clients will let us make the decisions but that's not Jerome. Personally, I think people aren't going to want to hear from Boston lawyers. They're going to want to hear from Jerome. And Daryl, he's a star. Can't be a whole lot of stars who've shown up in Meadowbrook. I don't know if Jerome can pull it off, but I'd bet a boatload of money he's got a better shot at it than we do. If Jerome wants us to do it, fine, that's his call."

I looked at my watch and turned toward the clubhouse. "Come on, time to head back."

We started walking again. Her arms fell to her sides and we didn't say anything for a minute.

"I can see your point," Jenny said. "I'm sorry."

"It's okay, I've been called a shithead before."

"It's still true sometimes, even if maybe not this time," she said.

"I'm not trying to take over the case, I just want the best thing for the client. You do, too. But we're not always going to agree on what that is. You're entitled to your view, I'm entitled to mine. We should hash it out ourselves before we talk to the client, though."

"I hear you," she said and took my hand. We walked back to the clubhouse through a peaceful golf course, only the sounds of bullfrogs from distant ponds and birds settling down in the trees for the evening breaking the silence. It would not be our last disagreement, I thought. Working with somebody I cared about had blown up on me in the past. But every time Jenny and I negotiated another personal or professional minefield together, I had a little more hope I could keep the explosions down to a dull roar this time around.

After leaving the golf course, we drove to the restaurant in Wellesley center. The trip covered about thirty miles but the towns were separated by more distance than that. On the way to meet Granger, we drove past affluent and stately Wellesley College, along with upscale women's clothing stores, pricey restaurants, a couple of antique stores, a host of other stores that wouldn't have stayed open for a week in Meadowbrook, and plenty of enormous houses with large, manicured lawns. Meadowbrook might have aspirations but Wellesley had long since arrived.

David Granger met us at a small Japanese restaurant he chose that was on the second floor of a Wellesley office building. Tall and lean, Granger wore steel-rimmed glasses and had a full head of curly brown hair.

The restaurant didn't serve alcohol, but Granger had planned ahead and brought a six-pack of Kirin beer to go with the food. He and Jenny ordered teriyaki; I ordered sushi.

Most of his work, he told us, was in the Wellesley area or in some of the adjoining suburbs. He handled mostly commercial properties. Granger took a bath in the late 1980s and early 1990s along with just about everybody else dealing in Massachusetts real estate back then. Things had picked up, though, and the late 1990s had seen a hot economy push real estate rents and prices back up again.

"Thanks for meeting with us," I said.

"No problem. Sorry I couldn't do it over the weekend—I'm out of here most weekends. I enjoyed working with Jerome, so I'm happy to help him out."

"How did you get involved with the property the Manns bought?" Jenny asked, after we'd gotten over the preliminary chatting.

"Simple story, though not my normal kind of deal. I grew up in Meadowbrook, knew Arthur Dennison, his whole family. I don't usually do land deals like this one, but when Jerome wanted some help, Dennison recommended me. Kind of a weird setup, but both guys were trying to be pretty fair about the whole thing, not trying to screw each other, so it worked out."

"Nice piece of land," I said.

"Yeah, it's gorgeous. Last place like it for miles around. I used to visit the farm with friends when I was a kid, do foolish stuff. A lot of people tried to buy it from Dennison before Jerome came along."

"You grew up in Meadowbrook?" Jenny asked.

"Yeah, my mom still lives there."

I looked up at him. "You knew Wells?"

"Yeah, can't believe he was killed. He was younger than me, but I knew him. We played on the baseball team in high school—when I was a senior, he made the team as a sophomore, maybe a junior. Hadn't seen much of him over the last few years, but still, I was shocked when I heard about him."

"You work with him?"

"No, just ran across him occasionally. He handled some real estate transactions for clients and was also a partner in some small deals."

"What kind of guy was he?" Jenny asked.

"Decent guy. We talked real estate, baseball, and women, about what you'd expect from guys who mostly connected over what they did in high school."

Jenny followed up. "What kind of practice did he have?"

"General practice. Some divorce and estate work, real estate, small business stuff. He never liked to work real hard, but he made a living at it."

"You ever hear about him having a weakness for women, drugs, or gambling?" I asked.

Granger looked at me over his beer glass intently for a moment. "Meadowbrook's a small town. I've heard plenty about just about every adult in the town and half the teenagers. Doesn't mean I pay it any mind."

"Sorry," I said. "I'm just trying to find out a little about Wells."

"How come? I know he represented Jerome—the police don't think there's a connection between Jerome's projects and Wells getting killed, do they?"

"No, we're just trying to understand the whole project better. You may have seen the Meadowbrook paper—there's some opposition to Jerome operating the camp the way he wants to. But Wells thought he could get the town to accept the camp, so we're just trying to find out what he had in mind."

"You call Gloria yet?"

"Jerome told us she's out of town for another week or so," Jenny said.

"Too bad. Anybody knows what Wells was thinking, she'd be the one. She lives in Meadowbrook, you can find her in the book there."

"Good, thanks. Do you live in Meadowbrook now?" Jenny asked.

"Hell, no. I left for college, never went back. I don't go back there now except to visit my mom." Granger shook his head and took a long drink of beer. "Place was okay through high school since all I cared about was sports. But the town had nothing going on and people didn't want to change. Now there are new folks in town while some of the old ones are looking for money, with the new office park opening up just down the road. It's not the same place anymore. Whether that's good or bad, it's not for me to say."

"The reaction to the camp surprise you?" I asked.

"Yeah. I never would have expected that people would raise such a stink about it."

"Why?"

"Well, not a lot of forward-looking folks there when I grew up and not a lot of activists either. So if somebody pushed hard to get something, people usually went along. And compared to other places around, it hasn't grown much economically. People wanted the golf course, thought it would help with taxes and a few jobs. I figured they'd just go along with Jerome on the camp since he was bringing in the golf course."

"So why are people so worked up now?" Jenny asked.

"Come on, you know the answer to that. Everybody

thought that Jerome would just rebuild the camp, make it a regular summer camp. Now they find it's a camp for inner-city kids. Meadowbrook's lily-white."

"Scared of black kids looting and pillaging? Seems pretty far-fetched," I said.

"Yeah, but it's more complicated, it's not just that they'll be black kids. I know, it sounds silly, but most of the people I grew up with have no use for Boston, won't go near the place. Some folks in town have never been there. So they're nervous, not so much racist, just anxious about kids who are different. They don't much care whether other people have green, black, or blue skin, just being different's enough."

"You know the town can block the camp if they want, and the golf course is closed," I said. "Things keep going like this, Jerome'll have to pull out."

"I know, he's told me. The turtles, that's just bizarre, I don't know how you fix that. But the town, Christ, it's such chickenshit stuff they're worried about. There's nothing but scraps to fight over in that town, so that's what people do, fight over scraps of power, control, money."

"If we want to try to move things along, who do we talk to?" Jenny asked.

Granger paused, then gave a short, flat laugh. "Couple of weeks ago, I'd have told you to talk to Wells. How he did it, I don't know, but he was pretty damn good at getting things done. With him out of the picture, there's nobody besides going directly to the town's officials who comes to mind."

"Can we ask you about some people who complained about the camp?" Jenny continued.

Granger gave a small nod. "Okay, but don't let on you got anything from me. I'm on talking terms with people in town, still do occasional business there. They won't be happy if they think I've been telling their secrets."

"All right. George Sheehan, Tom Jordan, and Linda Redmond," Jenny said. I knocked off a piece of tuna soaked in soy sauce, ginger, and horseradish.

"Sheehan's been in real estate there for years as well as a chairman of the Selectmen. Closest thing to a political boss there is, which isn't too close because nobody gives a shit about town politics most of the time. But if Sheehan wants something to go through, it usually does. If he doesn't, it won't."

"You think Sheehan will support or oppose the camp?" I asked.

"Sheehan will do whatever he thinks will help him, so I don't know."

"You saying he's for sale?"

"Nope. Can't say that. But from what I've seen, he's been rented on occasion." Granger smiled, but not happily. "And he's bought some people he needed to help a few of his projects out, according to the scuttlebutt."

"What about the other two?" Jenny asked.

"Kind of opposites. Jordan's a new guy, around for about the last five years. Kind of scrappy, from what I hear. Haven't met him. Heads up the homeowners' association of people living out by Echo Pond. Emotional, talkative, though not real polished."

Granger sat back in his chair. He gave a slight shake of his head and his expression softened. "Linda, well, her family's been around for generations. Her mother and aunt owned that old mansion, used to be a spa or hotel thing, with the carriage house out on the pond. Gorgeous girl, around my age. Then she disappeared."

Jenny sat up at the table. "Disappeared?"

"Yup. Disappeared. One day she was there, next she was gone. Her family never said a word about her. Happened when we were in high school—she was a year behind me. Big deal among the kids when it happened, but nobody knew anything about her for almost twenty years."

"Then what happened?"

"About five years ago, she showed up, back living with her aunt. Her aunt wasn't too healthy, Linda came to take care of her. She doesn't seem to socialize much, just takes care of her aunt and hangs out on their property."

"So she's still out there?"

"Yeah. The aunt's in a nursing home."

"I thought Jerome told us that somebody was renovating the hotel, making townhouses that are about to go on the market," I said.

"Yeah, Linda's living in the carriage house on the property and she's having the mansion redone. Never thought I'd see it, thought the aunt had all the money she needed, but maybe the medical costs are high or maybe she wants Linda to have some money in hand before she dies."

Granger looked at his watch and then drummed his fingers on the table. He hadn't finished his teriyaki shrimp, but whether it was our questions or something else, dinner was coming to an end.

"One more name to throw at you," I said.

"Shoot," he said, then added, "you mind if I try the sushi?"

"Go ahead," I said and he grabbed a piece of tuna maki with small chopsticks. "You know Stephanie Williams?"

"Heard the name, don't know her or anything about

her, other than she's an environmental activist. Hasn't done much in town so far."

At that point, he motioned the waitress over for the check. "Sorry I can't stay, but I've got somebody to meet," he said.

"No problem, thanks for talking to us," I said. Jenny excused herself and went off to the rest room, saying she'd meet us outside.

"You married?" he asked as we paid. "Or are you two an item?"

"We're working at it. What about you?"

He shook his head. "Used to be married. That's why I'm in a hurry. My ex-wife, I'd let her wait, but the one I'm meeting I'd rather not stand up. Or else she may not lie down later." He laughed.

As we walked out of the restaurant, Granger said, "I got to tell you, you, Jenny, and Wells are about the only lawyers I'd have dinner with."

"How come?"

"I meet a lot of lawyers, but between the ones racking up big fees unnecessarily on the deals I do, the lawyers for the banks that cleaned me out when the market went south in the early nineties, and the sharks that represented my ex-wife, I haven't met many I liked."

"Yeah, divorces can get pretty ugly."

"Ah, hell, it was just one of those things. When real estate crashed, so did we. One day she told me I had to give up my membership in a golf club I'd belonged to for years. The club is old, beautiful. I told her the golf club was ranked in the top one hundred private clubs in the country and she wasn't ranked in the top one hundred of anything. Next thing I knew, I had lawyers all over my ass. Got messy for a while, but I'm through it now, thank God." We stopped at his car and shook hands. I saw Jenny coming out of the restaurant.

"Anyway," he said and waved to Jenny, "call if you need more help," and he stepped into a Mercedes sedan.

"Why are you shaking your head?" Jenny said as she came up to me.

"Just sorry I don't have the same touch with women he has," I said.

On Friday night, I got home a bit early. Jenny was going out to a movie with a friend, so I decided to go for a run. Mike Steiner was at home in the unit downstairs in my two-family home. The Steiners had lived downstairs for a few years. I'd been in and out of their house a lot.

Mike and his sister Jessica treat me as an honorary, if wayward, uncle. Mike, like so many eleven-year-olds, is a fanatical sports fan. Unlike most other boys his age, Mike is generally confined to a wheelchair with cerebral palsy. When the Steiners moved in, we built a ramp to accommodate the wheelchair. Though he can't play any sports, Mike still loves to go to games of any kind. In addition, I had a special three-wheeled carriage built for him so he and I go running.

We took off and went, down Beacon Street and out a couple miles to Cleveland Circle. Mike kept up his usual patter throughout the run, talking about the Red Sox, who were good enough to tease us for another summer.

"Their pitching staff is pretty good," he said. "But I don't understand why they don't trade for some right-handed power in the lineup."

"For the same reasons they sold Babe Ruth to New York and let Carlton Fisk go for nothing, among others," I said.

He laughed. "I have another question," he said.

"Surprise, surprise."

"You play golf, right?" When Tiger Woods and David Duval came along, Michael started to pay attention to golf. Then Casey Martin, a professional golfer who had a serious problem with his leg, won the right to play professional golf while using a cart. Mike, like many people with disabilities, became really interested in the game. Martin's career had been spotty, to say the least, but Mike's interest had not faded.

"Yes, but I'm a pretty bad."

"I've been watching some tournaments and there are some things I don't understand."

"Like what?"

The list of things Mike didn't understand included: why some golfers used long putters and others used short ones; why crowds weren't allowed to cheer at golf matches; why, if professional golfers were athletes, they didn't have to carry their own golf clubs and always had caddies; and last, why in all other sports, the players had to use the same ball but in golf they could all use different balls. Good questions. The answers, to the extent I could figure them out, took us all the way home.

Later that night and still restless, I called Randy Blocker, my long-time buddy with the state police. We agreed on a time to play basketball the next day.

When we showed up at the Brookline gym in the morning, two four-man teams were already playing half-court games at each end of the court. We took winners at one end and picked up a couple more players while the game finished.

When Randy and I had played basketball back in high school, he had been quicker and the better shooter while I was the stronger rebounder and more energetic defender. Over time, our games had converged, or maybe collapsed. Randy had lost a step or more in the eighteen years or so since we'd played in the state tournament and I'd lost some of the desire needed to rebound and play defense. But we still enjoyed ourselves, especially against young studs. They took one look at us and laughed.

Our team started slowly. But then I decided to play some defense on the other side's scorer, a skinny black kid who never found a teammate he couldn't pass up in favor of a shot. He didn't like it when I started sticking with him, bumping and nudging him, and he got mad. He started rushing his shots and his team members started to stand around and watch.

Randy, meanwhile, hit a couple of shots from outside and then fed the other guys on the team with a couple of passes inside for easy buckets. Soon we'd gone ahead and the other team folded quickly.

Randy and I slapped hands as the players on the other team walked off, grumbling at one another. Randy gave me a grin as we shot around before the second game.

"Wondered when you were gonna wake up and take care of that boy," he said. "Figured you were going to jive me about your bad knee and bum shoulder."

"Yeah, well, took you long enough to knock one of those bombs down. Might hurt you, I know, but try a little running, maybe move without the ball or even play some D, this game."

"Nah," Randy said, "I leave that shit for hard-working, flat-footed, poor white trash."

We won the second and third games. Randy and I had both had enough.

"Beer?" I asked.

"Who's paying?"

"I am."

"Ah, shit, I guess so, but every time you pay, it ends up costing me."

"Just the pleasure of your company."

"Save that crap for the clients and judges, Kardon. I've known you too long."

We headed over to Mann's Best Hope for a sandwich and a couple of beers. For a long time we'd played together regularly. But as Randy had kids and rose to become a lieutenant colonel in the state police, he'd played less. Then in the last year I'd been worked over pretty good and still wasn't back all the way, so we didn't play together as much we'd like.

I heard about his family for a while; then he asked about Jenny. I said she was fine, but told him about her parents, and how it was difficult having her go back and forth.

"You know," he said, "if you're buying me a beer just to tell me you've messed things up with Jenny, I don't want to hear it. She's the best thing to happen to you since you met me. I find you fooling around on her, I'll arrest you for terminal stupidity."

"Hell of a friend you are. No, man, no fooling around. It's just a pain in the ass, this long-distance stuff, but that's not what I want to ask about."

"Good. You finally want in on the game of life, you got to get the hang of the relationship thing."

I gave a small laugh and shook my head. "Damn, I like the way you sugarcoat things."

Randy sat back in his chair, smiled, and grabbed his beer. "So to what do I owe this beer and the others that'll follow?"

"Nothing big, just whatever you can tell me about one of your investigations."

"Oh, no, not again. You sticking your nose in somewhere? Can't you just get paid lots of money to confuse, obfuscate, crap like that? And, dammit, you're a good friend, but you know I'm not giving you anything confidential."

"Yeah, I know, and I'm not involved in anything you got going on, at least as far as I know. Jenny and I just took on a project out in Meadowbrook. Lawyer before us turned up dead."

"That Wells guy? The lawyer?"

"Yeah."

"I can't believe it. I should have known. Trouble follows you like one of those goddamned sucker fish on a shark."

"You mean a remora."

"No, I mean you're an asshole. You're picking up a case from a dead guy, okay, but it doesn't give you a special license to figure out why he died and who did it."

"I know, we're not looking into the murder. We've just got some weird stuff going on in Meadowbrook. I want to make sure it has nothing to do with why Wells died."

"Well, I'm happy to tell you I know almost nothing, which is about all I could tell you anyway."

"Where are you in the investigation?"

"Still just talking to a lot of people. Could have been a robbery, but even that's not clear."

"No witnesses? Nobody saw or heard anything?"

"Big thunderstorms went through that night. They haven't found anybody who saw anything and most people weren't outside."

"I hear he liked the ladies," I said.

"Yeah, well, we've heard he had a bunch of nasty

habits, but we're still working on it. No main suspect, no clear motive at this point."

"Forensics tell you anything?"

"Whacked in the head with his own baseball bat. May have fallen and hit his head against a file cabinet on the way down. He'd been drinking. So why do you care?"

"Mostly I just want to make sure his death doesn't tie in to the projects we've taken over."

Randy wanted to know what the project was and his eyebrows lifted when I told him about the Manns, the golf course, and the camp. "I've heard good things about Jerome," he said, "but I hear Daryl's a punk."

"You know I can't talk about my clients."

"But I can talk about our investigations?"

"When you put it that way, I'd agree, Jerome's a good guy and Daryl's not a barrel of fun."

"You think somebody knocked off Wells over a kids' camp? Or a turtle?"

"Put in your usual subtle way, nope, I don't. That's too far-fetched. But there are grumblings about the camp in town. I just wanted to see if you'd nailed anything down yet."

"Nope, it's still open."

I paid as promised. Randy and I shook hands. On the way out, he talked to me about playing in a summer basketball league. When I didn't agree, he accused me of going soft. Then he told me I could make it up to him by getting him onto the Manns' golf course for free. I was about to say yes when it struck me.

"Damn, you set me up. You knew I wouldn't go for the summer league, then you went for what you really wanted, the golf."

"Hey, don't let anyone tell you you're slow just 'cause

you're JD-impaired. You catch on quick. So we gotta golf game?"

"I'll call you."

"Do that, buddy, or I'll tell Jenny you've been playing around. I do that, you're gonna wish you were in Wells's shoes."

After lunch with Randy, Jenny and I met at the office. We worked during the day to prepare for the hearing in Meadowbrook, checking out cases, zoning ordinances, and the file for any points we could find. The work took us until after six P.M. Jenny had agreed to meet with Jerome to go over some other questions we needed answered. She went off to dinner with him at Mann's Best Hope. She had a visit to the Museum of Fine Arts planned for the next day so I wouldn't see her until Sunday night.

I went home and went for another run, this one a little slower but longer, maybe ten miles altogether. Later, I turned on a late night NBA play-off game on television. Sacramento knocked off Minnesota by thirty-five points. I wondered if, on Monday night, Jerome, Jenny, and I would end up like Sacramento or like Minnesota.

CHAPTER————————
FIVE

J erome, Daryl, Jenny and I walked downstairs through the dingy corridors of the Meadowbrook town hall. We heard the Monday night meeting before we saw it. At first, only low-level voices and laughter drifted our way. As we approached the gymnasium that also served as the town's largest meeting room, the noise grew louder.

"Hold on a minute," I said to Jerome and Daryl, "let's take a look." I motioned them to wait before entering the room then Jenny and I stepped inside. We looked around the room, then I took a glance at Jenny. She looked back and gave a nervous little shake of her head. After a short survey, we went back to Jerome and Daryl.

"Bad news, counselors?" Jerome asked. Jenny looked at me.

"Big crowd. Got to be at least one hundred people there, maybe one-fifty."

"That's not a crowd," Daryl said. "Haven't played in front of a group that small since high school."

"Shit, Daryl," said Jerome, "this is no game. You get this many people in a small town like this, it means they're worked up about something. Maybe they'll be for us, maybe against, but it gives the real assholes among 'em cover, a crowd they can hide behind. I don't like it."

None of us said anything for a moment, then Jenny spoke. "You want to change what we planned on doing? You want us to take over, do the talking? Or we could still ask for a postponement."

"Nope. Gonna have to face these folks sometime, may as well be tonight. We run now, it'll look like we're scared. Come on, Daryl."

We walked in the door at the stroke of seven. Jerome went in first, nodding at people he knew, shaking a few hands. Daryl didn't smile, didn't acknowledge anybody, and simply followed along. Jenny walked behind them, holding herself tall but rigid, her muscles tensed.

Every person in the room turned and stared at us. We were the only ones in suits, the only ones with brief-cases, and Jerome and Daryl were the only blacks in the crowd.

The room had been set up with rows of folding chairs, now about half full with more people streaming in. Up front, five people sat at an old wooden folding table. A woman was at the far end of the table with documents, recording equipment, and paper in front of her, obvi-ously the secretary for the board. At the edges of the room and in the paths between the rows of chairs, small groups of people had gathered.

George Sheehan, the chair of the selectmen, stood off to the side of the table, laughing and red-faced. From the smiles all around, we had just interrupted a jovial chat he was having with members of the zoning board of appeals. On seeing us, the board members immedi-ately turned, almost in unison, to Sheehan, to form a huddle where they whispered among themselves, sneak-ing peeks at us.

The audience gradually went back to talking but we had quieted the roar. Jenny and I approached the head table. I stepped back and let Jenny take the lead.

"My name is Jenny Crane. Mr. Kardon and I are here with Jerome Mann for the hearing on the permit for his camp. Who's the chairman?"

The five members of the board looked at us but nobody spoke for a moment. Finally a round-faced man with glasses gave a cough.

"I am. Ed Brown."

"Can you tell me where we are on the agenda?"

He rubbed his hands together before speaking. "We weren't sure what'd you do, what with Chuck dead. That's too bad, by the way. Anyway, we weren't sure who would be here for Mr. Mann, we thought you might like more time, or maybe . . ." His voice trailed off.

Jenny let the board stew in its own silence for a moment before speaking. I glanced at a copy of an agenda for the meeting that lay in front of one of the board members. The hearing on the Mann project was listed as first on the agenda.

"No, tonight's fine. We're ready," she said, her voice strong and confident.

Brown cleared his throat again and threw a quick, almost furtive, look at Sheehan. "We'll take you last," he said, "after we finish all the other business and take a break."

"That's fine."

I stepped forward, as Jenny and I had agreed. "By the way, we're also taping the hearing. I assume that won't be a problem. We just want to have an accurate record of the hearing so we can review the concerns of the board and citizens later." What we wanted was an accurate record of the hearing in case we had to sue the town. By the closed, pinched faces I saw around the table, the message had not been lost on the board.

"Mr. Kardon," Sheehan spoke up and walked over so that he stood behind Brown, face-to-face with me across the table. "Do you or Ms. Crane intend to make a presentation?"

"No, Jerome Mann and his cousin Daryl Mann will address the board."

"How long will they need?"

"Ten minutes. But they'll take questions if you have them."

Again, silence for a moment. Behind me, the audience was aware that something was going on and people had started to take their seats.

"We'll talk further at the break," Sheehan said, and he walked back to a chair against the wall. "Let's get started," he said.

The board members took their seats at the table. Brown announced that the meeting was officially opened and parts would be taped. We then listened to a complaint about a homeowner who was keeping ten barking dogs at his house, much to his neighbors' annoyance. Another resident wanted permission to set up a small used clothing shop in her house. And so it went, a series of minor requests and small complaints involving only one or two residents, until it became clear that the audience was there for us.

The board took a break after an hour. As soon as they did, the board members made a beeline, with Sheehan, to a small office adjacent to the larger meeting room. They closed the door and the crowd started talking. Nobody approached us.

"What do you think they're talking about?" Jerome asked.

"I don't know," Jenny said.

"Maybe Sheehan really thought we were bluffing, that we'd end up asking for more time," I said. "Maybe they're concerned about the large crowd, too."

"First place I've been in a long time where nobody's said anything to me, not even something stupid like how's the weather up there," Daryl said.

"Yeah," said Jerome, "doesn't feel like a Welcome Wagon meeting here."

"Come on, guys," I said, "these people don't like anybody from the big city, whether they're black, white, or purple."

"Could be, but last time I checked, you haven't spent much time being black, having shit like this happen all the time. To you, they don't look friendly," Jerome said. "To me, they look like they're ready to run me and Daryl out of here on a rail."

The board members finally came back and the crowd settled down. I tried to read something from their faces. All I could tell was that none of them looked happy.

Brown called the board to order. "The board will now consider the project on the Mann property," he said. He picked up a piece of paper and started reading from it. His hand shook a bit as he read and he paused a number of times.

"The board is aware that there are two projects intended for the Mann property, one a golf course and the other a camp. The board has already considered and approved a special permit for the golf course. Tonight the board will consider a request for a permit for the camp. The property owned by the Manns that was used for a camp can no longer be used as a residential camp since such a camp isn't allowed in our by-laws. The Manns seek to renovate some of the buildings on the property, to construct a number of new buildings on the site, and then to operate a residential, recreational camp during the summers for young people. Apparently, though the Manns haven't told us this, most of the children at the camp will be from Boston. The applicants want a permit so they can proceed with construction and operation of the camp."

Brown cleared his throat and audience members whispered among themselves. "The board will now hear from those abutters who have noted their objection to the project to the board." His statement caught me by surprise— we should have had the first crack at presenting our case.

A tall, lanky, bearded man in blue jeans and a green, rugby shirt stood up. "I'd like to be heard," he said.

"Go ahead, Tom," Brown said.

"I'm Tom Jordan, head of the Echo Pond Homeowners Association." Jordan, too, read from a prepared statement. "Some of us live right near where the camp will be and we don't want it back in operation. The old-timers have told us about the noise from the camp and the problems that occurred when the camp was open years ago. The kids'll disrupt our fishing, our boating, and our enjoyment of the pond. They'll litter, leave things lying around, and make a mess." Jordan stopped and took a breath, then went back to reading. "Now, the Manns want to make the camp larger and bring in more kids. It will only cause big problems for our neighborhood. The camp also might cause environmental problems."

Jordan looked up from his paper and his voice went higher and louder. "I know some people won't like me saying it," he said, "but we might as well face it. The Manns say that most of the kids will be from Boston.

Now, I'm not racist, I'm just telling the truth—we don't want kids coming out here doing graffiti, shoplifting, selling drugs, breaking into our homes. I don't care what color the kids are. I lived in Boston for a lot of years and had to put up with stuff like that from all kinds of punks. That's one reason I moved here. We don't want these kids in town. They'll hurt our property values and businesses, threaten our own children, and damage the town. So we want the town to vote against the permit."

There was a lot of murmuring and few shouts of "Hear, hear," and "You tell 'em, Tom." I glanced at Jerome and Daryl. Jerome was frowning. When he saw me, he shook his head a little. Daryl sat there showing nothing and saying nothing.

Brown then pointed to the other side of the room from us. "Stephanie Williams," he said.

A black haired, deeply tanned woman in well-worn khakis and a green sweatshirt that said Free the Earth stood up. "All of you know what the Wild Woods Warriors stand for," she said. "The property owned by the Manns is the last, best open space in the area. They've had to stop work on the golf course because there are endangered turtles there. We can't let them go back to using the camp property. Since the old camp closed, the fields and forests have matured on the property, the shore has become more natural. And if they do figure out a way to redesign the golf course to avoid the turtles and open the course, then the camp property becomes even more precious as a place for all of us to savor the sparkle of the water, watch the rabbits in the field, listen to the woodpeckers, and smell the scent of pine needles.

"The camp property now has hiking and mountain biking trails on it. People go there to sit quietly by the water or to bird watch. That land should be preserved, not destroyed. Putting up new buildings, putting in a new parking lot and basketball courts, plowing and clearing the fields there, all that will change the character of the land dramatically. Having a lot of kids live there, if only for the summer, will unalterably change that land and probably the pond. We'll never get it back. The board must say no to the Manns."

More cheers, whistles, and shouts of support. Jerome leaned over and said something to Jenny. In the noise I couldn't hear what he said. Daryl still sat impassively.

Brown then called on Linda Redmond, whose family owned the mansion on the pond that was being converted to townhouses. I'd seen her letter in the file. She simply reiterated her opposition to the camp. It would, she said, diminish the value of the properties she was in the process of selling, but she didn't elaborate beyond that. Six more speakers stood up, all of whom spoke against the camp. Nobody supported it.

Finally Brown asked if there were any others in the audience who wanted to speak. When nobody volunteered, Brown turned in our direction.

"Mr. Jerome Mann, I understand that you'd like to address the board. You may proceed."

There was an undercurrent of whispering and murmuring when Jerome stood up. He paused for a moment, then walked to the front of the room and stood in front of the podium. The crowd quieted quickly as Jerome gazed around the room.

"Mr. Brown, members of the board, citizens of Meadowbrook, thank you for the opportunity to speak. I'm pleased to be here. The town has cooperated with us in our effort to get the golf course going. We're appreciative and hope to have the same relationship in dealing with the camp." The audience was still. Jerome's natural

baritone voice had gone lower. He ignored the microphone but could be heard in every corner of the room.

His shoulders relaxed a little and a small smile came
on his face. He stepped out from behind the podium and
moved closer to the front row of the crowd. "Now, I've
spent a lot of time in this town in the last couple of
years," he said. "I've been to your gas station," he said,
pointing to a man seated in the third row on the left.
"Had great pancakes for breakfast served by Shirley over
there," and gestured to a middle-aged woman with short
gray hair who blushed bright red as the audience turned
to look at her. "Bought some paint at Gus's hardware
store out past the lake, had ice cream at the drive-in on
Green Street. Doing all that, I've seen this town, the
people who live here.

"You folks aren't rich and you didn't come from
money. But you have nice homes, comfortable neigh-
borhoods, and a pond nearby. What you got, you earned,
paid for yourselves. You understand hard work, the importance of giving kids a good home and a strong community, and how good it feels to go for a swim on those
hot summer days."

Jerome paused and moved back behind the podium.
The cadence of his voice slowed, his voice dropped.
"Those of you who have lived here for a while will
know better than me, but the Dennison's camp on Echo
Pond operated for over thirty years. It was used by hundreds, maybe thousands of kids. We want to do just what
the Dennisons did, bring some pleasure and learning to
a bunch of deserving boys and girls." Jerome looked
taller, sterner. He spoke in a measured, precise way, a
manner I'd not heard from him before. He surveyed the
audience as he spoke.

"Arthur Dennison made sure the camp on his land

operated in harmony with the town and its neighbors. That's what we want to do. As far as I can tell, people tolerated the camp before without complaining. We promise to work with the town and all of you to make sure that we are good, responsible citizens. The kids that come to our camp will behave the way your kids do. And we'll be careful to protect the land and the pond."

Jerome paused and when he resumed, his voice took on an edge. "The board and the town, though, must know that the debate is not about whether the camp land will be developed or not. Let me make it perfectly plain—it will be developed. And the golf course will open. Ms. Williams can talk all she wants about preserving the land, but it's all a fantasy." The crowd stirred and a few boos were heard. "If this board prevents us from operating the camp, that land will go to the highest bidder. Maybe someone will ask you for permission to put in a big office building there. Or there will be a large development of townhouses and condominiums laying waste to the open space. Perhaps some nice big single-family homes will go in there and the rich folks that own them will fence you off their property. Whatever happens, if the camp does not open, I promise you that the land as you know it will disappear. So if you treasure it, you'd best give us a permit. If the camp stays, so do most of the forests and fields, and there'll be trails and access for all of you. Your choice, folks, not ours. We don't want to sell that land to a developer who will make it look like condo heaven. But we will, oh yes, we will." Jerome stopped and looked around. Voices began rising from around the room, some of them angry.

"Mr. Mann, the board will now—" Brown started to rise.

Jerome turned to Brown and stared down at him. "Mr.

Brown, I'm not finished." Brown sat right down and gave a feeble wave.

Jerome again surveyed the crowd and once more stepped away from the podium, moving closer to the front row of seats. The noise subsided again.

"You people have seen my cousin Daryl, I'm sure," Jerome said and turned his way. "Makes more money than all the rest of us in this room playing for the Boston Shamrocks. Drives an expensive car, wears six-hundred-dollar suits." A few people laughed. "Daryl, stand up." Daryl stood, still without expression.

"Daryl, did I have a big house in Boston when I grew up?"

"Nope. Two room apartment for you, your two brothers, and your mom in Roxbury."

"You used to come visit, right?"

"Yeah. I got to sleep on the sofa." A small laugh went through the crowd.

"How many jobs did my momma have?"

"Three, I recall. She used to clean houses, do some work at the church, and she cooked at a restaurant. Made the best fried chicken I ever ate." A bigger laugh this time.

"How about you, Daryl, where did you grow up?"

"Johnson City, Tennessee."

"You live in a nice house when you were a kid?"

"Nope, lived in a broken down trailer in a crappy trailer park, a mile outside town."

"What'd your daddy do?"

"Don't know. He left when I was about three."

"You ever go to camp in the summer?"

"Not till basketball camps in high school. I was good enough so I got scholarships to go."

"Ever learn how to swim?"

"Nope."

"Ever ride on a sailboat?"

"Nope."

"Ever sit around a campfire at night in the woods?"

"Only when the heater in the trailer busted a couple of times."

"How many jobs your momma work?"

"Two."

"How often she come home and cook you dinner before she went out again to work her night job?"

"Every night."

"Thanks, Daryl." Jerome turned back to the crowd and Daryl sat down. "See, these kids you're concerned about, the ones coming from Boston for a few weeks, Daryl and I know all about them. Most of them have parents working hard, just like most of you. But those kids live with asphalt all around them instead of grass. Some of them live with urine in the hallways instead of pine needles on the lawn. Pigeons crap on the cars and there are no woodpeckers in the trees. Those kids would love to hear the woodpeckers Ms. Williams mentioned, or see the rabbits she talked about. The kids in Boston don't have playing fields outside their doors, or hiking trails, or rowboats and a beach a short walk away.

"All Daryl and I want to do is give these kids a couple of weeks of what you folks have all year. These kids are going to be too busy on the pond, eating three full meals—some of them, for the first time in their lives— playing baseball or soccer, to do any of the things you're scared about. And if any of you have any problems, you call me any time and I'll make it right, whatever it takes.

"You have a chance to give some kids a look at a different way of living, give them some idea of why you care about woods and meadows, birds and animals. Sure, maybe it's a bit scary. But you tell me—you really want to write these kids off without even knowing them? Anybody here got the guts to tell any of these kids to their faces you don't want them coming to your town?"

Jerome stopped, to silence. He turned back to the board. "I'll take questions, comments, anything the board wants. This camp is important to me, to my cousin. We'll do whatever we can to make it work for us and for you." He walked back to join us.

For a long moment the crowd was silent. Then conversations started and the noise started to build. I heard some people say the camp should be given a chance while others insisted it should never operate on the pond.

I looked at the board. Four members of the board had their heads down, staring at the table or at documents. One, Brown, was looking at Sheehan. I saw Sheehan give a small nod of his head.

Brown cleared his throat and, speaking into the microphone, asked the crowd to be quiet. His voice had a noticeable quaver.

"Are there any comments or questions for Mr. Mann?" he asked. Nobody spoke up. "Do any of the board members want to discuss the issue?" More silence.

"Then we'll vote. All those in favor of granting the permit, raise your hands." None went up. "All those who wish to vote against granting the permit as requested for the camp, raise your hands." Five hands. "The request for a permit is denied." One of the other board members quickly moved to adjourn, it was voted on, and the hearing ended. Only a couple of people applauded. Most people seemed shocked at how quickly it was voted on. I heard a number of people say the board should have at least considered and debated the permit. Only a few, including Tom Jordan, seemed to be gloating, a testimony to the power of Jerome's presentation.

Jerome turned to us. "That's it? They don't have to talk about it or consider anything? Man, I can't believe it—these people got no balls at all."

The color had gone from Jenny's face. Anxiety and uncertainty had replaced it.

"Yeah," I said, "it smells, but they can do what they just did. You did a hell of a job, turned people around, but the board ignored it."

"We gotta do something," Jerome said, "can't let them pull this shit. I heard people in the audience, some of them want the camp."

"I know, but it's the board's decision, they don't have to pay attention to the audience. There's no law that says the board has to take any time to consider our case."

"So these two-bit pricks can get away with telling us to fuck off just because they don't like having black kids in town," Daryl said.

Jenny jumped back in. "Well, that's what we'll sue the board on—discriminating against the camp, after the camp for white kids operated out there, after the town's given permits to all sorts of white businesses and residents. But that's the only real legal recourse now, unless we can go back to the board and ask them to reconsider if we offer the town something."

"Ah, man, I've had it," Jerome said. "Back in a minute." He took off, showing a quick first step that would have made him strong on the basketball floor years ago.

"Damn," Daryl said, "I was afraid of this." The three of us followed in Jerome's wake through the milling crowd. As we worked our way through, I heard "sorry" and "good luck," as well as "should have stayed in Boston" and "get out of town."

We finally made it to the group that surrounded Brown and Sheehan. Sheehan had been holding court with the board members and a few others, with loud guffaws and back slaps all around. They fell silent when Jerome broke into the circle and we followed.

"I know what you pulled," Jerome said to Brown. "You had it wired all the way, a fucking kangaroo court. Bunch of white kids is okay, but nappy-headed black kids, they're not allowed. You think if white kids piss in the pond it's cleaner than black kids?"

"Mr. Mann," Sheehan said, stepping forward, "I hear you were a fine basketball player in Boston. You and your cousin are a little out of your element here. I understand you're upset, but let's not go around making wild accusations. The board considered the arguments and ruled on the merits of your request. The neighbors had complained and the board apparently believes that at this time, a camp is not an appropriate facility to put on your property. The ruling is legal, but if you want to take a fruitless case to court, go ahead."

"I'm asking you, man to man, bring the board back, talk about it, make things right," Jerome said.

"The board has ruled. We can't change that."

"You going to stand by that crap pulled on us tonight?"

"That's enough, Mr. Mann. We don't need to listen to obscenities and vilification. It's over."

"No, man, it's not over. You don't get it. You think it's over, but it's not."

"Is that a threat, Mr. Mann? This isn't a basketball court or a street corner."

"You don't know squat, Sheehan, and you sure as hell don't know basketball. Basketball's got rules, and a foul's a foul. You guys make up whatever rules you want. And Daryl and me, we don't talk trash when we play. We just do whatever it takes to win. You want to make sure you keep those poor, black kids away from your homes and businesses, you'll see the consequences, that's what I'm saying."

With that, Jerome wheeled around and walked away, leaving Sheehan's mouth open. He called after us as we walked away. Daryl kept walking while Sheehan all but ran up to Jenny and me.

"You saw him threaten me, Ms. Crane, so did you, Kardon," Sheehan said.

"He threatened to sell the land to the highest bidder and said we're not through yet, that's all," Jenny said.

"What the hell is he talking about?"

Jenny turned to me and shrugged. "I don't know. Do you?" I just gave a small smile.

"I demand you tell me right now what you and the Manns are planning to do. This is completely outrageous behavior."

"Cut the bullshit, Sheehan," I said. "You can't demand a thing from us. The board already screwed the Manns over, you were behind it, and it's obvious why. Whatever Jerome and Daryl do will be within their rights, just like you insist the board was within its rights. That's all you need to know." I turned and walked away thinking, Damn, I hope I'm right.

CHAPTER

SIX

By the time we'd walked back to Jerome's car after the hearing, Jerome and Daryl were deep into a conversation that stopped as soon as we arrived. Daryl was shaking his head.

"I'm sorry it all went so badly tonight," Jenny said. "Maybe we can let things cool down for a bit, then go back to the town and offer them something—build a Little League field, use of the camp facilities, things like that—before we sue."

"What kind of leverage will we have that we didn't have tonight?" Jerome asked.

"Now we've got stronger statements and evidence of discrimination," I said. "The town'll look pretty bad. But you guys were right, I was wrong—some of those folks don't want you in their town, period."

"You and Barbie figured it out a little too late, Ken," Daryl said. "And we're not going to court."

"Will you stop that Barbie and Ken crap?" I said. "We're on your side, case you haven't noticed."

"Okay, Ken, I'll—"

"Come on, Daryl, cool down," Jerome said.

"Jerome, what's going on with you guys?" Jenny asked.

"Ken—'scuse me, Mr. Lawyer, had it right," Daryl

said. "You guys fucked up. We walked into an ambush. You should have known about it. And you should have been doing the talking, not us. Should have threatened their asses, told 'em we'll sue every one of the sons of bitches on the board personally, make 'em spend all their money on lawyers, they don't give us the camp. None of that stupid oh-what-a-poor-black-boy-I-was crap we tried, Jerome. Kardon, we should have walked in there, you hit 'em upside the head with some heavy lawyer shit, we walk out of there with the camp."

"Now, Daryl—" Jerome said before Daryl cut him off.

"They fucked up, Jerome. Kardon's supposed to be good. He was, this wouldn't have happened."

"Daryl," I said, "yeah, I feel bad about what happened and maybe there are a few things we could have done better. I accept that. And you're entitled to your opinion. You think I fucked up, fine.

"But that board had its mind made up before we walked in there; didn't matter what we said. Maybe Wells had something to swing the board, maybe not, but Jenny and I sure as hell didn't know what magic potion Wells might have had. And Jerome did a great job, turned around a good part of the audience in a way we never could have.

"And another thing. You want us to intimidate people with phony legal threats, you got the wrong lawyers. First, it wouldn't work here—the town has perfectly competent lawyers who know legal bullshit, even if you don't. Second, it would destroy any credibility we might have. Whether you like it or not, that's important to me. You give me facts, arguments that make sense, and the law, I'll fight for you all day and all night. But you want me to blackmail somebody with a bogus lawsuit just so

they have to pay big legal bills, screw that. Go get one
of those suits that charge you four hundred and fifty
bucks an hour. I don't tell you how to rebound or play
defense, so I'd prefer you don't tell me how to practice
law."

Daryl and I were looking directly at each other. "So
now what, Mr. Lawyer?" he said. "Camp can't open and
we don't have time for court. Takes years for cases in
court and I'm not waiting. We gotta move this property,
cut our losses." Daryl turned and looked at his cousin.
"Jerome, you still want to build a camp, you find somewhere else to put it. This is ridiculous."

"No, Daryl, I'm not giving up yet," Jerome said. "I
know you got money on the line, but so do I. I'm not
going to mess around for long, but give me a few weeks.
Then if things don't change, I'll do whatever we have
to. Won't cost you, I promise." Daryl started to turn
away.

"And listen, you're wrong about Jenny and Kardon.
It was my decision, not theirs, that you and I talk tonight.
Actually took a lot of guts on their part—most lawyers
wouldn't do it because they don't like to give up control
and because of just what happened tonight. Things go
bad, the client gets pissed."

"Yeah, well, this is one pissed client," Daryl said.

"Daryl, you want—" I said but Jerome cut me off.

"Daryl, we got enough problems without you going
off on Jenny and Kardon. The board's the problem.
Lawyers wouldn't have moved them except with an Uzi.
By the end, we had some of the crowd with us and most
of them didn't expect the board to vote without discussion. Sheehan had those guys in the palm of his hand,
but they looked bad tonight in front of the whole town.
Sheehan, that's the guy to be pissed at. That's who

we've got to work on and I got some ideas on how to do that."

"What are you going to do?" I asked.

"Give me a day or two to think on it," Jerome said and turned back to Daryl. "Come on, man, give me a month."

"Jesus, Jerome, you better not do anything stupid," Daryl said. "You want a camp that bad, we can find you a place. Plus the golf course is still closed down."

"I know, but the golf course is just about done so we're not putting much more money into it. The site is perfect for a camp. Just give me a little more time—I won't put the money at risk."

Daryl and Jerome looked at one another, oblivious of Jenny and me or anything else. "A month," Daryl finally said. "Providing nothing else goes wrong." He gave me a last look, shook his head, opened the door to Jerome's SUV and climbed in.

"Dan, if you don't mind, I'd like a few minutes to talk with Jerome," Jenny said.

The discussion left me with a knot in my stomach and probably without a client. I took a deep breath. "Sure, but, Jerome, you want to tell me what comes next?"

He gave me a small smile. "Don't worry about tonight, Dan. You didn't do anything wrong. I've done plenty of deals where things got nasty, but Daryl's never been through anything like this. That board, though— they were exactly what I was afraid of, a lynch mob without a rope. A little more subtle up here but we're still fucked at the end."

Jerome gave me a cuff on the shoulder and I walked away. The knot in my stomach untied a bit. I stood in the parking lot by our car, waiting for Jenny, watching other people leave, listening to their small talk.

I'd underestimated the hostility toward the camp and misjudged the residents of Meadowbrook. And I didn't expect any more golf games with Daryl. But Jerome was right—on this night, neither Clarence Darrow nor Johnny Cochran would have changed the outcome. If Jerome had something better in the self-help department, there was no reason not to try.

There was, though, something we needed to do as well. Wells told Jerome he could get the board to grant a permit. Either he'd lied to Jerome, he'd badly misjudged the board, or he'd had something that would have turned the board around. I made a mental note to check with Wells's secretary when she returned and to follow up on locating whatever files Wells had. It seemed an awfully small thing to die for, but perhaps Wells had information that would have kept the board—that is, Sheehan—in line and somebody killed him to make sure it was never used. Unlikely, yes. But after what we'd seen tonight, I wanted to know the answer.

A few minutes later, Jenny came over and stood next to me, her body tucked in next to mine as we watched Jerome and the last remaining cars drive out of the parking lot. The building lights had been turned off and a few clouds swept over the silvery quarter moon. After the last car left, Jenny leaned into me and put her head on my shoulder. I put my arms around her.

"You okay?" I asked.

"Yes. Exhausted, kind of raw. I just wasn't prepared for this kind of a mess."

"How's Jerome?"

"Angry. Determined to keep going. He doesn't blame us, though."

"Shit, he wants to fire us, he's got grounds. We could

have been a lot better prepared, figured things out quicker."

"The real problem isn't us—it's that some of the good folks of Meadowbrook don't want black kids wandering around their fair streets."

"Yeah. Jerome and Daryl sniffed that out before the hearing started. I didn't catch onto how bad it was until too late."

"Stop kicking yourself. The board was going to deny the permit, end of story. Who was the one who taught me you can't win all the battles, you have to focus on winning the war?"

"Yeah, but I don't like getting caught with my pants down. Present company excluded, of course. And it's hard on you—Jerome's both a client and a friend. Bad combination, when things aren't going well."

"I know—it felt awful tonight. But Jerome and I talked about it a little. Jerome's a big boy. Daryl too. They knew what they might be getting into. Besides, they weren't in great shape before tonight. What's the worst that happens? Jerome and Daryl have to sell the camp, even the golf course, and buy a new camp somewhere else. Jerome wants to keep going, but he knows he can cut his losses pretty quick."

"He may have to. Even if he turns the board around, he's got problems on the golf course to deal with and I don't see Daryl keeping his money in the land for much longer."

Jenny gave a small laugh. "I know Jerome. If he has to sell, he'll try to sell the property to a used car dealership just so there's a big eyesore sitting on the pond."

"Come on," I said. "Let's head home. Can't do anymore tonight."

We drove home without saying much. I put Allison

Moorer's *Alabama Song* tape on and let her country hooks clear our heads and drive away the echoes of some of the drivel we'd heard.

I asked Jenny if she wanted to stay at my place. She wanted some time alone, she said, so I dropped her at her place. It was late when I arrived home, but too many dissonant thoughts kept sleep at bay. I ran down to Beacon Street, then west. The few people I saw disappeared altogether as I reached the reservoir. But then I ran through the campus of Boston College and found a few couples entwined in shadows and crevices. I took a shortcut off the college and headed back to the house, running harder into exhaustion.

Tuesday night, I ran home from the office. Jenny was going to meet me there—we planned to eat and then catch an Irish film at the Coolidge Corner Theatre.

I walked in the door to find Jenny hanging up the phone. She looked at me, put her hands over her face, and started crying. I hugged her and said nothing for a minute.

"What's the matter, honey?"

"I can't believe it," she said.

"What's wrong? Your dad in trouble?"

"No, my mother fell trying to help my dad and broke her hip. She's safe but in the hospital."

"Damn, I'm sorry." I held her for a couple of minutes while she sniffled.

"I'm going to have to go back there tomorrow," she said.

"Okay."

I held for a while longer, not saying anything.

"I don't know if I'm crying for me or them," she said.

"What's it all about?"

"Oh, I'm upset for my mom, she's been so devoted to my father. And I'm worried about him, because he's relied on her so much. I just never dreamed we'd have to deal with all this so soon. My dad's only seventy-three and my mom's sixty-five—I can't believe they're having all these problems. But I'm also so frustrated, upset about leaving work now."

"You mean Jerome's case?"

"Yes. A week and a half ago, I was excited. Now, things look difficult, and I'm not going to be around to work on it."

"It'll all be okay. You've got to do the important stuff."

"But it's all important."

"You'll have other cases, other clients."

"I don't want to let Jerome down, though."

"Don't worry about it. He'll have more work for you. And I'll handle whatever he needs to have done. We'll talk as we go along."

"I know, and I'm sorry—you have other work to do, and I know this will make life tougher. I'll call Jerome and tell him what's happening."

"Hey, with you gone, all I'll have to do at night is work."

Her eyes sparkled a little through the tears. "You got that right, buddy. You know, he told me last night he likes you."

"Who?"

"Jerome."

"He's a good guy. I'll do the best I can to keep your client happy with the firm, counselor. Now what about eating? What do you want for dinner? How about bar-becued ribs?"

"Hey," she said, "you told me to focus on the important things. There'll be more food, more dinners later."

She put her arms around my neck and we kissed for what seemed like a week and a half. We never made it to the barbecued ribs. We did make it back to the kitchen at around nine P.M. for ice cream. Afterward we went back to bed for dessert.

The phone rang in my office on Thursday afternoon. My secretary put Jerome through.

"Hey, Dan," he said. "I talked to Jenny. She okay?"

"Yeah. She's torn up, but she knows she's doing the right thing. Whatever you want me to do, just let me know. And I hope you're not calling from the Meadowbrook jail after doing something crazy."

"Man, you got no faith. I'm a good, law-abiding citizen."

"Then how come you're sounding happy? You get some good dirt on the board members?"

"No, but I think we can turn things around. Wanna help me out?"

"Happy to."

"What are you doing tomorrow morning?"

"Nothing I can't reschedule."

"Do that. Come on out to the golf course about nine A.M. I got something I want to show you."

I met up with Jerome the next morning in the parking lot of the golf course. He greeted me and waved me into his Pathfinder. One of the workmen sat in back. Jerome drove us out of the golf course and past the camp. We drove down near the pond on a back road I'd never traveled.

"You want to tell me what's going on?" I asked.

"Well, I got to thinking, we got it backward. I figured we'd do a deal with the board. But what I've seen of these guys, if they do a deal, they still might find a way to screw me. Sometimes you catch flies with honey, sometimes you use a flyswatter. Honey didn't work."

"You found a flyswatter?"

"We're going to look at it."

We pulled off the road into a small dirt parking area on the side of the road. Through a stand of trees, I could see the sun glinting off water. I followed Jerome and the workman on a path through the woods.

The trail emerged at the side of Echo Pond. To the right I could see homes, docks, a long beach, and, in the distance, a large mansion sitting up on a hill overlooking the lake. To the left there was an earthen dam with a stream running behind it. Along the shore I could see the golf course and camp. The face of the dam in the water was covered with stone. In the middle was a narrow gate that ran vertically down the face of the dam. Next to the gate, along the top of the dam, was a spillway, cut slightly lower than the top of the dam. Adjacent to the spillway and over the gate, a small metal shed stood atop the dam.

Jerome and the workman walked out onto the dam. It was about twenty feet deep across the top and the back sloped down at an angle toward the stream trickling behind the dam. The sloping back was covered by grass and the area along the base had been cleared of trees and shrubs.

At the shed on top of the gate, the workman stopped and unlocked a padlock on the shed door. Jerome looked over the edge of the dam at the center.

"At least three feet, maybe four," he called back to the workman.

"What are you talking about?" I said, moving up next to Jerome.

"My man Ronald here is about to make life unpleasant for our friends in Meadowbrook," Jerome said.

"You dropping some LSD in their water supply?"

"Nope. Ronald is about to open the gate to the dam. We'll let out a little water." Jerome looked at me and gave me a big smile. "Not sure the dam is safe. Right, Ronald?"

"Right," he said.

"You're going to lower the pond three to four feet?" I asked.

"Yeah."

I looked out on the pond. "How deep is it in the middle?"

"Not very. Maybe eight, ten feet through most of it. Shallower at the edges."

It took me a minute, but then I pointed to the long beach. "So the beaches and docks become useless. People have a swamp in their backyard. And if the water level stays down, probably property values go down and the town collects a lot less on taxes."

"Hell of a flyswatter, you agree?"

I shook my head. "Yeah, I do. But you better be ready for some heat. The water level goes down that much for the summer, you'll have everybody in this half of town after your ass."

"The hell with 'em. I'm not too popular as it is. Besides, this is small potatoes compared to what I thought about doing."

"Which was?"

"Just take down the whole dam. Breaching, they call it."

"Wouldn't do much for your campers who want to swim."

"Yeah, well, that's what stopped me. Anyway, folks'll still have their homes, they just won't have the pond to use, like I can't use the camp. If they're pissed enough, maybe they'll put some pressure on the town officials to back off. When they see the water coming down and summer on the way, people will have to work with me. This way, I can get a deal done and make sure these folks know not to mess around with us again. And maybe the state people won't be too happy either, might give me some leverage with them."

I looked out over the pond. It was a bright, cloudless morning; small ripples on the water showed a breeze moving west to east. The temperature had climbed to about 70 degrees, a nice day for May in New England. Leaves were filling in on the tree branches. I caught a quick glimpse of a muskrat scrambling up the bank down the shore.

"So why'd you call me out?" I asked. "Just to see you pull the plug?"

"Thought we might visit Sheehan, send a message. I wanted you along, keep everything cool. Then, depending on how things go, maybe next week I'll want you to contact the state, talk to somebody about the turtles."

"Sounds okay, but Jerome, I have to tell you, I think you're going to get people pretty riled."

He turned to me with a small, tight-lipped smile. "They got me pretty riled Monday night," he said.

The workman had entered the small shed and we could see him turning a wheel. Then the gates opened with a creaking sound. We watched as the water flowed through the gate, heading down the stream at the back that had been previously all but dry.

"Jerome, thanks. I'm glad you still want us onboard to help out," I said. "I'll keep Jenny in the loop."

"Listen, Kardon, I'm sorry if we gave you and Jenny such a hard time. I know we called you in late and the whole thing was a disaster. Daryl and I just got ticked off. And Daryl's used to blaming other people when things go bad. I tried to set him right afterward."

"You had a right to be angry. Don't apologize. I should have anticipated what happened better."

Jerome waved his hand. "Don't sweat it, man. You haven't lived with this kind of crap the way we have. You're black, particularly an athlete, they try to rip you off in business deals 'cause they think you can't even read a cereal box. When I bought my car, cops used to stop me for no reason—they couldn't believe a black guy could own an expensive car. Walk in our shoes awhile, you can smell shit coming a mile away."

"Okay," I said. "Let's go visit town hall."

We pulled up to the Meadowbrook town hall at about eleven A.M. Not many people were around, but it was a Friday, so the lack of activity was no surprise. Sheehan was in, though, and after greeting us he motioned us into his office. Before Jerome started back there, I held an arm up in front of him.

"We're comfortable here," I said, seeing out of the corner of my eye a couple of women watching us.

Jerome raised his eyes a bit, but then nodded.

Sheehan squinted at us. "I don't have time for games, gentlemen."

"Good," said Jerome, "neither do we. I'll be draining a little water out of Echo Pond over the next couple of days. Just thought you'd be interested."

"What are you talking about?"

"Just what I said. We're not sure the dam is safe, so we're going to take some pressure off it."

"How much water?"

"Three, maybe four feet. Maybe all summer. Maybe longer."

Sheehan's face turned white and his mouth dropped for a moment, but he came back quickly. "You can't do that. That's illegal, you're interfering with the town beach, with people's property rights. That's outrageous. The state agencies won't let you do it, either."

"So sue us," I said. "You and the townspeople got nothing to squawk about. Jerome's not taking anybody's property. He's just making sure he doesn't have an unsafe dam that might collapse in a bad storm. You just need the right attitude, Sheehan—you're not losing a pond, you're gaining a frog farm."

"Sheehan," Jerome said, "I don't want to fight with you and the town. I came to Meadowbrook 'cause I liked the land. I've liked the people I met. I want this thing over with as quick as possible, but I want that camp. The board's way off base, denying the permit. You know damned well that if I was bringing in a bunch of white kids to the camp, we wouldn't be having this conversation. So think on it while you watch that water go down. You want to work out something, you know where to call."

Sheehan stared at us for a full minute before turning around and walking into his office. At the threshold, he turned back to us. "Gentlemen, you'll find you've made a very big mistake. I suggest you think long and hard about this course of action." He walked into his office and closed the door. I glanced at the receptionist's phone on the desk near where we stood and I saw a line light up. We weren't the only ones who would be thinking long and hard.

The two secretaries stared at us without any pretense of working. "Have a nice day," I said as Jerome and I walked out the door.

"Thanks for keeping us out of his office. Those secretaries will have it across the town in a heartbeat. Now we wait," Jerome said. We were leaning against his Pathfinder, both facing town hall.

"Not much give in Sheehan. Let's just hope some others in town get to him, push him to move. Could be an ugly stalemate, otherwise."

"Difference is, I'm used to getting screwed and I'll do what it takes to fight back."

"I hope you're right, Jerome, but you don't have twenty-four hour guards on the golf course or the camp. People want to do some damage, you're in no position to stop them—you said that the other day."

Jerome nodded. "I know. If I can't have the camp, I want to get rid of that whole parcel anyway. I'll stick with this for at least a few days, see what happens, then decide what to do. I can handle starting over somewhere else if I have to. Right now, as the saying goes, when you got nothing, you got nothing left to lose. In this town, I got nothing to lose."

I shrugged. "All right, let me know what you need," I said. "But don't do anything stupid."

"That's something you and Daryl agree on. No, nothing stupid—I'm planning to have some fun."

Jerome and I shook hands. He took off in his new Pathfinder, I climbed into my five-year-old Blazer. Between the car and the skin, no cop would ever bother with me.

* * *

The phone rang at 3 A.M.

"Dan, it's Jenny, I'm sorry I'm calling, but I had to call. I'm scared, I need to talk, and I miss you."

I was a bit disoriented and fuzzy-headed, so could only come up with "Hi, what's going on?"

"My dad, he's had another stroke."

The fuzzy head disappeared. "Oh, Jesus, Jenny, I'm sorry. When?"

"Today. I got back from the hospital a little while ago and I couldn't sleep."

"How's he doing?"

"He'll live. He's unbelievably tough. But he's lost some of the function on his left side and the doctors aren't sure he'll be able to write or speak clearly."

"Damn. I wish I was there, just to give you a hug."

"God, I could use it. Seeing him lying there suffering was so hard. He's been such a rock for so long. If he can't communicate, to write, it'll crush him." Jenny's father, formerly an English professor at East Tennessee State University, was also an essayist. Among other things, he wrote about baseball.

"How's your mother taking it?"

"All in all, she's doing pretty well. But this makes things harder. Her hip is still in bad shape and Dad will need even more care when he gets home."

For a few minutes, I listened as she talked, until her fear and adrenaline dissipated. Then I told her about the events of the day with Jerome. Finally, we both knew we couldn't say a damn thing that would make either one of us feel better.

"Good luck," I said. "I miss you."

"I'm glad to hear it. I might have to stay longer than I expected now."

"You want me to come down, get some real barbecue this time?"

"Maybe. Thanks for offering. Let's see what happens."

"Whatever I can do. Love you."

"I know you do. It helps. I love you too," she said and hung up before any more tears started.

I tried to go back to sleep, but it took a while. I put on a Joshua Redman CD just to settle the buzz I felt.

Jenny was the only child in her family who didn't have young kids. It made sense for her to stay with her parents, at least for a while. She knew she could work in my firm whenever she wanted, so she didn't have a job at risk in Boston. All she had up here was me and neither of us had yet figured out exactly what that meant. If she was going to be in Tennessee for some time, it would take us even longer to do so.

I thought back to the time, a year ago, before I met Jenny, when I didn't enjoy my life, didn't know whether to keep my practice going, and didn't know some basic things about myself. I still had some tough learning to do, but Jenny had helped with a few big lessons. It wasn't that she was my teacher—it was that when the time came and I was ready to be a student, she helped. And painful as it sometimes was, I'd discovered I liked the learning, as well as Jenny.

Thinking about Jenny brought me back to Jerome. Both Jenny and Jerome had been close to attaining goals they'd worked toward when things fell apart. Jenny had wanted to stay in Boston and work as a lawyer and, I hoped, work things out with me. Jerome had been close to getting the golf course and camp he'd desired. Now, both faced serious setbacks. Jenny's sufferings were greater to be sure, but both were hurting. In *King Lear*,

Shakespeare wrote "The gods are just," but the fates of these two good people indicated otherwise. And I wasn't sure the difficulty would be over quickly for either one of them.

CHAPTER——————

SEVEN

With Jenny gone, the days, even Saturday and Sunday, took on something of a routine. Mostly I cranked things out as quickly as I could. I worked on memos, reviewed a few contracts, and engaged in some heated but ultimately productive settlement discussions with a difficult insurance adjuster—not that I'd ever dealt with an easy insurance adjuster.

After work, I'd have a quick sandwich before running or working out. Tuesday night, I skipped the running and went for dinner at Mann's Best Hope. I hadn't heard from Jerome and my calls to his office had gone unreturned, so I stayed through two sets of a truly awful fusion band, hoping to catch him. When he didn't show up, I went home.

On Wednesday morning, I got a call from the attorney for the town of Meadowbrook asking if we could meet with him—only with him—on Thursday morning. Just before heading off to court for another client, I put in call to Jerome and finally got through to him.

"How's it going?" I asked.

"Sorry I haven't called," he said, "too many things going on."

"You heard from people about the pond?"

He paused. "Took a couple of days before the water

went down enough for people to notice. Then I heard from a few people who think I'm the Grinch that stole Christmas. But you'd expect people who are pissed off to call, so no surprises."

"Who've you heard from?"

"Mostly fine, upstanding citizens who didn't leave their names."

"Great. Nasty anonymous calls. Any ones you're worried about?"

"Mostly I worry about whether any of these people ever graduated from high school. If they did, we got real problems with our educational system." He gave a laugh; I didn't. "Don't sweat it," Jerome continued, "I saved 'em for posterity—sometime when you want a lesson in how far we've advanced as a society, I'll play 'em for you."

"Anybody threaten you?"

"Nothing I'm losing sleep over." I wasn't reassured, but from Jerome's tone I knew I wasn't going to get anymore. "Finally heard from Gloria Duchesne, Wells's secretary. She's back."

"What'd she say?"

"She's devastated, but she's going to be cleaning up, closing the office. Police went through all sorts of things, including some of the files, so it's a mess. I told her you'd call."

"What about town officials? Any response so far?"

"I told a couple of 'em that we'll let the water level rise soon as we can get clearance on the camp. I gave the same speech to the reporter who ran the original story on the camp in the Meadowbrook paper. And there's a meeting of the Selectmen tomorrow night. Heat should be on the town to do something pretty quick."

"Might explain why I got a call from Tom Malone, the town counsel. He wants to meet tomorrow morning in Meadowbrook around ten to, as he said, 'explore options.' You interested?"

"Hell, yes. Set it up. When do you want to meet and where?"

"If the meeting's at ten, I might just go for a run first thing in the morning and meet you in Meadowbrook."

"Why don't you run at the golf course, shower there, then we can talk and have breakfast before we meet Malone? And just call me, leave a message, if we have to put off the meeting with Malone."

"I like it. I'll get to the course early and be back at the clubhouse by nine or so. One other thing. How about Daryl and the other investors? They holding firm?"

There was a pause and I heard a sigh. "They're still giving me some time, but nobody's happy. Daryl's supposed to meet me later this afternoon. It'll be okay." I heard a voice in the background calling Jerome, then Jerome said "Sorry, Dan, gotta go. Talk to you."

I put down the phone and got up from desk, gathering up material for a court hearing for another client. I had trouble letting go of Jerome's problems. We were walking a fine line. We needed the permit, the town wanted the pond back to normal. Should be grounds for a deal. But if we didn't get it done quickly, the relationship between Jerome and the people in town would be strained for a long time to come.

That evening I walked home along the Charles River. It was twilight and a cool, slight breeze was in my face. There were runners on the path along the riverbank, along with walkers, bikers, and rollerbladers, as well as a few rowing shells on the water. If a city could ever be lovely and playful, this was the moment—the last glow of the sun in the background, lights going on and off in buildings, the constant trail of headlights on the roads along the river, the reflections off the water. At that moment, if somebody told me that he was going to drain the Charles River, I'd be pissed.

That night, like the ones before, Jenny called. She had spent another day both at the hospital and taking care of things at home. By the time we talked, she was operating on fumes and without her customary defenses.

"My dad's getting better," she said, "more use of his arm, some of his speech coming back. But it's so slow, it's awful to watch."

"Probably a long road back for him. But he's working at it, at least, and hopefully his speech will improve over time."

"I know. That's the hardest part. I keep thinking about him, with a brain that works and a voice that doesn't, after all the words and wisdom he's given us. All the thoughts he's had, the places he's been, the things he's done, locked away. If he can just talk about those things, it'll mean so much."

"And it'll give you some time to talk to him."

"You mean, if he doesn't make it, or has more damage. I know. I just don't like thinking about it."

I waited for a moment, then said, "Damn, I'm sorry, I wasn't thinking. I didn't mean to make things harder."

"It's okay. I know it's there."

"Believe me, if you get the time, use it."

"You didn't get the time, did you?"

"Nope," was all I could say. Jenny knew that at separate times, three people who were close to me had died suddenly, without any goodbyes.

"God, I wish you were here," she said.

"I know the feeling. Today I'd have loved to have you here. Too much going on at the office, too little here at home."

"It almost sounds like you miss me."

"That's because I do."

There was a pause. "I like that," she said.

"You staying in your old room?"

"Yes," she said. "Same furniture from high school. Some of the same posters on the wall."

"Yeah, and you're just as cute as you were back then. You still wear that nice, tight cable knit letter sweater, made you look so sexy in those photos I saw?"

She laughed a little. "Oh stop it, I'm simply tired and worn out these last few days. Like some of those women up in the Appalachians who have eight kids and no teeth by the time they hit thirty."

"Have I never told you about my fetish for gaunt, haggard women? And teeth are highly overrated as a body part." She laughed some more and we broke off quickly, both sensing it wasn't going to get any easier to say goodbye.

The next morning, I put on my running clothes and was on the road before seven. Driving against the traffic, I made it to the parking lot at the golf course by eight. There were a few other cars there, presumably belonging to the workmen, but there was also one that looked like Jerome's Pathfinder. I stretched, warmed up, and went by the larger maintenance building. Neither of the two men there had seen Jerome, but it wasn't unusual for him to be out early somewhere on the golf course, they said.

Before heading out, I stopped at the clubhouse just to see if Jerome was there or whether he'd left it open so

I could grab a quick drink of water. The door opened and I walked inside to find Jerome facedown on the floor, next to a wooden table.

I said something out loud, but I have no memory of what it was. I took a deep breath and walked over to Jerome. His face was toward me, his eyes were closed. I looked for movement, felt for a pulse, and found neither. Below, I saw dried blood on the floor, on the side of him away from me. I walked outside. The bottom of my stomach dropped out. I felt nauseated and weak. I bent over with my hands on my thighs, breathing heavily, all but throwing up. After a minute or two I used my cell phone from my car to call the police, so I wouldn't handle the phone in the clubhouse. Then I walked back inside and knelt down next to him. Looking at him, my eyes burned and the lump in my stomach had ascended to my throat. "I'm sorry, Jerome. What happened? Why this?" I asked aloud.

I willed myself to look around. It didn't look like a forced entry—no broken glass, the door and the handle seemed intact. It appeared that Jerome had fallen right where he'd been shot—or stabbed, I couldn't tell—not moved from somewhere else since there was no blood trail or smearing. That meant that Jerome either knew who killed him or the killer sneaked in the door while it was open and Jerome wasn't paying attention. And since the blood was dried, and the lights were on in the clubhouse, I figured it happened late at night or early in the morning.

On the table adjacent to where Jerome lay papers and files were spread out, most having to do with either the camp or the golf course. Jerome must have been planning or drafting something, but whatever it was wasn't clear. Some of the papers had spilled on the floor, and a couple had fallen and were up against Jerome's legs.

Also on the desk was an electronic organizer, a little gizmo that plugged into a PC to back it up and kept addresses, a calendar, to do lists, and memos. I thought about picking it up, just to find out who Jerome might have been meeting with last night or this morning. I knew the police would look for fingerprints, so I didn't touch anything.

Within a couple of minutes I heard sirens and then a few police cars started arriving. The Meadowbrook police chief came along with a number of others. I met up with them outside.

"You call it in?" the police chief asked. He was beefy, with a florid face and looked maybe sixty-five years old. He squinted at me as he spoke.

"Yes."

"Who are you and what were you doing here?"

"Dan Kardon. I'm one of Jerome's lawyers, came here to meet with him."

"A Boston mouthpiece?"

I took a breath. "My office is in Boston!"

"You kill off Wells to get Mann's business?" The chief peered at me for a minute, then gave a wave at me. "Talk to him, get him out of here," he said to one of the cops with him. The cop rolled his eyes then pulled over just outside the clubhouse door.

"Lieutenant DeRosa," he said. He was balding, with a long, narrow face. His eyes looked me over without wavering.

"You got a sweetheart of a boss. He got a retirement party scheduled for later today that I screwed up?"

"He's okay. We got a few too many homicides going on right now, so everybody's on edge."

"Still nothing on Wells?"

DeRosa looked at me for a moment then gave a shake of his head. "Sorry, Kardon, we didn't come out to answer your questions."

"I gather from the chief Boston lawyers aren't highly regarded around here."

"What I hear, people in Boston aren't too thrilled with them, either," De Rosa said. "How about we skip this verbal foreplay, and you just tell me what happened, starting from the beginning."

He pulled out a small notebook and I told him what I knew while other cops worked inside. I heard the cops talking to one another, saw them looking at things, taking things in and out, using cameras, but nothing left an impression on me.

Slowly the police gathered up the other workmen on the site, all of whom looked shocked. From what little I could tell from their stories, nobody had gone near the clubhouse and nobody had seen anything.

Soon more police cars arrived, and then a couple of state police cars. I went over my story again when a pair of state troopers joined DeRosa, and then was told I could leave. I got in the car and headed back to the city. By 11:30 I was home. It was only then that I realized that I hadn't called Malone, the Meadowbrook attorney, to tell him that he'd never meet with Jerome.

I thought about making the call to the lawyer but didn't have the heart to do it. Besides, Malone would figure out what happened soon enough, if he hadn't already. I did call my office and tell them what happened. I was trying to decide what to do when the phone rang.

"Kardon? Is this Dan Kardon, lawyer who represents Jerome Mann?" The voice was deep, not one I recognized, but one sounding uneven and strained.

"Yes."

"This is Daryl Mann." He stopped again. It occurred to me that he had never called me by my name, only Ken or Mr. Lawyer. "Police told me you found Jerome this morning."

"Daryl, Jesus, I'm sorry." I went on to tell him the little I could. I asked him what the police had told his family.

"Just that he was found shot in the clubhouse, got no suspects right now. Police say they don't know what happened. They want me to come in for an interview this morning. My agent told me I need to check with a lawyer. I told him I want to use you and the lady, Jenny Crane, not the guy he wants."

"Daryl, I'm devastated about Jerome. He was a hell of a guy. I wish I'd known him better. And sure, I can help. But as far as the police are concerned, I'm a witness for the moment, so this is a little unusual. More important, we didn't exactly hit it off the other night. You just about fired us. You feel you need a lawyer, you better have one you have confidence in. And Jenny's back home—in Tennessee, actually—because of some family problems."

"I'm asking you 'cause of what happened the other night. And if Jenny's not around, I'd still like you. Argued with my agent over it. His guy, Dick Hooper, is smooth, lots of big words, but he likes to hear himself talk too much, loves to have control. He'll agree with me to my face, than do whatever the hell he wants."

"Hooper knows his stuff."

"Maybe, but I've met the man a few times and he doesn't listen."

"So why me, Daryl? I do this, you're going to have to let me do some things my way. I don't want to be looking over my shoulder all the time, thinking you're going to second-guess me."

"Yeah, that's okay. The other day, I liked it, you and Jenny didn't back down when I went after you. You admitted you might have screwed up and Jerome set me straight on some things afterward. And from everything I've heard, you're willing to get your hands dirty, do whatever it takes. Hooper, man, that guy wouldn't touch a dog turd with a ten foot shovel."

"Don't know that the fact I'll clean up dog shit is a great compliment, but I'll take it. You sure? You know damn well you can have any lawyer in this city. I don't want to go back to where we were the other night."

"Yeah, I'm sure. I got a bunch of things I'm going to need help with. And if the police can't find who killed Jerome, you do it, find the son of a bitch. I hear you've done that before."

"First things first. For the moment, that's the least of your problems," I said. "I'll do what I can. One ground rule here—you're unhappy about something, you tell me and we talk about it."

"Got it."

"Now, did the police say you're a suspect?"

"Nope. Just that they wanted to talk."

"Okay, you probably don't need me to go along. Did Jerome talk to you about phone calls he was getting?"

"Didn't tell me nothing till yesterday. When he told me about the calls, we got into it pretty good. I told him it was time to dump the property, find another place for the camp."

"You two had an argument?"

"Yeah."

"Where did you have it?"

"Clubhouse at the golf course."

"Anybody see it?"

"Some of the workmen were around."

"What'd you do after the argument?"

"We walked a couple of holes on the course, ended up over next to the pond, just to look around, talk about things."

"When you finished meeting with Jerome, where'd you go?"

"Listen, Kardon, I called you to help me out, not grill me."

"Daryl, you think I'm grilling you, you just wait for the cops to decide you're a suspect. Believe me, if the workmen saw you arguing with Jerome, then you're on the police radar screen. You want me to help, you gotta answer my questions. What'd you do after meeting with Jerome?"

"Went back to the clubhouse around five-thirty, then went into Boston for dinner, drinks."

"You stop anywhere on the way?"

"Yeah, stopped at a convenience store on the way back, bought some food."

"Anybody recognize you there?"

"Yeah. Somebody always does."

"Make sure you tell the cops about the store and the fact that somebody saw you. What about Jerome, what'd he do?"

"Don't know. He came back with me to the club-house, then I left. Said he wanted to check his messages, make some calls, then head out. I know he was nervous—the Selectmen are meeting tonight. He told me he'd called you, you guys were going to meet with the town lawyer this morning."

"You have any idea why he might have stayed at the clubhouse?"

"Nope."

"Any ideas about who he might have been meeting or who might have killed him?"

"I knew the guy, I'd be on the road now to break his neck. Had to be somebody from Meadowbrook. Nobody else had a reason to do it."

"Anybody around when you left the clubhouse?"

"Nope."

"Who were you with last night, your wife?"

Daryl didn't say anything for a moment. "No."

"You gonna tell me who?"

"Rather not."

"You sure you came back to Boston last night?"

"Yes, damnit."

"You going to be able to prove it?"

I heard only his labored breathing.

"Daryl, I'm not trying to give you a hard time. I know how you feel right now, but the police will be looking for evidence where Jerome died. They'll be talking to witnesses and they'll also be tracking down anybody who might have a reason to kill him, so—"

"Goddamnit, that's bullshit. Me kill Jerome? He's the only one I trusted, the only one . . ."

I heard more deep breathing, some clotted gasps, but Daryl held back the tears and seemed to pull himself together.

"Sorry," he said, "Didn't mean to go off on you."

"It's okay," I said. "Tell you what, talk to the police, answer their questions straight. If everything you told me is true, there's nothing to worry about. You have to withhold somebody's name, do it, maybe it won't matter. They can verify that you were at the convenience store. Given who you are and how close you were to Jerome, even if they know about the argument, they may not push you too hard, at least today. You bring me in now, the cops may wonder if you have something to hide. With any luck, they'll get some quick leads on the killer and leave you alone. You feel okay playing it that way?"

"Yeah," he said, after a moment. "I can do that."

"Give me a call tonight or tomorrow, whenever you're up to it. And anything you need me to do, just ask."

"Yeah, talk to you later, " he said, and hung up.

I sat there for a couple of minutes, feeling loss for Jerome and Daryl and some anger at myself. In the end, though I could have done things differently, it probably wouldn't have mattered. Jerome had fought his own fights long before I'd come on the scene. None of that proved a comfort, though, and the ache in my gut, the pain in my head, and the wetness in my eyes persisted.

I went to the kitchen sink and splashed some water on my face with hands that were shaking. I wanted desperately to go for a run or go back to bed. Instead, I picked up the phone to make the call I most hated to make. Part of me hoped she'd be away at the hospital.

"Hi, it's Dan."

"Are you okay? Your voice sounds funny."

"Jenny, God, I hate to be telling you this. Jerome was killed—"

"What? Oh, no, no, I don't believe it. No, no, no—" I heard her gasp and she gave a keening cry before, in a ragged voice, she asked what had happened. I told her the little I knew, including the phone calls Jerome had told me about.

"Has anybody figured out why he was killed?" she asked.

"Not that I've heard."

"Do the police have a suspect yet?"

"I don't know, but Daryl has asked me to talk with him, help him through the criminal investigation. Far as I can tell, the police haven't identified him as a suspect, but they might take a look at him. You feel okay, having me represent him? I don't know yet what he's going to want to do with the camp, the golf course, but he might want to dismantle the things Jerome wanted to establish."

I heard her pause. "Oh, God, right now I'm not sure I give a damn about the camp or the golf course. I cared about Jerome. Daryl was an asshole to us, but I know how much he meant to Jerome. Maybe Daryl figured out we weren't the problem at the hearing. So if he wants you, that's okay with me."

"What if the police develop evidence pointing to Daryl killing Jerome? How do you feel about my representing him then?"

There was a pause and I heard only uneven breathing for a moment. "Oh, Jesus, I don't even want to think about it. If Daryl killed him and you represent Daryl . . ." Her voice trailed off and I let the silence sit for a moment.

"I know I'm a lawyer and part of the system," she finally said, "but I don't want you doing a damn thing to help whoever killed Jerome."

"Look, if you—"

"No, it's okay, I'm upset and not making much sense. I'm sure you'll do the right thing."

"Believe me, I don't want to be representing Jerome's murderer. I don't have any sense that the police have focused on Daryl and from what he's told me, he was in Boston when it happened. But I'll talk to you as we go along, and if things change, we'll figure out how to handle it."

"Okay. I'll come up for Jerome's funeral, and we can talk more. It's just impossible to believe Jerome's dead, you're so far away, my parents are in tough shape."

"Look, you're more important to me than Daryl. You want me to come down there? I can take a flight later today, be there by evening and stay for a few days."

"No, I'll be all right. Thanks. I just wish I could borrow your arms for about three days and have a nice, long hug."

We talked for a while. I said more things to try and ease her mind. None of it helped or mattered. She didn't want to give up the phone, so I finally told her I had to go.

I was just getting a sandwich when the radio played an oldie, Creedence Clearwater's "Bad Moon Rising." Instantly, I saw Jerome that first night at his bar, sweat running off his head and the harp nestled in his hand. I turned off the radio, sat down, and leaned back on my sofa, closed my eyes, and listened in my head to Jerome play the blues riffs and then his solo on "Bad Moon Rising." He'd been right to play the song—he'd seen trouble on the way, but more than he ever imagined.

I went out for a run. It was great weather for it, maybe sixty degrees with a slight breeze. I ran through Coolidge Corner, where people checked in and out of stores, coffee shops, and restaurants, sampling the wares and enjoying life. All seemed normal, nothing out of the ordinary. Except, of course, for Jerome's murder, which would make the television news shows for twenty-four hours, be featured in tomorrow's paper, and then be lost in the daily torrent of noise that passes for news.

As I turned and went out Beacon Street, I couldn't run freely. I had trouble breathing where normally air flowed easily and I had a knot in my side. I ran faster up a small hill. Hard as I ran, the knot remained. I listened for a harmonica but heard only car engines and horns.

The sun arcing upward warmed the air as I ran, just as I'd grown accustomed to Jenny's presence warming my home, my bed, and my life. But now it looked like a cold summer ahead.

Chapter

EIGHT

Just before six P.M., Daryl called. After telling me his meeting with the police had gone about as well as he could expect, he asked me to come to his house later that night.

Daryl lived in a massive gray Tudor home set well back from the road in Weston. Weston has little commercial development in it. Instead, it is one of the wealthiest suburbs in the Boston area. It also has a great soft ice cream stand that opens for the summer. Before getting to Daryl's house, I stopped for fried clams and a large soft vanilla cone for dinner.

I entered through a gate mounted on stone pillars at the head of the drive, giving my name to a disembodied voice on an intercom. After a drive up to the well-lit house, I parked behind a green Range Rover. A deep blue Lincoln Mercury Navigator sat further away on the driveway next to a red Porsche Carrera.

It was around nine P.M. when I rang the doorbell. A slender black woman, standing around five feet ten inches, opened the door. She wore blue leggings and an oversized gray sweatshirt. She appeared to be in her late twenties, around Daryl's age. She had a finely drawn face with a slightly upturned nose, a delicate chin, and a natural curve to her lips. On a normal day, she would have been gorgeous. But the red, puffy eyes, the stare that looked past me, the compressed mouth, the disheveled hair, and her silence as she let me in and led me down a hallway made clear this was not a normal day.

The hallway had a number of rooms off it. A few of the doors were closed but I caught a glimpse of a large kitchen with an island built around a high-tech steel and glass stove in the middle of a room full of other new appliances. I also peered into something that looked like a large den, holding a couple of bookcases, two desks and two computers with large monitors, and a television set.

Without a word, the woman led me to the threshold of what looked like an enormous family room and gestured me into the room with her hand. Then she turned and walked away silently.

I peered into a room that was softly lit from one side, with only a couple of track lights directed against a wall. A Bang & Olufson high end stereo system was built into one side wall with massive speakers placed in various corners and crevices. The far wall consisted mostly of a large picture window with vertical blinds over much of it. Hanging on the last wall was an enormous high definition TV, only a couple of inches thick, with a basketball game showing on it. The screen looked about five feet across. Arrayed at an angle to the television were a large, electronic treadmill and an electronic stationary bike. Right in front of the television was an unusually long sofa covered in rich, chocolate-colored leather.

As I walked in, Daryl Mann unfolded from the sofa. He pushed a button on the clicker in his hand and the television went silent, though the picture stayed on. He stood up and towered well above me.

"Yo, Kardon," he said, "want a beer, soft drink?" He pointed to a small, built-in refrigerator I'd missed over by the stereo. His eyes, like those of the woman who had brought me in, were red and puffy. We both sat down on the sofa and looked at the silent men in short pants running around a basketball court.

"No, I'm fine." I waited for him to speak.

"Jerome's dead," he finally said. "Can't get my mind round it, just blows me away. Always thought I'd be the first to go, not him. He was always so smart, always in control."

"Your family okay?"

"My aunt's pretty busted up, my mom too. He was the best of all of us and now he's dead just 'cause he tried to do something good."

I waited for a moment and gave him a sidelong look. Daryl stared at the television screen, the flickering lights playing off the angles and seams in his face. He was still shy of thirty years old, but in the fluctuating glow, he looked over forty.

"Cops give you a hard time?"

"No, not too bad. Bunch of questions about what Jerome was up to, who he hung out with, people who might be pissed at him, what I knew about the flack he was getting over the dam. They asked about the argument we had. Also, about last night, where I was, who I was with. I told 'em I spent the night with somebody who wasn't my wife and they didn't push further."

"They still might."

"Yeah, I know."

"Who was it, local cops or state troopers?"

"Local guys, they kind of stumbled around a lot. I heard somebody say that state troopers were doing the search out where Jerome was killed."

"Yeah, the locals will be over their heads on this, so the state police will help out."

"I don't care if they get help from the Psychic Hotline, they gotta nail the bastard who did this. They asked to see Jerome's office out at the golf course, so I let 'em go ahead."

At that moment, the woman who had let me in the door came back into the room and sat on an ottoman next to the sofa, holding a drink in her hand. Daryl looked up at her briefly.

"My wife, Wanetta," Daryl said, and gestured with his hand toward the woman. She nodded and sipped from her drink.

"You want to tell me more about this argument with Jerome?"

"Nothing unusual. We argued a lot. I'd want to do things, spend some money, he'd give me a hard time about it. Or he'd want to invest in something I didn't want to touch. Sometimes one of us backed off, sometimes not. But it always passed, we'd go on. This time, though, he'd poured a boatload of money, a lot of it mine, into the golf course and the camp. We got freakin' turtles, racists, asshole local politicians—the whole thing's impossible, I told him we ought to find another place."

"You told him that yesterday?"

"Yeah. Who needs shit like this? Sell the damn land, cut our losses, find something else."

"Anything unusual about the argument yesterday?"

"Nope, we both got worked up for good reasons. We had a lot of money tied up in the property and Jerome had his heart set on the camp. I didn't like the threats against Jerome, wanted him to bail on the camp right away. If he'd wanted some time to see if the golf course could go, I'd have gone along. But he wanted time for the camp, too."

"You threaten him at all?"

"No, man, Jerome's family—better than that, he's my best friend. Jerome's the only one around me who talks sense, doesn't kiss my butt. Everybody else feeds me bullshit, hoping I'll throw 'em a bone. But Jerome, he talks straight. Pisses me off sometimes, but he never gives me jive, doesn't feed me lines."

I didn't correct Daryl's grammar. If Jerome was still alive for him, it wasn't my place to correct him. And if Daryl was right about Jerome's role in his life, Daryl would have a big hole to fill.

All of a sudden, the woman spoke up, her voice low and somewhat husky, but insistent and intense.

"This the guy you want, right? You tell him yet?" she said.

Daryl didn't say anything.

"Jesus, Daryl, you got to tell him," she said. "Even if the police don't follow up about last night, this whole thing's a mess. You gotta be ready for publicity you don't like. Can't hide forever, boy. You gonna need help. You trust him, you'd better tell him," she said, and walked out of the room.

I didn't say anything. I didn't have a clue about what she was saying. Daryl kept looking at the screen, his face impassive and immobile for a couple of minutes.

"Something I ought to know?" I finally said. "I don't want to wade into this thing, then get blind-sided. That won't do either one of us any good."

Daryl leaned back into the sofa. "Kardon," he finally said, "did you like Jerome?"

"Yeah. Can't say I knew him well, but what I saw, I liked."

"What'd he tell you about me?"

"Not much. He told me to leave you alone. He said your personal life and how you did things wasn't my business."

"Yeah, he was good about that, trying to protect me. So what do you think, you like me?"

"Daryl, what's going on here? We had one argument the other night. You itching for another? What does it matter what I think? I'm a lawyer, not a shrink. I work hard for my clients, like them or not."

"Just asking a question. You'll know where I'm going soon enough."

"I don't know you well enough to know what I think. Sportswriters don't like you, you don't look like you're having much fun out on the basketball floor, and you don't seem to do much beyond playing basketball. That's all I know."

Daryl sat up and looked at me, as if for the first time. His brown eyes stared at me for about a minute. I held his gaze, but just barely.

When he spoke, his voice was deep and his cadence slow. "Kardon," he said, "you're right, you don't know shit about me. You see a bunch of guys hanging around here, acting like punks? You see me wearing lots of jewelry, ridiculous clothes? You see any cocaine on the table top, any weed lying around? You read about me going to nightclubs, getting into fights, having lots of kids with different women?"

"If that's a question, the answer is, I don't know about any kids and no to the rest of it."

"Right. That stuff's what you see with too damn many of the guys in the league. Nobody sees that with me. Instead, people see a big, black guy not sucking up to anybody, not taking shit from anybody, and everybody thinks I'm an asshole."

"Look, Daryl, you don't owe me any explanation. You don't like something I said and you don't want me to represent you, fine."

"No, dammit, you're not getting it." Daryl sighed and sat back in the sofa. "I've wanted to make sure nobody knows me. Except for Jerome and Wanetta, I've deliberately kept people away."

Daryl looked away from me for a moment. I saw his head and shoulders droop just a bit. His face became quiet and sad.

"What you don't know, Kardon, and what I don't want to tell you, is that I'm gay. I'm queer."

I sat there for a minute, trying to formulate a response. The best I could come up with was, "No shit."

"Yeah, no shit."

"Jerome didn't say a word about it."

"He wouldn't. Jerome's one of the few who knew, about the only guy, straight or queer, I could really trust, really let go with. Now I've lost the guy who helped me with pretty much every big decision I made."

"Daryl, I'm sorry. This must hurt like hell."

"Yup. And it's going to get worse. I'll be in the spotlight, at least for a while. Been hiding from that for years—just wanted to keep a low profile."

I gave a little, mirthless laugh. "You think it's funny?" he said.

"No. Just the idea of you hiding. Your wife talked about it before, now you bring it up. The only All-Star on the Shamrocks, almost seven feet tall, hundreds of articles and film clips about you every year. And you're hiding in plain sight."

"You got it. That's what it feels like. After every game, some little piece of me waits for a reporter to ask me something that'll make it all come crashing down."

"But you're married." The minute it came out of my mouth it sounded stupid.

"Big deal. Guys do it all the time. I needed a cover. Wanetta and I've been friends a long time. She's discreet, we work it out so she has a social life. We're pretty close and care about each other. She kind of likes being my wife—people don't hassle her and the pay's pretty good."

"So when you were out last night, it wasn't with a woman."

"Catch on fast, don't you? Yeah, it was with Mark Barton. And he's not out of the closet, either. So besides keeping me out of jail, keeping the businesses going, and making sure the police find out who killed Jerome, part of your job is to help me keep a lid on everything."

I tried to keep my jaw from dropping but without much success. Mark Barton was the high-priced, popular, and handsome sports anchor for Channel 8, the leading Boston news station. Other stations had openly gay news personnel, but I'd never heard a whisper about Barton. There'd been an occasional gay sports reporter in Boston but nobody close to the stature of Barton.

"Your family know?"

"Only Jerome, though he thought my mama and his suspected."

"Your agent, lawyers, teammates—nobody knows?"

"Not that I know of. Damn, this game's hard enough, I don't need people knowing."

"What's the big deal? Guys have come out all over the place."

"No big deal for you, you ain't a gay black man.

Think about it. I'm hanging around locker rooms, some guys'll make stupid comments. Guys on other teams will get on my ass. This comes out, the few endorsements I got will go faster than you can fart. Fans'll say stuff that'll peel paint. Then I go to church, preacher says homosexuality's a sin and everybody goes Amen. Most black guys don't even want to think about it, afraid they'll catch the homo disease."

"But guys in the league do stupid, even criminal, things all the time, nothing happens."

"That's what I was saying before. Guys get caught with drugs, with guns, beating up women. But they got money and it gets covered up. The league and the union work together to protect the bad guys so they don't screw up our precious image. You think the league and the union gonna be there for me, it comes out I'm queer?"

"Hey, Dennis Rodman got away with wild stuff."

"No, Rodman got away with being a sideshow freak. He wore dresses and did crazy stuff, but he made sure everybody knew he slept with gorgeous women."

"But you've got a big contract—guaranteed, right? You can handle the small stuff people will throw at you."

"Ain't always small stuff when you see it, hear it every day, when it changes the way you live, the way you work. The contract makes it nice, but it's hard to remember that when people spit in your face, call you names." Daryl turned to look at me, a little more life in his eyes.

"I hear you," I said.

"You willing to deal with all this, help me out?" Daryl asked.

"Yeah, but I'm a lawyer, not a public relations guru or therapist, any of that."

Daryl nodded his head just a little and blew out a deep breath. "It's cool, man. I need those guys, I can buy 'em. For stuff in Meadowbrook, I need somebody I can talk straight to. Jerome trusted you. I got to do the same."

"I'll do my best, but I'm not Jerome."

Daryl shook his head and gave a small laugh that turned into a muffled gasp. "No, you're not. Nobody is. Man had a bad knee, but he could carry the whole damn world on his shoulders when he wanted to." Daryl stretched back on the sofa and closed his eyes again.

"Why don't I get out of here? You look exhausted," I said. "I'll call you tomorrow. I'll talk to the cops, see if somebody will tell me what they've got."

"Thanks. Couple things you can do for me."

"Sure."

"I'm going to get a lot of questions about operating the restaurant, the buildings, and the golf course and camp. Far as I know, Jerome and I owned most of it together, so I should have control now. People call me, I'm going to send 'em to you till we know what's going on. Jerome's got an assistant, Fred Bender, he's pretty good. I'll tell him about you. Talk to him, check out the businesses and figure out what we need to do. Bill me for your work."

"Okay. I'll probably need some help."

"Do what you need to do. And the police want anything, take care of it."

"No problem. Anything else you want?"

He drew a deep breath and then closed his eyes. "What I want is Jerome to walk in here about an hour from now, when he's done at the restaurant, and tell me I'm an asshole for buying another big-screen TV." He opened his eyes and looked at me. "Any chance you can get me that?"

I shook my head.

"Thought so," he replied, continuing to look at me with a hooded, intense glare. "If I can't have that, I want the son of a bitch who killed him put away forever. I got time and money, Kardon. The police don't do it, I want you to find his killer." He closed his eyes again.

"You going to be okay?" I finally asked.

Daryl sat up and passed a hand over his face. "Yeah. I'll be all right. Sure as hell better off than Jerome right now."

At that point, Wanetta came back in, still with a glass in her hand. She didn't say anything but sat down next to Daryl and gave him a quizzical look.

"Told him," Daryl said.

"Good," she said. "You gonna need all the help you can get."

Daryl lay back on the sofa. "I expect you're right about that."

"Your mama called again," she said. "Aunt Becky's with her. Becky's pretty upset."

"Yeah, I was afraid of that," Daryl said. "I'll call them."

Wanetta put her hand on his arm and stroked it. It looked like a small leaf on a massive branch. Daryl, his eyes closed, reached over and rubbed it as if it were a lucky amulet. Wanetta reached up with her right hand and softly stroked his cheek.

"It's okay to hurt," she said.

"Come on," Daryl said, "cut it out. You're gonna make me cry."

"Uh-uh, baby," she said, "won't be me. Doesn't matter how tough you try to be. You cry, it's that ol' heart of yours, filled up with all the pain and hurt it can stand. It's got to let go."

She stood up, reached over and hugged him, hard around his neck. He buried his face in her shoulder. I saw his head and shoulders shudder and heard a stifled sob. I walked out of the room, past the lights from the fleeting, bright images on the silent screen that illuminated the entwined forms of Daryl and Wanetta.

First thing in the morning, I called Randy Blocker.

"Hey," I said, "just checking in—"

"Damn, I knew this was coming. First thing I said this morning when I heard about Jerome Mann was, guess who'll call me today."

"Sorry our relationship has become so predictable. But yeah, I'm really calling about Jerome Mann."

"Sorry, Dan, can't give you much, and you know it."

"I'm representing Daryl Mann. That help?"

"We heard it was Dick Hooper."

"Not according to my client, who met with me last night."

"Hope you get a nice piece of his contract."

"That plus he promised to help with my jump shot."

"The man can't shoot himself, I'm not worried he'll do anything for you. Anyway, still can't tell you much. Too early, and it's too hot right now, we got people on it."

"How'd Jerome die? I found him, but couldn't tell from what I saw."

"Shot, looks like close range, is all I can tell you right now. A lot more tests and reports still due back."

"When?"

"First guess was real late Wednesday night or early

yesterday morning, but no official word yet from the medical examiner."

"Any suspects yet?"

There was a pause. "Not yet."

"Close to naming somebody?"

Another pause. "Nobody's in, but nobody's out yet, either."

"Daryl have anything to worry about?"

"You on the level about representing him?"

"Yeah."

"All I can tell you, go over with him real good what he told the investigators and what he was doing on the golf course. Somebody saw something and we've got people looking for it right now, that's all I'll say."

"Looking where?"

"Near the golf course. Some of our boys might take a swim, you catch my drift."

My turn to stay silent for a moment. "Thanks, Randy, I owe you one."

"Bet your ass you do. Have a good talk with your client, counselor."

As soon as the call ended, I phoned Daryl on the unlisted number he'd given me. I got nothing but his voice mail. I said it was urgent that Daryl call me, then picked up the phone again.

I knew I needed help. Jenny wasn't around, so I put in a call to Al Thompson.

I'd met Al on a recent murder case. Al, now retired, had been the police chief in Wettamessett, a small town in southeastern Massachusetts. Al spent his time fishing, boating, and keeping active in the community and church. When I was pursuing leads on the other case in the Wettamessett area, Al helped out. He kept himself in shape, his hair short, his boat trim, and his opinions to himself until asked. And he did the things he said he'd do. Last time we'd talked, he'd offered to help me out if something came along.

On the phone, Al said he'd love to help. He also said stripers were running at the Cape Cod Canal. The Canal cuts across the base of Cape Cod and lets ships avoid having to go around the tip of the Cape. Al and I had fished before on his boat, *Serenity*, but the engine was in the shop for repairs. Al suggested we try the Canal so he could combine three of his favorite activities, storytelling and catching both fish and bad guys.

He proposed I meet him near the Massachusetts Maritime Academy in Bourne, close to where the Canal spills into the northern end of Buzzards Bay. We settled on a time late in the day.

Waiting to hear from Daryl and to meet with Al, I did a little work on some documents we had to produce in an age discrimination case. After about forty-five minutes, my secretary broke in to say that Daryl was on the line. I told him I needed to meet with him and we agreed that I'd come by on my way down to meet Al.

When I drove through the gate, Daryl's house looked pretty much the same, though this time the red Porsche was gone. Daryl himself met me at the door. I'd seen him less than twenty-four hours before but time had not been kind. His face was lined and unshaven, his eyes dark and shadowed, and his voice flat, without affect.

We sat down on the same sofa we'd been on before. The television was on again, this time showing a rerun of a stock car race. Daryl watched it without seeming to see anything.

I told him what Randy had said to me.

"Don't know what he was talking about," Daryl said.

"Let's walk it through. You met Jerome at the club-house, right?"

"Yeah."

"What time?"

"Supposed to meet there at two P.M. I was on time, he was a few minutes late."

"What'd you guys do then?"

"Walked around the clubhouse, some of the buildings. Jerome wanted to show me the progress we'd made. We checked out the practice green, the first hole. Then we talked about the camp. That's when we had the argument I told you about."

"Any kind of a physical fight or horsing around?"

"Nope."

"Were there other people around?"

"Sure, some workmen, the course superintendent."

"So they could have seen you or heard you?"

"Yeah, could be."

"Then what?"

"I went for a walk on the golf course, just to cool down."

"Where'd you go?"

"Walked across a couple holes, went down to the pond."

"Did you take anything with you?"

"What do you mean?"

"Did you carry anything, hold anything while you were walking the course?"

"No—wait a minute, just took a beer."

"What kind?"

Daryl looked at me with a frown.

"Just answer the question, if you can," I said.

Daryl looked up at the ceiling. "Coors Silver Bullet,"

he finally said. "Don't much like it, nothing to it, but it was the only thing there."

"What'd you do when you finished it?"

"Put a rock in it and chucked it in the pond."

"Why'd you bother with the rock?"

"Jerome. Every time we went out on the golf course or the camp, he'd give me a hard time if I littered."

"What'd you do after that?"

"Walked a little, went back to the clubhouse."

"You and Jerome talk?"

"For a minute. I had to get back to town. We agreed to talk after the next day, when you guys were supposed to meet with the town attorney and the Selectmen were meeting."

"He tell you about meeting anybody, anything he had to do after that?"

"Nope."

We were both silent for a minute or two.

"All right," I finally said. "Thanks for all this. I know it sucks to talk about it. Now, can I use your phone? I want to pass some of this on to the police."

"Why? What's wrong?"

"Nothing. You give me a chance, I might convince the cops to charge you with littering. Or you can wait, see if they charge you with murder."

Daryl shot me a look, then pointed to the wall. "Phone's over there."

I went over to the wall and picked up a cordless phone from a cradle on the wall. I punched in a number. Randy Blocker wasn't there but I left a detailed voice mail telling him that Daryl would be happy to talk with the police again and the police searchers would probably find a Coors Silver Bullet with a recent brew date and a rock in it on the pond bottom near the golf course.

I came back and sat down on the sofa. "Sorry," I said, "I just wanted to get the information to them."

"You want to tell me what's going on?"

"What I hope is, somebody saw you with the beer. It was late afternoon, sun shining at an angle and it hit the beer can. Somebody saw the silver reflection and told the police they saw you with something metallic down by the water. Now, the timing was wrong—you couldn't have shot him without workers on the course hearing it. But still, cops have to check it out in case it's a gun. Hopefully they find the beer can and you're off the hook, when they add it to the fact you went to the convenience store on your way back to Boston."

Daryl looked at me, raised his eyebrows and nodded. "Sounds good. I like that."

"You had any more thoughts about the water level, the camp, any of that?"

"I'll worry about that after the funeral. I'm not deciding anything right now."

"Fine. I'll be in touch with Fred Bender and get started on the businesses tomorrow."

"Glad you mentioned that—I want to give you an extra set of keys Jerome kept here. Has keys for his house, the office, the golf course clubhouse. My house, too, maybe some others. You'll have to figure out what works on the different places."

"Thanks. I'll be in touch."

I took off after that, heading south. Around five P.M., I met with Al Thompson in a parking lot near the end of the Cape Cod Canal. We walked along the bike path adjacent to the Canal for a while then settled on some large boulders in the riprap that lined the Canal shore. Soon summer visitors would fill the bike path. Families, retired couples, kids, and young lovers would walk, bike, and rollerblade next to the Canal. Fishermen would spread out along the six miles of banks lining the waterway. But today, even with a bright sun and a sparkle off the currents flowing through the Canal, people were sparse.

Al and I baited the fishing lines, then cast out into the Canal. We put the butts of the rods into short plastic tubes stuck in among the rocks and sat back to drink beer and eat a couple of salami sandwiches that Al had brought along. We ate; the fish didn't seem hungry.

Al told me about a trip he'd gone on with his wife over the winter. She'd wanted to cruise in the Greek islands for a few years and he finally consented. Most of the story was about things that went wrong. First, his wife disapproved of the nude sunbathing on many of the beaches. Then, they had to sail through a storm on the way back. Al was delighted to report his wife was now planning a trip to Alaska, with no cruises.

Soon we turned to Jerome's murder. Al knew nothing of Jerome and little of Daryl, so I spent some time telling him what I knew, including that it sounded like the police didn't yet have a prime suspect but were at least considering Daryl. I also mentioned my interest in the Wells murder.

"You know of any funny business between Jerome and Wells?"

"Don't know but everything I've seen and heard about Jerome is that he was honest, tough sometimes, but never crooked. On the one hand, they were both working on getting the town to allow the camp, which turned out to be real controversial. On the other, they were killed in quite different ways," I said.

"Well, let's start by making it easy on ourselves. Who would have wanted Jerome out of the way?"

I talked to Al about the opposition to the camp and each of the individuals who had formally protested against the camp. For the first time, I also voiced my suspicion that somebody in the town government might have had a greedy palm and had tried to work a deal with Wells. I didn't have enough information on anyone to point fingers but I also didn't want to wait around and see if the police cleared Daryl on their own. If they didn't find the killer quickly and didn't clear Daryl, it could very well affect Daryl's personal and business life.

Al and I both agreed that checking the Meadowbrook people was worth doing. And Al happily agreed to do a little of the tracking himself.

"What's your rate?" I asked.

"Rate for what?"

"Rate for working on this. I'm working for Daryl, I'll be billing him. I want you to get paid, too."

"No, Dan, no need to pay me."

"I know there's no need, but—"

"Hey, don't sweat it. We'll see how it goes. It turns out I feel like I'm really working, I'll let you know."

"All right."

We agreed that Al would do some background work in Meadowbrook because he wouldn't be linked to Daryl or Jerome. Al would also go to work with his network of friends and former colleagues. I'd do a database survey and some computer searches, and try to meet some of the people involved, so we could start putting together material on each of the Meadowbrook people involved.

We finished the evening in darkness, with no fish to show for our effort. I thought Al might have been disappointed, but he gave me a cheerful goodbye and promised to be in touch in a couple of days. He didn't catch a fish, but maybe he'd caught the scent of something with an even bigger kick.

CHAPTER——

NINE

The next morning, I spent some time cleaning up at the office. I'd finished up the most important projects, but still an assortment of correspondence, phone calls, small memos, and administrative tasks kept me busy. I'd also arranged to talk with Fred Bender. I'd planned on a phone call, but he wanted to meet so I headed out to Jerome's office in Copley Square.

Bender, a short, round black man with a scraggly goatee, looking about thirty years old, met me at the door of Jerome's office with a weak handshake. We sat down in a small conference room to talk. Bender fingered his goatee constantly as he answered my questions.

"Where was Jerome's main office—here or at the bar?" I asked.

"He kept most of his things here, had most of his meetings here. He was a cell phone fanatic, but he'd give out the number for this office and he'd check here for messages."

"Did he move around a lot to check on the properties and businesses?"

"Yeah, he never spent the whole day here. We were always looking at new properties or dealing with problems at the ones we had. He also liked to go hear bands play, try out new menu items for the restaurant, plus he had all the basketball clinics. And during the last year or so, he was out at the golf course and camp all the time."

"Did he talk to you about the problems in Meadowbrook?"

"Boy, I heard about it. He'd worked hard developing the course, but when the time came to work on the camp, he became almost obsessed."

"He told me about phone calls he was getting complaining about the camp. You hear any of those?"

"No, I'd refer people to him or to his voice mail."

"You know if Jerome recorded any of the calls?"

"Once he told me he'd saved some, but I never listened. He never wanted me to know about his private calls."

"You know if he ever identified any of the callers?"

"If he did, he never told me."

"The Wednesday night he was killed, did he talk to you that day, tell you what he was going to do, who he was going to meet?"

"He said he was going to meet Daryl out at the golf course, that's all I know."

"You talk to the police yet?"

"Yeah. They asked if I knew who Jerome was going to meet, whether anybody had threatened him, whether he had a calendar or diary, stuff like that. They called me after they searched the golf course office and the car in Meadowbrook. From what I gathered, they hadn't found anything and I couldn't help them much."

"I saw an electronic organizer out there, near where he was shot. Nothing helpful in it?"

"The police asked me about that. I heard Jerome cursing at it, I guess the batteries had died. Maybe he had it out to remind himself to pick up batteries. He'd asked if we had any here and we didn't."

"Without batteries, the database in the handheld unit would be wiped out, but it plugged into his computer, so the information should be there, right?"

"Right."

"Fred, I know you must have thought about it. You have any idea who killed him?"

Tears welled up in his eyes and he shook his head. It took him a minute to talk. "God, he was such a wonderful guy. Whoever did it is sick, real sick."

Bender took a moment to compose himself. He gave me a short memo he'd prepared, summarizing the various properties and businesses they had, how the document files were organized, a quick and dirty index of their computer files, and how I could access Jerome's voice mails.

Bender and I talked for a few minutes about running the businesses. Bender agreed to keep working but to check in with me every day or two just so I knew what he was up to and whether he'd encountered any problems. We also scheduled a meeting for more serious planning. I told Bender that he had a job for at least two months and probably more while we sorted out what to do with everything. His voice almost cracked with relief when he thanked me. Then he left.

After Bender left, I prowled around the other rooms first, finding little of interest. Then I opened the door to Jerome's office.

His desk was a simple, old square table with a single central drawer. It had little on it, only a telephone, computer, and pad of lined yellow paper, all the pages empty.

A credenza held a computer printer on top along with

a few slim files. Below, on a shelf, there were a number of eclectic books, among them a biography of Mississippi Delta bluesman Robert Johnson, Bill Russell's *Go Up for Glory*, and a management book titled *Total Project Control* by Steven Devaux.

A tall bookcase full of files and documents along with two filing cabinets stood against the one remaining wall. Fred Bender's notes gave me brief summaries of what was in there, so using the notes as a guide, I scanned the bookcase and then pulled out some files to review.

Jerome had organized his affairs meticulously. The bookcase had files, reports, and a wide variety of business, real estate, restaurant, travel, and sports materials carefully arranged in folders.

I started skimming some of the files he kept for his businesses. I also found a copy of his will, making Daryl his executor and leaving his estate to family members. The will's provisions simplified the situation but reading it didn't make me feel any better. Jerome had prepared his affairs well in the event of his death; it was just his family and friends who weren't prepared.

Finally, I pulled out a number of file folders on the camp and the golf course. By the end of two hours or so, I had a better handle on his businesses, but no better idea why he died or who killed him.

Then I sat down and fired up Jerome's computer. The program directory listed an organizer, so I clicked on that. After clicking on an onscreen tab that said Calendar, the screen showed me Jerome's schedule for that day. I experimented with the program for a couple of minutes to understand it better. Then I went to the monthly planner and clicked on the day Jerome died. It came up on the screen and so did "Redmond—clubhouse" written in next to six P.M.

I sat there, surprised, for a minute, then had the item printed out. I looked at my watch and then shut down the computer. As important as the calendar item was, I wanted to check something else.

It was close to 4:30 when I picked up the memo from Bender and, following his instructions, plugged Jerome's code for retrieving messages into his voice-mail system. A female voice told me that there were twenty new messages. Probably would have been more if the system had the capacity to hold them.

I took the names down and saved the new messages. All of the calls came in after Jerome had died from people who did not know about it. Most were straight business calls but a number were more personal. I involuntarily shivered, thinking about returning those calls.

The message system said that Jerome had saved an additional fifteen messages. I started replaying those as well.

The system retrieved from the oldest to the most recent. The first message dated from the day after the article in the Meadowbrook paper appeared. Later messages concerned the water level of Echo Pond.

That first message, and the next fourteen I listened to, varied in terms of gender, voice quality, vocabulary, verbal dexterity of the speaker, and the intensity of the vitriol, but they all made much the same point.

An early caller said, "I want to deal with black kids doing graffiti and shoplifting, I can go to a Boston school. Keep those goddamn kids out of our town." A later caller said, "Get the water level back up before we plug the dam with your fat, black ass. Or maybe we'll cut off your dick and stick it in the eighteenth hole." Another practically spit into the phone, "My family's been in this town for generations and no nigger black-mailer will get away with this." Those were not the most offensive messages.

I didn't know why Jerome had saved the messages but I didn't erase them. I sat there listening, not recognizing either the voices or the bile and hatred spilling out of the phone. By the fifth call, I was sweating on the outside, nauseated on the inside, and all but shaking.

I had to tell the police about the calendar entry as well as the phone threats. With the phone threats, I doubted there was much they could do. There was nothing distinctive about the calls and none of the callers left their names. Had Jerome been alive, the police could have put a trap on the phone and figured out where the calls were coming from, but now a trap would be useless. Besides telling the police, I decided to keep the calls and record them onto a tape later in case the voices or language triggered some recognition as I worked in Meadowbrook.

In addition, though, Daryl might want to hear the messages. He had a big decision to make about whether to continue the golf course and camp. Which way the tapes would tilt him, I didn't know, but he had a right to know about his potential new neighbors. And the right to know just what his cousin had endured.

I thought about calling Randy but decided I needed to establish some good contacts with the local cops, so I called the Meadowbrook police station. When I told the dispatcher what I wanted to talk about, I was referred to Lieutenant DeRosa. He said little in response to the information I gave him about the calendar, but he did ask me to fax him a copy of the calendar printout.

Then I walked him through the messages Jerome had left. DeRosa expressed anger about them and promised to get on them right away. I gave him the directions and code so that the police could access the messages themselves. He promised they wouldn't erase the messages.

Having given him something, I asked about what the police had found to date.

"Not much," he said.

"Where have you looked?"

"Golf club and the area around there. State troopers have checked his house, talked to a lot of people in Meadowbrook and friends, people he worked with."

To earn more brownie points, I told him I could help with getting access to the Boston office. Then I asked, "Anybody in particular on the hook right now?"

"Nope."

"What about Daryl?"

"Kardon, look, we know what Daryl told us, we found the beer can you reported, we know the Manns were close, and we've tracked down Daryl's story about a convenience store. But we also know they had a big argument out at the golf course. We're looking at everybody, including your guy. But thanks for all this stuff— it may well be helpful. We'll follow up on the calendar entry."

"Anything else we get, I'll give it to you."

"Okay," he said. "You know, it's nice you found this, but we have good people working this case, and enough of them. We would have tracked this stuff down. No need for you to spend time on it."

"Thanks for the advice," I said, "but I've got a client who's devastated his cousin and business partner was killed, not to mention he's a potential suspect. Before that, his lawyer in Meadowbrook was killed. We've got some real questions about what the hell's going on around the town. Soon as we get the answers we're looking for and Daryl's in the clear, I'll be out of the picture."

"Suit yourself. By the way, has Daryl Mann decided what he's going to do about the water level in the pond?"

"Not yet. Why? You live near there?"

"Yeah, I have a small three-bedroom Cape. Nice backyard, runs right down to the pond. Bought my ten-year-old son a small fishing boat last month. He asked me last night if we'd ever get it out of the mud."

"Sorry. Nothing to report."

"I figured. It won't stop me from doing my job."

"Let me ask you," I said, "if you'd been in Jerome's shoes, what would you have done after the board rejected the permit? And if you were Daryl, what would you do now?"

"I know why Jerome did it. Hell, I give him credit, it was pretty clever. Problem is, a lot of innocent people are getting screwed while the Manns and Sheehan piss on each other. My boat's sitting in mud, my home's value is about to go down the tubes. I don't care much who's right, I just want the water back."

"I hope you're telling your town officials."

"Oh yeah, first thing a cop does to advance his career is to complain to town officials about how they've made a hash of things."

I put down the phone and packed up my things. I took off my windbreaker and sweat pants and headed out of the office, locking the door behind me. Only the run home began to dissolve the film of filth and disgust left by the messages I'd heard.

CHAPTER

TEN

Gloria Duchesne was at the receptionist work station in Wells's office when I walked a few minutes later than the time we'd agreed upon on Tuesday morning. Her brown hair was short, just over her ears, and she wore a large blue sweatshirt over tan slacks. She had tortoiseshell glasses on her round, pale face. Though seated behind a desk, I could see she was relatively short and plump. White smoke from a cigarette in her hand curled to the ceiling as she worked her way through the file on her desk.

"I'm Dan Kardon," I said.

"Gloria Duchesne," she said, looking up at me.

She waved me into a chair in front of the desk, finished looking at a file in her hand and shook her head. "Damn, another one. Here's a file, Chuck never got the releases he should have. I sent him two notes about it. A hell of a lawyer when he wanted to be, but he never bothered with the details." She tossed the file onto a tall pile of other folders and sighed. "May have to fix that before the client sees it."

"You were the one in the practice who paid attention to the details, I assume."

"You got it. Sorry, didn't mean to be abrupt. Chuck's death was such a shock. And then Jerome. I didn't know

148

him well, but he was always good to deal with, even when I could tell he was mad. It's just been pretty difficult all around. Doesn't feel like an office any more, it's a cemetery, only we're burying files, not people. Things were in terrible shape when I got back."

"The office was still messed up from the night Wells was killed?"

"Yes. And the police went through the whole office—files, computers, desks, everything."

"I'm sure it's been hard. I appreciate your talking to me. I'd like to know about Wells, his practice, any thoughts you have on what happened, then I may ask you about a few people in town. I assume the police have already talked to you."

"They interviewed me the day I got home. I sure didn't have much to tell them."

"How long did you work here?"

"Eight years. Took us a while to get along. He was used to somebody a bit quieter. Took him time to get comfortable with me."

"You liked him, it sounds like."

"Sometimes he drove me up a tree, but yeah, in a funny way I liked him. Things were always happening. It was never dull around here, he had so many different clients and different projects and cases going on. Even when stuff went wrong, he kept a good attitude and figured out ways to fix it. He was never mean or nasty and he could be generous. I knew he liked to take chances, cut some corners, but clients liked him and he got things done. I also knew he was doing some things he didn't tell me about, but I thought they were personal."

"Like women?"

"Yeah, I didn't always know who, but I could tell when a new one came along."

"Gambling too?"

"Sure, he traveled to Foxwoods, Mohegan Sun, Atlantic City, but that was no big deal. A lot of people around here do it."

"You ever get any sense he was in over his head with the gambling?"

"Nope. Police asked me the same thing. Never heard him worry about money he'd lost. It was funny, I did a little of the bookkeeping. Every time things looked a little tight, he'd find a way to bring money in."

"What about drugs?"

"Nah, I don't believe it. I know, lots of rumors about him using marijuana and cocaine, but I don't believe it. He liked to drink, go to parties, have a good time—can't do cocaine and be real social in these parts or anyplace else I ever knew him to go."

"What's his background? Has he always practiced here?"

"He grew up around here, went to Boston University Law School. He practiced in Boston in a small firm for a year or two, I gather, but didn't like it. He got an opportunity to join another lawyer here in town. Then three or four years later, the other guy let Chuck buy him out. That was well before I came along."

"He had a general practice, right? Litigation, real estate, small business clients?"

"Yes, though he'd been cutting way back on the litigation. He did some divorces too."

"Did he do any really nasty divorces?"

"Well, we had plenty of angry people, but most of the couples weren't rich, didn't have lots of money to spend on lawyers."

"So you don't have any idea why somebody killed him?"

For the first time, she pulled a tissue out of a box and

dabbed at her eyes. "No. I mean, I knew he made people mad sometimes, but nothing big enough to kill him over."

"Okay. You mind if I ask about some people?"

"No, I'll tell you what I can."

"Linda Redmond, Stephanie Williams, George Shee-han, Tom Jordan. Any of them clients of his?"

"Oh, sure. He did things for all of them. One or two, he might have represented the bank in closings on their houses, so technically they weren't our clients, but still we did some work for all of them."

"The bank—you mean the Meadowbrook Savings Bank?"

"Yes. I remember now—we did real estate closings for Tom Jordan and Stephanie Williams. I remember the Williams one—he waived the fee on that one."

"How come?"

"Well, it was when Stephanie came back to town. She didn't have much money and wanted to buy a small house. I think he had a little crush on her from high school, so he didn't charge the fee to be nice to her."

"What about Linda Redmond?"

"Oh, Chuck represented her aunt for years on some things before he did work for Linda. Linda also came in once for some kind of a closing. Whatever he did, it didn't generate much paperwork, so I don't know much about it, but I do know he did things for the family."

"And Sheehan? What did Wells do for him?"

"Over the last few years, he represented George in some real estate deals. They argued sometimes—they each liked to have things their way—but most of the time, they got along. George did a couple of the bigger projects in the area recently so Chuck was glad to have the work."

"How about David Granger?"

"I know he's in real estate, but I don't know much about him. I don't think he was ever a client or recall him at any closings."

"What are you doing with the files now?"

"We're contacting clients, offering to give them back. Those that people don't claim, I guess we'll have to keep in storage for a little while, anyway."

"You still have billing records, client lists, that sort of thing?"

"Oh, yes, one thing about Chuck, he let me buy good computers and software, so we kept things right up to date. At least, those things he told me about. We have all sorts of information on the computer. We're still trying to collect unpaid legal fees for the estate, but you know how it is. Once people know what happened to Chuck, they don't pay their bills."

"Any chance I could get copies of some of the office records?"

"Oh, I don't think I can do that, unless you get permission of the executor."

"That's Wells's brother in New Hampshire?"

"Yes, Dick Wells."

"Is he using a lawyer in town?"

Gloria gave another smile. "There are only a few other lawyers in town. Chuck didn't get along with most of them too well, so Dick Wells hasn't selected a lawyer yet. Dick knew Roger through Chuck, so for the moment, Roger's sort of informally advising Dick. Dick's been down to look things over. You know," she continued, "the police made copies of a number of documents, I understand. Maybe you can get things from them."

"All right," I said, "I'll check with either Wells, Vaneck, or the police. How about the files for Jerome's

projects? Do you have anything on the real estate transactions?"

"A lot of those files disappeared along with files for
about six or seven other clients. Things were such a
mess in the office after Chuck was killed—I don't know
whether things were stolen or destroyed."

"Can you give me the names of those clients?" She
did. They were all real estate deals, she said, but none
of them meant anything to me.

"What about his correspondence file? Wouldn't that
contain copies of all the materials he mailed out?"

She nodded. "Yes, it would."

"Could you pull out the material from the correspondence file on the Mann projects and give it to me?"

She took a deep breath. "Sure, but it'll take awhile."

"I'll wait."

She pulled down a series of binders, each one con-
taining copies of the correspondence and accompanying
documents sent out for the preceding month. I waited as
she went through each monthly file and compiled a small
stack of documents from the available binders that went
back to August of the previous year. Correspondence
files older than that, she said, were in storage.

I took the stack she gave me and spent a half hour
going through it. It was all straightforward business correspondence and copies of the documents used in the
various transactions. Some of it I'd seen in Jerome's
files. There were documents I needed, but nothing gave
me any new insights. There was no correspondence from
Wells to the Division of Fisheries and Wildlife and, as
well, the file didn't include incoming correspondence.

I gave back the documents and asked her to make a
set of copies and send it to me.

"Wells told Jerome that he thought the zoning board

would approve the camp without any trouble. You have any idea what he was talking about?"

"Huh. First time I heard that. Just before it came out in the papers, I know Chuck was worried about a permit for the camp. I remember he told somebody on the phone that getting a permit for the camp would be a problem. But he never said anything to me about it."

"You remember who he was talking to?"

"Sorry, I don't. I didn't think much of it at the time. Might even have been Mr. Mann."

I'd run out of questions so I thanked Duchesne and told her I appreciated her help. I wanted the firm records, but I didn't push it with her. I figured, with Randy's pull, I could get them from the police or maybe through Dick Wells and Vaneck, although they might not see any reason to turn them over and would have valid reasons for not doing so. When I left the office, Duchesne was pouring over another file and grimacing. Probably another one for the to-be-fixed pile. Chuck Wells and his inattention to detail might keep his secretary working for a while after his death. I wondered if it had also contributed to how and why he died.

With a little time on my hands before meeting Daryl, I figured I'd see if I could meet with Lieutenant DeRosa. He was about to leave the police station but he said he had a few minutes for me.

"Already followed up on the Redmond entry in the calendar," he said. "Normally, I wouldn't tell you, but you gave us the tip."

"Thanks. What'd she say?"

"She says she never showed for the meeting."

"She have an alibi?"

"Says she went to the nursing home, had dinner with

her aunt, then visited a couple friends in town. We're working on confirming it."

"If it checks out, she couldn't have been out at the golf course until late. And Jerome wouldn't have hung around all night waiting for her. If she's telling the truth, maybe he met somebody else out there a bit later, he just didn't put it down in his calendar. Redmond tell you guys why she was supposed to meet with Jerome?"

"Supposedly she wanted to talk to him about the water level in the pond since she and her aunt are selling townhouses out there. Said she got nervous and upset about meeting Jerome, and skipped it at the last minute."

"So you're back to square one."

"We're looking at a number of things." We both walked out, neither one of us more sure of anything than when we started.

Wednesday night at the airport, Jenny gave me a long, long hug when I met her. Her eyes were red and puffy, but there were no tears. We didn't talk much as she held my hand all the way to the car. Just as on most of her previous trips, Jenny went directly to bed upon arriving at my house. Before, however, she had done so with passion in mind and me in tow. This time, fatigue and pain had etched lines and shadows in her face. I held her in bed until her breathing was steady.

She slept until almost noon the next day. When she walked into the kitchen, her eyes were clear and the lines were mostly gone from her face.

"Hi," she said to me with a small smile as I stabbed at a waffle I was trying to extricate from my old-fashioned two-slice toaster. "Nice to be here." She came close and I pulled her in.

I pulled back the hair on the side of her face and

kissed her cheek. "Nice to have you here. I have a gourmet brunch planned."

"Toasted waffles with peanut butter, accompanied by a Harp Ale?"

"No, I'm going all out. I bought real maple syrup."

"I don't suppose you have anything I might like, maybe some fruit, granola, or yogurt."

"Usually I'm opposed to that kind of stuff. Against my principles—life's too short for fruits and vegetables. But for you . . ." I pointed over to the end of the counter, where I'd amassed all the things I knew she liked.

I pulled a chair out from the small wooden kitchen table and waved her into it. "Allow me, madame."

"That's mademoiselle to you."

"What would mademoiselle like?"

She looked up at me. "Healthy parents and Jerome here for breakfast," she said. I sat down next to her and hugged her as she lay her head on my shoulder.

We had nothing scheduled that afternoon. Jenny wanted to go back to the golf course as something of a memorial to Jerome.

When we arrived at the clubhouse, there were no cars in the lot and we didn't see anybody else around. Jenny said that she wanted some time by herself to take in the area, think, and remember, so I grabbed my camera.

I strolled out past the first tee, then cut over a number of other holes and through some woods to reach the fourteenth hole. The sun was bright and high with the temperature in the low seventies. The maple and oak trees had filled out, and ferns and bushes were coming alive on the forest floor. Up above, two red-tailed hawks wheeled around, scouting for food. By turns, I could smell new-mown grass, evergreens, and, every once in a while, the odor of skunk cabbage from some of the lower-lying wooded areas.

As I approached the tee on fourteen, the wind came up just a bit. The tee was elevated maybe thirty feet above the hole. It was a par three, with the hole, according to a marker, 160 yards to the green. Just before the green, on the right, the infamous turtle pond jutted a little way into the fairway. Tough hole for any golfer with a slice—which was probably three-quarters of those who would play the hole. If the course ever opened, the turtles would appreciate their shells.

I approached the pond and then sat down about twenty yards away. I checked out the rocks on the edge of the pond as well as a small branch on the border of the pond. I pulled out my camera and extended the telephoto lens, just in case. No turtles. I waited awhile, thinking they might come out to sit in the sun.

Mostly I played on golf courses full of people. It was an unusual pleasure to have time simply to sit back and look around. The red-tailed hawks continued circling in the sky, riding the thermals in and out of my view. Squirrels played in the trees and I saw a red fox patrol the edge of the fairway for maybe fifty yards before going back into the woods.

After thirty minutes or so, the turtles had not appeared. My legs and back began to protest so I moved on. I walked through a band of woods separating the fairways of fourteen and sixteen, and then headed out to the field I'd traversed with Jerome in the golf cart toward the buildings of the long-abandoned camp sitting on the pond shore.

I started out at the back, wandering in and around some larger buildings and the cabins. I passed an all-but-disappeared, weed-choked baseball diamond and a cracked asphalt tennis court. I had a little more time to look at things than I had during my quick trip with Jerome. As I worked my way toward the lake, it was clear that some of the bigger buildings were in decent shape and could be used with relatively minor work. But even if the town had granted a permit, Jerome would have been hard-pressed to get everything done by the time summer ended.

I checked out some of the smaller cabins. Wooden and empty inside except for bunks, they had large windows on the sides, most in need of wire screens. The open windows helped to cool off the cabins in the summer, while the screens kept the bugs out and kids in. And the counselors and camp director could listen at night from the outside to make sure everything was okay. Some of the windows still had shutters that could be closed in case of rain, but many had long since fallen off. Screens were bent and broken in places and some of the front doors on the cabins were gone.

A number of the cabins each had a hole in one corner. I remembered that feature in some of the cabins I bunked in. Lazy counselors in charge of younger kids put the holes there so the counselors wouldn't have to get up in the middle of the night to escort the kids to the latrine or risk letting them pee out the front door.

I had only to walk into one cabin to remember the first time I went to overnight camp. I ended up in an after-hours pillow fight, causing the whole cabin to be punished with the loss of candy privileges for a day.

There were a couple of sheds, probably for athletic and maintenance equipment. One cabin looked like the old camp canteen. It had no windows, but had a split door, with the top and bottom opening separately and a counter built on top of the bottom section. Camp employees would have distributed mail to the campers from there and would also have sold the kids candy, snacks, and small personal items. It had been a lot of years since I'd manned a canteen, but I still remembered how we schemed to get our hands on extra candy.

I worked my way down to the main office building, which sat just back from the pond. Before the building stretched what had been, and what might be again someday, a lawn leading to a beach. Next to the beach, a pier sat in considerable disrepair, and just beyond it, the old boathouse that Jerome and I had wandered into. Both the boathouse and the pier looked like they'd already endured a few too many storms and kids pounding on them.

I rounded a corner of the main office building and almost walked into an old, weathered, gray wooden picnic table sitting to the side of the building. More to the point, I almost walked into a woman sitting at the table with a book in front of her, facing the sun. She wore blue jeans, a plaid red flannel shirt, a well-worn brown leather vest over it, and beat-up hiking boots. As I came around the corner she looked up but her face remained impassive. Her brown hair was cut short, framing a round face with deep-set, brown eyes. Though it was still early spring, her face, hands, and forearms were all deeply tanned. The hands looked hard, with callused palms.

"Sorry," I said, "didn't mean to interrupt you."

"You didn't," she said, "I heard you barging around back there for a while." She looked me over for a moment with narrow eyes and a frown. "You look familiar."

"Just out for a walk," I said, recognizing Stephanie Williams, the environmental activist who had opposed the camp at the zoning board meeting. I pointed to the book she was reading, *The Monkey Wrench Gang*. "You an Edward Abbey fan? Personally, I liked *Desert Solitude* better, but it was a different kind of book."

She gave me a slow smile. "This one's my bible," she said, holding the book aloft. "I go back to it every couple of years, just to keep grounded in what I'm doing."

"Well, this place isn't as empty as Ed would have liked, but it's still a damn pretty spot. Gonna be different with the golf club open and kids here."

"No need to worry," she said and laughed. "They'll never open the golf course. And the town won't let the camp open up."

"Huh. How do you know?"

"A small pond over there," she said and pointed in the direction of the course, "has some endangered turtles in it, so they'll have to close off some of the holes, soon as the process of designating the turtles is done. Nothing the owners can do, now that the state knows about the turtles." Her smile broadened. "And most people don't want the camp here, bringing in all sorts of people from outside."

"Ed Abbey would have appreciated the notion that a few turtles might keep overweight guys in ugly shorts from knocking little white balls into the woods."

"Exactly. I think he would have liked it a lot," she said and laughed loudly.

"You know this place pretty well?" I asked.

"I grew up around here—swam in Echo Pond, chased my dog all over these hills. I moved away for a while. When I came back, the sons of bitches were trying to destroy it. So some of us are doing what we can to preserve it."

"Interesting. What's the name of your group?" I asked.

"We're the local chapter of the Wild Woods Warriors. You probably haven't heard of us. We're national, but sort of low-key."

"Kind of like the Monkey Wrench Gang?"

"No. I wish we were that ambitious and brave," she said with a small laugh, "and times have changed. Can't do all those stunts anymore."

Ed Abbey's *The Monkey Wrench Gang* was a funny novel about the first environmental saboteurs, people who, in the name of protecting Mother Earth, tore down offensive billboards and spiked trees so they could not be safely harvested by loggers. Monkey-wrenching became a term of art for radical environmental activists as they took the fight to those they thought were despoiling the land. In the last decade or so, the environmental movement had increasingly turned to men and women in suits and government agencies to fight their fights. Stephanie Williams was right—most people thought the time for monkey-wrenching had passed.

I knew all of this only because, for a time at the beginning of law school, I'd been involved with a woman who was a rabid environmentalist except, it turned out, for when she was in the environment. She gave me a bunch of books to read, including a few by Abbey. I heard from her about different environmental groups and their strategies. We had endless debates about the importance of recycling plastic bags and the merits of paper versus cloth diapers. We broke up when I tried to take her camping. After one night out in a tent, she insisted on going to a motel so she would not go another day without a long, hot shower. Things with her were never quite the same after I pointed out how much water she had polluted and wasted by her change in venue.

A quick look at Stephanie Williams's tan, boots, and

clothes made it clear that, unlike my former girlfriend, she'd done time outdoors. And the close scrutiny she gave me made clear that the time she'd spent with people, or maybe with men, had left a mark as well.

"Planning anything exciting around here?"

Her eyebrows lifted and her head tilted to the side a bit as she focused on me with a quizzical look. "Anything's possible," she said. Then she paused for a moment and gave me a hard stare. "Are you with a paper company or a logging outfit?"

I raised my hand and shook my head. "No, no, I just know a little because I used to belong to a couple of environmental groups in the past. I'm not trying to pry."

Tension drained from her face, the lines around her eyes softened, and a smile came back. "Okay," she said, "just can't be too sure. I've had friends burned pretty bad by trusting the wrong people, so I'm pretty careful. A lot of people don't like those of us committed to saving the earth."

Saving the earth was a noble cause and all, but Daryl and Jenny, each in their own way, needed help of a less grandiose nature. I also didn't want to overplay my hand or get Stephanie Williams too interested in checking up on me before I checked out the Wild Woods Warriors.

"Good luck, hope you succeed," I said, "I've got to head back."

She stood up, filling out the blue jeans and vest fully and admirably. "Maybe I'll see you out here again some time," she said. "We're always on the lookout for new members, particularly fans of Ed Abbey." She held out her hand again. "I'm Stephanie Williams."

"Dan Kardon. I'll keep that in mind." She kept my hand a second longer than necessary before letting go.

"I'm in the book in Meadowbrook, if you ever want to find me," she said.

"Thanks," I said, and walked away, willing myself not to look back. Damn, I thought, as I stepped up the pace, Jenny's only a short walk away and yet Williams had looked quite appealing.

Walking back to find Jenny, I thought about whether to tell her about meeting Stephanie Williams. If I'd learned anything in the last few months with Jenny, it was that it was easier to talk with her about most things than not. It was when I didn't talk about something that she got nosy, concerned, pissed, or all three.

Not talking as a response to things going bad had served me well when I was younger. Over the years, it became easier just to keep on that way. But with Jenny, not talking was not an option.

At the same time, there were still things I needed time to mull over before talking with Jenny or anyone else about them. So I'd developed another strategy—hide things in plain sight. Bring something out, then let it sit, fade into the woodwork or get buried in the humdrum of the everyday events, available for me to think about but unnoticed by others. In that way, I was, perhaps, more like Daryl than I'd like to admit.

But I hadn't come out to the golf course to ruminate about my social life. I'd come out in part to be with Jenny and in part to get a better handle on the problems that Jerome had faced. How Stephanie Williams set off the male chemicals in my brain and groin was a mildly intriguing personal question I could look at in my leisure. Whether Stephanie Williams was involved in the effort to stop Jerome's plans, or even participated in his killing, was a far more compelling and timely question. Between Linda Redmond, mysterious mistress of the

mansion, and Stephanie Williams, radical environmental
activist, the town of Meadowbrook was serving up some
unusual women. And while I didn't plan to join the Wild
Woods Warriors, I wanted to discover all I could about
those who had.

CHAPTER

ELEVEN

Jerome's funeral took place on Saturday. The funeral was just as unique as Jerome had been. Mourners filled the solid brick church on Blue Hill Avenue in Roxbury. Limousines double-parked in front of the church cost more than some of the battered, broken-down neighboring homes. Inside, the crowd included athletes, businessmen, real estate moguls, kids who Jerome had worked with and their families, as well as most of the members of the church congregation, many of them elderly and poor, since Jerome and his family had worshiped there for years. With substantial numbers of blacks and whites in attendance, as well as some Hispanics, the crowd made for an unusual sight in Boston.

The service was full of gospel songs, emotional testimonies to the impact Jerome had had on those around him, prayers, and an impassioned sermon. My favorite speaker was Andy Dennison, the same young man who had flourished at Jerome's camps and whose grandfather sold Jerome the Meadowbrook land. Dennison, in college but no longer playing serious basketball, talked about how Jerome treated the teenagers at his camp.

"It took me a little while, but I finally figured him out. At first, he'd only play ball with us. He didn't talk much, except about basketball. Instead, he'd listen to us and

watch. When things got slow, he'd play a few riffs on
his harmonica. He didn't say much about himself but we
figured out pretty quickly he was a cool guy.

"As camp went along, he found something good to
say about every one of us. He'd get into our games just
to have fun with us," Dennison said. "After a while, kids
started to ask him about his life, the choices he'd made,
how he got where he was. That's what we were hungry
for, information about how to get to where we wanted
to be, but we wouldn't talk to our parents or our teachers
about stuff like that. After all, they weren't cool—or at
least we didn't think so. But Jerome, he had it together.
And suddenly, he had us asking him about the things he
wanted to talk about. But if he'd just started talking,
trying to lay stuff on us, man, we would have blown
him off from the start.

"He gave us respect, answers to our questions, some
insight about how people grow up, and a model of how
an adult could still be cool. It may not sound like
much—but if it doesn't, you're not a teenager."

The tears flowed, the hymns resounded with grief and
loss. And all the while a part of me surveyed the crowd.
In particular, I looked to see if I recognized anyone from
Meadowbrook, anyone who might have been Jerome's
killer.

The crowd was too big, though, with too many un-
familiar faces, for me to make any real headway. I decided I was being foolish trying to do detective work
during a funeral. At least until I noticed, standing against
the wall on the side of the church, Lieutenant DeRosa
from Meadowbrook wearing a suit. After the funeral I
tried to catch up with DeRosa, but he seemed to melt
away. Nobody I saw made an impression, and in the

end, I learned nothing about who killed Jerome. Instead, I learned how much others lost when he died.

I had plenty to keep me busy over the next few days, between talking with either Fred Bender or Daryl about various business issues, spending some time with Jenny, and doing some work at the office. Messages piled up, some about cases and some about Jerome's businesses. All it meant was that I had little time to think about investigating what happened to Jerome.

By Wednesday afternoon, Jenny was withdrawn and remote. While we drove to the airport, I said, "You're awful quiet. Anything going on I need to know about or is this about Jerome and going back to Tennessee?"

She was silent for a couple of minutes. "I can't tell you," she said, "although you get some points for asking." She gave a fleeting, small smile. "I feel as if somebody turned me upside down and emptied everything out so there's nothing left to give anybody. But whatever's left, I'll need in Tennessee. So I guess I'm saving my strength for that. Sorry. You deserve better."

"Hey, you're the one deserves better. Anything i can do to help, just whistle."

"Thanks," she said as she reached up and stroked my neck for a moment. Then she returned to staring at the light rain outside. She didn't say anything further until we arrived at the airport. There we checked her bags at the gate. In a reprise of her arrival, I hugged her for a long time on the curb. When we pulled apart, I looked at her face and saw that it reflected all the pain she felt inside. I could only say, "Love ya—call me tonight," before my throat closed up.

"I will," she said. She turned and walked through the doors into the airport.

* * *

On Saturday, Daryl called. He asked me if I'd meet him out at the golf course the next day. He said he wanted to play a little and talk about some things.

I arrived before Daryl. Everything was still green and beautiful but a closer look showed that maintenance was falling behind. The practice green next to the clubhouse hadn't been mowed in a while. What I could see of the first tee and fairway showed little evidence of any up-keep.

Daryl showed up in his Lincoln Navigator. He stepped out, took off his sunglasses, and nodded at me. "Thanks for coming," he said.

We each grabbed our clubs. "What do you have in mind?" I asked. "Doesn't look like the course is in tip-top shape."

"I figured. Thought we'd take a cart, visit some holes, and hit some balls for Jerome. He'd like that. Between the funeral and all the family stuff this week, I haven't had much quiet time."

"Whatever you want."

"Might be a nice memorial to Jerome, we knock some balls into the turtle pond." I gave a small laugh. He didn't.

So we drove around the course. It wasn't golf, really. We played only a few holes fully. We hit some balls from spots that Daryl thought Jerome had loved. When we got to the fourteenth hole and the turtle pond, we each took a handful of balls. I still didn't see any turtles. From about fifty yards away, we lobbed them into the pond.

When we had each exhausted our supply of balls, we were both silent for a moment. Then Daryl turned to me.

"Like to check out the camp. You mind?"

"No problem."

We took the golf cart over. When we got there, things looked pretty much the same. But when we drove over by the main building, we found graffiti in large, black, spray-painted letters on one of the walls: GOOD RIDDENCE. I watched Daryl as he stared at the wall. Then he jammed his foot on the golf cart brake and jumped out of the cart. He strode quickly down to the water and walked out onto the pier. He stood on the wooden dock, looking out over Echo Pond, his arms folded across his chest. I didn't follow him.

Daryl stood there for at least five minutes, maybe more. If he moved a muscle while he was staring at the water, I didn't see it. Finally, he turned and walked back to the cart.

"Some pretty sick people out there, plus they can't spell," I said. "I'll call, get the wall cleaned up."

"Thought I was coming out here for the last time. Planned to tell you I wanted to sell the property, get rid of the complications." He paused for a moment.

"You changing your mind?" I asked.

"I got out here, took a look around, realized this is all we got left," Daryl said, sweeping his arm to include the camp shorefront and the pond. "This is what we got that's really Jerome's. The businesses, the restaurant, hell, those were just investments to him and I don't want the hassles. But this place, it grabbed him. We can do a camp, we can run a golf course, the state lets us. Won't be the same without Jerome, but we can still get it done just the way he'd like."

"Nothing's going to be easy about it, Daryl. That graffiti tells you people out here aren't going to roll over for you and make a martyr out of Jerome."

"I hear you. But I walk away, I'm making it easy for

them. Any moves we got left to make sure they don't drive us out of here, let's make 'em."

"This is no basketball game. We don't know why, but people are dying. No rules or referees in this game."

Daryl was quiet for a moment. "Paintball without boundaries and with real bullets."

"No. In paintball, at least, you know the difference between the good guys and the bad guys."

Daryl shook his head and sighed. "Ah, hell, I can't worry about what happens next. More shit goes down, I'll deal with it. But I want this place to be what Jerome had in mind."

"What about the other investors?"

"No problem. They'll stay in, so long as I do. Things don't get better, we still got the land to sell. For now, we do what we got to do to get these places up and running. Costs money, I'll pay."

"Okay. We can get going on selling some of the other properties. With the camp and golf course, mostly it'll just be dealing with the town and the state. What about the dam, the water in the pond?"

"Any reason to let the water back up?"

I thought for a moment. "Not if you're prepared for the heat."

"Somebody killed Jerome. No heat left worse than that."

"Good enough. I'll put the word out we still want to open the camp. We keep the water level down, start legal action against the town, and maybe offer the town some incentives to settle, we might generate enough pressure on Sheehan so he gives something back."

"Sounds good. About Jerome, light a fire under the cops if you can, but if you can't, check it out yourself. Cops aren't doing anything wrong that I know of. But

with all the bad stuff happening out here and the Meadowbrook folks involved, I gotta believe some of the
cops don't want to find out the truth."

"I wouldn't sweat your situation. The state police are
in on this, plus the town looks pretty bad right now. I
expect the locals will want to do it right."

"Yeah, well, we expected the town officials to do the
permit right, and look where it got us."

"Can't argue with that. All right, I'll see what I can
do."

We took off in the golf cart and headed back. Daryl
left as soon as we got to the parking lot. Before I left,
I went back to the turtle pond one more time. The sun
was out and it was warm, but the turtles still hadn't
emerged.

Back at home, I called Al Thompson. After I filled him
in on what had happened over the week, Al told me he'd
found a friend of a friend, a retired cop in Meadowbrook. The guy didn't have much use for the current
chief of the Meadowbrook police. The chief had passed
over Al's new-found buddy for promotion once too often. The retired cop was happy to have Al come by, give
him some background on the people in town, including
the police chief. And that would give Al an excuse to
do some checking around. Al and I agreed to meet later
in the week in Meadowbrook.

After talking to Al, I tried to find things to keep me
busy in the house, but I couldn't stay there. The front
closet had a jacket of Jenny's. A couple of her books
were in the living room. She had taken over a bedroom
closet and part of a bureau, both of which were still half
full. The toothbrush holder held her green toothbrush
right next to my orange one. The sink was cleaner than

it had been since I'd moved in years before. Instead, I called downstairs and then put on my running clothes.

Mike Steiner liked the idea of a run, so we headed out. There was still a lot of light left as we headed toward Coolidge Corner, took Harvard Street to Brookline Village, and then went on a long, slow run around Jamaica Pond before heading back.

Mike started off talking about the Red Sox. When we finished discussing why the Red Sox had approximately six guys who could play first base or could DH, but couldn't play anywhere else, Mike hit me with a question seemingly out of left field.

"Dan, where's Jenny? I saw her once, but she didn't say much."

"She only came here to go to a funeral. Then she had to go back to Tennessee. Her dad's not well and her mother was hurt badly in a fall so Jenny needed to go home and help them."

"How long will she be gone?"

"Don't know, probably three or four weeks. Maybe longer." Much longer, I almost said.

We stopped to cross a street and Mike went silent for a moment. When I was back running, he asked, "Do you miss her?"

"Sure," I said.

"Are you going to marry her?"

"I don't know."

"Well, do you love her?"

"Yeah, I do."

"Then why don't you know if you'll marry her?"

I ran for a minute or two before I answered. "Sometimes getting married isn't just about love. She has to be in Tennessee for a while to do some things and I'm not sure either one of us wants to get married right away."

"Mom says you might never get married, that you like living alone too much."

I shook my head and smiled. I'd never talked to Terry Steiner about my social life or about Jenny. But Terry was a bright woman and I'd been in and out of her house enough to become part of the furniture. "Your mom's right about most things. I hope she's wrong about this one." I stopped at an intersection and moved forward to see Mike. Then I played the card I knew would divert him. "You know who I played golf with the other day?"

"No."

"Daryl Mann."

His whole body become tight and rigid with excitement. Between golf and the Shamrocks, he couldn't figure out what to ask about first. Most important, the diversion worked.

"Wow. Daryl Mann, that's great. Where did you play?"

I gave him a little of the background and asked what he thought about Daryl.

"He's the Shamrocks' best player. A lot of people don't like him, but I do."

"How come?"

"I'm not sure. When he makes a great play, he doesn't make a big deal about it. He's good on defense and he doesn't complain to the refs."

"Some people say he isn't friendly."

"I don't care. I know he's different from some of the other players, but he plays hard and I think that's the most important thing. Is he a good golfer?"

"He's okay, not great. He'd be much better if he could putt."

"Are you a good golfer?"

"Not really. I'm about as good as Daryl. I'm a better putter than he is, but he hits the ball a lot farther than I do."

"Do you know how they make a golf course in a desert?"

Mike had watched part of a golf tournament played on a course in Arizona sometime over the winter and he'd been puzzling over how they built the course in the middle of the desert. I talked to him a bit about irrigation, grass nutrients, pesticides, and the like until I had no more to say. Happily, we were in Coolidge Corner and I could slow the flow of questions by buying him a cup of chocolate chip ice cream. We sat outside and watched people go by as I fed him his ice cream with a spoon in between more sports talk.

By the time we got home, my legs and Mike's jaw were sore. I went upstairs, put a Richard Shindell CD on the stereo, and knocked off a Bass Ale.

On Monday, I received calls from David Granger, Roger Vaneck, and George Sheehan. I called them back in that order and, to my surprise in a time of pervasive and endless voice-mail and answering systems, reached each one of them. The calls were all variations on the same theme.

Granger had come to Jerome's funeral but we'd not had a chance to talk. He apologized for bringing up business so quickly, he said, but he'd already had inquiries about the golf course and camp land. With Jerome dead, people figured that Daryl would sell. Granger was calling just to let me know that he would have no trouble finding Daryl some buyers. In fact, he said, he had one particularly eager party wanting the land. I told Granger that at least for the moment, Daryl was not inclined to sell but that I'd get back to him if things changed. I heard the surprise in his voice after I told him that Daryl intended to carry on what Jerome started. Okay, he said, good luck. If he could help in any way, let him know.

Sheehan expressed his extreme remorse over Jerome's death in a single, clipped sentence, then said that the town would like to talk to Daryl before he sold the camp property. I told him Daryl had no plans to sell.

"He's never been involved in the camp. He can't possibly be interested in pursuing it. He's worth millions—what does he care?" Sheehan said.

"You think people with millions don't care about anything? I suppose you could be right. To find out why he cares, you've got to talk to him. To figure out what he plans, you can talk to me. We're going forward with the golf course. We also want to proceed with the camp and I'm authorized to sue the town, if it becomes appropriate."

"Don't threaten me, Kardon."

"I'm not. I'm stating a fact."

There was a pause. "What about the pond? Mann's not going to keep the water level down, is he?"

"What about the town? You going to let him renovate and operate the camp?"

"The zoning board of appeals voted and that's all there is, Kardon. We won't be intimidated."

"I guess you could say the same goes for us."

Sheehan all but sputtered into the phone. "You want us to contact the companies he endorses, maybe even the Shamrocks, to tell them how he's hurting the working people in this town?"

"Jeez, now that scares the hell out of me. That'll give the town great publicity. All those townhouses, new homes you're trying to market—newcomers will certainly pour into a blatantly racist town that has a swamp for a town beach. You want to contact the press, the team, we'll give you some phone numbers. Come to think of it, maybe we should be contacting the press. It'd be a nice story—corruption and racism in a small New England town. Thanks, I like the idea." Sheehan hung up on me.

Roger Vaneck, the president of the Meadowbrook Savings Bank, called to find out what Daryl was doing as well. With a loan out to Daryl and Jerome to finance the land purchase and projects, he was, he said, just checking on what would happen with the projects and the land. When I told him, the line went silent for a minute.

"Am I to assume that even though neither the golf course nor the camp are opening, payments on the loan will be made on time?"

"That's the plan. No need to worry about the payments." A shorter silence followed.

"This has been a much more controversial project than we ever imagined," Vaneck finally said.

"I'm not surprised."

"Frankly, the bank is in an awkward position here, supporting a project that has divided the town so badly. We're always supportive of our customers, but we've been a part of this town for generations and we hate to see this kind of disruption."

"You want us to pay off the loan immediately so you can get out of the project? Is that what I'm hearing?"

"No, not exactly. We have considerable investments in this community. I guess I'm wondering if I can meet with you and Mr. Mann to discuss the future of these projects."

"You going to push us to drop the camp? I don't mean to be rude, but if that's what you want to tell us, we don't need a meeting for that."

"It's not that we don't want the camp or the young people, it's that this debate about the camp, and the lowering of the pond, is devastating to so many people in the community. As one of the representatives of the business community, I'd like the opportunity to talk to Mr. Mann about the situation, to see if there are some creative solutions we can come up with."

"I'll talk to Daryl about it, but I can't make any promises."

Vaneck made more noises about wanting to find an amicable solution to the impasse between the town and Daryl, but I ended the phone call pretty quickly. Maybe there were some compromises available, but the one that Vaneck could offer most readily—forgiving Daryl part of the loan if he'd forget about reopening the camp—would help the pocketbooks of Daryl and the investors but wouldn't satisfy Daryl's interest in carrying out Jerome's wishes. I knew, though, we had to meet with him, if only to preserve good relations with the businesspeople in town. And maybe Vaneck and others would come up with something more than I anticipated. Daryl would then have to decide whether Vaneck truly wanted to help us find a middle ground or whether he was a smoother, smarter Sheehan.

In the end, the phone calls made clear that the leaders of Meadowbrook hoped Daryl would bail out. Time for a little digging, I thought, to see what some of the other folks in town thought.

I'd kept the copy of the article in the Meadowbrook paper that Jerome had shown me, the one that described for the first time the plans for the camp to host inner-

city kids. The article had a byline, Marie Riley. I thought
I'd start with her to see if she'd tell me who had put her
on to the story.

But a couple of emergency phone calls came in from
clients and then I had to spend some time on a memo
due in court the next day, so I never made the call to
Riley. Instead, when I left the office just after six P.M.,
I decided to stop at Jerome's office to play on his computer. I wanted another look at his calendar.

Fred Bender was not there when I let myself in the
office. I parked myself in front of Jerome's computer
and took some time to go back through his schedule—
the last time, I'd looked at the day he died and little
else.

The daily responsibilities of his life made me simultaneously a bit guilty and sorry. All that I'd heard about
Jerome was right there—plenty of business appointments but also numerous meetings with people about
basketball clinics, appearances at schools, and the like.
Typically he had meetings three and four nights a week,
at churches, at social service organizations, or at cor-
porations, some obviously for fund-raising.

I began by skimming through his schedule for the full
year before, just to see if there were any patterns. It was
easy enough. Just click on each day and the appointments came up. Jerome was pretty good about giving
more than just a name. He usually gave one or two
words to give an idea what the meeting was about and
something to note where the meeting was.

The months I looked at showed Jerome met with
Daryl, Wells, Vaneck, and others out in Meadowbrook
whose names I did not recognize, although I surmised
that some of them might be people doing work on the
golf course. I printed out the appointments I had ques-

tions about so that either Daryl or Bender could tell me who the people were.

Meetings in Meadowbrook slowed down considerably after October, presumably because most of the work on the golf course was complete. Then, after March, things picked up again. There were more appointments out at the golf course and a few with Wells, presumably as they started talking about the camp.

When I got to May, I saw an entry indicating that Jerome had met with Jenny and then found another for the night Jenny and I met Jerome at Mann's Best Hope. I went through all the May entries with some care, including the one for the meeting with the zoning board of appeals. Seeing it gave me a quick flashback to that night, and I had to stop for a moment before finishing the entries. After that, there were a couple of meetings with Daryl and others, probably investors.

And there was another meeting listed with Linda Redmond—not at the golf club, but at her home. The meeting had been scheduled a few days after Jerome began draining the pond and three days before he died. So what was the real reason, I wondered, for Redmond's failure to show up for her meeting with Jerome on the day he was killed? She'd met him already, according to his calendar. There was no reason for her to be intimidated, as she apparently told the police. Maybe she told the police of that first meeting and disclosed what they talked about. But if the meeting took place and she didn't tell the police about it, I sure wanted to know why.

Nothing else of interest showed up on Jerome's schedule. I ended that program and called up my internet access provider. His computer was newer and faster than mine so I wanted to do my web surfing on his computer.

In particular, I was looking for the web site of the Wild Woods Warriors. Even if—indeed, especially if—it wasn't an established, mainstream environmental group, the group would probably have a web site. It took a while, but I finally found it—www.wildwoodswar.org.

It was a great place to start for any aspiring ecowarrior. In addition to pages devoted to the philosophy of the organization, the web site included a whole slew of different pages—discussions of environmental activism and the art of monkey-wrenching; the importance of taking direct action against those who would despoil the environment; places where environmental protests were underway; and, of course, the page that sold books, tee-shirts, hats, patches, and bumper stickers, which would presumably biodegrade on your solar-powered car.

Perhaps the most interesting page on the web site was devoted to a camp that the group had held the previous summer to teach budding ecowarriors how to focus their energies. In addition to learning how to fashion the most effective blockades and protests, the campers, living in tents in an unnamed Oregon forest, learned how to handle the press. They were taught that the most effective sound bites were nine seconds or shorter, that they should send out press releases a week before their environmental protests, and that they should rehearse what they would shout when they were dragged off by police in front of the news cameras. If professionalizing our protestors was happening, I wondered whether unionizing was next on the list.

The story about the camp made clear that the campers learned some interesting tricks as well. The instructors, long-time radical environmentalists, talked with some fondness of stealing distributor caps and sugaring the gas tanks of construction equipment. Spiking trees was the subject of great debate though. Some old-timers had spiked trees about to be logged with large nails to deter saw-wielding loggers from cutting down the trees. But if a spiked tree wasn't marked and a logger didn't know about the nails, the nails might blow up the saw and cause the logger serious injury. According to the activist quoted in the website story, just such an accident in 1987 had substantially undermined the influence of the radical environmental movement.

All in all, though, the message to the campers was clear. Taking disciplined, public action against any individual or institution that threatened harm to the environment was the only way to reclaim the earth and to keep one's soul pure.

Finally, just as any recreational camp would advertise using shots of happy campers, the camp page finished with pictures of the activists in training from the summer before. Photos showed campers hoisting circular plywood platforms about two hundred feet up Douglas firs and installing them there for people to live on to stop logging of the trees. Other campers were shown learning to climb trees with ropes and carabineers and then traversing cables tied between trees, telling stories by a big campfire, and taking chilly, nude baths in a stream.

At the end of the camp web page, I found a spread of about twenty photos of campers, mostly young but some middle-aged, fairly evenly split between men and women. Some smiled; others had their dour ecoactivist faces on. None of the men had shaved for some time. Grinning at me from a photo on the left margin was Stephanie Williams.

I knew that Jerome didn't die from a stolen distributor cap or a spiked tree. Williams was not a murderer just because she went to a radical summer camp—indeed, perhaps she fully accepted the nonviolent creed of the camp. But her presence at the camp suggested she would go well beyond reading her letter to the zoning board to defend the lands she cherished and the Manns had purchased.

Over the years I'd wasted a lot of time on the computer, checking out ridiculous websites, playing games, waiting for documents to upload, download, and sometimes explode. This evening, the time had been well-spent. What Stephanie Williams would do, or did do, to protect the land on the pond was just as interesting to me as why Linda Redmond scheduled two separate meetings with Jerome and may have shown up for neither.

the bank. Sheehan thought he was going to end up leading the bank, but the board picked Vaneck instead. Sheehan went into real estate, began as a broker, then started doing some small developments."

"Has he been active in town government for a long time?"

"Yeah, and he's helped a lot of people over the years with favors."

I finished off my beer and munched on a couple of pretzels while Riley ordered another beer and a hamburger. She looked like she was just getting started.

"Let me switch gears on you. Wells—any ideas floating around about why he was killed or who did it?"

"Nothing official. Police are checking out drugs, gambling, women, angry clients, but so far doesn't seem like they're making progress." Riley took a generous gulp of her new beer.

"Pretty busy guy, if he was into all that."

She shrugged. "Couldn't tell you. He never did any of it with me."

"From what I hear, he wasn't such a popular guy."

"Wells rubbed a lot of people the wrong way over the years, but he represented probably half the people in town on different matters. People may not have liked him, but they sure as hell used him as their lawyer. He didn't hide the fact he was smart or that he made money. In a small town where most people don't make a lot money and a lot of the smart ones leave, he stood out. And he wasn't always, let's say, tactful. But I don't think he got killed over a lack of tact."

"Last question."

"Don't ever say that. Lawyers I've talked to never have a last question."

My turn to laugh. "Fair enough. The story you

CHAPTER

TWELVE

In the middle of the week, Al Thompson saved me from the bankers, realtors, creditors, and others, even musicians, calling to know what was going on with Jerome's businesses. Al phoned after spending some time in Meadowbrook. We agreed on dinner out there in a neighboring town on Thursday night.

I also called the reporter at the Meadowbrook paper I'd been meaning to track down. Marie Riley agreed to meet me late in the afternoon, before my dinner with Al.

By four, I'd billed some hours, so I headed out to meet with Marie Riley.

The *Meadowbrook Chronicle* was housed in a small, plain brick building, much like the one on the other side of the town square where Chuck Wells had maintained his office. The young receptionist, a brunette in her twenties chewing a wad of gum, was just picking up her bag and coat to leave when I arrived. When I told her my name, she gave me a quick second look, then called Marie Riley and told her I was waiting in the lobby. I smiled at her but she didn't smile back as she walked out the door. The counter of the reception area had a sign with her name—Donna Sheehan. It didn't take a super sleuth to figure out there was a decent

chance that George Sheehan was a relative. I added the
question to the short list I had for Riley.

Riley emerged from a door into the lobby in another
five minutes.

"Sorry," she said, "had a story to finish up. Marie
Riley." She looked between twenty-five and thirty, with
black hair, a round face, and glasses. She was stocky
and had a low voice. She extended her hand, shook mine
with a firm grip, and gave me a brief smile.

"Thanks for meeting with me," I said.

"You want to go grab something to eat?"

"Can't do dinner, but if you want to eat, I'll have a
beer. And I'll buy."

"Beer sounds better than dinner right now, the day
I've had," she replied.

She said I should follow her in her car to a local bar.
We ended up at a place called Christopher's, which was
a lot nicer inside than the battered wooden exterior
promised. We grabbed a well-built and elegant wooden
booth with a high back and I ordered pretzels and two
draft beers. I started to give Riley a little background
about who I was and what I was doing in Meadowbrook.
She laughed.

"I know all about you," she said.

"Word spreads, huh?"

"That, plus I'm a reporter, remember? You gave me
a little time, so I checked you out."

"Nice to be notorious somewhere, I suppose."

"Hey, it's a small town, not much going on most of
the time. Somebody makes George Sheehan look bad,
word spreads quick. You and Jerome Mann did a pretty
good job of that."

"He nailed us pretty good at the zoning board hear-

ing." I shook my head and downed some ⟨   ⟩ to
douse the memory.

"Yeah, Sheehan controls the board, but J⟨   ⟩
Daryl, they turned around some people at the ⟨   ⟩
You took a vote of that crowd before those guy⟨   ⟩
you'd have had no chance. Afterward, it migh⟨   ⟩
been close. Then, when you told George about the ⟨ ⟩
being lowered—hell, that went around town in a⟨ ⟩
five minutes."

"Actually, since we planned it that way, I'm glad ⟨ ⟩
know it worked. You mind if I ask you a few question⟨ ⟩
about the town, some of what you've written?"

"Nope—I figured that's what you wanted. Kind of
reversal of form for me. But this is my town, too, and I
depend on a lot of people, so I may not give you what
you want."

"George Sheehan—can you tell me anything about
him?"

"Only stuff that doesn't matter. They've got their eyes
on me already, so I gotta be careful."

"Donna Sheehan, the receptionist?"

"Yeah, she's George's niece. Tells him damn n⟨ ⟩
everything, as far as I can tell. But also I've got an ed⟨ ⟩
who's in tight with local officials, so you won't ⟨ ⟩
anything negative from me."

"Okay, whatever you can tell me would be helpf⟨ ⟩

"Sheehan grew up in this town, went to work a⟨ ⟩
bank after college."

"The Meadowbrook Savings Bank?"

"Yeah."

"Did he work with Roger Vaneck?"

"Vaneck started later. The story I've heard, V⟨ ⟩
had been a lawyer for a while in town. But he'd w⟨ ⟩
in a bank before becoming a lawyer and ended up

wrote—the one about the camp operating for inner-city kids. How'd you find out about the camp? Can you tell me who your source of information was?"

She waved the bartender over and ordered another beer. I ordered a ginger ale. This woman could keep up with some of her big city newspaper colleagues at the bar.

"What kind of reporter do you think I am, giving up sources? Hell, I gotta keep my sources confidential," she said and gave something between a sigh and a snarl. "Sources. At this piece-of-crap newspaper, I got sources of stress, I got sources of heartburn, I got sources of bullshit, I got sources of assholes, but I got no sources of information. Everything I get, I dig for. That story, some concerned citizen with nuts the size of ball bearings sent an anonymous letter to my editor. He gave it to me, I checked with Wells, called people. That was it, and we blew up a camp for kids. Great journalism in the name of the public's right to know. More like the public's right to act like idiots." She stopped suddenly and said, "Excuse me, I have to visit the little girl's room."

"Marie, I've got to get going, have to get to that dinner meeting. I'll pay up front—thanks and take care of yourself."

"Hey, I have some questions for you."

"Sorry, I really need to head out."

She frowned for a moment. "Some weird stuff is going on, I can feel it. Anything you can tell me?"

"Sorry, can't help," I said and went to the front of the bar.

I couldn't say she'd given me much that was new but that was okay. I didn't know who publicized the camp and the police had nothing hard yet on Wells. I had a better fix on Sheehan and maybe a better picture of the town. If we could separate Sheehan from the town, or isolate him from the board, we might have a shot at getting the board to change its mind. How to do that, I didn't yet have a clue, but it gave me a place to start.

Al and I met at an Italian restaurant, Mike's. It was an old wooden building sitting back from a side road, and not far from a small bridge with a stream under it. The front parking lot was full so I went around back, next to a small patch of woods and some picnic tables that would be in use in a few weeks. I could hear the stream babbling. Nice place to eat pizza and to be eaten by mosquitoes.

Inside, the restaurant had the requisite red-checked tablecloths, posters of Italy on the walls, and old, round wine bottles with unused candles in them. The menu had all the spaghetti, pasta, and pizza one would have expected.

There were only a few diners in the restaurant when I came in. Al had already grabbed a table and waved me over. After exchanging pleasantries and uncovering a basket of stale Italian bread, we ordered beers and an antipasto plate. Then I gave Al a short summary of the few things that had come up since we'd talked, and Al gave me an update.

After locating the retired cop, Joe Renheart, in Meadowbrook, Al had come up over the weekend. He stayed at the local Motel 6. I told him that next time he could upgrade his accommodations and I'd pay. He visited with Renheart a couple of times, just to get his take on different people and the town. Then on Renheart's advice, Al spent some time at a popular breakfast place where he could sit at the counter and gab with the waitresses as well as a luncheon spot where a bunch of the retired guys—some former town workers, a couple of letter carriers, and tradesmen—hung out, smoking, drinking beers, and telling stories and lies.

Al himself told some great stories about his childhood in a blue collar fishing city, New Bedford, and from his years as a cop working his way up to police chief in the town of Wettamesset. He'd have held his own in the gabfests. Combine that with his buddy Renheart's knowledge and a little old-fashioned detective work, it didn't surprise me that in a few days, he'd learned quite a bit.

He said there was plenty of speculation about the murders as well as both the camp and the lowering of Echo Pond. He'd also gleaned a great deal about the individuals we were interested in. After a long wait for our dinners, Al ran down the list with me over his watery chicken cacciatore and my large mound of overcooked spaghetti, sausages, and marinara sauce.

"This Sheehan guy, he's one of these small-town power brokers," Al said. "What I hear, he chased after the Dennison property for years. Arthur Dennison wouldn't sell him a broken alarm clock, let alone the land. Sheehan's still hot for the land, figures he's got a shot if Daryl has to sell. Plus, Sheehan's a realtor for a development under construction somewhere else on Echo Pond. Those properties are already down in value, according to brokers in town."

"Does he run the town?"

"In some areas, looks like it. Heard a few stories that he's got the zoning board in his pocket because he sold some of them land at ridiculous, giveaway prices, but nobody's gone after him for it."

"I like it when naked greed drives public policy."

"Yeah, ain't capitalism grand. Now this Tom Jordan,

the guy heading the homeowners' association, likes to think he's a stud but people really don't like him," Al said.

"You find out what he does?"

"A contractor. He's built some homes for Sheehan, but he also does a lot of repairs, renovations, additions. Does good work and mostly reliable, but people say he's a rough guy, likes to talk tough and crude."

"Must have been on his best behavior the night of the hearing."

"Renheart says Jordan was involved in one barroom brawl when he first moved to town from Boston—maybe South Boston—a few years ago, but he's been okay since. They checked out his record back then—a couple of convictions for disturbing the peace, one assault, but all minor league and no jail time."

"How'd he end up out here?"

"Married a local girl. So far, he's still married, though people think he's pushed her around a bit. There's some talk the marriage may not last long."

"What about my environmentalist friend, Stephanie Williams? Any word on her?"

"Not much. Apparently she was always something of a loner as a kid, taking on causes and not much involved with other kids. Left town for a while to go to college, came back with a kid when her marriage broke up. Has a job running a large farmstand at a nearby farm. Talks about this environmental group she's in, but nobody knows what they do or who else is in it. Far as people here are concerned, there aren't any burning environmental issues in the area anyway. The town isn't all that developed, so even if the golf course and camp are on the prettiest open space left, there's still plenty of fields and woods around."

I told Al what I'd learned about the Wild Woods Warriors and the summer camp Williams had attended.

"So maybe, if she's working with other members of the group, there's good reason for them to keep quiet."

"Yeah, I guess," I said, "but maybe she's a group of one. What can a radical environmental group do in this part of the world? Out West, you want to live in a platform in a tree for a few months to stop logging of an old-growth forest, you can do it. Or you can find dams to protest, or sacred Indian burial grounds that some highway will destroy. Do things like that, TV cameras will give you your fifteen minutes of fame. But here, we've farmed, logged, built plants and mills, created dumps, and beat the crap out of every inch of the land for a couple of hundred years. No unspoiled land to fight over, so no TV time. I'm betting she's pretty much on her own."

"Still," Al said, "she could be doing some low-level stuff—harassment, vandalism of guys developing properties, things like that. And trying to stop the golf course and camp might be the opportunity she's looking for."

"Jeez, Al, you might be right, but if she did something, or is going to do something, won't she want credit for it, even if just within her movement? She can't tell anybody she killed Jerome, even if she did it. Seems like a stretch to me."

Al shrugged. "You're probably right. You look at most people, you don't think they'd be able to pull a trigger. But fact is, people do it everyday. Not just ex-cons, drug addicts, gang members, or hit men, like in the movies, but regular folks like you and me. And people in towns just like this one go to restaurants like this one and say, I thought he was a decent guy, what the hell happened?"

Al was right, of course. I'd been reluctant to look at Williams, but how much of that defense was based on logic or how much based on the handshake and the smile she'd given me I couldn't say.

"Okay," I said, "we'll have to do more with her. What about the lady of the pond, Linda Redmond?"

Al sat back in his chair. "There, my friend, you have a real mystery, according to people around here."

"I heard a little. Granger told me she left school, and the town, I guess, when she was fifteen. Came back just a few years ago to take care of her aunt, live in the big mansion out on the pond."

"Apparently she disappeared one day, reappeared about twenty years later, and nobody had any contact with her in between, including the aunt. If anybody knows where she was, what she was doing, they're not saying. But there are all sorts of stories about her, most of them about how she married some rich guy in Hollywood who died, leaving her with lots of money."

"What does Renheart say?"

"Not much. The family was rich. If things were wrong, the police never knew about it. Renheart doesn't know why she left or why she came back. Lots of rumors, but facts are few and far between."

"If she's rich, why did she have the mansion developed into townhouses and sold off?"

"Good question. Nobody knows. But remember, nobody's really sure whether she has money or not."

"I can see her being upset about the pond going down if the townhouse prices are taking a hit, but that's still a long way from killing somebody."

"Unless she thought Jerome was going to harm her for some reason."

"If there's anything I can promise you, Al, it's that

Jerome wouldn't threaten or harm anybody, unless they were threatening him first. I don't give a damn about the mystery behind her leaving and coming back, but I sure as hell want to know what she and Jerome talked about."

Al and I had each stopped eating, both leaving large portions on our plates. Everybody else in the restaurant except for the staff had left. We ordered desserts just to see how badly those would turn out.

"I got something else that might interest you," he said.

"Yeah?"

"Yesterday, some of the guys were shooting the shit about Daryl, wondering what he'd do with the property. Some guys thought Sheehan would get hold of it. But one guy said he thought this guy you've been talking to, Granger, would get his hands on it, one way or another. Then a couple of other guys said Granger could never swing it because he's a gambler, can't hold on to his money. From what I learned, his mother loves everything from Bingo to taking the buses to Foxwoods and Atlantic City to play the slots. She brags about how Granger is a big gambler, makes a lot of money. Renheart didn't know anything about him but he might be worth checking out."

I shook my head. "Daryl finds out that Granger was involved, after Jerome brought him into the deal, we're going to have another homicide."

"Maybe whoever Granger owes is calling in the debt and it involved the property."

"Damn," I said. "Granger called the other day to say he had a client who wanted to buy all the property. I wonder if he's trying to dig himself out with somebody by getting the property at a cheap price quickly."

"Well, you think about all this, tell me what I can do

to help. Turned out to be nice little vacation. My wife went off to visit her sister. I didn't have to go, plus I got to fish a few of the ponds around here. Met a bunch of nice people, now all we have to do is figure out a murder or two," Al said. We both gave small laughs, left money and a small tip, and walked out. The hostess locked the door behind us.

We talked for a few more minutes in the parking lot by Al's car. He then drove off to a last night of cable television at the Motel 6. The lights in the main dining room of the restaurant and over the front door went off. It was a clear night and the sky was full of many more stars than I could see in Boston. Over the creek and the small patch of forest, I saw a three-quarters moon rising, silver and cool, and millions of miles away, a place I'd never visit. I'd seen Sheehan, Redmond, Jordan, Williams, and Granger, most of them up close and personal. But right now, I felt a hell of a lot more certain about the moon than about any of the people I'd met in Meadowbrook.

I walked back to my Blazer, hidden from the light of the moon by the restaurant. And out of that darkness, from against a restaurant wall, came three men, all with baseball hats pulled low so I couldn't see faces. Two of them grabbed me from behind, one putting some kind of towel or cloth over my mouth and nose. The other stepped in front of me and threw a punch at my head. It glanced off my cheek as I jerked to the side and struggled to pull away. I smelled alcohol from the men holding me, and one said, "Damnit, stand still or we'll really fuck you up."

As the guy in front of me reloaded for another punch, I relaxed a little and stepped backward until I felt a leg. The hands on me and the cloth across my face loosened up just a bit. Then I lifted my foot and stepped down hard on the foot of one of the guys behind me. At the same time I jerked my torso down and forward. Both the guys behind me shouted, one in pain, the other in anger. The guy trying to punch me missed. The gag around my face wrenched my neck, but one set of hands on me came loose. Freed up a little, I came up hard and fast out of an awkward crouch by pushing off the foot I had landed on. With that, I heard another yell and got an arm free to grab the guy who had punched me. As he twisted away, I pulled at his hat to see if I could see his face. But just as I got the hat, I was tackled from behind and knocked onto the parking lot pavement. All three men started kicking me in the head, the chest, the kidney. I curled in a ball on my side as best I could and, with the cloth gone from my face, tried to yell in between kicks. A light came on suddenly.

"Somebody's still in the restaurant. Let's get out of here," I heard a voice say. I was still lying on the ground, not able, or wanting, to move.

I felt somebody drop beside me and then a hand grabbed my hair and lifted my head a few inches off the pavement. I opened my eyes and held tight against the pain. I could see pieces of a face to the side, but I couldn't get a clear picture.

A low voice with a Boston accent said, "Tell Daryl Mann there's plenty of this to go around, you guys don't stop fucking around here. Sell the land, get the hell out." The hand bounced my head off the pavement, it hurt for a flash, and then I felt nothing.

CHAPTER

THIRTEEN

I woke up to pain in my chest and back, a headache, and a soothing hand washing my face with a cool, damp cloth. Hands and arms, I couldn't tell how many, were propping me up in a sitting position from behind. I opened and closed my eyes to make sure they worked. As far as I could tell, I was still in the parking lot behind the restaurant.

"Take it easy," a voice said, "you're pretty banged up. Want some water?"

"Thanks," I croaked out. "Give me a minute, though."

"You're going to need more than a minute. We're going to call an ambulance."

"No, look, would you just call the Motel Six, ask for Al Thompson, tell him what's going on and ask him to come out."

"Go ahead, Sherrie," I heard footsteps take off.

"It's okay," I said. "I can sit. Don't know if I can stand just yet, but I can sit up."

A lean, pale, and bald man in his late sixties or early seventies moved from behind me into my view. "You sure you don't want us to call an ambulance?"

"No, I'll see a doctor at home, but I don't think too much is wrong. I'm not spitting up blood or anything.

Could I have that water?" I took a long drink. It hurt to move but the drink felt good going down.

"Thanks."

"Your friend comes, you should go to a hospital right away. You were knocked out when we got here. Also, the side of your face don't look so good."

"Yeah, you don't see many people using parking lots to perform their facials. You own the restaurant?"

"Yes. I recognize you—you had dinner."

"Yeah. Good dinner." Under the circumstances, it was the least I could say.

"Ah, bullshit," he said. "When I was the cook, we served good food. Now, I'm too old to stay in the kitchen all the time. This new cook, he don't pay attention. I have to fire him. It hurts me to come to the restaurant now."

"Well, I'm glad you did, but now that you mention it, the food wasn't that great." I took another drink and lay back down on the pavement, short of breath. I had trouble moving my neck without pain, my chest was sore as hell, and my back and shoulder ached. But most of all, my head hurt, both on the inside and the outside.

"You know who did this to you?" Mike asked.

Eyes closed, I shook my head just a little. "I got ideas, but I didn't recognize anybody."

"This hat, is it yours?"

Mike was holding a dark blue baseball hat in front of me. On the front of it, in white block print, was the name Jordan Builders.

"Nope," I said.

"You need anything?" Mike looked at me and gave a small shake of his head.

"Maybe some more water."

"Okay," he said, "I'll see if Sherrie found your friend and I'll get you some water."

I closed my eyes and lay there semiconscious for what seemed like hours, even though I knew it was only a few minutes.

Mike came back with water and Al drove up right after that. Al took one look, then with Mike's help got me into his car. Disregarding my protests, we went off to the closest emergency room.

By the time they finished checking me out, running some X rays, and treating the various cuts and scrapes, it was close to midnight. They agreed to release me on Al's word that he'd stay with me. It was too much to drive back to Brookline, so we went back to his cozy motel room, where he had a pair of double beds.

"You know," Al said, once I had climbed into bed clad in my underwear and tee-shirt, "you want to spend the night with me, you could have found easier ways to set it up. I'm easy."

"Of all the things I want to do in life, spending the night with you is not in the top ten thousand."

"You want to tell me what happened? Mike said he heard yelling, came out and saw three guys knock you down and kick you. You know who they were?"

"Didn't get a good look. One of the voices sounded like Jordan, and I pulled a hat off one of the sons of bitches, might be worth something."

"What'd they want?"

"Just friendly messengers. Told me and Daryl to get out of town quick." I gave an enormous yawn.

"Okay, Dan," he said, "go to sleep. We'll talk in the morning."

"Al, you gonna respect me in the morning if we sleep together?"

"Who said I respect you now?"

I had a witty retort ready, but my tongue felt big and awkward and I couldn't move it out of the way to say the words. I struggled with it for a while because I knew how wonderfully funny and pithy the comment was.

I woke up to sunlight streaming in the one big window in the motel unit. Al was sitting in a wing chair, clean clothes on and reading a newspaper.

"Hey, Sleeping Beauty," he said.

I gave a grunt and tried to sit up straight.

"Go easy there, young fella. Doctor said you'd have a tough time moving today. Want some help?"

"No, thanks," I managed to sit up on the edge of the bed. "Nice bedside manner, but if I need someone to help me piss, it won't be you."

I shuffled into the bathroom. The face that looked back at me in the mirror was not one I'd seen before. I had bandages on my right cheekbone where the pavement had abraded my skin. I had two black eyes, bruises all along my chin, and red marks on my cheeks and forehead. Al came up to the bathroom door and watched me appraise myself.

"I've been prettier," I said. "I don't recall much of what happened in the hospital. Want to fill me in?"

"Basically, they said you're damn lucky. Doesn't look like any internal damage, just lots of bad bumps and bruises."

"The restaurant owner, what's his name—"

"Mike."

"Yeah, Mike, he came along before they had a chance to do any heavy damage. By the time they started kicking me, Mike had put on the light, called out. Probably saved my butt."

"More than your butt from the report I got. How you feeling? You want to go back to the hospital?"

"No, that's okay. You can take me back to my car, I'll drive home, have my regular doctor look at me."

"Son, you take me for a fool? I'll drive you home. You can get Daryl Mann to spend some of his big contract money to have your car brought back to you. Go ahead, get dressed; we'll talk in the car."

We stopped at a convenience store. Al bought me some orange juice to wash down a couple of painkillers. They worked nicely, so we didn't talk in the car, at least until we got to Brookline. Al woke me up at that point so I could give him directions to the house, then helped me in when we got there.

My downstairs neighbor Terry Steiner was home. She saw Al helping me, then she got a look at my face. She joined us in an instant and helped me get comfortable. She took over for Al at that point, arranged an appointment with my doctor, rustled up some food, and reassured Al that she could handle things.

I told Terry that I wanted to talk to Al for a minute. Fine, she said, she'd go downstairs and do a couple of things that needed doing before her kids got home. "But," she said, "this time the male bonding looks more like male bandaging." Al laughed a lot. I tried not to, since it hurt.

"Can you tell me what you remember of what happened? I didn't get too much detail from you last night," Al asked.

I told him what I remembered, in as much detail as I could.

"You sure there were three of them?" he asked.

"Yeah, pretty sure."

"And what about Jordan—you certain of the voice?"

"I thought so, but I'd never be able to swear to it. Whoever it was only spoke a few words and things were happening too fast. Did the restaurant owner recognize anybody?"

"If he did, at least at this point, he's not saying anything. By the way, I called in and reported it to the police in Meadowbrook. Told 'em who I was, what happened, and that you'd call in later to confirm."

"I would have gotten around to it."

"Yeah, maybe in the next century. Incidentally, you recognize this?" Al held out a paper bag, reached in, and pulled out a dark blue baseball hat with white letters saying Jordan Builders.

"Yes, officer, I do, that hat was on the head of one of the assholes who beat the crap out of me."

"Probably plenty of these hats around. You don't have enough to go after Jordan and his buddies for assault."

"I know, but I got enough for me."

"Be careful, huh? Hard to know if they wanted to kill you or just warn you, so they may or may not be the ones that nailed Jerome and Wells. But if they're not, then you've got even more slimeballs on your tail than we thought. Get some rest, I'll call you in a couple of days and we can sort out what we do from here."

"I'll be careful. But I'm also going back. The unfinished business out there seems to be piling up."

"I know you well enough, I know you're going back. Be careful, is what I said."

Al finally left. I called the office, dealt with a couple of things, and told people I'd be out for the rest of the day. Finally, I checked my voice mail. Jenny had called a couple times, both at work and home. She didn't say anything explicit, but I could tell she'd been concerned when I hadn't answered her call near midnight. And

Roger Vaneck, the bank president, had called once more, requesting a meeting with Daryl to discuss the golf course and camp.

I rested awhile before Terry took me to the doctor. He found what I hoped—some ligament strains, deep bruises and cuts, the aftereffects of a concussion, but nothing that wouldn't heal with time outside the hospital. With instructions and another prescription in hand, Terry and I headed home.

We stopped on the way for Chinese food. I ate with the Steiners. Mike had me run through my story of what happened about three times, with a separate set of questions each time. I didn't mind—it prepared me for the discussions I'd have with Jenny, Daryl, and Randy Blocker, among others.

Finally, stories finished and dinner done, I went upstairs.

First I called Daryl. He listened quietly while I told him what happened, glossing over my injuries, and also what we'd learned from Al's efforts and my talk with Marie Riley.

"Sorry, man," he said. "Not supposed to happen this way. This damn town's got the same kind of vermin I knew back in Tennessee."

"Yeah. Different clothes, nicer houses—"

"White skin."

"That too. Anyway, we're at least narrowing the field, figuring out who's in and who's out."

"Yeah, well, sounds like you ain't a member of Meadowbrook's in crowd. Look, you want to bail out on this Meadowbrook thing, that's fine. You've paid your dues. I'd appreciate help on the businesses, get things in shape with Bender and all, but if you want to let things in

Meadowbrook go so you don't get more shit kicked out of you, that's okay."

"Thanks, but I'm in, don't worry about it. Jenny and I agreed to represent you and Jerome, so we'll stick with it. I have no idea how this will all play out, but even if the good Mr. Jordan doesn't end up in police custody, my time with him will come. How about you? You still want to try to make a go of it with the camp?"

"You the one they beat up, not me. I'm in it till I tell you otherwise."

"That's the case, I think maybe we should send a message."

"What do you have in mind?"

"Kind of like *High Noon*. You and me wander around, show the bad guys they haven't run us out of town. Maybe push the buttons of a few people."

"You got a devilish mind. I like that. So long as it's after my workout, I can go any day."

I thought for a moment. "How about next Tuesday? Meet you out in Meadowbrook?"

"Yeah, Tuesday afternoon works." We finished with some business items. I promised to call Bender in the next couple days and hung up.

The next call went to Jenny.

"Hello?" Even that single word carried anxiety and concern.

"Hi, it's me. I'm—"

"Dan, what happened to you?"

"Nothing much. I had to go out to Meadowbrook last night to meet with Al Thompson. He and I talked pretty late, had some beer, so I decided to stay out there with him, then—"

"Cut the bullshit. When I called your office and they ducked my call, I called Terry. She told me you'd been hurt. Tell me the whole story. All of it."

So I gave it to her, all of it, cutting the bullshit. "And did Terry tell you the doctor said I'd heal just fine?" I finished.

"No, she said the doctor said everything would be fine except you'd still be a stubborn jerk on occasion. Like tonight. Weren't you going to tell me what happened?"

"I wasn't going to lie."

"But?"

"But maybe I wasn't planning on telling the whole truth. A big difference there."

"I hope, someday, I'll have the chance to know you when you're not a lawyer."

"Watch it, lady, you're a lawyer yourself. Look, I'm sorry. I figured you had enough on your plate, you didn't need to worry about me."

"I'm old enough to figure out for myself what to worry about and not worry about, thank you," but her voice softened a bit. "How hurt are you, really?"

"A couple of Tylenol works magic. Mostly bruises, bumps. No broken bones and no long-term damage. I'll take it easy. I'm pretty sure I got a couple of good licks in on the other guys, no real damage to me, so to coin a phrase, all's well that ends well."

"Just because it comes from your buddy Shakespeare doesn't make it true. All is not well. Jerome's still dead, so's Wells, now you're hurt."

"You put it that way, I probably should have quoted *Measure for Measure*."

"Daryl hanging in there?"

"So far."

She was quiet for a moment. "You know, you can stop this, leave it to the police, let Daryl fight his own battles. I hope you're not doing this for me, because I originally brought in the case with Jerome."

"Nah. You know I can't just walk away from something like this."

"I could have called that one. But I'm not thrilled about this. I'm not sure I can handle another one of the people I care about most—"

"I'll be careful, I promise. How're your parents?"

"Actually, there's a little good news. Mom's progressed enough so they're giving her a lot more therapy and exercise. She'll be home soon. And my father's doing much better with his speech. It looks like he'll lose some of the function on his left side and his memory is affected, but he understands things, he'll be able to write, and the doctors think he can get some retraining so he'll be able to communicate—not to where he was, but pretty well."

"That's great."

"I know, but we still have a long way to go." She paused, then continued. "God, I can't stand hearing myself talk to you now. We used to have things to talk about. Now, I'm either whining or bitching to you or you're telling me about all this stuff I don't have any control over anymore. It's so depressing."

"I know it's no fun, but it's not your fault. You had to make a choice between two tough situations. Things will get better," I said.

"I know that in my head. It's just hard to believe it sometimes. And I don't feel any better when I think you're in danger."

"I'll be careful."

We talked for a while longer. I offered to come down to Tennessee to convalesce there for a few days, but she rightly pointed out that the traveling would do me more harm than good. And it was a bad time for her to come up again, so I promised her I'd go south in a week or two, "When I have my boyish good looks back."

"If I have to wait for that, you might as well move to Mongolia," she said. We broke off, finally, and her voice sounded freer, happier than when we first began talking.

I needed something to wash down the medication, and beer was forbidden. I pulled out a new pint of mint chocolate chip ice cream and finished all of it in front of a late night Red Sox game televised from the West Coast. I never made it to bed and never turned off the television, just fell asleep on the sofa. I woke up at about three A.M., in the middle of a dream in which I played a large harmonica while a man I didn't recognize cowered in front of me, covering his ears and begging for mercy.

By early Saturday morning, the soreness in my upper body and neck had subsided a bit. My legs were fine so I took a long walk out around the Brookline Reservoir and back. It wasn't the same as running, but every time I broke into a run, the pounding hurt too many body parts. I tried it twice, then quit.

On the way back from the reservoir, I cut off Cypress Street and went into the gymnasium on a hunch. Playing in the weekly basketball game on a team with a bunch of teenagers, I found Randy Blocker. I watched from the door for a while.

"Thought I might find you here," I said to Randy. "Lost pretty quickly without me, I see."

"Kardon, mostly I'm lost trying to keep up with you," he said, then did a double take when he saw the colors on my face. "Either you gotta get a new razor or Jenny finally beat some sense into you, boy. What the hell happened?"

"You got time for a cup of coffee?"

"No, man, sorry, but I can talk a few minutes here."

"Okay."

"Jesus, you got to find another profession. Maybe a school nurse or a pastry chef, somewhere trouble can't find you." He shook his head. "All right, let me take a shower, I'll meet you in the lobby."

We walked outside and sat on a bench, watching some kids play baseball. I laid out the story, including my own suspicions about Jordan. Randy asked a bunch of short, precise questions. At the end, he simply shook his head.

"Just wish we had something. We got nothing good on either murder," he said. "This doesn't give us any more that we can act on, though I'll have some people look at Jordan. But it's hard to figure. Whoever took out Mann and Wells didn't leave anything behind, while these bozos practically put up a sign."

"I know. Doesn't make sense to me either," I said.

"All the more reason for you not to get any more of your body parts destroyed out there. Leave it to us," Randy said.

I shrugged. "Come on, I can't do that. You wouldn't either."

"You mean because a few guys beat you up? Hell, yes, I'd walk away. You know damn well I've walked away from fights I could've won when I had too much to lose."

"Yeah," I said. "I'll give you that. Couldn't believe it a couple times, but it worked for you. But that doesn't mean it'll work for me."

"Damn, I got more to teach you, boy. But my tae kwon doe teacher said it best. 'When the student is ready, the teacher arrives.' Whenever you're ready, here I am, man, your personal tutor in the book of life."

"Long as I can get the book in paperback. Couldn't afford the hardcover."

"Seriously, watch out for Jordan. The guy may or may not be a killer, but you got to be careful. Can't bring him in and charge him based on what you've told me. And if he's got buddies to pump him up, help him do the dirty work, you can't predict. Watch your back, my friend."

I nodded. "I got some ideas about how to confront Jordan but I hear you."

Randy stood up. "By the way, Daryl's not a suspect."

I looked at him. "That official?"

"You heard it right. We're not looking at Daryl anymore. We have him leaving the area from a number of witnesses. The medical examiner has given us a harder fix on Jerome's death, and it's right around midnight Wednesday. We got nothing pointing to Daryl."

"Glad to hear it."

"Anything new comes up on him, obviously we'll look at it, but you can tell him we're looking elsewhere."

"Thanks. I've got some looking planned myself."

CHAPTER————

FOURTEEN

Back in the office on Monday, I scheduled a series of meetings in Meadowbrook for Tuesday, the day Daryl and I had arranged to be there. I set up a meeting with Vaneck at his bank. I also determined the hours when Sheehan was usually in his office at Town Hall. As a contractor, there was no telling where Jordan was, but I figured our best shot was to track him down at the end of the day.

After I had the meetings in place, I had another brief phone call with Daryl. We talked about strategies for a couple of the meetings in Meadowbrook as well as what we could do with the town to move the negotiations along.

First thing Tuesday morning, I stopped by the golf course. There were more workmen out there than I'd seen in a while. I tracked down the golf course superintendent, Rich Grant, in one of the large supply sheds giving some instructions to a couple of workers. Each worker had a small electric truck with some pesticides and fertilizers in the back. Grant was instructing them on where to put everything. After the workmen left, I introduced myself. He gave me a quizzical look so I told him that the bruises and cuts on my face were from a small car accident. He nodded and, since Daryl had told him about me, he was willing to talk.

I asked if anyone had vandalized the golf course. Grant reported that he'd found no harm done but he was concerned. There'd not been many people working on the course in the last few weeks and it had been closed. But now Daryl had instructed Grant to get the course in shape. The notion they might open the golf course, Grant thought, might inspire somebody to retaliate.

I also asked him about the contacts with the commonwealth over the blue spotted turtles. He'd first heard about the turtles from Jerome. Grant had then been around on the two occasions when a woman sent by the state Division of Fisheries and Wildlife had come by to confirm that the turtles were in the pond. The first time, Grant had taken the specialist out first thing in the morning and found a couple of turtles. Grant said he couldn't tell a blue spotted turtle from a chocolate cashew turtle, but the specialist had gotten a good look with binoculars and confirmed that they were blue spotted turtles. The second time, the wildlife specialist had gone out there later in the day and had found no turtles. Grant got the rest of his information from Jerome, who told Grant he'd had Wells follow up with the Division of Fisheries and Wildlife.

I asked Grant how long he'd worked on golf courses. Twenty years, he replied.

"Ever seen a problem like this?" I asked.

"Nope, but I've read about it happening. Somebody was building a golf course designed by Jack Nicklaus in Florida a couple years ago. It was delayed for a while when they discovered bald eagle nests in some trees they planned to take down. I never did hear what finally happened with the course. Then there's a real expensive course on Nantucket where there were plenty of battles with the local conservation commission."

Seeing the workmen drive off in carts with fertilizer and pesticides triggered a memory of Mike Steiner's question to me about how people make golf courses in the desert.

"You've treated the fairways out there by the pond with fertilizer and pesticides, haven't you?" I asked.

"Yeah. But we're a new course, and we've fallen behind on maintenance in the last couple of weeks, so they haven't been used too heavily out there. And we know enough so that anywhere there are wetlands nearby, we go light on the stuff. We've tried to limit the use of chemicals."

"But some pesticides would run off into the pond."

"Probably."

"The other courses you worked—did the ponds have fish, frogs, other kinds of wildlife, or were they too contaminated?"

"Most of the small ponds are too contaminated, but not all of them. Depends on the source of water, how big the pond is, how much of the hole is surrounded by treated land, the kind of wildlife, that sort of thing. Out here we got wild animals all over the place—deer, foxes, lots of birds. Even saw a coyote on the third hole a couple of weeks ago. Some of them will disappear once we get the course opened and we get a lot of people out there. You figured out what we need to do to open the course?"

"I've got to check with the agency," I said. "Last I knew, they generally try to work with landowners, find ways to compromise, so I'm surprised they came down so hard here. But I haven't seen the reports or recommendations yet, so I want to do that. I need any more help or if we make some progress, I'll get back to you."

I walked back to the car more confused than before. Given the fertilizer and pesticide runoff, the pond seemed an unlikely place for turtles, though you could store all I knew about turtles in the shell of a mighty small turtle.

Without the files from Wells, I was at a loss, but I'd contact the agency and check out their reports. I wondered, though, after reading the Wild Woods Warriors website, if Stephanie Williams had played a role in this. What she could have done, how far she would have gone, were questions I couldn't answer. After I talked with the Fisheries and Wildlife people, I'd start looking for the answers.

After a quick Coke and a pair of large cheeseburgers at a small diner, I walked over to where I'd arranged to meet Daryl just after two P.M.

"Did a number on you, didn't they?" Daryl asked when we first connected.

"You think my career as a male model is over?"

"Anything you need to help nail the suckers who did it, you let me know."

"Thanks. Your workout go okay?" I asked, eager to get to another topic.

"Yeah, I guess."

"From what I read, some of the other guys on the team don't work too hard on their games over the summer, maybe just play in a summer league. What about you? You work on specific things or just stay in shape?"

He didn't speak for a moment, just looked at me with his shades on.

"Daryl, I didn't mean—"

" 'S'all right. Most summers, I'd go back to Tennessee for a while, Jerome would come for a week or two. We'd chill—drink a few beers, catch some flicks, play ball with some of the college kids. When Jerome wasn't around, I'd play paintball with my buddies, maybe do some road trips. Time passed quick. This one's gonna be a long summer. Be up here in Boston, in the gym, most of the time. I'm tired of losing, having fans and other teams dis us. Gonna kick some butt this season." Then he looked around. "All right, how about we do that here, too?"

We walked over to the town hall, reviewing our strategy for the meeting. We passed by a few people on the way and without exception they stared or started talking among themselves. I felt like I was in an old Western, walking into a showdown with the bad guys—except, of course, to the people looking at us, we were the bad guys going up against Sheriff Sheehan.

Last time, Jerome and I had talked with Sheehan in front of the office staff about the pond. This time, he looked a little surprised when he saw Daryl, but then he ushered Daryl and me into his office. On the way I dropped an envelope on his secretary's desk. Car accident, I told Sheehan when I saw him eye me with concern.

"I'm sorry about your cousin," he said as we sat down. Daryl just nodded.

"We wanted to meet with you to see if the zoning board of appeals has changed its position and will give the camp a permit," I said.

"I can't presume to speak for the board," Sheehan said, "so—"

Daryl stood up and took a step for the door. "You gonna play games with us, I got other places to be."

With another stride he had his hand on the doorknob and started to open it.

Sheehan looked at me. I shrugged and stood up.

"Now, hold on a minute," Sheehan said, "I don't think you understand." Daryl turned and looked at Sheehan.

"I'm not a member of the board, it's an independent board, but I have talked with the chairman and some of the members and they'd be happy to have me talk to you, explore some options. Then maybe I can talk to the board and make some recommendations."

Daryl looked over at me and I nodded. He came back and sat down. "What I hear, you make a recommendation in this town, that's how it goes."

Sheehan gave a blustery response, a cross between "I don't have that much power" and "You better believe it." Then he launched into a short set piece about how the town valued the Manns, wanted to work with them cooperatively, and were delighted to do anything they could to help with the state in terms of opening the golf course.

"Obviously," Sheehan concluded, "many of us are upset about Echo Pond and want the water back. But there's also a strong feeling that we can't give in to the kind of negotiating tactic that Jerome used. And while we don't know who killed him or why, his murder should give you some idea just how deep emotions are running. So we're hoping that you, Daryl, will take a less, shall we say, confrontational approach than Jerome, and that we can find a way to work things out."

I looked at Daryl and he nodded at me. "We're here. We'll listen," I said.

Sheehan sat up on the edge of his chair and pulled some papers in front of him. He rubbed his hands together.

"Excellent," he said. "Now, please understand, the issue of the camp is not about the kind of campers you'll have there. The zoning board has assured me that they would not grant a permit to any kind of camp on the lake." With a lawsuit hanging over their heads, I was sure that was true.

"What we'd like to explore," he said, "is whether we could work with you, come up with some compromises about the land."

"What kind of compromises?" Daryl asked.

"We've located property elsewhere where a camp would fit nicely. We were thinking that perhaps we could have some kind of agreement that the camp be set up at another location in the town, or a neighboring town. Or perhaps we could do a land swap, your property for another one."

"Town property or private property?" I asked.

"We've identified one piece of town property that might be suitable. We also have a private citizen who will consider selling his land at a greatly discounted price, or swapping it, to accommodate you and the town."

"Where's the town property?"

"It's a park area now, in the northwest corner, a beautiful area, not much development out there yet."

I had an idea why. A lot of towns had developed nice parks on their outskirts in the last twenty years. "That the site of an old dump the town had to close down?"

Sheehan's face reddened. "Yes, but that was years ago and it's a beautiful park—"

"Where's the private property?" I asked. "In town?"

"No. It's just across the town line in Buxbridge."

"Either locations on water?"

Sheehan shook his head.

"Sheehan," Daryl said, "I don't pretend to be no crusader, but I've done my time in crappy places. You're not sticking me where there was a dump. Either you're unbelievably dumb or unbelievably arrogant. You want me to give up a waterfront camp property for an old dump or a spot in another town. That's real consideration and cooperation."

"Look," Sheehan said, "we're trying to work with you, help you with the camp. I understand you might not like these sites, but you really ought to see them. We can also throw in some tax breaks, make things easier on you. Remember, without the town's permit, you don't have a camp."

"You been fishing in Echo Pond recently?" Daryl asked. "What we're thinking is, the camp don't open, we'll turn the old cabins into a spa, give all sorts of rich ladies from Boston, New York some nice mud baths in Echo Pond. Keep their complexions soft and clean."

"I gather you're trying to be funny, but you don't seem to understand, Mr. Mann. The town has the right to insist that the land has only approved uses on it. The town has not had a camp on that site for many years and has no intention of having one now. If you try to use the property for any other impermissible use, that too will have to meet with board approval."

"The golf course required a special permit. Why did the board give that one?" I asked.

"Obviously, that's a different situation. A golf course is beneficial to the town in many different ways."

We went round and round for a little while, Sheehan trying to get us to consider at least checking out the other sites, Daryl and I not biting.

Finally, Sheehan sat back in his chair and folded his

arms across his chest. "I did hope that you'd be more agreeable than your cousin."

"I think you'll find that Jerome was, and Daryl will be, eminently reasonable," I said. "Let's look at this another way. The town doesn't want the camp there, okay, we understand that. What if we put some sweeteners in the pot? We couldn't help notice that the outdoor tennis courts and basketball court near the high school are in bad shape. We're willing to put in new courts, fix it all up. We're willing to offer some free space at the camp for Meadowbrook kids. And we're willing to let Meadowbrook residents play at the golf club at a reduced rate. Maybe a really reduced rate."

A frown crossed Sheehan's face. "Echo Pond is a special place in this town. People feel very strongly about it. You can't buy our approval just by putting a few dollars on the table."

"Bullshit," I said. "You told us Jerome did just that when he got a permit for the golf course. The golf course was fine for you guys—new tax revenues, a few jobs for local folks, people stop on the way at gas stations and convenience stores, and property values go up in town with the nice golf course nearby. Now, we're just haggling over the price for the camp."

"You're clever, Mr. Kardon, and it may stand you in good stead as a lawyer, but you simply do not understand this town or the people who live here."

"Fair enough," I said. "How about we agree to this? We'll publicize the offer we just made to you. We'll notify the paper, send flyers out to people, all that sort of thing. Then you have a special town meeting, let the town vote on whether they want the deal or not. We'll even pay the expenses of the special town meeting."

Sheehan shook his head. "I'm sorry, gentlemen, I

don't see how we can come to an agreement on anything if you stick to wanting the camp on the pond."

I shrugged. "Have it your way. You'll get a letter confirming the offer we just made to you. If there are other points that town officials want to discuss, we'll be happy to talk. And if the town wants to put it to a vote, with a special town meeting, we'll abide by that. The camp loses on a town-wide vote, we'll give up on it."

Daryl and I stood up. Sheehan continued sitting, his hand fidgeting with his ear. He had a sour look on his face. "When your letter comes in," he said, "I'll discuss it with the board."

"Oh, the letter's in," I said. "We dropped it off with your secretary on our way to see you." We started to go, then I turned back. "And we prepared a letter to the editor of the paper outlining our offer as well. I believe we left that one with your niece." Daryl and I walked out, keeping our game faces on as we walked past the questioning eyes of the town hall workers.

"The man looked like he had a bad stomach when we left," Daryl said with a grin, outside town hall.

"You played that perfectly when you threatened to walk out." The day before, we had planned a number of different actions and reactions, depending on Sheehan. Daryl had played his part beautifully.

"Tell you what, I almost walked out for good when he came up with those offers to move the camp."

"First, I don't think he expected you to be here. I didn't tell him you were coming, so he was probably prepared to pitch things to me, not you, and there are things he could say to me he wouldn't say to you. Second, I think he figured you're a basketball player, period, and this was Jerome's deal not yours. He probably thought you'd want out of this with as little mess as possible, so the town only had to hang in there a little longer until you'd cave."

"Yeah, I hear you. But we got him boxed in now."

Daryl had it right. Sheehan thought we'd called to concede. Instead, we'd put him in a tough spot, and he knew we knew. Some townspeople would never agree to the camp, but others had already been agreeable after Jerome and Daryl spoke at the last meeting. If people thought about what Daryl was offering—and figured they might negotiate a bit more—then some people on the fence about the camp might well jump our way. The golfers in town would make Sheehan's life miserable.

From everything we were hearing about the townspeople, Sheehan had to know by now that the only people who felt strongly about the camp were those with properties on the pond. And even they had to be questioning whether it was better to have a full pond with a camp on it or a pond they couldn't use.

Sheehan would have to take the offer back to the zoning board and the selectmen. It might not be enough to change the tide for us, but it was likely to make Sheehan's life difficult in the coming days. But then, if he was the one who killed either Jerome or Wells or both, political skirmishing with us was not likely to be his most pressing problem.

Daryl and I walked over to the bank, both of us laughing about the meeting with Sheehan.

"This stuff's not so hard. Maybe I'll be a lawyer," Daryl said, "when I finish playing."

"Hey," I said, "I can make a free throw. Doesn't mean I can play in the NBA."

"Mann and Associates," Daryl went on. "Got kind of a nice ring to it. Or maybe Mann and Kardon."

"Since when does your name go first?"

"You oughta see the offices we'd have, before you squawk. But nah," he said after a pause, "don't think I want to be a lawyer after all."

"How come?"

"I'd have to hang out with other lawyers."

"Most lawyers aren't any worse than a lot of the players you hang out with, I'm guessing."

"Yeah, but I'd have to spend all day with the lawyers. Right now, I only spend two, three hours with my guys, then I'm gone."

"Nice work if you can get it."

"It's a great country, man, a great country."

We walked into the large brick building that housed the Meadowbrook Savings Bank. We were guided to the back of the bank and then taken into Roger Vaneck's office. It was large, with an oak table on one side as well as a desk. A number of original art works hung on the wall, two landscapes and one portrait. Vaneck had a couple of windows, one that looked toward the green in Meadowbrook center and another that looked out back, to a street of plain old wooden frame houses that the bank had probably financed in its heyday.

Vaneck wore a gray suit, a white shirt with blue pinstripes, and a red bow tie. He was thinner than me and shorter by an inch or so. He had sandy hair and a long but neat mustache, which he twirled at regular intervals. "Thank you for meeting with me," Vaneck said and turned to Daryl, "and my deepest condolences on the loss of your cousin. I didn't know him well, certainly, but he struck me as very smart and very principled, an uncommon man in my experience."

"Thanks," Daryl said. "Good word for him, uncommon."

"And you, Mr. Kardon, I hope you weren't seriously hurt in whatever befell you."

"Thanks. Small car accident, no real damage. By the way, I met with Gloria Duchesne about Chuck Wells's practice. I gather you're helping his brother close things down. I may have to call you about some items later on, if you don't mind."

"By all means. I'm only helping until Mr. Wells chooses a lawyer," Vaneck said. "As you know, gentlemen, the bank has extended a loan for only a small part of the costs of these projects. We were quite appreciative that Jerome wanted to work with us. Certainly he didn't have to. What concerns us now is not simply the matter of the loan, as we have no reason to believe that there will be any trouble repaying it. We pride ourselves on our support of this community, though, and I do want to convey our concern that this project, and the lowering of Echo Pond, is driving a deep wedge through the people of this town."

"That's refreshing," I said. "We've just come from meeting with George Sheehan. He didn't want to acknowledge that some people out there support the camp."

Vaneck gave a small smile. "I've known George for many years. I've never known him to give an inch until he has to. But that, of course, is precisely one of the things that concerns me. Mr. Mann, if I may ask, what are your intentions for the pond and the camp?"

Daryl shrugged. "Gonna try to finish what Jerome started. If we got to keep the water in the pond low to do it, that's the way it goes."

Vaneck looked at Daryl intently. "Interesting. I would

have guessed that you had no interest in all this, that only Jerome had been behind it."

"Would have been a good guess, before. But Jerome's gone, so you got me."

Vaneck gave a little nod.

"Well, let me ask some other questions, if I may. How did your meeting with Sheehan go?"

Daryl and I both laughed. "I'd say we agreed to disagree," I said. "But we may as well tell you the offer we put on the table to the town. You'll hear about it soon enough." Vaneck cocked his head and his eyes went wide when he heard what we'd offered.

"That is most intriguing. In a sense, then, you've anticipated my concerns by giving people in the town additional reasons to support the camp."

"Yes, and we made clear that if the town officials wanted to negotiate further, there might be some additional room to move."

"But, of course, none of what you have proposed will appease those who live around the pond."

"Not much we can do if those people are truly scared that a bunch of black campers is going to pollute the pond or whatever," I said.

"Mr. Kardon, with all deference to your adversarial skills, I was once a lawyer myself, and one of the things I learned is that there is always another side to things."

"Absolutely," I said. "I agree with that. But just because there's a second side, doesn't mean we have to agree with any of it."

"Well," Vaneck said in a low, almost soothing tone, "I think perhaps you've not talked with many of the people who live out there. They're not concerned just about who uses the pond. They're concerned about the quality of their lives as well as who's going to have access to their neighborhood, to their homes."

I shrugged. "There was a camp out there for years. People lived with it."

"Yes, Mr. Kardon, but the world has changed. As you know, there's an old railroad bed out there that serves as a perfect bike trail. When the camp ran, years ago, the bed still had railroad tracks in it. The tracks were taken out more recently. Now, with the bike trail and all these new mountain bikes, people are concerned about strangers of any kind coming into the area. They feel vulnerable." I'd said much the same thing to Jerome what seemed like years ago.

"If there are security issues with the camp, those are things that can be taken up when the camp starts up," I said.

"That may be," Vaneck said. "I'm not telling you what to do, I'm just trying to make you understand that there are some legitimate and deeply felt concerns out there."

"People out on the pond want to meet with us, try to figure out ways we can make them feel better, we can do that," Daryl said.

Vaneck nodded. "That would probably be helpful. Maybe we can set up a meeting. I'm thinking about something else, though, a show of good faith to let people know you're willing to work with them. Close up the dam, let the water level begin to build up. It won't happen overnight, but it will send a message. In some ways, right now, the low water level is more inflammatory than the camp could ever be, simply because every time people look out on the pond, they see the problem."

Neither Daryl nor I spoke for a moment. "I see that closing the dam helps the town and people on the water," I said, "but how can it possibly help us?"

"First, it means you're extending a hand, showing a desire to find a solution. That should go a long way with at least some people. And second, it doesn't hurt you, because you can always lower the water level again if you don't get what you want."

Again there was silence.

Vaneck continued. "You've already made your point. Anytime you want, you can turn the pond into a swamp. You have your bargaining chip to play and it's a mighty larger one. You negotiate all the time, Mr. Kardon. Sometimes you walk in with nothing backing you up, sometimes you walk in with a big gun on your side. If you have a big gun, you don't use it—you just let the other side see it. Let the water back up, you might just win some friends without giving up your big gun."

Just as we'd boxed in Sheehan, Vaneck tried to box us in. All of his arguments made sense. I wasn't ready to give in on the spot, but Vaneck had given us something to think about. I watched Daryl. He was looking at Vaneck, his face devoid of expression as usual.

"You said our offer to the town is interesting. I'd say the same about your take on things," I said. "We can't make a decision here. We'll go back, consider it, and then let you know."

"I'd strongly suggest you think about it and talk it over. Closing up the dam will do you a world of good with the town officials, restore a good relationship with the citizens, and leave you with all your options."

"Don't need to talk about it," Daryl said, shaking his head. He pointed his finger at Vaneck. "You made it sound good—give people something positive, give 'em a reason to come around. If Jerome were here, that'd be something for him to think on. But he's not here, he's dead, as far as I know because of the pond or the camp. Somebody else already brought a gun to the table, Mr. Vaneck, so mine's not going back in the holster."

Vaneck blanched and there was momentary silence. "Oh, damn," he said, "that's a terrible analogy I made and I'm sorry for it, I just wasn't thinking. I apologize, it's just that I'd like you to think about—"

"I don't take offense, just telling you how it is. There was a time, maybe your idea could have worked. Might still be good for people in this town, Mr. Vaneck, but it's way past time for me. I do appreciate your meeting with us, though." Daryl stood up and within a couple of minutes we were out the door.

We had walked most of the way back to the car before either one of us spoke. We hadn't scripted this one because we didn't know much about Vaneck or where he'd be coming from. Daryl had again performed well. Better than me.

"Sorry, I should have checked with you before responding to Vaneck," I finally said. "I got caught up in the negotiations, not in what all this means for you."

"It's okay. You're supposed to do what you did— think ahead, keep me from committing. I understand. But sometimes there's nothing to discuss. Man was smooth, maybe even right, just talking to the wrong guy."

We drove in separate cars to our final meeting. We stopped at the head of a short driveway leading to a recently finished large, wooden Colonial, white with blue trim. The house was one of the first group built in a small development that looked like it would one day hold twelve, maybe fifteen more new homes. I'd been told that a group of small cottages belonging to three families had been on the land. The developer had come in, taken down the cottages, and was putting up much bigger homes. About half of the homes backed up on Echo Pond and there was a small beach area for the development.

A sign at the entrance to the road leading to the development said the owner of the development was Echo Pond Shores Realty Trust and the realtor was George Sheehan. The sign didn't say it, but with one of three or four of the homes already built in the development, the odds were pretty damn good that Tom Jordan was the general contractor on the site.

Through a hole in the trees at the back of the property, sunlight reflected off the water. There wasn't quite as much of a reflection as there would be when the pond was full.

The mailbox in front of the house said JORDAN. My secretary had called and arranged for us to meet with Jordan after he had finished his work for the day. She told him that we wanted to meet at his house because we were from out of town and would be traveling around to look at some properties during the day. I got a little grim glee out of having her tell Jordan that Mr. Jerome and an associate would be stopping by.

I had Daryl standing by me when Jordan opened the door. His mouth flew open.

"Get the fuck off my property," he said and tried to slam the door.

Daryl stepped up and stuck out his hand. The door hit his massive palm and stopped.

"I'll call the police," Jordan said as he pushed futilely on the door.

"We'll be just a minute," I said, "and you might not want to call them just yet. Unless you want them to show up and finding me wearing this hat." I put on the Jordan Builders hat that I'd been holding behind my back.

Jordan saw the hat and reached for it. I pulled back and Jordan stopped short, inches away from slamming into Daryl. Jordan stepped back again, half concealed by the door.

"I don't know what your game is, Kardon," Jordan said, "but I don't know anything about that hat. You and your domesticated gorilla better get your asses off my property."

Daryl shook his head. "World's becoming damn un-civilized, you ask me. We knock on your door just the way we're supposed to. We weren't civilized, we'd do like some people do, just barge in, like this."

Daryl pushed the door hard and fast, though it looked like only a small wave of his forearm. The door flew open and Jordan staggered back, his nose bleeding where the door had hit it squarely. His feet hit the base of the central stairs behind him and he sat down. He shook his head, pulled a handkerchief out of his back pocket for his nose, and staggered to his feet.

"Fuckers get out of here. You can't pin anything on me."

"Not right now, maybe," I said, "but that's the name of our game."

"What?" Jordan said with a muffled voice.

"Pin the tail on the asshole," I said. "All you need to know, Jordan, is I'm on to you. I'd watch my step, I were you."

The door slammed in my face.

We walked back to our cars and then leaned against Daryl's SUV, looking back at Jordan's house. We saw Jordan looking out at us through a large picture window.

"Wave to the nice man," I said and we both waved. Jordan disappeared.

"Okay, we pissed him off, now what do you do with him?"

"Don't know and right now, I'm hoping he's the least of our worries. I figured he'd either get a little nervous and back off, or he'd go over the edge and do something obvious and stupid. I hope he'll just leave us alone. But what the hell, I got a kick out of it. 'Course it helps to have you around as a sidekick."

We talked for another few minutes about things we had to do and what we had to follow up on. Daryl took off quickly. I lingered a little while, watching the curtains move every few minutes, happy to be unsettling Jordan. A couple of cars drove past into the development, the drivers eager to get home and not even noticing me. Finally, I gave a little wave to the shades in the window, stepped into my Blazer, and drove off.

Driving home, I went over everything in my head. We hadn't learned as much as I would have liked, but I had enough new angles and people to pursue that the day had been quite productive. We'd thrown down the gauntlet, as Shakespeare might have said.

But Meadowbrook was a small town. Perhaps things were getting stirred up too much. As I drove, I mused on the line from *The Taming of the Shrew*, "A little pot and soon hot." So far, we had a hot little pot of a town, but Wells, Jerome, Daryl, and I were the only ones burned.

CHAPTER——

FIFTEEN

The next day, I turned to finding somebody at the Division of Fisheries and Wildlife who knew what was going on out at the golf course. Calling the Division's central office, I was given a number for an outlying office that dealt with endangered species. When I reached that office, Jill Connolly told me she was the staff person assigned to the case.

I explained who I was and told her I hadn't had the chance to see the file, but I was trying to find out what the agency intended to do about the pond.

Connolly told me that a written report had come in from someone in the Meadowbrook area describing blue spotted turtles in the pond on the golf course. The report itself was not remarkable. Blue spotted turtles were an endangered species and were found in four other ponds within a few miles of the golf course. If the report had come in from a individual known to be reliable in identifying the turtles, the office would have immediately prepared a form called an Environmental Occurrence and sent it off with a copy off to the landowner and then negotiations would have begun over protecting the turtles' habitat.

In this case, Connolly said, the reporter was not known to the agency. As a result, the office then asked a herpatologist they trusted, a Ph.D. student at Harvard, to go to the site and try to confirm the presence of the turtles. If the scientist confirmed the presence of the turtles, the same procedure would come into play. Connolly gave me the name of the graduate student—Susan Gannon. And the person reporting the turtles was Stephanie Williams.

I could hear Jill Connolly getting short with me so I apologized for taking her time.

"It's not that," she said, "it's just that I went through all this with the first attorney for the golf course. I don't remember his name, but I walked him through the process we would be following."

"Charles Wells? From Meadowbrook?"

"Yes, that's the one. Isn't he still working on this? I don't want to have to deal with too many different people."

"I understand, but that won't be a problem. Mr. Wells died recently and I've taken over the case. We've been unable to locate the files that Mr. Wells kept, so we're backtracking, trying to fill in the blanks."

Her voice came back without the edge. "I'm sorry, that's too bad. All right, what can I tell you?"

"Did the graduate student, Gannon, find anything?"

"Yes, she found the turtles at the site."

"So what happened then?"

"Well, we filed the Environmental Occurrence form and sent a copy to the landowner."

"Jerome Mann."

"That sounds right. Then Mr. Wells contacted me. I explained to him that we always send out the form."

"What does the form say?"

"Oh, it says we'll have to monitor the identified species and take actions to preserve them and their habitat from any harm from human activity or development. It can sound pretty threatening to people, like we're going to take over their property. The laws are quite strict. They do prohibit anyone from harassing the identified species or doing anything that might interfere with their breeding or living peacefully. But we work with land-owners to come up with approaches everybody can live with to protect the species and the land. And we're try-ing to buy more undeveloped land to protect species."

"You told Wells that?"

"Yes. And I also told him that we were doing more work on confirming that the turtles actually lived in the pond. This case was a little—unusual, I guess—and Su-san Gannon wanted to do more work on it. I told Mr. Wells that we would contact him soon with more infor-mation."

"Did you tell Wells that the golf course would have to close down three holes?"

"No, I said we might have to close some holes. But first, we needed the data from Gannon."

"Have you gotten it?"

"No, not yet."

"Do you mind if I call her?"

There was a pause. "We can't stop you, of course, Mr. Kardon, but we have had instances of people threat-ening our staff members and researchers, hoping to in-timidate them or influence their reports. We do not view that as working responsibly or cooperatively with the agency."

"No, no, I just want to ask some questions, see what Ms. Gannon has so far. I've got some ideas that I'd like to run past her, as well."

She told me how to reach Gannon. I hung up and sat back in my chair, wondering what in hell Wells had been up to. He'd given Jerome only a small part of the story. And the way he had presented it was as negative as possible from Jerome's perspective. Had Wells just misunderstood the situation with the agency? Or had he deliberately misrepresented the agency's intentions and misled Jerome?

If Wells had simply confused what the agency intended, then it had no bearing on all that had followed. I hoped that we could still work out a solution with the agency. But if Wells had deliberately misled Jerome, then a logical series of questions followed. Why? What did Wells have to gain by helping to close down the course? Was he working for somebody else in an attempt to get Jerome to leave town? Was he killed because of his actions or because somebody was afraid he might change course again? If he was acting with somebody else, who was it and why the conspiracy? And what were the conspirators up to now?

My head was spinning trying to sort out all the questions. All I knew for certain was that instead of helping to make the golf course operational, at the end Wells was doing his best to stymie efforts to open it.

In the face of all these new questions, I decided to try another tack before pursuing the elusive turtles and the problems they were creating. Maybe, I thought, Linda Redmond would be easier to track down.

I called Information and found no L. Redmond listed. The phone was probably under her aunt's name, which was a problem since I knew the aunt's first name but not the last. But I went on the Internet and fairly quickly found a database I'd used before that gave me phone numbers by addresses, not by names. I had Redmond's address so I was able to match it to a number.

When a female voice answered, I asked for Linda Redmond.

"Who is calling, please?"

"I'm Dan Kardon. I'm a lawyer representing Daryl Mann. And before that I represented Jerome Mann. I'm quite anxious to talk to Ms. Redmond."

"Sorry," the voice said in a low voice not much above a whisper, "she's not at home." The woman on the other end of the phone didn't say much, but what I heard didn't sound like a woman ready for a nursing home.

I tried again. The same female voice answered.

"Hello, this is Dan Kardon again. It's quite important that I speak to you, Ms. Redmond. I'm not interested in giving you a hard time—I'm just trying to help my clients. Would you—"

"Goodbye, Mr. Kardon," she said and the phone line went dead.

I tilted my chair back and studied the ceiling for a while. The few other people in my office were gradually heading out. More calls to Redmond would prompt her to switch on an answering machine, disconnect the phone, or contact the police to complain that I was harassing her. Instead I decided to try to meet her later face to face.

It was after five P.M., but I only had a home phone for Susan Gannon, so I went ahead and called. I figured she spent her days in classes, tracking turtles, or dealing with obnoxious academic advisers who wouldn't give her the support she needed. She might not mind a call at home from someone who actually had an interest in what she did.

Gannon was cautious and didn't say much initially. But after telling her who I was and how I'd found her, she agreed to talk. When I asked her to tell me a little about blue spotted turtles, it was like turning on a spigot.

Blue spotted turtles grow fairly large and are the second largest freshwater turtles in New England, she told me. Adults grow to about ten pounds and live as long as eighty years. The vegetarian turtles have a tough time in the winter. In addition, over the years, they've graced many a menu—Native Americans dined on adult turtles while skunks, herons, foxes, and bullfrogs snacked on the young ones. With pollution and land development narrowing their habitat over the years, blue spotted turtles now resided only in a handful of ponds in the Meadowbrook area.

Because of their rarity, Gannon went on, they are valuable on the black market. Turtle collectors in Asia and Europe would pay more than two hundred dollars for a blue spotted turtle.

"You know your stuff," I said.

"Oh, it's nothing, I specialize in turtles so I should know them well. These have been really interesting to study."

"I gather you went out to the pond on the golf course and found the turtles there."

"Well, I went out twice. Once I found them, once I didn't."

"Did that surprise you?"

"Well, no, I mean, it's not as if I could make an appointment with the turtles or be certain where they'd be."

"One thing I wanted to check with you about. Since the pond is on a golf course, it's got to receive at least some runoff from the fertilizers and pesticides they use. Did you check the water quality?"

"No, I haven't yet, but that's one of the things that I need to go back and do. To be honest, I didn't expect to find them there partly for that reason. Also, that particular pond is so isolated and clean—no vegetation, shrubs, the stuff that makes the ponds attractive to turtles. I wasn't sure if the turtles actually were at home in the pond, or whether they were just passing by. Turtles can really truck all over the place, you know, even aquatic turtles. Anyway, I was uncertain about a couple things, so I want to go back."

"This was the first time the blue spotted turtles had been found in that pond, right?"

"Yes."

"Did you ever interview the person who reported finding them?"

"Stephanie Williams? Oh sure, I talked with her, to see if her report was credible and to get all the information she had on her sighting."

"I spoke to Rich Grant at the golf course, so I know he met you on your visits. Was Williams with you?"

"No. She asked me to let her know when I was going out there, but then couldn't make it either time."

"You let her know exactly when you'd be out there?"

"Yes, just as a courtesy. Plus if we confirmed the sighting, we'd take that into account on later sightings."

"What are you thinking now about the turtles?"

"To be honest, I'm not sure what we'll do. Once I've finished all my work, even if I'm skeptical, if the turtles are there, the Division will negotiate with the golf course to protect them."

"You think the turtles will like having golf balls rain down on them?" I tried for levity, but Gannon was deadly serious about her turtles.

"Oh, they won't like that at all. In fact, that could be considered illegal. They're easily frightened by noises from motors, homes, construction, boats, anything like

that. And high stress levels have affected their repro-
duction rates, so that—"

"Ms. Gannon," I said, "I'm sorry. I have to go shortly.
You've been immensely helpful. A final question—do
you have any more site visits to make?"

"I don't have anything scheduled. Why?"

I told her what I had in mind and asked if she could
schedule another visit out there, letting Williams and
Rich Grant, the golf course superintendent, know about
it. She agreed to go out there on Friday, which gave me
time to work things out. I thanked her and hung up.

I thought about what Gannon told me. She had questions about the presence of the turtles in the pond. I had
questions about Stephanie Williams. The site visit we
had planned might give us some answers.

At home, I knocked off a smoked turkey sandwich and
a Foster's beer. Then Daryl called. He wanted to talk
about how Bender and I were handling a couple of the
properties, as well as the restaurant. We wanted to spend
some money to fix some things before we put them up
for sale. Bender had sent Daryl documents that set out
the plans. Daryl was going through them. I could hear
frustration in his voice as he tried to understand what
we were doing. I asked if he wanted me to come over,
and within a few minutes, I was on the way to Weston.

When I drove up to Daryl's, twilight was fading fast.
As I stopped at the entrance to Daryl's driveway and
announced myself, I saw a dark car—it looked like a
large, late-model American sedan—parked along the
side of the road just thirty or forty yards past the stone
gate at the head of the drive and on the opposite side of
the street. While I waited for Daryl to buzz me in, the

car started up and slowly drove away without putting on its lights.

I pulled in and parked my Blazer in front of Daryl's house. Then I walked back down the drive. Keeping cover behind the gate, I looked down the road to where the car had been. I could barely see it parked on the same side of the road but further down.

As soon as Daryl opened the door, I asked, "You hire anybody to watch out for you?"

"You mean a bodyguard?"

"I mean somebody to sit outside your house, check it out, make sure you don't have problems."

"Hell, no. Waste of money. Nothing every happens out here and that's the way I like it. Why? What's going on?"

"Probably nothing, I'm just a little paranoid. Can I get out of here without going through the front gate?" Daryl told me there was both a side gate and a back gate in the stone fence surrounding the house, neither locked because they were fairly well hidden by woods and shrubs.

"Give me a few minutes, I'll be back."

I went outside, found the side gate, and worked my way to the road. I followed the road until I could see the large sedan still parked on the shoulder. I backtracked away from the house and the parked car. Then I crossed the road and walked back toward the car, parallel to the road, but just in the woods where I couldn't be seen.

The woods by then were fairly dark, so it would have been tough for anyone to see me. Nonetheless, I walked carefully, hiding behind trees and bushes. When I got to the edge of the woods, there was still enough light to locate the sedan. I had trouble seeing inside, but I didn't see any light or movement, so I left the woods, kept low, and moved toward the car.

I could feel my pulse quicken as I got to the passenger-side door. I expected at any instant that someone would pop up out of the backseat. But nobody did.

I took a deep breath and raised out of a crouch to look into the car. The interior looked a lot like mine often did—the floor and seats were full of junk food wrappers and soda cans. There was a closed canvas brief case on the front passenger seat and nothing else I could recognize. Once I was satisfied that I couldn't see anything useful, I jotted down the license plate number on one of my business cards and walked back to the house.

I had just walked through the front gate when I heard rattling and something like a car door closing. I ran back out through the gate and up the road in time to see a large male slam a trunk door and throw a full garbage bag into the back of the sedan. I thought about running after him, but he closed the door quickly, jumped into his car, and took off immediately. So I went back to the house and found Daryl sitting in the kitchen.

"I just saw a guy drive off in a late-model Chrysler New Yorker with a trash bag. Any chance he got in the house?"

"Nope. Back door might be open, since I was out there this afternoon, but I've been sitting here and didn't hear a thing."

"You got anything valuable in the back of the house?"

"Only things I got back there are the TV, stereo. Also, there's a closet full of sports gear. Don't think anybody's going to get much for my collection of old basketballs and paintball guns."

"What about outside?"

"Grill, patio furniture, nothing fancy."

"And trash cans?"

"Yeah, of course. A couple outside, near the back gate in the wall. You think the guy took a trash bag? Why the hell would anybody do that?"

"Old private eye trick. They rummage through your trash, see if they come up with anything. A guy I used on some private injury cases called it 'dumpster diving.' So now here's the big question for you. Anything in your trash that worries you—letters, bills, pictures, credit card statements he can use to track down personal information?"

Daryl shook his head for a moment. "Nothing that I can—oh, shit," he said. He put his head in his hand and just held it.

"Magazines. I just threw out a bunch."

"What kind of magazines?"

"Gay magazines. Some tame stuff, some not so tame stuff. Maybe ten, twelve magazines. Also, might be some letters in there. I got a guy keeps writing to me. I met him once, he wants to get back together. I don't even read the letters anymore. Wanetta takes them and throws them out."

Ouch, I thought, but I kept that to myself for the moment. We'd deal with the problem when and if it came along. "Not proof of anything, but it puts somebody on the right track if they're looking for information. So we know someone's checking you out."

"For what?"

"Maybe they'll try and pressure you to drop the camp, raise the water level, pay money, who knows? We'll see if they want to negotiate or blackmail you."

Daryl just shook his head. "This situation just keeps getting worse."

"Hey, in a perverse way, it's good news if somebody's trying to blackmail you. It means you're too valuable to kill or they think it's too risky, at least for now. And let's face it, you've been afraid something like this would happen for a long time, so now you get to figure out how you want to play it."

"Yeah, thanks for the positive spin, but right now I'd prefer not to have to deal with this shit. I'd prefer to beat the crap out of the son of a bitch who stole my trash."

"Don't get too upset yet. I got the license number of the car so we should be able to track the guy down."

"Hey, nice work."

"I'll find our trash collector and go visit him in the next day or two, I hope before he can get anything other than a few magazines on you."

We went through the business items for about an hour and a half. When I left, I first walked down the driveway and looked up and down the street. I didn't see any sign of the Chrysler New Yorker so I took off in my car.

Heading home, I cranked up some vintage Springsteen. I didn't like the new turn of events—that was taking matters in an ugly direction, an indication that he might be targeted as Jerome was. But at the same time, I liked it that things were happening. Even if we didn't yet understand who or why, we would have a chance to capitalize on mistakes, intercept the action, or pick up the trails of the people involved. People on the move leave trails. It's those willing to lay low, stay out of sight, who are harder to track down. Tonight, somebody moved.

It was after eleven P.M. when I finally walked in my door, too late for me to call Jenny but, with all that happened, too early to sleep. I grabbed a beer and sat

down in front the television and a night game from An-
aheim. The Red Sox, with Pedro Martinez pitching a
two-hitter, were playing against the California Angels,
for whom Mo Vaughan had a double and a home run.
Why couldn't the Red Sox get a first baseman like that,
I wondered.

Just before midnight, with the score knotted at one
and my eyelids digging into my chin, the phone rang.

"Hi," Jenny said. "Sorry I'm calling late. I just wanted
to hear your voice."

"Glad y'all called, little lady. I'm trying out a new
one. Like it?" I said in my best Southern drawl. It got
a little giggle out of her.

"You can be such a jerk."

"Can't argue the point. You okay?"

"I'm fine," she said. The tone belied the words.

"Problems?"

"Nothing you haven't heard before. And I hate having
the same conversation over and over."

"I'm listening."

I heard her sigh. "I keep thinking things will get easier
but somehow they don't. My parents are doing a little
better. But we don't know whether we can expect much
more from my Dad and he's still at risk for more strokes.
I get to the end of some days and just wonder how we'll
get out of this mess. Meanwhile, I've dumped my career
down the toilet."

"Come on, forget about the job. You'll have plenty
of years left to work. Might take some effort to get
things back to where you want 'em, but it'll come. Taking care of your parents, though, dealing with doctors,
hospitals—that's put you in a tough place. You have to
have faith things'll get better."

"God, I hope you're right. My parents seem to be in

better spirits than I am. I just hate seeing what's happening to them."

I was silent for a moment.

"Damn, I know I sound whiny," she finally said. "People you cared about died young and here I'm bitching because my parents are getting older and things are going wrong."

"I'm sure it's hard to watch, but yeah, like it or not, things could be worse. And maybe that's what your folks have figured out, what they've come to terms with. Maybe they've figured out what's most important to them, so their expectations are different."

"Meaning I don't know what's important?"

"Hey, I'm not giving you a hard time. Look, you went home, gave up pretty much everything, to take care of your parents. You've decided what's the most important for you. But you're still struggling with it, second-guessing yourself. Screw that. You made the best decision you could. Stick with it. Sometimes you can't do it all, you have to do one damn thing the best you can. And another thing. If I remember right, somebody once told me to give myself a break. That's what I'm telling you."

"Seems like so long ago, I was lecturing you."

"Yeah. One more thing for you to chew on. Could be your parents feel pretty good these days 'cause you're around. I sure as hell feel better when you're around here."

She was silent for a moment. "All right, you're not always a jerk," she finally said, with a small laugh.

"You're with your folks. Stop worrying about what's going to happen. Enjoy the time together. Take your dad to a ball game or read him a book. Go with your mom somewhere she'd get a kick out of."

"Look what happens. I leave for a little while, you turn into a New Age guru."

"No chance. You never see one of those guys with a nice cold brew in his hand."

"Thanks. I know you're right, it's just hard to keep things in perspective sometimes," Jenny said. "What's going on with Daryl?"

I told her what Daryl and I had been up to, describing the meetings with Riley, Sheehan, Vaneck, and Jordan. She asked a few questions and voiced her disapproval of our confrontation with Jordan.

"You like that, don't you?" she asked.

"What?"

"Barging in, doing the bull-in-the-china-shop thing."

"Hey, the guy beat the crap out of me. What's wrong with getting in his face?"

"Who's getting defensive now? I didn't say there's anything wrong with it. I just said you like it."

"Well, let's say that sometimes I think that's the way to get things moving."

"Just remember, when you go in banging and shouting, you won't be able to predict all the reactions."

"I hear you. You're telling me my bull-in-the-china-shop act might break more than just the china. You thinking of somebody in Meadowbrook in particular?"

"No. But when you're dealing with the other people, you might think more about how you approach them. Contacting a witness in a lawsuit is one thing—you can depose or subpoena them, most of the time, even if they don't want to talk. But here, you've got no leverage over anybody. You make a stink, push too hard, or cause a stir, you may drive some people underground.

"Between Jerome's murder, the racist messages, your beating, and the hassles Daryl's going through, I know how badly you want to make things right. Just use your head, don't make so much of a scene you miss things, is all I'm saying."

This time I was quiet for a moment. "Whoever knew there was a brain behind all that blond hair?" I finally said.

"Watch it, pal, or I'll prove to you that blondes really do have more fun, only I'll do it here in Tennessee." We talked for a while longer, until her questions and comments petered out.

"I guess I'd better go," she said. "I miss you."

"Miss you, too. Talk to you soon."

I felt better since she sounded stronger at the end of the conversation. But I was aware we'd talked about her parents and her job as the two most important and troubling things to her. She hadn't talked about me; we hadn't talked about us. Either that was good, because Jenny didn't perceive any big problems, or it was bad, because I fell fairly far down the list of important items. For the first time, I recognized that I'd like to make it to number one.

I grabbed another beer and sat down in front of the last inning of the baseball game, which the Red Sox lead by a run. Martinez struck out Vaughan for the last out. I chanted, "We're number one! We're number one!" Whether for the Red Sox or for my desired status with Jenny, I probably couldn't have told you. Game over, I walked down the hall to the bathroom, there ending my stint as a holding tank for the beer, and into the bedroom, where I fell into a cool and empty king-size bed.

CHAPTER————

SIXTEEN

Late the next day, I aimed the Blazer west again to Meadowbrook. I'd taken Jenny's comments of the night before to heart and planned on a quieter trip this time.

I put on an old George Jones tape and listened to the world's greatest rendition of "Bartender's Blues." It didn't help me figure out how to help Daryl get the camp going or who killed Jerome, but it sure made the time pass more quickly. I intended a surprise meeting with Linda Redmond before the site visit to the pond on the golf course. I had some special accessories in the back of my car.

The only two places I knew to look for Redmond were at her home or with her aunt at the nursing home. I struck out at the carriage house on the lake. No cars in the driveway, no lights on in the house, and nobody answered the bell. On the way out, I did take a quick look at the adjoining mansion that had been converted into a series of townhouses. A sign on the lawn said that the townhouses were for sale by a realtor, George Shee-han. As far as I could tell, Sheehan had the listings for most of the new homes around the pond, which meant most of the commissions from the sales as well.

A kid at a gas station on the way sold me a two-liter

Coke, a large bag of Doritos, and a box of chocolate chip cookies for dinner during my stakeout. He also gave me directions to the one nursing home in town.

The nursing home was a large brick building, at least forty years old, sitting a short distance back from the road in front of a circular driveway. It had a nice lawn in front of it, with a small garden to the side. In the warm evening, a few people walked outside. I parked in a small parking lot, then headed over to the nursing home, past a large maintenance shed and a Dumpster receptacle. I didn't go much farther. I'd seen Linda Redmond at the hearing, so I recognized her sitting outside on a bench next to an older woman in a wheelchair who I presumed was her aunt. They were talking intently and didn't see me. Instead of approaching them, I went back to my car for my gourmet repast. From the parking lot, I could just see them in front of the building.

After twenty minutes or so, the Redmonds went into the nursing home. Another hour passed, giving me enough time to knock off all the soda and the junk food. I wondered how cops ever made it through long stakeouts without gaining twenty or thirty pounds. I also wondered what they did for bathroom breaks.

Finally, Linda Redmond walked out of the nursing home alone. I waited, out of my car, until she was in the driveway to approach her directly. When I was about twenty feet away, I spoke up. "Ms. Redmond? I'm Dan Kardon. I'd like to talk with you." She had been looking down, preoccupied, but when I spoke her head snapped up. She stopped and her hand went into the purse hanging from her shoulder. I had no desire to find out what she had in there. Her face looked cold as steel in the warm, humid spring evening.

"I'm sorry to meet you like this," I continued, "but

the phone calls weren't working and for the sake of my client, it's very important that I talk with you."

"Mr. Kardon, you are nothing if not persistent, much like a toothache. It may be important for you, but it isn't for me. I'd like you to leave me alone, please." She spoke forcefully, looking directly at me and not backing away. Her hand stayed in the purse, which I took as a mildly positive sign.

"Ms. Redmond, I can't force you to talk with me and I wouldn't want to do that if I could. You say no, that ends it. But Daryl Mann has lost a dear friend and cousin in Jerome Mann. Chuck Wells also died. And recently, not far from here, I was beaten up by a small gang of thugs." She gave a small start at that. "I just want to talk to you, try to get some information I can't get elsewhere. Maybe you don't have anything useful, which is fine, but maybe you have a little knowledge that would help me. I'm here to help a man try to do some good things. I'm not here looking to pin anything on you or anybody else."

"Mr. Kardon, I've talked with the police. They seem satisfied with what I had to say. Why don't you just check with them?"

"I know what you told the police. You didn't meet with Jerome the night he was killed, though you had arranged a meeting."

"That's correct." Redmond was hugging herself as if it was cold, but it was not and she wore a sweater.

"And you had scheduled a meeting with Jerome about a week earlier, which I believe you also missed."

She was slower responding this time and looked at me fairly intently before answering. "I told the police I didn't go to that meeting either."

"Did you call Jerome beforehand and reschedule the first meeting to the later date?"

She looked away. "No."

"Why not?"

She didn't answer me. The light from the streetlights wasn't strong enough to allow me a good look at her face. She looked frozen in place, not ready to talk but not willing to leave either.

"See, Ms. Redmond, that's what's bugging me here. I think you arranged two meetings with Jerome, then skipped them. The meetings are in this calendar, but Jerome never talked to me or Daryl about meeting with you, even though he was willing to meet with anybody who had property on the pond. And Jerome was a pretty busy guy. If you blew him off the first time, I don't think he'd have been quick to reschedule unless you gave him a good reason. What I'm guessing is you set up a meeting and asked him not to tell anybody. Something got you concerned, you didn't go the first time. But you felt strongly enough about seeing him to contact Jerome again, gave him a pretty good story so he agreed to meet you."

She gave a small shake of her head. "Speculate all you want. It doesn't matter now. I never met with Jerome Mann. And if it will reassure you, Mr. Kardon, I don't have any idea who killed Jerome Mann or Wells. Or who beat you up, for that matter. It wasn't me." She hunched her shoulders and pulled at her sweater as if to ward off more internal chills. Then she pulled at her purse as if she was about to leave.

"I don't expect a confession, Ms. Redmond, or answers to all my questions. But everything helps, any piece of information you can give me I can use as a bridge to get more information. The more you withhold, the longer it will take me to make the connections I need.

"You can walk away from me tonight and I won't contact you again until I know what this is all about. What I will do, though, is keep at it, to understand what you're hiding. I don't know if it has anything to do with Jerome or Daryl. All I can tell you is, I have you on my radar, at least until I know enough to move you off screen. So you have a choice. Give me a hand, on terms that work for you, or wait until I find things out."

She turned away from me and walked to her car, parked out on the street. I watched for a moment, then walked back to the parking lot. I had a guilty feeling in the bottom of my stomach and I reproached myself. First, I thought, as Jenny had prophesied, I'd come on too hard and Redmond had been skittish. Then I thought, hell, I didn't threaten her enough. I needed to go back and tell her she had to cooperate or we'd really make her life miserable. But by the time I climbed in the car, I'd given up the tongue-lashing. Maybe I didn't do things quite right, but Redmond hadn't seemed intimidated in the least.

I watched her drive off, then started up my Blazer. I turned on the George Jones tape and then ejected it—I hadn't done enough, I thought, to earn the reward of more George. Maybe the Monkees or the Spice Girls.

As I was rooting through a few tapes to figure out what to play, I saw a car's headlights coming down the road. The car stopped next to mine and the window came down. Linda Redmond looked out at me, tears streaming down her face.

"Mr. Kardon," she said, "if you'd like to follow me, I'll talk to you at my house."

"Sure," I said and she turned around and drove off. I

followed. It was around nine P.M., so the night promised
to be long. I had no illusions about what I was bringing
Linda Redmond—pain and hurt showed in the face I'd
seen in the car window. But thinking about questions to
put to Redmond, I had a sense of movement, of energy
and excitement. I had the chance to be the hunter, not
just the hunted; to be ahead of the curve, not behind it.
In Meadowbrook, these were new feelings.

We parked in front of the carriage house. It was a small,
two-story Victorian, painted tan with green trim, that
looked squarely out on the pond. It had a wraparound
covered porch and three wide steps leading up to a center door. Linda Redmond went in ahead of me and
turned on a porch light. She held the door open for me
and I walked into a small foyer full of bare oak and a
few scatter rugs. A small room went off to the left. A
set of stairs was directly in front of me.

   She motioned me into a room on my right, a living
room with an old leather couch and matching armchair.
Glass-covered bookcases full of old hardcover books
covered one wall. Another had an antique table and next
to it, a small cabinet held a radio. In one corner, small
bookcases had been built into the wall and now held a
host of photos, mostly black and white, that, like the
books, were old. In front of the couch was a round antique wooden coffee table with a single portrait of a
young woman in a silver frame. The only light was from
a pair of dull brass floor lamps in opposite corners. The
room looked as if it had not been touched for years.

   Linda asked me in a soft, low voice if I wanted coffee.
I declined but asked for the bathroom instead. She
pointed to a door off the hall.

   When I came back, she was seated on the leather

armchair. The tears were gone, but her eyes were still red. She sipped from a cup of coffee or tea while one of her hands tapped the side of her mug. She stared at the Oriental carpet on the floor for a moment after I sat down on the couch and then looked up at me.

She had brown hair, gracefully curved cheeks, a slender nose, and full lips. Add in full breasts, a slender waist, and smooth, tan skin, and only the crow's feet at the corners of her wary gray eyes made clear her age. On appearance alone, she was an unlikely candidate to be living alone in a house filled with older and antique furniture and set in a small, middle-class town.

"Beautiful home," I said.

"Thank you. It was my aunt's. It's been in the family since the turn of the century," she said.

"Is that your aunt?" I said, pointing to the photo on the coffee table.

She nodded.

"How is she?"

"Her mind is in fine shape, but she needs a fair amount of caring for."

"Must have been hard for her to move out of here."

Redmond nodded. "Yes, but she's unusually tough, pragmatic. We tried bringing help in, but the service was erratic and we couldn't always get what she needed. One day she just decided it wasn't working. Once she makes up her mind, that's it."

"The nursing home okay for her?"

"Oh, it's not great. But she's made friends there and overall the care is better than she could get here. And I make sure the staff knows I'm paying attention—that seems to help."

"Your aunt is lucky to have you."

She gave a small smile and looked at the photo. "No,

I've been fortunate to have her." She turned back and looked at me. "I agreed to talk with you, Mr. Kardon, but I'm having trouble deciding whether I have anything to tell you. Or whether I can trust you. You think I had a hand in Mr. Mann's death?"

I shrugged. "I'm not accusing you of anything. But I do believe there's something you're not telling me.

"As for trusting me, all I can tell you is what I've said before. I'm a lawyer, from Boston. Originally, I represented Jerome Mann. I came in to help him just after Chuck Wells was killed. Once Jerome died, I continued to represent Daryl Mann. Mostly I'm trying to resolve things so the camp opens and you folks get your pond back. But Daryl is awfully torn up by his cousin's death. The police haven't figured out what happened. If we can determine why Jerome was killed, Daryl would feel a little better. What would help you make up your mind about me?"

"I don't know. Tell me where things stand with the camp and the town."

I gave her a short version of the discussions we'd had with Sheehan and Vaneck and the offer we'd made to the town.

"You said you'd been beaten up recently? What happened?" she asked.

I told her.

"Do you know who did it?"

"I have a pretty good idea."

"And that is?"

I paused for a moment. I'd accused Jordan face-to-face and I didn't see him as likely to bring a defamation action, so I did.

She gave a small laugh and shook her head. "You've seen the townhouses just down the drive?"

"Yes."

"You know who did the renovation work to build them?"

"Let me guess. Jordan?"

"Yes. And do you know who the realtor is?"

"That I know. George Sheehan. They're still for sale, I noticed."

"They haven't gone as fast as George thought they would. Or at anywhere near the price he expected."

"He thinks it's because of the camp and the water level?"

"There's a small beach area for the townhouses that is now useless. The view isn't as attractive, and walking on the shore is not very appealing right now. Meanwhile, the bike path runs near here so George has visions about who'll be on the path and why."

"So Sheehan's unhappy because the prices on his properties are going down. Jordan's pissed because he has a house on the pond and won't get as much new work if the properties don't sell."

"To be fair, George is also angry about the town beach. He's a selectman, and the town has run nice swimming programs there for the last few years. George takes these things seriously."

"I'm getting that sense." I shook my head. "Everything's connected. Close-knit community, I gather."

"I don't know if you could call it close-knit, but it's certainly small and people try to get along."

"You think there's a chance Tom Jordan or George Sheehan had anything to do with Jerome's killing?"

"Hard for me to believe that of any of my neighbors." Redmond walked over and looked out a window. "But who knows who they really are?"

"People in town say the same about you."

She turned and gave me a small, sad smile. "I imagine they do."

I waited for a moment. When she didn't speak, I did. "You want to tell me why you scheduled meetings with Jerome? I assume it was about the pond."

She turned back to the window. With her eyes closed, she tilted her head back and took a deep breath. "It's not that simple, Mr. Kardon," she said.

"Call me Dan. Things rarely are."

She gave a slight shake of her head.

"This where the question of trust comes in?"

"Yes," she said.

"Until you tell me what you're scared of, I can't do much to reassure you. But tell you what, I want to call someone and have you talk to her. You don't know her from Adam, and it's only a phone call. But she might be able to answer some of your questions. She's a lawyer, she's someone I care about deeply, she's trying to take care of parents with health problems, and she's been through some tough times herself. Seems to me you and she might have things in common."

Before Redmond said anything, I walked over to a phone that was sitting on a small table in the hallway. I put the call to Jenny on my phone credit card.

"Hi," I said. "How you doing?" We talked for a minute or two. Jenny had some progress to report for each of her parents so her voice was strong, her mood more relaxed and upbeat.

"I have a funky request," I said. "I'm out in Meadowbrook, talking to Linda Redmond. I'm trying to do it your way—you know, no grenades or broken china. She's not sure she should trust me. You willing to talk to her?"

Jenny laughed. "Sure. Trying to get me to give you

the sisterhood seal of approval, huh? And who says I think you're trustworthy? Is she good-looking?"

"Very."

"Then why should I tell her anything that will keep her in your company longer?"

"Because you're more so."

"Good answer, counselor. Put her on. And call me later to tell me what this is all about, okay?"

I motioned Redmond over and told her I would wait outside while she talked with Jenny. I walked out the door and sat on the front steps.

I saw some dark shapes fly out from under some trees, looking more like bats than birds. Along some stretches of shoreline, lights shown in houses. But along much of the shore, there was only darkness. In the bright moonlight, the pond was silent and silver. These particular still waters ran shallow, not deep, and gave no hint of the fierce battles people were waging over them. Looking out over the pond on a clear, warm spring evening, with frogs croaking and insects buzzing around, I could understand that people wanted to preserve it. I could understand that people felt a strong attachment to it. But I couldn't understand how someone had killed over it.

After perhaps ten minutes, the door opened and Redmond told me I could come back in.

"Thank you," she said. "Talking to her helped."

"It usually helps me so I'm not surprised."

Redmond walked over to a window overlooking the lake. "It looks like such a peaceful spot at night," she said.

"Looks like? I'd say it is peaceful."

"This place is many things for me, but not always as peaceful as it looks. I've thought about whether I could tell you only a piece of the story, but I don't know that it makes sense unless I tell you the whole thing. Only a handful of people know most of it, so I need to ask that you keep it confidential." Still standing, she turned and looked at me.

I thought for a moment. "You're not a client, and there's at least some chance that you and Daryl are going to be in conflict, so I can't simply make you a client. And you know there's a criminal investigation going on, so I don't know whether I'll ever have to talk to the police. What I can promise is that I'll keep it confidential as long as I possibly can, and I'll let you know if I have to disclose any of it. That okay?"

She thought for a moment then nodded. "I don't know if this has anything to do with either of the killings, but I'll tell you the story and let you decide whether there's a connection."

She remained standing, looking out the window. Whether the pond gave her strength or the moon gave her detachment, I couldn't say, but she told her story with composure and a calm, steady voice.

She had spent many of her early years in the mansion that had been converted into townhouses. Her mother and her Aunt May were sisters. Her father died when she was three and her mother moved back into the mansion with her parents and May. Her grandparents died within a couple of years of each other.

By the time Linda was twelve or so, she realized she was different from a lot of other girls in her class. She was slender, taller than a number of the boys, and had breasts bigger than girls two and three years older. She endured a lot of teenage humor and harassment. She took to wearing oversize sweaters and sweatshirts and ignored boys altogether. She had a few girlfriends but she much preferred walking in the nearby woods and meadows, catching frogs, fish, or butterflies, working in the large vegetable garden in the back of the carriage house with her Aunt May, swimming in the lake, or canoeing.

Then Linda's mother remarried. The family stayed on in the mansion and Aunt May moved into the carriage house. Soon Linda chose to avoid not only some of her classmates, but also her parents. Her stepfather, a respected dentist in town, insisted that the household run on a firm timetable that did not allow much time for Linda's outdoor activities when the weather turned warm. And he insisted that he would maintain order in his home.

When, as a fourteen-year-old, Linda broke one of his rules by coming home late for dinner, he punished her by grounding her. When she broke another rule by talking back to him, he decided a spanking was necessary. He took her into his study, pulled her over his knee, and spanked her. It hurt, not so much physically as emotionally. And she noticed that he seemed red and flustered when he finished.

So began his sexual abuse of her. She didn't tell me the details, other than that it happened at irregular intervals in her bedroom. Accompanied with dire, explicit threats, he ordered her never to tell anyone. At the same time, he became even more controlling of her. When she went to her mother to complain that her stepfather was too strict, her mother supported her stepfather. Feeling betrayed and alone, Linda could never tell her mother what was happening.

In the meantime, her Aunt May and her mother, once close, became distant. Her aunt would not tolerate the authoritarian ways of Linda's stepfather and made no bones about it. Linda knew that her aunt worried about

her, but because of the growing conflict between her
parents and May, Linda was scared to tell her aunt what
was happening.

Time passed slowly. Linda barely spoke around the
house. She began performing badly in school and started
hanging out with the tough crowd. She alternated
screaming at her mother and stepfather and refusing to
talk to them. She had a boyfriend, more for companionship than anything else, but she implied it was much
more to her mother and stepfather.

On her sixteenth birthday, after a small party with her
family and a few friends, her father came into her bed
late at night. She didn't tell me exactly what happened,
but I gathered she used a knife to keep him at bay. He
forced the knife away from her and told her never to do
it again, he'd be back.

After he left, Linda got up and packed a bunch of her
things in a bag. She went to the carriage house and
knocked on the door. Sobbing, she told May what had
been going on and that she had to leave. May asked her
to stay with her but Linda insisted she had to leave, she
was scared. May convinced her to stay for the night.

Linda and May talked for hours. Sometime in the
middle of the night, May realized that Linda was determined to leave and that neither the police nor Linda's
mother were likely to believe Linda's story. In the morning, May drove Linda into Boston and set up a bank
account for her with five thousand dollars. She arranged
for Linda to stay with some friends in another town who
had a teenage girl. She told Linda to do whatever she
needed to save herself and that she could have money
or a place in May's home anytime she wanted.

Within two days, Linda left Boston. She took a Grey-
hound bus west to Los Angeles. People had always told

her she was beautiful enough to be an actress. Now was her opportunity.

And so, over time, she became an actress. It didn't happen right away. She had to work up to it. She worked days in a department store and nights as a waitress, until she could afford some of the gyms, the bars, the restaurants, and the nightclubs where she might get noticed by film people. And she did get noticed so that some bit parts came her way, as did a steady flow of drugs, alcohol, hot tubs, and sexual adventures.

Within six years, she became a star, but one who would never go home. She thought about her aunt, but never contacted her. Linda took a new stage name and left Meadowbrook behind, never telling anyone where she ended up. In part, she never wanted her stepfather to find her. And she never wanted people who had cared about her to know that when she became a star, it was in B-movies built on, as she put it, "thighs, spies, bikinis, and ballistics."

She had a number of successful years, but the business demanded an endless supply of new, young, naïve, and star-struck bodies. Soon enough she didn't qualify. Unlike many others in the business, though, she didn't spend all her money putting cocaine up her nose or spirits down her throat. She deliberately set some money aside. When the film opportunities began to diminish, and the invitations to fancy parties became fewer, she had some money to fall back on. She had also listened and learned over the years to all the businesspeople around her, many of them lacking any conscience but with sharp financial eyes. She put a chunk of her money into the stock market and found she had a knack for making it grow.

She spent her early thirties doing occasional B movies, investing carefully, and making enough to stay comfortable in L.A. On occasion, she backed or coproduced a few movies, making money but always staying in the background in the male-dominated industry. She had expected to remain there for life.

"So how'd you end up back here?"

For the first time in her narrative, Redmond hesitated and then spoke haltingly, with pauses between the sentences. "My thirty-third birthday, May called, out of the blue. She told me that my parents had died in a car crash and she was having some health problems. She asked me if I'd like to come back."

"How had she tracked you down?"

"All she said was that she hired a private investigator who found me and gave her my address and phone number."

"Why come back here?"

"I didn't, at first." She was whispering and I saw tears begin at the corners of her eyes.

"You did well in L.A."

"No, it wasn't that, it was almost the opposite. I talked with May a few times, then gradually realized I was afraid."

"Afraid of what?"

"Afraid of who I'd turned into, the life I'd created. And scared that I could never go back, not so much to Meadowbrook, but to being a person I liked, a person I wanted to be."

"You had reasons for what you did."

"Yes, but I've been an adult for a long time, free to make my own decisions. I couldn't blame all my bad choices on my stepfather forever. And I realized I didn't want him to control me anymore."

"What do you mean?"

"So much of what I'd done, what I'd turned into, was in response to him. I didn't want him to have the power to control how I lived even after he had died."

There was silence for a moment but I let it sit. I wanted to walk over and put my arms on Linda's shoulder, give her a hug, tell her it would be okay. But I had the sense at that moment, with her face pale and still in the moonlight streaming through the window, despite the enormous strength it had taken her to survive, Linda was composed of fragile crystal. One touch and she'd shatter into pieces. I waited.

She finally spoke again. "Things fell apart for a while. I went into a deep depression. But finally, after I reached bottom, I began to put things back together. And once May and I started talking again. I realized that though I hadn't seen her in close to twenty years, I was closer to her than to anybody in California. And I could manage my investments from anywhere." For the first time, she turned away from the window and walked back to sit on the sofa, then continued. "Finally, there was nothing to keep me in L.A., but here I had Echo Pond and May. I came back about six years ago. And it's been good."

"You were brave to leave, but maybe braver to come back. Not too many bright lights, nightclubs, or ritzy parties around here," I said. "And lots of curious locals around to pass judgment."

She shook her head. "I had all I could take of L.A. I'm happy to be here, locals and all. I've got a few good friends. Overseeing the building of townhouses has been a fun project."

"I was going to ask you about that. How did that happen?"

"We decided to renovate the mansion and turn it into

townhouses maybe two years ago, before May went into the nursing home."

"I'm surprised she was willing to do it, since it was the family homestead."

"It was her idea. She knew I could never be comfortable there. 'It can't make us happy,' she said, 'so let's allow somebody else to enjoy it.' We could have just sold the whole thing, but we knew we could make more money if we did the work, then sold the units. I've tried to reassure May that I'll be all right financially, but she wanted me to have the money from the house. Maybe she figures that's some retribution for me."

"You oversaw the work?"

"Yes. I did most of the planning and arrangements, but May was involved in all the big decisions. The mansion had been in the family for years so there was no mortgage. We got a construction loan from the bank and started work."

"The Meadowbrook Savings Bank?"

"Yes. Roger Vaneck was good to work with. Things went well, we were on time and close to budget. Tom Jordan did good work."

"I've heard that."

She nodded. "It's too bad he's a pig."

"He make a play for you?"

She gave me a close-lipped smile. "The man has the subtlety of a mule, not to mention a wife."

"And I expect you have the kick of one, if you want to keep somebody away."

She gave a small laugh. "A mule or a wife? A mule, maybe. Probably not a wife."

We were both silent for a moment, then I spoke. "From things you've said, I gather something happened in the last few months."

Her face quickly settled into a frown. "Just a minute," she said. She left the room and came back with an envelope. Pulling a sheet of paper from it, she held it by one corner as if it was tainted.

"In February, May's health was bad and she had to be hospitalized for a few days. I was pretty upset. Then I received this."

It was a letter written on a computer.

Dear Ms. Redmond,

The town was pleased to have you return to your hometown. And my compliments on the fine job you have done on the mansion.

I also have considerable respect for your business acumen, as evidenced by your substantial bank account in L.A. and your work on the renovations. As a result, I'll go straight to the business proposition I have for you. If you are willing to deposit $9,000 every two months by wire transfer from the Wells Fargo Bank, I will be happy to make sure that the town, and your aunt in particular, never become aware of how you spent your time in L.A. That seems a fair price to pay for the tranquility and peace you are now experiencing.

In case you think I am not serious, I enclose some still photos taken from a couple of your fine cinematic productions. You are very lovely now, but I must say you were truly a beauty fifteen years ago. Personally, I'm disappointed that you have wasted your beauty on other women, more than with men, but I concede your sexual preference is not my business. I also have records of your two arrests for cocaine possession. All in all, you were a busy lady in L.A.

Within another day or two, I will provide further evidence of my resolve, followed by instructions as to how to make the fund transfers. Should you not make the transfers, much more information about you will become public quite quickly—as will occur if you seek assistance from the authorities. And I am smart enough to know that once your aunt has died, you may not care about publicity, so you will need to make no more transfers after her death.

An admirer

Redmond was staring at the rug when I finished, but looked up and gave an almost imperceptible shake of her head. "If you don't mind," she said, "I won't show you the photos."

"Not interested," I said. "No question they were taken from one of your movies?" She nodded.

"The drug arrests—"

"They happened. I never went to prison, but I have a record, was on parole and did some community service. And I'm bisexual. Mostly I've had relationships with women, but not always. Not a pretty picture, I know, but I was pretty normal for a lot of the people I knew in L.A."

"All great Americans, I'm sure. You never told your aunt about any of this? And the investigator never told her?"

"She said she'd deliberately asked him not to tell her anything about my life. If I wanted to share things, fine, but she'd never ask. She was just happy to have me back."

"What happened after you received this letter?"

"Two days later, my aunt got a package in the mail, a video of one of my B movies." She gave a mirthless laugh. "*Bimbos on the Beach*, it was called. One of my finer T and A performances. She was bewildered about it and showed it to me at the nursing home. I told her somebody was playing a joke and took it. She didn't look at it, thank God."

"Then what?"

"In early March, I got another letter. I was given instructions to wire transfer the money to a bank account in the Cayman Islands."

"Jesus," I said. "Blackmailers used to be satisfied with a suitcase of cash in the dead of night. This guy had it all figured out. He checked out your background, then he sets up the payments so it'd be no fun to find him. The amount was under $10,000 so the bank didn't have to report it, plus it's an offshore transfer. Maybe traceable, maybe not, but only after getting a lot of people involved."

"The only good thing is that he seems not to have discovered other funds I have located elsewhere. I can afford the payments for now, but it's a painful and difficult situation. I have to be careful about how much I help my aunt financially, at least until we sell the townhouses. And there's this horrible tension of me not being able to tell my aunt."

"What about your aunt? What about her assets?"

"When I got back here, I was surprised at how little she had. Based upon the property and money I thought the family had, May should have had more. But she didn't, so she agreed to let me take control of her stuff and I moved her money out of Meadowbrook. We've done better with it, but she's still not rich, particularly now that we're paying for the nursing home. I kick in something every month for some of the extras."

"She know you're doing it?"

She shook her head.

"So you've made only two payments so far?"

"Yes, the second just a week or two ago."

"Before Chuck Wells died?"

"After, I think."

"Have you had any more contact from the blackmailer?"

"Right after the paper came out with the story about the camp, I got another letter telling me to oppose the camp at the public hearing. Maybe he was scared that if we can't sell the townhouses for the price we planned, I'll be in financial trouble."

"Is he right about that? How much damage will the lowered pond cause you?"

She looked me square in the eye. "A lot. But not enough to kill Jerome or anyone else over it, if that's what you're wondering. If the water level stays down, we figure our prices will drop at least ten, maybe fifteen percent. Some realtors have estimated that other properties are down as much as thirty percent, because the houses weren't great and the pond was a prime attraction. But our homes are good and I'm confident that we'll make some money. Maybe not what we expected, but something."

"You never went to the police?"

"I can't bear the thought of May learning all of this. She's been through so much, lost so much, I don't want to hurt her more. I can't tell the police, because then there's no way to keep a lid on things."

"Hard to believe you'd give up a big chunk of change like that."

"It's money, nothing more," she said, and flashed something that was a cross between a challenging stare and a frown. "When I left Meadowbrook, I had the bank account from May with five thousand in it and nothing else. I never took another penny from her. If it would buy peace and ensure that May was not disturbed, I'd pay a lot more than fifty thousand per year."

"I'm sorry I'm upsetting you, but my job is to figure out what's going on, who killed Jerome and why he died, and get the golf course and camp on track. Right now, I'm pretty skeptical of everybody in this town."

"I've told you what there is to know about me. You can't possibly understand how difficult the last few years in L.A. were, how deep in a hole I was, how hard I had to dig to get out. If you could see that, you'd understand that for me, selling the townhouses is a game, nothing more and nothing to get upset over, let alone kill. What's real are my relationships with May and a few close friends, this house, my garden and the woods I walk through, the beauty of this place. It took a great deal to get to the point where I feel, most of the time, whole. I'd never jeopardize that over the sale price of a town-house."

I nodded and was silent for a moment, conscious that Redmond was watching me intently. She sounded sincere, but then she'd been an actress. Could she simulate honesty with me in the same way she had simulated sexual pleasure with onscreen lovers? I'd sort out the truth later.

"Is the blackmailer right that you won't care about his threats after May dies?" I asked.

She sat quietly for a moment, looking at the hands in

her lap. "Absolutely." I could see her working to hold back her emotions.

I sat back in the chair and thought a bit. "So Wells, Sheehan, Jordan—any of them could have been in on this."

"Yes."

"You think Jordan was upset enough to retaliate when you turned him down?"

She shook her head. "I don't think so. This takes some thinking and planning and that doesn't seem to be his strength. But everything has all been so shocking, I don't pretend to have any good ideas about what's going on."

"Tell me about Jerome. Why did you want to meet with him?"

She gave a soft, sad smile. "I was out walking around the pond one day last fall, maybe in October, and I met him. He was sitting over by the dam, having a sandwich and a beer. He was friendly and we started talking. He was so happy with the land and so excited about the golf course and the camp. He didn't tell me much about his plans, but I enjoyed seeing him take so much pleasure out of the area.

"When the letter came telling me to oppose the camp and I did, I felt awful afterward. I wanted to tell Jerome I didn't really care about the pond, so I made the appointments. But I never kept them because I was too confused and scared of what I might say."

"You never told Jerome about the blackmail?"

"No. We had that one meeting last fall, then I saw him again at the meeting at town hall. He did a wonderful job, he and Daryl. They made me feel ashamed to oppose the camp. I never saw him again after that."

"We've talked about Wells, Sheehan, and Jordan.

Anybody else who might have an interest in blackmailing you?"

She looked away.

"Linda," I said, "if you don't tell me, I can't do anything to check it out."

"David Granger," she said.

"Granger," I said. "How is he involved?"

"I don't know that he is. But he was my boyfriend
when I left Meadowbrook in high school. I never explained to him what happened to me, why I left. When
I came back, I saw him a few times. First, he wanted an
explanation. Then he wanted to get back together. I said
no to both. He was pretty angry."

"And, putting it bluntly, maybe he got even angrier if
he found out what you'd been doing in L.A. and now
wouldn't go to bed with him. You know, I had dinner
with him recently and asked about you. He never mentioned you'd been his girlfriend. What a cast of char-
acters in this town." I could see tears starting in her eyes
again. "I'm sorry," I said, "I didn't mean to be so—"

"It's okay, this whole thing is so sick, I've never told
anybody about the blackmail. It's just upsetting. Give
me a moment." She left for a few minutes.

Upsetting was an understatement. She was holding up
remarkably well under a whole series of painful events.
Whoever the bikini queen had been, it was hard to see
her in the Linda Redmond before me now.

When she came back, we talked for a while longer. I
got a few more details but nothing more of import.

As I was leaving, she said, "Is all this helpful?"

"Yes," I said. "It's confusing as hell. But you've given
me a whole new angle as well as ideas and people to
check out. Thanks for talking to me."

"I'm glad I did. You probably ought to thank your

lady friend, Jenny. She was quite convincing, said some mighty nice things about you."

"Proves you can fool some of the people some of the time, I guess, but I'll pass the thanks on."

Linda Redmond opened the door and shook my hand. "Between blackmail, murder, and assault, somebody is turning a nice, comfortable town into a human cesspool. I only hope you can fool someone into telling you the truth," she said.

"So do I," I said, then got into the car planning to do just that.

CHAPTER———————

SEVENTEEN

"**I**f the damned grad student won't show until eleven-thirty, why are we here so early?" It was nine in the morning. "We could have slept another hour, fooled around a little, had breakfast, and been here on time."

"Gary, you're cute, but leave the thinking to me. First, if you haven't learned it yet, you wanna fool around with me, you better plan on an hour, no quick hitters for this girl. Second, I want to make sure everything's the same on the course and near the pond, and keep track out where the workers are. Some of the guys out here have seen me wandering around before," said Stephanie Williams, "but still we've got to be careful. We don't want them to see us when we do it. Last time, things got screwed up—it's important we work this one right."

"What do you want to do now?" I'd never heard the man's voice before.

"Let's look at the fairways next to this one. They're supposed to be marked off and I want to see if they did it right. Also I want to see how many guys are actually working on the course. Supposedly more people are back, but I don't hear any machines and we haven't seen anybody. I want to see if I know any of the guys so I can talk to them later."

"You sure this makes sense? I mean, this is the fourth

time we've done it. How many more times we gonna have to come here?"

"Gannon said that if she gets a good sighting today, she'll have enough to report to the Fish and Wildlife people. Today goes well, we'll be done."

"I hope so. These early mornings are killing me."

"That's only because you were playing pretty late last night. I don't hear you complaining about that."

"Not a chance."

"Come here." There was silence and I took a look out from under the evergreen tree where I was lying. The leaves were blooming so I couldn't see much, but what I saw looked like Stephanie Williams wrapped around somebody.

They finished the kiss after a time—a long enough time that I was afraid they were going to start the hour Williams needed—and then giggled together a little. They each shouldered a backpack and took off across the fourteenth hole. In a few moments, I moved to the edge of the woods and, with my camcorder, followed them across the green expanse. My camera with a telephoto lens was ready as well. I'd already trotted out an extrasensitive tape recorder to try to pick up the conversation I'd been able to hear, though that was less of a concern. If all went as I hoped, the pictures alone would get Stephanie Williams thrown out of the Wild Woods Warriors faster than an Oregon logger.

I'd driven to the golf course right from Linda Redmond's and then stayed in the woods overnight. I didn't know if Williams would show up at all but if she came early, I didn't want to be visible. As a result, I'd slept in a small clearing in the woods near the fourteenth fairway in my sleeping bag on a foam pad but without a tent. I didn't look great and probably smelled worse, but I'd been lucky. No rain, no wind, not too many bugs, and the temperature had stayed in the fifties.

Since I'd seen her at the camp before, and I figured she'd worry about who might be around, I thought Williams might come over to the golf course from the camp and make her way through the woods to the turtle pond. After stashing my sleeping bag and small duffle under a tree and downing my sumptuous breakfast of two granola bars, I stayed in the woods near the pond and scanned the adjoining areas.

When I finally saw two figures approaching, I took cover under an evergreen. Williams and her escort walked around the woods a little, looking for people on the course, before stopping within earshot of where I lay.

That I was part of a small group of people running around in the woods trying to fool one another reminded me of scenes from *A Midsummer Night's Dream*. Shakespeare was right. Lord, what fools these mortals be.

I was hungry and tired, but quite content to wait. After the two visitors left, I climbed back into my sleeping bag and snoozed for a while in the warmth of the morning.

When I awoke again, it was about 10:45. I didn't see anyone around, but to be safe I stayed in the woods. Unfortunately, the pond was out in the open. I'd like to have been able to get closer, but with the camcorder and the telephoto lens, I thought I could get some good shots from my current location. For my purposes, I didn't need perfect photos, just shots that showed Williams at the right spot at the right time.

At about 11:10, I saw Williams and a man with a mustache, about my height but younger and blond, come walking down the fourteenth fairway from the direction of the clubhouse. They walked over to the edge of the woods, not far from where I was. The young man picked up two broken branches, each about four or five feet long. He carried them over to the pond. From what I could see, he laid the first one down so it was half in and half out of the water. The second one he placed perpendicular to the first, at the base.

I had moved to a position in the brush at the edge of the woods so I could videotape and photograph. I was too far away, maybe 150 feet or so, to hear them talking.

With the branches arranged to their liking, I saw each of them reach into their backpacks and pull out a large turtle, which they then placed on the ground next to the branches. I couldn't see the turtles at that point, but Williams and her companion slipped into the woods a little further down the fairway from where I was. I videotaped most of it, putting the camcorder down long enough only to shoot a series of photos.

A few minutes later and right on time, Gannon and Rich Grant came walking down the fourteenth fairway, just as Williams and her co-conspirator had. When they got near the pond and could see the turtles, Gannon did some gesticulating and then took a bunch of pictures with her camera. I also saw her doing something at the water's edge. After maybe fifteen minutes of note and picture taking, Gannon and Grant walked past me, heading back.

I stayed in place. After another five minutes, Williams and her friend came out very cautiously, looking all around. Through the lens of my camera, and then through my camcorder, I watched them scoop up the two turtles and put them back in the backpacks. They walked towards the camp. I collected my stuff and walked back to talk with Gannon.

Susan Gannon was sitting inside the clubhouse filling out a form when I arrived. We introduced ourselves. I helped myself to a glass of water, then sat down next to her at the table.

"What did you see?" she asked.

"Take a look."

I played back what I'd captured on the camcorder. The distance was too great to pick up details, but what Williams and her boyfriend had done was obvious. Gannon shook her head and frowned as she watched.

"I'm glad we did this," she said. "Otherwise, I wouldn't have known what to do."

"Why?"

"The way I found the turtles. That just wasn't right. If you see them out in the sun, it's on a log or a rock near the water's edge, not sitting on the grass in the middle of the day. They'll go on land to travel to other bodies of water or to search for food, but it was bizarre to see two of them just sitting there. If you hadn't been around to see how the turtles got there, I'd have had to confirm the sighting."

"I overheard them say they'd been there a couple of times, but something went wrong the second time."

"Makes sense. They must have brought them over the first time from some other pond and Williams took some pictures of the turtles in this pond. Then she knew when I was coming the second time and brought others over. The second time, I remember I ran late, so probably the turtles made it into the pond. I stayed around for a while but never saw them."

"You test the water out there?"

"Sure, just did a couple quick tests today and I've got

samples to bring back, though we don't need them now. Tests I did today can't tell me precisely what's in there, but whatever it is, there's a lot of it."

"What're the chances those turtles that they didn't retrieve are still alive?"

"Hard to say. We're learning that turtles have a powerful homing instinct. They might have headed off for whichever pond they'd been take from. But if they went into the pond on the course, between the pollutants and the lack of food, chances of survival are about the same as my appointment as a full professor at Harvard."

"Zero."

"I'll report what we observed. The Fisheries and Wildlife people aren't going to be happy."

"Neither will her activist friends. I'll send a story, with photos, on e-mail to the Wild Woods Warriors. They solicit environmental stories on their web site. Once they realize Williams may have killed a couple of endangered blue spotted turtles, they'll be tougher on her than the state people."

"You want me to have somebody from Fisheries and Wildlife talk to her right away?"

"No, I'll pay her a visit later today." We talked for a while longer. Gannon was disappointed she wouldn't get a paper out of the new location for the turtles, but she was happy to have her confusion cleared up.

Once she left, I ate the remaining cookies and soda I'd brought along. I checked in with Rich Grant to tell him where things stood. Then I called Daryl, who was, for him, almost exuberant. "Hey, man," he said, "that's pretty wild stuff. But damn, that's good news about the golf course. Kardon, you're doing okay."

"That's Mr. Lawyer to you," I said. He laughed.

I called Al Thompson as well. I gave him a rundown

of what had occurred. I asked him if he could track down the guy who'd taken Daryl's trash and gave him the license plate number I'd grabbed. I figured Al had connections. He was happy to do it. Though it was early Friday afternoon by this time, he figured he could get information about the plate by the end of the day. We agreed to talk that night.

I left the golf course and stopped for a hamburger and fries at the town diner. I asked one of the guys behind the counter how I could find Meadow Road. He gave me directions and a short while later, I pulled up in front of a small green ranch house badly in need of painting. I thought about bringing my camera but decided I didn't need it.

I rang the bell. Stephanie Williams answered. In the back, I heard a voice call, "Who is it?" The voice was that of the man accompanying Williams earlier on the golf course.

"You may not remember me. I'm Dan Kardon, an attorney for Jerome and Daryl Mann."

Her mouth was tight and her eyes narrowed. "I recognize you. I don't remember you telling me before you represented the Manns."

I shrugged. "You should have asked me the right question. What I'm here about are the turtles and the golf course."

"Sorry, Mr. Kardon, our group doesn't do deals, if that's what you're here for. I wondered when you'd try to buy us off. We're not interested in negotiating over the golf course. Those turtles are too precious. The golf course has to go. And I have no interest in talking with either lawyers or liars. You're both." She started to close the door.

"Ms. Williams, I just came to give you a sneak preview of what I'm going to tell the Fisheries and Wildlife people about your little adventure this morning. You want to wait for a copy of the video, or the letter and the pictures from this morning I'm going to send to them, that's fine."

The door opened back up and the blood drained from her face. "What are you talking about?" she said.

"I was there when you and your friend brought a couple of blue spotted turtles to the pond on the golf course this morning. The party is over, Ms. Williams."

"What are you talking about? We've been here all day, right, Gary?"

The blond man, at least ten years her junior, walked up wearing only blue jeans and pushed in front of her.

"What's going on, man? You bug Stephanie anymore, I'll kick your ass."

"Calm down, Gary," Williams said.

"I'm not bugging anybody, pal. I just came to tell you your turtle scam is over. You might want to think hard about what you do next. I won't be your only visitor. It's a crime to kill an endangered species."

Williams's hands flew to her face. "What are you talking about?"

"That second set of turtles you brought to the pond, the ones that Gannon didn't see and I expect you didn't retrieve? If they stayed in that pond, there's a reasonable chance they're turtle soup by now. It's also illegal to harass an endangered species. Even if you don't go to jail, our buddies from the Wild Woods Warriors camp aren't going to be too happy about the story I'll be sending them."

"Hey, asshole, you got nothing on us, get the fuck away from here. We haven't done a damn thing and you can't prove we did." Gary started to close the door in my face.

"That's fine, I'll let you argue about the videotapes with the authorities. You look pretty good on camera in that purple North Face fleece jacket you had on when you and Stephanie did a little kissie-face, Gary. 'Course, the jacket didn't match your backpack—you should have switched backpacks so you had Stephanie's black one. Would have looked much more elegant."

"How the fuck you know what I wore?" His red eyes narrowed and his nostrils flared. He opened the door and stepped forward. He pulled a wrench out of his back pocket. I looked right at him and didn't back up.

"Gary, cut it out. He saw us." She put a hand on his shoulder and pulled him back.

"Ms. Williams, you and I should talk," I said.

"Don't tell him anything," Gary said, "just let me—"

"Gary, I'll handle this. I got us into it, I'll deal with it. Go in the back room so I can talk with him." He grunted, threw the wrench down, and sent another malevolent stare my way, then walked toward the back of the house.

Williams opened the door and motioned for me to come inside. I followed. She went into the kitchen and sat down at an old wooden table. I sat across from her. She tapped her fingers on the table for a moment.

"How did you know we'd be there?" she asked, looking up at me with little trace of the vibrant, confident woman I'd seen before.

"I didn't know. Susan Gannon and I agreed on when she would show up at the pond. I spent the night out in the woods near the pond just in case you came along."

"Why did you suspect anything?" I told her what I knew.

She nodded. "I knew it might look a little funny leaving the turtles on the grass, but it was the best we could do. If we left them on the branches or rocks, they'd have been in the water too quickly, we'd have lost them."

"What happened to the second pair?"

"I don't know. We left them on the grass. Gannon was late, I couldn't wait the whole time, and when I got back the turtles were gone. It didn't occur to me that the pond would be that bad. I mean, the golf course has only really been operating this spring, and . . ." Her voice trailed off and tears started coming down her face. "Pretty stupid, huh? Hell of an environmental activist I am, killing off endangered turtles."

"What about Wells and Jerome Mann? You kill them, too? It's not as if they were endangered species."

Her mouth flew open and her eyes went wide. She put both her hands on the table. "Is that what you think? That's ridiculous! I had nothing to do with either one of them. I never even met Mann."

"He was making you pretty angry, wasn't he, trying to open the golf course and the camp, then lowering the pond?"

She took a deep breath and composed herself. "Mr. Kardon, if I went around killing all the individuals who anger me with their waste, pollution, destruction of wildlife, forests, and plants, I'd make Jeffrey Dahmer look like a Boy Scout. I may not obey every law but I believe strongly in peaceful civil disobedience. I've never done anything violent to people and I never will. I didn't like what Jerome Mann wanted to do, but I didn't kill him."

"Fair enough. What about Gary? He was eager enough to take me on. Didn't look like he fully absorbed Gandhi's teachings."

"Forget Gary. He's just being macho because I'm

here. He's never even been in a barroom brawl. And
he's not really an activist." Except maybe in the sack, I
thought, but didn't say anything. Williams's face was
suffused with pain, her voice quavered and hands shook.
She pulled her hands from the table and wrung them in
front of her.

"What are you going to do?" she asked.

"Gannon already knows. She and I will both check in
with the Fisheries and Wildlife people."

"Do you think I'll be charged with anything?"

"I don't have a clue. But Daryl Mann won't press
charges, if that's what you're worried about. You should
feel pretty damn lucky. The Manns have lost a lot of
time and money because of your screwing around. And
the golf course delays contributed at least a little to Jerome's lowering the pond." I was laying it on a bit thick,
but it was all true. "I am serious, though, about writing
that letter to your group's leaders, maybe sending them
some pictures."

She was looking at the table. Tears fell on the wood
surface. "I'd almost rather go to jail," she said.

We sat in silence for a moment. In the background, a
soap opera was on a television.

"Tell you what," I finally said. "I'll make you this
deal. I won't notify them so long as you do. At the least,
you have to tell the basics of what you did. Make it an
apology, a 'what I did wrong' story, I don't care. And
it doesn't matter to me if you tell them you may have
made toxic turtle soup, but you have to send a letter to
the group leadership. You do that, and show me it's
done, I'll hold off sending anything out myself. That
work for you?"

She grabbed some tissues and dried her eyes. "Yes,"
she said in a scratchy voice, "I can do that. Thank you."

"One last thing. If the camp ever gets to a vote in Meadowbrook, I expect you to be there supporting it and telling any of your friends to do so. If that camp doesn't go forward, I don't know what Daryl will do. He might sell the land. With the golf course next door and the new demand for housing in the area, that land will be carved up into a development in a heartbeat. You want to protect that land at all, a camp is the best deal."

She nodded.

I stood up. "Are you clear about our understanding?"

"Yes," she said in a whisper. "Tell Mr. Mann I'm sorry. And you must believe me, I didn't kill anyone, Mr. Kardon. If I killed anything, it was those turtles. Along with my reputation and everything I've built up over many years."

I left her sitting at the table, as I walked out the door. I wasn't proud about how I'd broken Williams down. I thought it quite possible that overall, in her activism over the years, she'd done far more good than harm. But she'd played with the truth. If I'd learned anything as a trial lawyer, it's that people who play with the truth run a big risk of getting burned. It has little to do with morality and everything to do with human nature. Lying, covering up, and concealing are difficult. It's hard to remember everything the same way every time, it's hard to cover all the bases with a tarp of lies, and it's hard to anticipate all the questions and problems that will arise when you start a chain of falsehoods.

Sometimes, of course, nobody cares much about the events or people behind the concealment or the coverup. But in this case, Jerome and Daryl had both cared. And I was certain that Williams would have nightmares about blue spotted turtles for a long time to come.

* * *

It was about four in the afternoon by the time I pulled into Wells's office. I'd thought about calling Gloria Duchesne before arriving but didn't want her to have the chance to tell me not to come. I knocked on the door and was pleased to find her there. One look at her face made it obvious she didn't share my feelings.

"Hi, Gloria, I wondered if I could come in and check out a few things."

"I was just planning to close up the office. And Mr. Vaneck told me we can't release any files without permission from the clients, so—"

"That's okay, I don't need to look at any client files." I stepped up close to the door. "There are just a few things I'd like to look at, if I could."

Her face showed obvious reluctance but she opened the door slowly and let me in.

"You must have a list of clients on the computer."

"Yes."

"Do you mind if I take a look at it?"

She bit her lip for a moment, then sighed. "I'm sorry, but you'll really have to speak to Roger Vaneck. He's in charge."

I nodded. "I understand the rules, but I'd like to get this taken care of quickly. How about I take a quick look at the stuff, then call Roger if I want any follow-up. I don't need copies or to look at individual files."

"No, I really think it's better if you talk with Roger."

"Okay, I'll call right now."

"I don't know if he's around and—"

"Let's give it a try. What's the number?"

She gave it to me and I gave an internal sigh. I'd hoped to bluff her, avoid the call.

"Roger, Dan Kardon here. I'd like to look at some of

the records Chuck Wells kept in connection with my work for Daryl Mann."

Vaneck cleared his throat. "Now, Dan, I appreciate you're trying to help your client, but you can't just go barging into the Wells files, particularly the ones that have attorney-client material in them."

"I know, I know, I'm not looking for anything that's privileged. Just a list of clients."

There was silence for a moment. "Don't know about this. It's pretty unusual."

"You've got to remember, I represented Jerome. Daryl, as a partner of Jerome, was also a client of Wells, so he's got rights that somebody off the street might not have." What that had to do with an attorney-client privilege I didn't know, but it sounded good. An old professor of mine taught me that if you have the law, argue the law; if you have the facts, argue the facts; and if you have neither the facts nor the law on your side, just argue like hell.

"Interesting point. I hadn't thought about it. But we could debate the point for a long time and get nowhere. Put Gloria on. I'll tell her to let you look at a client list. I don't see any harm in that."

"Thanks, this won't take long. I appreciate it and Daryl does as well."

"Daryl coming around yet on the pond?"

"No, can't say that he is."

Vaneck gave another small sigh. "I'll give it to them, the Mann boys don't lack for balls."

"Some might say conviction."

"Some might. Let me speak to Gloria."

I gave the phone to Gloria. She listened for a moment, then hung up.

"I'll get the client list off the computer," she said.

"Thanks a lot," I said, "and one other thing. How did Wells keep his time records?"

"We have a billing system on the computer. He would write down his hours and I would put the time entries into the system."

"And the system would generate rough bills at the end of the month that he would review."

"Right."

"Could I get a computer printout showing his time entries for two different weeks?"

Gloria gave me a dark look. "Dan, we're going to have the same problem—I can't give you privileged information and those time entries are full of that kind of information. You should have asked Roger."

I raised my hands. "You're right, sorry, I wasn't thinking. I've got something quicker. I'll give you the names of four people. You tell me if he had meetings with any of them in two separate weeks."

"All you want me to do is check on the entries during the two weeks and see if Chuck met with any of the four, or did any work for them?"

"Yup, that and one other thing. Can you just give me an idea of Wells's schedule on the day he died? I don't want anything confidential, I just want to know what he did that day."

She looked at me for a moment and then put a hand over her face. When she moved the hand away, her eyes were tearing. "I'll try. Every time I think I'm okay with things, it hits me again. Tell you what. We've got two computers here. I'll set you up with the client list on this one. Then you give me the names and the weeks, and I'll check the system on the other computer. Finally I'll give you what I know about his schedule. And then—"

"I'll stop bugging you and you can go home." She gave me a small smile and pointed to the client list she'd brought up on the screen. I told her I wanted to check on one week in the winter—the week before Linda Redmond got the first blackmail letter—and also the week before Wells was killed. I asked her to check if Wells met with Sheehan, Jordan, Redmond, Williams, or Granger.

I found Sheehan, Jordan, Redmond, and Williams on the client list. That Granger wasn't there didn't matter since he'd already told me he had at least some professional contacts with Wells.

Trusts, depending on how their names were alphabetized, were interspersed among all the other clients. I clicked on a couple just to see the information they contained. I might have been breaking Gloria's rules, but she hadn't told me I couldn't.

Most, but not all, of the trust entries carried the name of some individual to contact on behalf of the trust. George Sheehan was the contact on at least three or four of them. Echo Pond Shores Realty Trust didn't have any individual named—indeed, the entry had nothing more than the name. It wasn't unique. A few other trusts I checked out were similarly barren of information.

I was tapping my fingers lightly on the keyboard trying to figure out if there was any way to attack the problem when Gloria came back.

"I went through the time entries for those weeks. George Sheehan is the only name to show up," she said. "Chuck had meetings with him in both of those weeks."

"Interesting," I said.

"As for his last day, I've been over it with the police. I was away but I checked on his schedule and his time sheets. He had a meeting first thing in the morning with a client who wanted to buy a small motel. Then he met with an elderly couple, he'd handled their affairs for years, about some estate planning issues. After that, he made phone calls in the office for maybe an hour. He went out for a quick lunch and came back around two P.M. He wrote up a couple of short letters and did a real estate closing. When he came back from the closing, there was a meeting here with our client and another attorney and his client to discuss the sale of a local building supply business."

"Did any of the people I asked you about—Sheehan, Redmond, Jordan, Williams, or Granger—meet with Wells or contact the office that day, do you remember?"

"No meetings that I know of. I don't know if any of them called."

"How about Roger, from the bank?"

"Oh, Chuck and Roger talked frequently. I don't know about that day."

"How about Jerome Mann? Did Chuck talk with Jerome either that day or the day before?"

She cocked her head to the side. "You know, Mr. Mann did call a couple of times that week, looking for Chuck. And I remember that Chuck appeared nervous about talking to him. He seemed to put off calling him back. I remember because it was unlike Chuck. But if he actually talked with Mr. Mann that day, or even the day before, I didn't know about it." She took a deep breath and wiped an eye.

"I'm sorry I've upset you, Gloria. I appreciate the help. I promised I'd leave you alone and now I'll keep to it."

"It's okay. Part of it is that I'm just about finished here, so I'll be working somewhere else soon. It's been a hard time."

I nodded and shook her hand. "Good luck," I said and walked out door.

The little I learned didn't help at all. Wells had handled Echo Pond Shores Realty Trust but I knew nothing more about the trust. Certainly any of the people I was interested in could be tied to that trust or others. And while none of the individuals showed up in the billing entries, Wells might still have talked to one or some of them in those weeks—it just meant he didn't bill for it.

There was little time left in the afternoon when I finished with Gloria Duchesne. First, I put a call in to my office from my car. I got a message that Al Thompson had called, so I called him right back.

"Henry Werner," he said.

"That's who owned the car I saw outside Daryl's?"

"Yup."

"You get his address?"

Al gave it to me. It was in a relatively low rent section of Waltham, a suburb west of Boston. "And I went a little further, got one more thing," he said. "Werner had a private eye license, then lost it. Haven't been able to find out why. But if he's been operating as an investigator, it hasn't been with a license."

"Al, that's good. Gives me something to go on. I can track this guy down."

"Be careful, huh? Hard to know who you're dealing with here."

"I hear you. And I'm not going to approach him right away—I've got some connections to make first and this helps."

Al and I talked awhile longer and then he signed off. I left my car and walked over to the Meadowbrook police station. DeRosa was there, so I told him what had happened with Williams and the turtles, more to put him in good humor than anything else. Then I asked about progress on finding out who killed Jerome.

He gave a small shake of his head. "Nothing yet."

"Identified any particular suspects?"

"Not yet. We're still looking at a bunch of people."

"Daryl's off the list, we've been told."

He hesitated, then nodded.

"You looking at people in Meadowbrook mostly?"

"Yeah. We don't know if this was one person or more, so maybe somebody was involved outside too, but we figure there's a Meadowbrook element. Your client's not on the list but we haven't named anybody else, that's all I can say."

"What about Wells? Any progress on that one?"

Again he shook his head.

"You established any links between the two killings?"

DeRosa didn't say anything for a moment. I could tell he was struggling with how to respond. "I can't comment," he finally said.

"Look, if there's something there, I can—"

"Kardon, I can't tell you anything else. We got rules and I play by 'em. I know who you represent, I know the Mann family has the right to know what's going on, but I can't tell you any more. That's the way it is. Somebody else wants to tell you, fine."

"The name Henry Werner mean anything to you?"

"No."

"Okay, thanks," I said.

DeRosa's response confirmed for me that the police had found a link between the killings of Wells and Jerome. I hoped Randy would tell me more.

With all the different threads, though, I was having trouble keeping track of things. Did everything tie together? Or were a number of different people with dif-

ferent agendas acting independently? I thought about it
for a few minutes, while sitting in my car, but my eyes
closed pretty quickly, and I realized I needed some food
and sleep before I did anything else. After a quick dinner
before the drive home, I planned to do just that, get a
good night's sleep. Just rewards for a productive day.
The sleeping bag was safely stowed in the trunk and I
looked forward to a real bed.

CHAPTER ——————

EIGHTEEN

I walked over to a modest pizza place and sat down to a small sausage pizza with onions and green peppers. I thought about Wells as I ate. He seemed connected to everything and everybody. Not only had he done work for each person I was interested in, he was also tied to Jerome and properties out at the pond. Were he and Sheehan in cahoots? Sheehan could get favorable treatment from the town for developments, Wells could act as the representative up front, and any conflicts of interest or illegality would be well-concealed.

But the same was true of others as well. Jordan could be engaged in some construction scams or development schemes that required the use of a lawyer. Redmond could have a deal going on with Wells to rob her aunt; he got too greedy, she killed him, and then killed Jerome when he lowered the water level and the value of her property. Granger and Wells might be connected in any number of ways, whether through gambling together or through real estate deals. Even Stephanie Williams had a connection to Wells. All in all, it felt like Wells was at the center. I just didn't know what he was at the center of.

I was musing about Henry Werner when it occurred to me that if Wells was at the middle of things, maybe he was also connected to Werner. Linda Redmond, when we'd talked the other night, said that her Aunt May tracked her down using a private investigator. And Wells had worked for both May and Linda. Where would an elderly single woman in a small town go to find a private investigator? Her lawyer, Chuck Wells.

I got up in a hurry, knocking over an almost-empty container of root beer. It was still early in the evening. Gloria Duchesne might know whether Wells ever used Werner as a private eye, but I didn't know where she lived and I'd already put her through enough today. Instead, I thought I had time to visit Linda Redmond's Aunt May at the nursing home. Linda said her mind was still sharp. Maybe she could make the connection that had so far eluded me.

I parked the Blazer in the small parking lot I'd been in before. It was just twilight. Though it was warm, this time just a couple people sat outside as I approached the nursing home. At that moment, I realized I had a problem—I knew her first name was May, but I had no idea what Redmond's aunt's last name was.

I walked up to a woman seated behind the reception desk. She had the phone to her ear and put it on her shoulder as I walked up.

"Yes?" she said in a tone that said go away.

"Hi," I said. "I'm Dan Kardon, a friend of Linda Redmond's. I've just come to say hello to her Aunt May—I've known Linda for some time, she told me May is here. Can you tell me where to find her?"

"Room one-twelve, that way. Visiting hours end in a thirty minutes."

She was back on the phone before I could even say thanks. I walked down the hall, past rooms on both sides. Out of some I heard televisions or radios, out of a few I heard talking, and out of one I heard some moaning. The place was old, though it looked clean and fairly well maintained.

The door to 112 stood open. A sign on the outside said May Dern. I knocked and a firm woman's voice told me to come in.

The room had two beds in it, but only one occupant. May Dern sat in a wooden rocking chair, rocking back and forth, with an open magazine in her lap. She was heavy-set, with grey hair just above her shoulders and glasses. A walker stood on one side of the bed near the wall. She wore a cotton nightgown and a heavy purple terry cloth robe over it. On her feet she had plain white socks and slippers. A photo of Linda Redmond, looking quite glamorous, sat on the windowsill along with some more magazines and books. May Dern gave me a quizzical glance, not hostile but not welcoming.

"Hello Ms. Dern, my name is Dan Kardon. I met your niece Linda Redmond recently and she told me you were here. I'm a lawyer and I wanted to talk with you because I have a problem I think you can help me with. I'm working on a couple of projects out on Echo Pond."

May gave me a big smile. "Oh, you can call me May. Are you a friend of Linda's?"

"Not really a friend, but she and I have become acquainted recently. She speaks so well of you and I know it's meant a lot to her to come home."

"It's such a blessing to have her back after all those years. She's a wonderful girl, don't you think?"

"Yes, she is."

"Mr.—I'm sorry, what's your name again?"

"Just call me Dan."

"Well, Dan, are you a lawyer from around here? I don't think I've heard your name before."

"No, I work in Boston and live in Brookline."

"Are you married?" Aunt May didn't waste any time.

"No, but I'm not really single, either."

She sighed. "Too bad. Well, it's really none of my business, but I do hope Linda finds a good man sometime soon."

"She seems fairly happy to me. And finding a man won't necessarily ensure she's happy."

"Yes, I know that, all too well. But I know she'd only stand for a man who was good to her. And I worry that she spends so much time alone."

"If she wanted to be around people, she would have stayed in California."

Aunt May looked at me with piercing eyes. "Did Linda send you to tell me to stop pestering her and worrying about her?"

I laughed. "No, May. I didn't even tell Linda I was coming. I was just trying to say that Linda seems to feel good about her life. And I guess that if Linda really wanted to have a man, from what I've heard and seen, she could probably accomplish that pretty quick."

May beamed. "Yes, she's a beautiful girl, isn't she? And smart."

"Yes. And she has spirit, a lot like her aunt, I daresay."

May gave a little laugh. "Oh, that girl had spunk from the start. She was always my favorite, of all my nieces and nephews." May leaned my way a little. "People say you're not supposed to have favorites, but that's hogwash. You just don't get on the same way with all the little ones. Linda and I always got along so well."

"I know your family has been here for generations. It

must have hurt when she left for California."

A cloud crossed her face. She sat back and crossed her arms. "Oh, that was a terrible time, a terrible time. The family, I mean, it was . . ." Her voice trailed off and she stared out the window into darkness.

"Linda told me she was having troubles with her parents when she left and that you were her only friend. You helped her a great deal, if I read Linda right."

She gave a little smile. "Well, I tried. I loved that little girl."

"I gather things weren't always easy at home for her."

"Her stepfather, well, there's no word I could use to describe that man. Odious, just an awful man. Her mother was the sweetest woman. She just fell in love and couldn't get herself out. It killed them both, finally, in a car crash. He was drunk. It was so tragic."

"And after Linda left, you had no contact with her for years, I gather?"

"No, nothing. It was so hard. It felt like that man came into our lives and drove away all the people I loved."

"Did you know where Linda was during that time, or what she was doing?"

May gave me a sideways look. "Is something wrong with Linda? Is that why you're here?"

"No, nothing like that, I promise. I'm just interested in a little of the story, not anything you consider too private. It must have been hard for both of you."

"It was for me. I'm sure it was hard for her to leave home that young, though I've never talked with her about it. I know she must have done well out there, though, because she keeps telling me she has enough money."

"I gather you're the one who finally contacted her."

She nodded and looked at her lap. "Yes, I thought she needed to know about her parents."

"How did you track her down after all those years?"

She looked back up at me. "Oh, goodness, I didn't do it. I had a private detective do it."

"Do you remember the name of the detective?"

She narrowed her eyes and cocked her head, rocking all the while. "Is this what you're after with all these questions, Dan?"

I laughed. "Part of it."

"Are you going to tell me why?"

"I can tell you a little of it."

She nodded and rocked for a minute. "I don't remember his first name. His last name was Werner."

"How did you find him?"

"My lawyer, Chuck Wells, recommended him. You've heard about Mr. Wells, have you? That was a tragedy. He was sweet on Linda, you know. After she came back, he'd ask me about her, but she never had any interest."

I smiled. "I never met Wells, but yes, I knew about his death. I'm now working for somebody he used to represent, Daryl Mann."

"Oh, I've heard about him. He's related to the black man who was shot out by the pond. They started that golf course and want to start another camp on the lake."

"Yes."

"That's such a wonderful idea, rebuilding that camp to bring kids out from the city. I used to love swimming and fishing in the pond. Kids from the camp would be all over it, swimming, fishing, or rowing, all sorts of things.

"Other folks in town don't see it quite the way you do."

"Some people in this town have their heads up their rear ends."

I laughed. "You're right. Anyway, I'm now helping Daryl Mann, Jerome's cousin, trying to get the golf course and the camp going. As you know, we've had some resistance to the camp. Daryl also wants to know why Jerome was killed, and who killed him. So far, the police haven't come up with a solid case against anyone."

She gave me a keen look. "Is he going to keep the pond water down?"

"For the moment."

She gave a little smile.

"You think that might get people's heads out of their rear ends?" I asked.

"Well, I shouldn't say it, since Linda tells me the problems at the pond make the townhouses we're selling less valuable, but some people in town had it coming to them."

"May, I have just a couple more questions. Did the detective tell you how he found Linda?"

"No, we met once, and then a couple of months later he gave me an address and phone number. I told him that's all I wanted."

"Was Wells involved in your discussions with the detective?"

"Oh, no, I just met with the detective. He told me he wouldn't say anything to anybody."

I thought for a moment but I didn't need more questions. I had as much as I could expect. We talked awhile about Meadowbrook, her house, and some other things. Then visiting hours ended and it was time to go.

"Thanks," I said, "you've been a big help. And it has been a real pleasure to meet you."

"I hope you'll come back sometime, Dan, and tell me how all this turns out. And why you needed to find out about the private detective."

"I'll be happy to do that."

"Perhaps I won't tell Linda about our little talk. And," she smiled at me, "if you ever get to be really single, I hope you'll come visit Linda."

"I don't know, May. If I was really single, I might come visit you more often."

I walked out of the nursing home with both new information and more confusion. Werner was connected to Wells and he knew about Linda Redmond. Whether it was Wells and Werner who were blackmailing Linda, or Werner on his own, or Werner and somebody else—Sheehan, Jordan, or Granger, perhaps—the information about Redmond had to have come directly or indirectly from Werner.

But even if I had that part of it right, that still gave me only some insight into Linda Redmond's situation. It didn't help with figuring out what was going on among Meadowbrook officials that lead them to deny the special permit for the camp. How did the two situations fit together or were they in fact separate? Did Wells die because he was tied to a blackmailer while Jerome was killed because he antagonized corrupt local officials? I had no answers but a visit to Henry Werner had just zoomed near the top of the To Do list.

I walked down the drive to the parking lot, past the maintenance shed and the large Dumpster. Dark forms—two people, I thought—came at me from the gap between the shed and the Dumpster. Arms grabbed me and pinned me from behind. I started to shout and a rough cloth bag went over my head. A hand forced some of the bag into my mouth. I started to pull at the arms holding me back and to struggle. Then, for an instant, I felt a sharp, severe pain on the right side of my head. After that, I didn't see or feel anything.

When I regained consciousness, I still had the bag tied over my head. My hands were in front of me, bound together at the wrist. I lay in the back of a moving vehicle, whether some kind of van or a sports utility vehicle I couldn't tell. I heard nothing except road sounds.

I passed in and out of consciousness briefly. When I finally managed to stay awake, I had a terrible pain in my head. Rolling around to see if I could get a hand on anything that would help, I found nothing. Shortly the vehicle stopped and I heard doors open, then slam shut. Close to me, I heard another door open. Hands grasped my legs and roughly pulled me out of the vehicle. I felt at least four hands on me.

"Stand up," said a raspy voice I didn't recognize.

"Walk," the voice said. Somebody behind me put a metallic object against the back of my head. I didn't know if it was a gun, a crowbar, or something benign, but I didn't want to find out. I walked. This was not the same group that had jumped me at the restaurant. These guys knew what they were doing.

I walked over uneven ground, not pavement or gravel. The men pushing me along said nothing until one finally barked, "Stop." I heard the squeaks of a door opening. Then, "Step up here."

I took three tentative steps up until I could feel no more steps in front of me. Suddenly hands pushed me hard from behind. I took a few off-balance steps, banged against a wall or something, and fell down. I heard a door close behind me and the clinking of metal.

I heard some footsteps and whispering, along with a kind of splashing sound. My first instinct was to get the cloth hood off me. It was tied on, but while my wrists were bound, my hands were free. I untied the strings holding the hood in place and pulled it off. I could breathe more easily, hear a bit better, but still could see nothing in the completely dark room.

Sitting down, I felt around with my hands. The floor was wooden. I moved against a wall, also made of wood boards. I walked, or staggered, around against the walls, feeling for windows and doors and to get some sense of the size of the building. It was a small structure with no windows. I found only one door. It seemed larger than normal and had a horizontal seam in the middle cutting between the vertical edges. I pushed on it and got nowhere. I walked blindly, arms extended, across the room a couple of times, finding no furniture.

A building in the camp was all I could figure. All wood, unused, and a long way from other buildings. The other thing I realized as I heard a whooshing sound, was that somebody had set the building on fire.

I heard some crackling sounds. Through cracks in and around the door, I saw orange flames flickering upward. A voice said, "Let's go." A car engine started up and soon the engine noise faded away. With my head pounding and my wrists bound, I wanted desperately to sit down quietly and get rid of the pain and the rope. But the flames started to spread at the end where the door was. The splashing sound had obviously been gasoline. On the wooden walls, it did what was intended.

The door, surrounded with flames, was still the only obvious way out. I pushed the shoulder of my lightweight fleece coat up to my mouth and worked my way toward the door. Again I pushed, harder this time, hammering the door with my shoulder. Nothing moved. I fiddled with the handle, pushed it, pulled it, turned it, and twisted it. There was some play there, but it stuck, no matter how hard I worked it. I suspected that whoever had thrown me in there had also jammed some kind of padlock or bar on the door.

I worked at the door for a minute more and then the flames and smoke drove me to the other end of the room. I did a quick tour of the walls again, staying away from the end where the flames were most intense. Finding no chinks or busted boards, I slunk back down into the corner of the room farthest from the flames, staying low. Smoke started to fill the room. For a moment, I wondered if my life would pass before my eyes. Mostly I was coughing and thinking that if I had to die, this was a really sucky way to do it.

I tried to calm down, to get my addled and scared brain to think. If it was a camp building, it wasn't a cabin—no bunks and no windows. But given the split front door, it could be the canteen.

When I'd been a senior counselor at a summer camp, a couple of buddies and I had regular canteen duty and loosened up some floorboards in the building. We'd pull up the floorboards and drop things through the floor during the day, then crawl underneath and pick them up at night. If we'd figured it out, there was a good chance other depraved, sugar-addicted teenagers in other camps had figured it out as well. Or maybe the damp, termites, and carpenter ants had done some damage over the years and I'd just plain get lucky.

I lay on my stomach and scrabbled my fingers over the floor. I had to take the fleece coat away from my mouth, so I took in more smoke, but with my hands bound, I had no choice. I started in the corner I was sitting in and found nothing to get a grip on.

I moved along the back wall, searching with my fingers for a hole, depression, an edge, anything that might indicate a loose board. I scooted along the back wall, my hands moving faster and more erratically. I looked back and the flames had moved from the other end of the building down toward me.

I pulled myself up a bit and my fingers caught what felt like a large knothole along the edge of a board. I stuck a couple of fingers into the hole and yanked. The board moved a little, but not enough. I sat up to get a better angle and pulled as hard as I could. One end of the board came up. I grabbed it and twisted, using my body, and with more effort, the three foot board popped out.

The first thing I did was to put my face down where the board had been and breathe better air. With a quick hit of clean air, I pulled at both adjacent boards. Neither one moved. But I took the board I'd pulled up and inserted it in the space that I'd created. I stood up and stepped on it hard, near where the fulcrum was, using it as a lever to force up the edge of one of the adjacent boards. With both hands tied I was clumsy and scraped my hands and legs on a couple of nails coming out of the board I'd removed. But after I stamped on the free board twice, the edge of the board in the floor came up a little. I took the board I'd pulled out and hammered the end of it against the raised edge of the board still nailed down. The board twisted up some. I felt where it was, crawled across from it, took both feet and pushed as hard as I could. The board came up with a ripping noise as the nails released.

The boards felt like they were about six inches wide.

That meant I had about a foot wide hole, too large for me to create much leverage if I tried to use one board to remove a third board. Meanwhile the flames had spread down the walls near to where I was. I slid my feet into the hole through the floor.

My feet hit the ground with my knees at about floor height. At first, I was wedged between the boards and couldn't move. But I leaned over to the side to get my waist and torso down, while simultaneously bending my legs and splaying my feet to the side. Going down, I banged my side, my chest, and my face on floorboards. But the flames spreading to the wall in front of me provided a powerful incentive to ignore a few more nicks on my face. Forcing my shoulders down and wriggling hard, I finally dropped my torso below the cabin floor into the dirt and rolled quickly out from under the floor at the back end of the cabin, the only wall not on fire.

I lay on my back in the grass for a moment. After the dark of the cabin, I felt like I could see everything clearly—other buildings, leaves on the trees, clouds moving across the sky. I was coughing, gasping for air, and breathing hard. I sat up and watched as the flames engulfed the small cabin.

With the fire and the moon coming out from behind clouds, I could see enough to recognize the large administrative building. My guess about the canteen had been right. The moon reflected weakly off the pond. Along the shore, I saw a few lights go on. The distant whine of a fire alarm started up. Out of breath and weary, I lay back down. This was the second straight night I'd spent outdoors in Meadowbrook. Under the circumstances, I hoped it would be the last. I dearly missed my bed.

I was still lying down, listening to the wail of the

sirens approach, when I heard a woman's voice call out, "Are you all right? Hello, are you okay?"

I saw the beam of a flashlight play over me and I sat up.

"Thank God you're all right," she said, "I saw the fire and called the fire department, they'll—Dan, Dan Kardon? Is that you? Are you hurt?"

"Yes, Linda, it's me." My voice was full of croaks and wheezes, and my throat was dry and hurt, but I could talk. "I'm okay. Something of a smoked sausage, but happily not a crispy critter."

"What happened to you?"

"Tell you later. Here come the firemen. I've got to get them to cut the rope on my arms."

A couple of firefighters came over. One of them cut the ropes while the others went about extinguishing the fire. They asked if there were any other people in the cabin. I told them I was okay and gave them a brief description of what had happened. The fire was quickly doused, so they hung around for a while, inspecting the woods and the other buildings. They were perfectly happy with the evening—a nice diversion from a quiet night in the firehouse, a good story for their friends and families, but no risk.

Somebody would have to decide tomorrow whether to investigate the cause of the fire formally, given my story. Since the canteen had no real value, there would be no insurance claim. And I couldn't help them pin a criminal charge on anybody. Happily for me too there were no injuries. The investigation, if any, would be perfunctory.

A few moments later, a police car pulled up alongside the fire truck. Lieutenant DeRosa stepped out from the car.

"When I heard from our fire boys you showed up at this weinie roast," he said. "I had to take the call. My house is just across the way. You want to tell me what happened?"

I walked away from Linda Redmond and told him the story. He asked good questions and figured out pretty quickly that I couldn't give him any information that would help identify my attackers.

"You had a similar problem at a nearby restaurant, I heard. Couldn't find those guys either. Whatever you're doing, I'd say you're not making friends around here," DeRosa said.

"Yeah, I can see that."

"Looks to me like you're making somebody pretty damn nervous. You want to tell me whatever you got that I don't know about?"

I thought about it for a minute and then shook my head. "I've told you what I know. I don't have anything new and I don't have a clue about what I've got that has people pissed off."

DeRosa looked at me for a moment. "Okay, tough guy, have it your way." He walked away to talk to the officer in charge of the fire squad.

Linda Redmond walked back over to me. "How are you doing? Do you have a car here? Can you even drive?"

I laughed, a nervous one even to my ears, and patted my pockets. "I've got the keys and my wallet, amazingly enough. But the car's not here and I'm not sure what I'd do with it if I had it. I'll see if I can catch a ride into town with the police."

"You can come back to my place now if you want, it's just a short walk."

"No, it's okay, I need to grab some extra clothes."

"Look, the police and firemen will be here for a while. I've got some old things a friend left behind. I think they'll fit. Why don't you come along? I'll get you something to drink and you can get some sleep and head into Boston in the morning."

I didn't have the energy to argue with her. She walked over and talked to DeRosa. He nodded, spoke to her briefly, and turned back to talking with the firemen.

"He said he just wants you to stop by the station in the morning and give them a statement. Come on this way."

We walked back around the pond toward her house. At one point, I stopped and looked back. The frame and base of the canteen still sparked and glowed in spots. The scene looked far more benign than the blaze in my memory but it still had a magnetic beauty in the dark.

The fire diminished altogether as we moved along the shore, but the smoke odor didn't dissipate. When we got to Redmond's house, she led me straight to the bathroom and gave me a large plastic bag. "Dump your clothes in there," she said. "There's no detergent that'll get rid of that smoke odor. Here's some other stuff."

She was right. Some friend of hers about my size had left everything I needed. I didn't make a wisecrack about it but gratefully took it instead and stepped in for the longest shower of my life. When I emerged, wearing a tee-shirt and shorts for pajamas, I still smelled of smoke. Only more serious scrubbing and shaving my head bald would get rid of the smell entirely. But at least I had washed away some of the ash, dirt, sweat, adrenaline, and fear.

Redmond had lemonade and cookies waiting for me on the table in the kitchen. I swallowed the glass of lemonade without a break and she filled up the glass again.

"Thanks," I said. "Guess the least I can do is tell you the story." So I did, including telling her about my visit to her aunt. Since my car was in the parking lot at the nursing home, I didn't see a way around it.

I wanted to see how she reacted, to know what she was thinking. But as I listened to one of her questions, I felt my eyes close and my head drop for an instant. I caught myself and straightened up but Redmond had seen it.

"Okay, enough for now," she said.

"Sorry, I guess I'm a bit tired."

"I'm not surprised, you've been a busy boy. Come on, I'll show you to your room."

She led me upstairs into a room with a couple of bookshelves, an armchair, and a double bed.

"Looks great to me," I said.

"You know," she said with a smile, "it's been a long time since I've had a good-looking man alone in the house. If you hadn't had me talk to your Jenny, I might be tempted to take advantage of you."

"Thought you preferred girls."

"Mostly yes, but I make exceptions."

"First, if you ever called her 'my Jenny' to her face, she'd probably give you a right to the chin. Second, the way I smell and look, the shape I'm in, I can't think of any advantage you could take of me right now, but thanks for making me feel better."

Linda laughed a little and closed the door. I thought about Jenny for a moment. It felt like forever since I'd had a good, long talk with her, let alone held her. I lay

down on the bed, recalling that I'd thought about Jenny
at the bleakest moments in the cabin, when I wasn't sure
how to get out. I struggled to remember just what those
thoughts were, then I struggled no more.

CHAPTER———

NINETEEN

Light was streaming in the bedroom window when I awoke. It took me a moment to get my bearings, but a quick whiff of smoke and a cough brought things back quickly. I heard either a radio or television downstairs. There was, though, a new towel piled invitingly by some clean clothes. I took another shower, scrubbing my hair even harder, and put on the blue polo shirt and khakis left for me. I still had to wear the running shoes from the night before and it was pretty obvious that those would be trashed when I got home.

I walked downstairs around eleven A.M., according to my watch. Linda Redmond was sitting in the living room reading the paper when I came down.

"Morning," I wheezed. My throat still ached and my voice was raspy.

"Good morning. Everything okay?" she said.

"Must have been. I don't remember a thing after getting into bed. Thanks for the clothes, they're just about right."

"They look better on you than they did on him," she said, and then directed me into the kitchen, where she had assembled juice, fruit, muffins, and bagels for breakfast. Though anxious to get moving, I ate a little of everything. We talked more about the events of the evening. News of the fire had already spread throughout the town, with all sorts of wild rumors and speculation attached. Redmond had already received a bunch of phone calls. We laughed at some of the stories Redmond had heard. But neither of us laughed when she asked me if I had any idea who had hijacked me and then tried to burn me to death. I said no.

A short time later, Redmond drove me over to the nursing home so I could get my car. I thanked her, told her I'd be in touch.

"And I'll send the clothes back," I said.

"Bring them yourself. Then you can tell Aunt May and me how things work out."

"Somehow, in this town, I expect you'll learn all about it before I do."

"That's okay, we'll be happy to hear your side of it. Take care, and say hello to Jenny for me. Tell her she was right. And lucky."

I watched her walk into the nursing home to visit with her aunt. She wore dark blue slacks and a white polo shirt that set off her tan, and everything else, beautifully. Her aunt was the fortunate one, as would be the person Linda chose, if any, to settle down with. But Linda, too, was fortunate. I'd had a moment to watch her when I came down to the living room from the upstairs bedroom. She looked perfectly at ease and at peace in a living room that no one in L.A. could ever conceive. Whatever she hadn't found in California, she'd discovered something good when she returned to Meadowbrook. I made a note to make sure I never checked out one of her videos.

I stopped at the police station and gave them my report of what had happened. They had uncovered nothing helpful at the site or elsewhere in the vicinity. Nobody

visiting the nursing home reported seeing the men pull
me into a vehicle. There was no evidence at the now
destroyed canteen that would help identify anybody.
With Wells and Jerome Mann dead, I could tell they
weren't taking the incident lightly. But I could also tell
that the fire had already been categorized as one that
would never be solved.

While I was at the police station, I looked up a Meadowbrook address. Before heading back to Boston, I
drove a roundabout route to make a quick stop.

I'd had a little time to think about things. It seemed
logical that Sheehan was behind the attack and the arson.
I hadn't seen or heard much from my assailants last
night, but what I'd experienced put them in a very different league than Tom Jordan and his boys who jumped
me at the restaurant. Even if Jordan was involved last
night, he was following someone else's orders. Sheehan
was a planner. Jordan was not.

Further, Sheehan had an awful lot at stake. As a small-
time politician, he faced losing credibility with everybody. If the water level stayed down, many
Meadowbrook citizens would be pissed at him and he'd
cost the town plenty of tax revenues. At the same time,
if he caved in to Daryl, he'd look bad to other town
officials who had followed his lead in staking out a very
public, hardline position. Similarly, for Sheehan as a
broker, the lower pond level would continue to drive
down the prices of the houses he listed in the area, hurting both his income and his stature among prospective
sellers.

And finally, Sheehan could be both the broker and the
developer of the new homes going in at the site owned
by Echo Pond Shores Realty Trust, the site where Jordan
owned a house. In Massachusetts, with a nominal trust

owning the properties until homes were built and title transferred to new buyers, the owner of the beneficial interest in the nominal trust—the one who got the money when the property sold—would not be identified anywhere publicly. Sheehan worked with Wells on other developments, he was the broker on this one, so there was a pretty good chance he was behind the trust. His motives, when stacked against the others, stood much higher.

For example, I didn't see Stephanie Williams and her boy toy pulling off murder, hijacking, and arson without leaving a nice bright trail. After all, they'd bungled the handling of defenseless turtles. Jordan also had strong motives, but this seemed beyond him, as well. Besides, I was pretty sure that Daryl and I had managed to scare him off. Granger, I knew little about, but I could probably find out if he'd been gambling elsewhere last night, a Friday night.

I even thought about Linda Redmond. I still had no corroboration of much of her story. Neither of my assailants the night before had been Redmond, I knew that. But that didn't mean she wasn't participating in some way.

With all of that in mind, I decided to stop by Sheehan's home, like I had Jordan's. Probably it would just rile him, but maybe seeing me unexpectedly, and perhaps after he tried to kill me, would jar something loose.

Sheehan lived on a large lot in a big, boring, and bland Colonial executive home. There were two cars in the driveway so I decided to give it a try. I could have called, but for my purposes, I wanted to see his face, check him out personally when he spoke to me.

I rang the doorbell. The door opened and Sheehan

stood in front of me in brown pants and a tan sweater.

"Morning, Mr. Sheehan. Nice day to be alive."

Emotions played across Sheehan's face. Surprise, anger, confusion all showed in the head snapping back, the sharp intake of breath, the narrowing of his eyes, the tight set of his mouth, and the arms he brought tightly across his chest. I willed myself to stay silent.

Finally Sheehan spoke. "From what I've heard, you had a rough night. What do you want?"

"A quick piece of business."

"What?"

"We want to know where you stand on the camp. Ready to negotiate yet or is the board keeping its head in the sand—or mud, perhaps?"

"When the board decides to change its position, I'll let you know. If you hear nothing, you can assume the board will stick with its decision. But it should be pretty obvious to you and Mann that, whatever you think of the board, this community simply will not accept another camp on the pond. Even if you get a permit, no camp will succeed there. Just operate the golf course, leave the camp property for some other use, that's what we want."

"Fine, I'll take your message back to Daryl. But you should tell the kids in town not to plan on swimming lessons at the beach. And one more thing. If I find out you were in on what happened to me last night, you'll be a most unhappy camper. You'll be selling berths in prison cells, not prime real estate."

"Don't threaten me. I don't know what you're talking about, I wasn't involved with any of it, though if it'll drive you out of town, I won't be unhappy."

"With all your commissions out there and property values falling, you have more to lose than anybody else. And I know you're connected to the Echo Pond Shores development and to Wells. I'm digging for the rest of it."

"Kardon, if you're accusing me of murder, you're way off base. Go see a doctor. Smoke inhalation can be a real serious problem. I had nothing to do with what happened to Wells, to Mann, to you. High water, low water, it's not a big deal. I control so much real estate and have so many deals going on, I'll make money no matter what. I wouldn't risk all that over you and the Manns."

"Keep rehearsing your lines, Sheehan. It's not me you're going to have to convince, it'll be the district attorney and a jury. Remember, people who play with fire get burned."

"I'm going to tell you one more time, it wasn't me. And I won't sit back if you go around falsely accusing me of things I didn't do." He paused and I expected him to close the door. Instead, he looked at me for a moment.

"I'm going to try to ignore your outrageous comments for a moment to make one last attempt to resolve things. As long as you're here, I'd like you to convey a different offer to Mr. Mann."

"Better improve on the last ones."

"Tell him I've had a number of people and companies contact me who would be interested in buying the land. I'm willing to put you together with somebody who'll buy the property at full market price so Mann and his investors can get out quickly and with the least loss, and I'll waive my fee. On a property that size, that's worth a hell of a lot."

I smiled. "I've got to hand it to you, Sheehan, you don't give up. I'll pass it on to Daryl. But he's not interested in cutting his losses right now. This isn't about money. It's about building something of value for a community and for kids. It was Jerome's dream and

Daryl wants to make it happen. Adding a few zeroes to your offer doesn't change it, Sheehan."

Driving away, I thought about the encounter. I had really hoped the board might be coming around. At some point the threat of having a permanent swamp instead of a pond had to make an impact. At the same time, Sheehan's not-so-subtle point was valid and one Daryl had to consider. What price or consequence was too much for the camp? We weren't talking about the principles at issue in desegregating the South or busing kids to desegregate the Boston schools. We were talking about a few weeks of sunshine and swimming for a small number of kids. If the community wouldn't tolerate it, how much more suffering should there be? Should we risk another death? How many more buildings would go up in flames? My bravado was fine, but I wouldn't be there to protect the camp or the kids. In fact, thus far I'd done a lousy job of protecting Jerome and myself.

And Sheehan's speech about his motives also contained at least a grain of truth. Sheehan would make money, no matter what. Even his offer at the end reflected that. If he put together a deal that Daryl went for, it would cost Sheehan nothing and raise the value of his properties. I'd left my meeting with Jordan more certain I'd been right about him. I couldn't say the same for my encounter with Sheehan.

Finally back at home, feeling stiff and sore from the activities of the previous two nights, I went for a long, slow walk. I stopped in at the Steiners' and Mike perked up. The Red Sox were winning on television, with a rookie pitching a three-hitter for them through six innings. The hurler for the White Sox was also pitching a three-hitter. Mike decided to skip the rest of the game, figuring that he'd rather come back and have the happy surprise of a Red Sox win than stay to view the more likely loss.

It was a bright, sunny Saturday afternoon. Coolidge Corner was choked with traffic as well as pedestrians doing errands and finding companionship in coffee shops and fast food restaurants. Mike had much to tell me about his summer plans and the Boston sports scene. Mostly I just listened. My night in the dark, almost surrounded by fire, had seared more than my clothes and hair. The orange flames, seen through seams and holes in the walls, seemed to intermittently burst into my vision even as I walked with Mike. I'd shake my head, or look hard at something right in front of me, and the flames would go away . . . for a little while.

But the flames seemed to have melted away things too—so many small things I needed to do for work, or the house, or the car. All the things that I'd promised to people that I now didn't have time for, all those things that disrupt the normal flow of life. It felt like the flames left standing only the things that most mattered.

One of which was that I was still walking, though slowly. I was glad, too, that I'd walk in the office on Monday and have some decent work to do and good people to work with. And I wanted to call Jenny, to hear her laugh or cry, whatever she needed to do, and to tell her that the flames had not burned away her picture in my mind, the memory of her scent, the secret thrill I still felt at her touch, or the delight I took in her smile.

On the way back, we stopped and bought a soda for Mike. We walked over to a Little League game. I held the cup as Mike drank from the straw. He cheered for a couple of his friends on one of the teams. He didn't once comment on the unfairness that an eleven-year-old boy was a captive on the sidelines, unable to get into a baseball game. I knew he had times when he felt isolated from his often insensitive friends and angry at his limitations, but this afternoon was not one of them and I was happy to share it with him.

That night, I called Jenny at about 9:30, figuring her parents would be asleep by that time. She picked it up, said hello, and I felt a catch in my throat as I replied.

"Dan, are you okay?" Her voice had a funny catch of its own.

"Yeah, I'm . . . I'm fine," I said. "I'm sorry I didn't call you back last night."

"I tried you a few times last night, then at the office today. I guess you never made it home after we talked."

"Jenny, you're right, I didn't get home, I ended up at Linda Redmond's after—"

"You don't have to explain. You don't owe me anything."

"Don't owe you anything? What are you talking about?"

"You just told me you never made it home from Linda Redmond's. What really pisses me off is, I can't believe you had me talk to her, then you slept with her. Makes me look pretty foolish, don't you think? Or is that what you wanted? You want to sleep with somebody else, you might at least have the decency of not flaunting it in my face. I'm—"

"Whoa, whoa, will you cut it out? I never said I slept with Redmond, because I didn't. If you give me a chance, I'll explain."

The line was silent.

"I could have slept with her, I suppose," I said, "except for three things. First, she's bisexual but prefers girls to boys, which is definitely a scene I'm not into. Second, I had a little mishap earlier in the evening when I had to escape out of a burning cabin at the camp, which left me just a little out of shape for sexual escapades. And third, while I was on the way to becoming lawyer flambé in the cabin, thinking I wasn't going to get out of there, I had a few thoughts about how much I missed you. All that kinda put a damper on the evening. Linda Redmond found me when I got out of the cabin, she took me to her house, and I went to bed. Alone."

There was only silence for a moment, then her voice came back, this time more strained and halting.

"Oh, Dan, I'm sorry, I . . . I guess I got a little crazy, over the top, when I couldn't reach you. I just latched on to what I thought was the worst-case scenario. But what you're telling me—that's much worse, just horrible. I feel so bad about how I reacted, but I got so scared and angry all at once, and things have been hard here, and—"

"Hey, it's okay, you don't need to explain."

"I'm so, so sorry. But what happened? Are you okay?"

So I told her about Linda Redmond and the fire. Or tried to, anyway.

"So you're not hurt?" she asked.

"No, but I'll probably pass on cooking on the grill tomorrow."

"Will you please stop that bullshit, at least with me? I'm not interested in hearing jokes, I want to know how you are."

I hesitated. "I'm fine, I really am. And lucky, real lucky. I know that."

"You sure are. How you keep coming through these things, I don't know."

"I meant that I'm lucky in other ways, I think the whole thing helped me see that. Kind of got me to focus. I'm sorry we haven't talked in the last few days and I'm sorry I haven't gotten to Tennessee to spend some time with you, help you out. But I'm awfully happy to have you in my life."

She was quiet for a moment, then went through some tears and laughter all together. We talked for a long time about her, and her parents, and the slow progress they were making. We talked about how much we wanted to see each other, how much we could each use a hug. I told her I hoped to get down there the next weekend, but I could tell she didn't completely believe it. "Why do I think something will come up?" she said.

Finally, she asked me to go back over all that had happened in Meadowbrook before the fire. Even with all the emotional roiling, she had the instincts and desires to be a damn good lawyer. I went back over everything with her. She asked pointed and incisive questions that helped me sort things out.

So much had happened, so quickly. I'd been focusing on the cabin and the fire. But as I talked about what had occurred with Stephanie Williams, the meeting with Gloria Duchesne, what I'd learned about the private eye, then finally the fire and the confrontation with Sheehan, I could feel my brain getting back in gear. We still needed the approval for Daryl's camp. I also wanted to see Sheehan, or whoever it was, behind bars for trying to kill me and killing Wells and Jerome Mann. Jenny, of course, saw it a little differently.

"I just wish," she said, "I was in Boston and could help you. But I'm worried, too. You're turning this into a crusade."

"Hey, it's no crusade, I'm just helping Daryl."

"Yeah, and Michael Jordan was just another basketball player."

"That's not fair. Daryl's getting screwed out in Meadowbrook. The golf course will be back on track. Now I just want to see what we can do about the camp. It's not like I'm making any of this stuff up."

"I know that, but won't you acknowledge that some of this is knight errant Dan Kardon, tilting at windmills?"

I sighed. "Okay, I won't argue the point. But some of these things that I keep thinking are windmills keep tilting back."

We talked awhile longer, until I heard a hint of laughter and lightness in her voice. After we said goodbye, I was even more hoarse. I medicated myself first with a Red Hook beer and then with a pint of Wavy Gravy ice cream, then went to bed. Not even a late-night baseball game could keep me up.

I woke to the phone ringing. I glanced at the clock—nine a.m. precisely—as I reached for the phone.

"Don't move from that house," a voice said. "I'll be there in ten minutes."

"Make it twenty, I got three women to make happy first," I said to Lt. Col. Randy Blocker of the State Police.

"You're trying to make 'em happy in seven minutes each, I understand why you're still single and Jenny's in Tennessee."

"You wouldn't believe what I can do with those seven minutes. It's Sunday—what's up?"

"What's up? I'm checking some messages, having a nice muffin and coffee, and what do I hear? You again, in the middle of a hijacking, arson, attempted murder.

And you didn't even call me. So now I'm coming over to arrest you."

"For what?"

"Hurting the feelings of an officer. Making me miss church."

"I hope you're bringing some of that coffee."

"And bagels and doughnuts. I know I can't eat the shit you got in your kitchen."

Marcia Ball was playing and singing some Texas blues on the stereo when Randy came in. As promised, he had food. After he gave me a critical visual inspection and found no parts missing, we sat down and talked and ate. I went back over the things I'd discussed with Jenny, but in less detail. I described the meetings Linda Redmond scheduled with Jerome, but not the blackmail. When I was done talking, he was finished eating and I hadn't started.

"Let's see," he said, "I've heard about Williams, Sheehan, Jordan, Redmond, and Granger so far, but you're tilting toward Sheehan as the guy behind things. Two guys jumped you the other night—you think he was one of the pair?"

I thought back for a moment and then shook my head. "You want an honest answer, I don't know. I don't remember anything familiar about the guys who jumped me at the nursing home."

"You sure it was two guys?"

"You mean instead of one?"

"Instead of one, three, whatever. Or instead of one guy and one woman."

I thought about it. "Yeah, I'm pretty sure it was two guys."

"But you can't identify anything about 'em."

I shook my head slowly.

"No idea who was involved? Did the pair talk? Did it look like they'd worked together a lot?"

"They didn't say much. But I do have an idea about one of them," I said. "I just can't tell you where the information is coming from."

Randy rolled his eyes upward. "Lord give me strength," he said. "I'm here trying to help and you're holding out on me."

"Sorry, no can tell," I said. "You don't want to hear it, that's okay."

Randy gave something between a snort and a moan. "All right, just give me the name."

"Henry Werner, a former private investigator."

Randy looked away for a moment, seemingly concentrating on a far wall. "Hold on," he said after a minute. "Got somebody to call."

He went into the kitchen and came back about five minutes later. "He's a scumbag. Lost his P.I. license about five years ago due to a couple of little things like getting nailed for cocaine possession and theft. Guy I talked to said Werner still seems to work as an investigator, but the guy doesn't trust him. Said that nothing would surprise him about Werner, that he's always looking for a score. Now, you want to tell me if I can do anything with all this?"

"I don't know. Werner's name's came up. I think he's involved, but I'm not sure where or how."

"You think he was one of the guys that threw you into the burning cabin the other night?"

"Could be. He's connected to a couple of people in this mess."

Randy just shook his head.

"I've got a question for you," I said. "I talked with DeRosa, one of the Meadowbrook cops, earlier this week. He wouldn't tell me, but something's linking the Wells and Mann killings. Can you tell me what it is?"

Randy was silent for a moment. "I guess so. Can't see any harm in it. We recovered the gun, an older thirty-eight, somebody used to kill Jerome Mann. A couple of teenagers wandering around golf course found it in the woods, under some brush, just a few days ago."

"Any usable prints on it?"

"Nope. Wiped clean."

"You traced it? Who did it belong to?"

"Wells."

I leaned back in my chair. "I'll be damned. But Wells was killed when somebody whacked him in the head with a baseball bat."

"Yeah. Somebody clobbered him, then he hit the other side of his head on furniture on the way down, and the combination got him."

"So how does the gun figure in?"

"We figure that whoever killed Wells messed the place up to make it look like robbery, or maybe to cover up something they wanted to take. Drugs, money, files, who knows? Maybe they went through the desk, found the gun, and took it. Then the guy wants to knock off Jerome, he realizes that's a good gun to use."

"That one of the reasons you cleared Daryl?"

"Yeah. He was never high on the list. But with the gun, it nails the connection between Wells and Mann, so we're looking at people from Meadowbrook."

An electronic alarm went off. Randy looked at his belt and pulled out a beeper. He grabbed the phone again.

"It's Blocker," he said into the mouthpiece. He listened for about a minute.

"On my way," he said into the phone.

"Gotta go," he said. "We got more to talk about, but

it'll have to be later. You be damned careful. We're starting to figure this thing out, but meanwhile somebody wants your ass dead. You keep it up, you might just give it to 'em."

After Randy left, I did some things around the house and returned some calls that had come in over the last few days while I'd been out in Meadowbrook. One was from David Granger. He had called both the house and the office on Friday. Just checking to see where things stood, he said, because his commercial client continued to have a strong interest in buying some or all of the land on the lake. I could call him on Monday, he said. He'd be gone over the weekend. I looked at the phone and wondered whether he'd delayed his weekend gambling junket until after he set fire to the canteen with me in it. But all I had against Granger was an assortment of potential motives and speculation.

For a while, I spun out different theories. It gave me nothing definitive to tell Daryl. I also realized, with a start, that I hadn't talked to him since Friday and he might not even know about the canteen. I called and left a message for him asking him to call me.

It was around noon when my phone rang. I picked it up, thinking it might be Daryl. Instead, Al Thompson said hello, then invited me down for the afternoon to fish on Buzzards Bay in his boat, now back in Wettamesett harbor.

"After the other night," I said, "being around a lot of water sounds pretty good right now, but I've got too much to catch up on here."

"What do you mean the other night? I talked with you Friday after the turtle thing—that what you mean?"

"No, sorry, things have been moving so fast I can't remember who I've told what." I went on to tell him about the fire. I also told him what I'd learned about Henry Werner, the private detective.

"So my next move is to go to Werner," I said, "to see if he'll tell me anything about what the hell's going on."

"Can't imagine he'll talk much, but, yeah, you need to figure out what his involvement is. Sounds like he might be a bit nasty and not too happy to see you. You want me to come with you?"

I paused. My normal response would have been, no thanks. But things were not normal. "Sure," I said.

We arranged that Al would call Werner and try to set up a meeting for first thing Tuesday morning at Werner's office in Waltham. If that time worked, Al and I would meet at a nearby restaurant for breakfast first.

Al went off to fish. I went to the refrigerator and pulled out a beer, and sat down in front of television with a turkey sandwich and potato chips. When I finished lunch, I flipped channels between golf, baseball, and tennis until I closed my eyes for a quick rest.

When I awoke to a ringing phone, the six o'clock news was just finishing and the Red Sox had won another game from the Angels. It took me a moment to clear my head and remember how I'd ended up asleep on the sofa. When I played my phone messages, I discovered Daryl's call was the one that woke me.

I called him back. He sounded tired, more down than I expected given the good news on the golf course front. I told him about the gun linking the killings of Wells and Jerome. When I told him about the fire, he asked a lot of questions. Rich Grant, the golf course superintendent, had called him about the fire, but he wanted the details. He was quiet for a moment after I described how I wormed out of the canteen.

"I know I said I wanted to see the camp through, make it a memorial to Jerome and all, but it's not worth more people dying over it. And we sure as hell can't have security out there the whole time to keep people from destroying the place," Daryl said.

"I know. But my sense is the police feel like they're making progress. We've narrowed the field, at least."

"But if police find out who did this, and nobody else is injured, we still need to get a permit."

"Yeah, but this kind of violence looks bad, probably will get a lot of publicity. Maybe the board will change its mind."

He paused and I heard nothing for a moment. "Got another problem," he finally said.

"A letter?" I asked, my stomach clenching.

"How'd you know?"

"Shit. I've been afraid of it since Werner took your trash the other night. I thought if he found anything he might want to act on it right away. What's the letter say?"

"I'm supposed to pay a hundred grand immediately, in cash, and he wants me to drop the request for a permit. Otherwise, copies of magazines and letters go to the Shamrocks, the papers, all over the place."

"How are you supposed to pay?"

"Letter came on Saturday. Says I should have the money in cash by Tuesday or Wednesday morning. I'll get a phone call Tuesday night telling me where to deliver it Wednesday night. Any hint the cops are involved, he won't pick up the money and he'll release the information."

"He enclose a copy of anything from the trash?"

"Nope, but he gave the name of the guy who wrote the letters I threw out. It's legit."

"You got a fax machine at your place?"

"Yeah."

"Can you fax me a copy of the letter tonight? The number is 429-3522."

"Okay."

"Daryl, I'm sorry, this really sucks. This project is like a deadly virus—anybody who touches it is getting killed or hurt somehow." We were both silent for a moment.

"You decided what to do?" I asked.

"Nah. The money's not the big thing, I can get that no problem, but damn, it feels dirty, cowardly to give in, after Jerome getting killed, now you getting attacked."

"Yeah, well, neither Jerome nor I would be plastered all over *Sports Illustrated* or *People* if the letters come out. It's your decision. What happened to Jerome or me doesn't matter, except we know that somebody out there plays rough."

"I know I don't want to call the cops. That's no different from stiffing the guy, 'cause I'd have to show the cops the letter. So either I pay or I call the guy's bluff and hope nobody pays attention if he sends stuff out. Or maybe I pay, but go ahead with the permit and the guy doesn't really care about the permit and he walks. You think I should pay?"

"Daryl, this one's all yours. I can't tell you what to do. I'll help any way I can. You want to talk it through, you want me to participate somehow, fine. This kind of blackmail's tough, 'cause you won't have a guarantee that the son of a bitch won't do or say something even if you pay. But no way am I telling you what I think— whatever the consequences are, you're the one who lives with them, not me."

"Yeah, don't I know it. And just so you know, I'm

starting to get some other heat about the camp."

"Who's putting the pressure on?"

"Apparently some of the town officials have bitched to state officials, so some state senator called me as well as a guy from an environmental agency. The team's asked me about it too."

"The Shamrocks are getting involved?"

"Not so far, they just asked me what was going on. They know better than to push me. But I gather some of these political types are contacting them as well. I also got a call from a *Boston Globe* reporter. The message said she was doing a story for a Sunday edition, maybe this week or next."

"You're getting to be high profile."

"Bad news, man, bad news. This asshole releases the stuff to the right people now, the story'll get bigger real fast. Any bright ideas about these officials calling me?"

"Can you stall 'em for a bit, have your agent call them, see what they want and tell them you'll get back to them shortly?"

"My agent doesn't know squat about what's going on. I haven't told him too much about the camp, and I sure as hell don't want to tell him about this other stuff. I'd rather have you make the calls."

"All right, I'll call, give them some general bullshit, and put them off for a few days. But you can also declare victory and walk away from everything if this is getting to be too much of a circus for you."

"No, man. I got to decide about this scumbag and the hundred grand first. For the moment let's hang in there, see what happens. If people outside are starting to talk to me, they got to be going after the town as well. Maybe that fire you were in will wake people up. I just wish I knew why the camp's such a big deal, why Jerome died, why they went after you—even if the town's full of racists, this stuff is pretty far out."

"Yeah, I can understand that. Most of the time, you want to solve a case. Here, we got a bunch of things that happened, but we sure as hell don't know who was involved, what the connections are, or what people are really after. So maybe we need to focus more on why, on how things are related."

Daryl sighed. "Okay. I talked to Fred Bender. He's put together the information on the businesses you and I talked about, so I got decisions to make. Most of the properties look good and we can probably sell them pretty quick."

"Sounds good. With all this pressure on you, you're still dealing with the business issues. Careful, you're starting to sound like Jerome, a real executive."

Daryl gave a little chuckle. "Yeah, only peace and quiet I get these days is working out in the gym. But the more time I put into the business crap, the more my jump shot looks like an executive's too. Okay, man, stay cool. I'll talk to you tomorrow night, tell you what I decide about paying the money."

CHAPTER————————

TWENTY

D aryl didn't have to tell me what he was going to do. He'd pay the money. It would eliminate one more mine in a field of them that Daryl was now walking through. At the moment, Daryl didn't have the heart to do anything but acquiesce, at least in terms of the money. But if he pursued one option, giving the money but not pulling the permit, where would that leave him? Out the money and also outed? Or would the blackmailer hold off, figuring he still had some leverage to play with?

In a few moments, I heard the ring of my fax machine. I walked over and picked up the letter Daryl had faxed over.

Dear Daryl Faggot Mann,

If you don't want your loyal fans, the Shamrocks, the Boston Globe, and the Boston Herald to know you're queer, get together $100,000 in cash by Wednesday morning. I'll call you by Tuesday night at your home (yes, cocksucker, I know your un-listed home number) and tell you how to deliver the cash to me Wednesday night. As soon as I have the cash, I'll destroy all the papers I have—you'll

330

*have to trust me on that. And withdraw your re-
quest for a permit for the camp in Meadowbrook.*

A basketball fan

*P.S. Say hello to your buddy Phil Brown for me—
bet he's got a cute butt.*

I dropped the letter on the table and walked over to
the window. The style of this letter was not at all like
the letter Linda Redmond had received, but that proved
nothing. If it was the same person, a different style letter
and different payment mechanism could be a deliberate
ruse to confuse an investigator. As well, Daryl's blackmailer seemed more interested in cash than the permit;
could the same person be blackmailing Linda and Daryl
and also be the killer of Jerome and Wells?

That evening, over a Foster's beer and a tuna sandwich, I sat down with a pen and a pad. I hoped to outline
the information I had along with a rational plan for dealing with the town over the camp and finding the bad
guys in Meadowbrook. After half an hour, I looked
down at the pad and saw only a series of doodles. Un-
answered questions, many of them unconnected, kept
swirling around in my brain.

Did Jerome have a meeting set up at the golf clubhouse with somebody else after he was scheduled to
meet with Linda Redmond, a meeting he never put in
his calendar? How about Stephanie Williams, who
clearly wanted the golf course and camp stopped? She
denied killing anybody, but could she have worked with
others to protect the land by killing both Wells and Jerome? Granger had been fine with me but was he black-

mailing his one-time girlfriend who now avoided him? And if so, would he have also killed Wells and Jerome? And if Granger wasn't behind the blackmail, who was? Tom Jordan didn't want the camp in his neighborhood and Sheehan had money at stake. How far would they go to protect their interests?

I opened another beer but that didn't help me figure it out. More doodles appeared on the note pad but no notes.

When Jenny called, she was in a better mood. Other family members had helped out during the day, so Jenny had gotten in a long walk, a swim, and had seen a movie with an old high school friend. She sounded better than I'd heard her lately so when she asked if there was anything new, I said no. There was no need to tell her about Daryl's situation yet. I told her I still planned to be with her for the next weekend.

Afterward, I sat down with chocolate chip cookies in front of a late night James Bond movie from the 1960s. Bond, played with duende by a young Sean Connery, got into and out of scrapes with nary a thought about the consequences of people dying around him. I wondered about the people I was now dealing with. Linda Redmond, George Sheehan, Tom Jordan, David Granger, Roger Vaneck, Stephanie Williams, whether victims or perpetrators, how were they feeling as violence became the norm in their peaceful town?

Most of all I reflected on Daryl, assailed from so many sides yet without Jerome, the one man he'd leaned on in the past. This time, Daryl couldn't simply play better defense, rebound, and run harder. How would he hold up to the flood of trials and tribulations engulfing the too-shallow Echo Pond and anybody near it?

* * *

Monday night as promised, Daryl called. He said he'd decided to pay the money. I didn't press him on it. His voice was low, his speech tentative and without affect. I hung up and reflected on the blackmail letter. Daryl was buying only a temporary reprieve. Maybe the blackmailer wouldn't come back for more, but the chances of the blackmailer destroying the material were pretty small. Time was getting short for Daryl's secret, I thought.

In the meantime, I had my own problem to deal with. I hadn't told Daryl that Al Thompson and I planned to meet with Werner the next morning. I went back and forth on it, even trying to figure out if I had an ethical obligation to let him know. But Daryl never asked what I was doing, I had no proof of Werner's involvement, and we'd set up the Werner meeting before the letter to Daryl arrived, so I decided not to say anything. I thought Al and I could meet with Werner, make clear we knew that Werner had worked for Wells, and that we were following some leads regarding the murders of Wells and Jerome. I wanted to warn Werner off doing anything to Daryl without actually confronting him about the blackmail. It was ticklish—I didn't want to scare Werner off, then have him retaliate by mailing out word of Daryl's homosexuality to the world.

I didn't know Werner at all and we had to be careful how we played him. Some people you negotiate with, it's best to leave them a way out because they're okay until you put their backs to the wall. Others, you get the chance, you have to squash them like bugs.

On Tuesday morning, Al and I met around eight in a restaurant just off Route 128. I brought Al up to date, leaving him shaking his head. We agreed on how we'd approach Werner and talked over various scenarios.

Werner had an office in a peculiar old wooden house set between a major street and a small, seldom-used side street. Next to the building was a small parking lot so that Werner's office sat as something of an island in a sea of traffic. The buildings around it were all commercial—in a quick glance I took in a convenience store, a dry cleaner, a beauty salon, and a pizza parlor.

I parked on the main street near the door to the wooden house, which had been converted to two offices. One office had a sign for a chiropractor and the other one housed Werner's office. Paint peeled off spots on the siding. A length of gutter was missing. Three or four windows showed corrosion from aging storm windows.

Al and I tried to enter the front door. It was locked and ringing a buzzer at the side of the door brought no response. I took a look through a small window in the middle of the door but could see nothing.

After about a five minute wait with no sign of Werner, we got antsy. We walked through the empty parking lot and around to the back of the building, where a door opened to the side street. Parked on the side street not far from the door was the same late-model Chrysler New Yorker I'd seen at Daryl's. The driver's side window, closest to the building, had been smashed. Small pieces of glass still stood in the bottom corners of the window and shards of glass on the ground below the window reflected the rising sun.

We walked over and looked inside the car. The front seat and floor were covered with more glass. Papers and documents lay strewn about. I recognized pleadings from court cases, but none of the documents I saw involved Daryl. A couple of manilla file folders sat on the car floor. The glove compartment was open and items from it were on the floor. It looked like somebody had picked the car up, shaken it until everything was tossed out of its normal place, then put the car back down.

After surveying the car, Al and I went over to the back door of the building. White curtains stood behind four small windowpanes in the center of the door. As we got closer, my shoe crunched on some glass and I could see that one of the windowpanes had been broken. The door was closed but when I grabbed the doorknob and pushed, the door opened.

Al grabbed my forearm. "You want to call the cops? I'll get the cell phone from the car."

"I'd rather go in first, see what we find. Maybe Werner's injured inside."

"Don't touch anything, Dan—we're walking into a crime scene here."

"I know. But anything we can find might make a big difference."

Al thought for a minute. "Tell you what," he said. "Let me get the phone. If need be, we can call from inside without using the office phone."

"You sure? You don't like this, I can go without you and pick you up later, you want to take a walk."

Al shook his head no. "No, I'm in. It's funny, it's the first time I've done this without the badge or the uniform." He started to walk away, then turned back. "And Dan, be a good boy, wait there, huh? If we're going in, should be me first. We end up explaining anything to the police, they're more likely to listen to me." He was right so I waved at him to go.

I heard and saw nothing while I waited. Al came back in a couple of minutes. We went inside, slowly and quietly. In front of us was a small hallway with unmarked doors to the left and right. The only difference between them was that the one on the left was open a bit, so we walked in.

We entered the back of a workroom, which contained some file cabinets, a water cooler, a small refrigerator, and a couple of tables holding a small copier and fax machine.

"Hello?" Al called. No one answered. He called a second time and we still heard nothing.

Al, with me right behind him, walked through the workroom into a single large office. To the right were a couple more file cabinets and a door, presumably the one to the front of the building. In front of us were faded landscape prints mounted on the walls above an old brown sofa, and adjacent to it, a battered coffee table. The sofa and table had files, papers, books, and other items strewn about.

An old wooden pedestal desk sat to the left. Partially obscured behind it, on the floor, a man lay on his back wearing black pants and a green long-sleeve shirt. Al and I looked at one another, he nodded, so we approached. The man had a chest full of blood and wasn't moving. I took a deep breath and knelt down next to Al to take a closer look.

With his sallow, lined face, the thin man could have been anywhere from forty to fifty-five. At the temples, his brown hair was graying.

Sitting back on my knee, I looked around. The desk next to the body was mess, but I saw no other evidence of what happened or why.

As soon as Al felt for a pulse and confirmed the man was dead, he called the Waltham police. While we waited, I tried to look for anything helpful. I scanned a bunch of the papers on the sofa and some of the documents both on the desk and inside file drawers, without touching anything. As the sirens sounded, I conceded defeat. Documents and files were in such disarray that it would have taken hours, if not days, to find anything useful.

A handful of police cars pulled up. A large, beefy, balding cop with a florid face came in with others behind him and took charge, ordering everybody about. He directed two cops over to us and they started asking a host of questions. Al identified himself as a former police chief and explained we'd simply wanted to talk to Werner about a case. They asked him why we didn't call from outside and Al said we wanted to get inside as quick as we could to help anybody who might be injured. They listened, then told us to wait outside while they looked around.

Soon we heard more sirens, and more cops showed up. Al had established a pretty good rapport with one of our interrogators, who confirmed that the dead man was Henry Werner. He said that some of the cops knew him and none were surprised at how he died, only that it hadn't happened sooner.

We had to stick around while they took our formal statements. Two hours after the appointed hour we were supposed to meet with Werner, we left.

Al and I were both silent as we drove away. I pulled in to the parking lot of the restaurant where Al had left his car after breakfast so we could drive together to Werner's office.

"Thanks," I said. "We prepared for a bunch of scenarios, but none of them covered finding Werner dead."

"Seems like somebody's getting pretty desperate. Where you off to now?" he asked.

"The way I see it, both Wells and Werner were involved with somebody else, whether together or separately. My money's on Sheehan, but that's just an intuition. I need something to connect all these people. Right now Werner's files are a mess and we'll never get in there, so I'm going to make a couple calls and try to get some of the files Wells kept out in Meadowbrook. I'm hoping there's something that will give me an idea of who else is involved or what the purpose of all this is."

"You want me to ride shotgun on this little adventure?"

"Well, I'd love to have you come along, I can get through more paper that way, but this may be pretty boring. You've got to have better things to do. If I remember correctly, you're retired, you don't have to do this kind of stuff anymore."

"The body's retired, son, not the brain. As for boring, somehow boredom doesn't seem to be a problem when I hang out with you. If you don't mind dropping me back here later, let's go."

"All right."

First, I called Daryl. "It's Dan, I'm on the road," I said. "By the way, a friend of mine, an ex-cop, Al Thompson is with me—I had to tell him what's going on with you; hope it's okay."

"No problem, you do what you gotta do."

"No calls about the payment yet?"

"No, but the guy said he might not call until tonight."

"I'd say the odds are pretty good that you won't get a call at all."

"What happened?"

"Nothing. We just showed up at the office of a private investigator, Henry Werner, and found him dead. Shot. Werner's the guy who stole your trash."

"You shitting me? That guy's dead?"

"Yup. Maybe he passed the information on to some-body else and maybe he's not the blackmailer, but there's a chance you're going to be off the hook. Listen, I've got some things to look into today—I'm hoping to go out to Meadowbrook. I'll check in with you later, okay?"

"Yeah, man, but be careful, huh?"

"Thanks. I've got Al with me, we'll be okay."

I called my office to let them know I wouldn't be in later. Then I tried Linda Redmond. But she didn't an-swer. I'd wanted her to call Gloria Duchesne and have her waive the attorney-client privilege so that I could read the files Wells kept on her concerns. I put the cell phone down in the car for a moment and drummed the steering wheel with my fingers before making the call to Duchesne. Then it occurred to me there was another way to skin the cat, or catch a killer.

I called the nursing home where May Dern lived. It took a staffperson a few minutes to find her and get her on the phone, but I finally was able to speak to her.

"Hi, Ms. Dern, this is Dan Kardon. You may remem-ber me from the other night—I came by to ask you about the private investigator."

"Oh, I remember you, Mr. Kardon. And I've heard all about your being kidnapped from our parking lot and thrown in that cabin that burned. My, my—we've never had such excitement out here. And of course, now I'm a celebrity because you met with me before all that hap-pened," she said and laughed.

"I'm glad to give you some fame and notoriety, Ms. Dern, and even happier I'm around to hear about it from you. I wondered if I could ask you a favor?"

"Certainly, I'd be happy to help. This is all so interesting."

"That's one word for it." For a moment I thought about not telling her the Werner story, but she seemed pretty strong and would learn soon enough. "And it's getting more so. Mr. Werner, the private eye you hired to find Linda, has just been murdered."

"Oh, my goodness, that's awful! What's happening, Mr. Kardon? Have people in this town just gone crazy?"

"I don't know, Ms. Dern. Maybe that's it. But I think somebody's crazy like a fox, and I'm hoping we're getting close to finding out why. It might help me to look through the files that Chuck Wells kept concerning your legal matters and Linda's. Would you mind if I took a look at the files? I'm not looking for personal material, just information that might help me understand what's going on."

"Of course you can look at the files. I don't mind what you see—Linda says you're a very nice and honorable man."

"Thanks, Ms. Dern. I'm going to call Gloria Duchesne, who—"

"Oh, I know Gloria well. She did almost all the work in Chuck's office, I always thought."

"I'm going to try and reach her, and have her call you. If you can just tell her to release your files to me, that would be great."

"I'd be happy to."

"I appreciate it. I tried to reach Linda just now and she didn't answer. I hope you'll tell her we talked."

"It's no problem, Mr. Kardon."

"Could you also ask Linda whether she'd let us look over her files as well and then call Gloria Duchesne?"

"Certainly. But I do have one question for you."

"Sure, Ms. Dern."

"Are you sure that the lady in your life approves of this dangerous life style of yours?"

I laughed. "No, she doesn't. But if you're asking if I'm going to be available to go out with Linda anytime soon, I don't think so. And I don't expect she'd approve either. Sorry."

"Well, no harm in asking. I hope I don't offend you."

"No, Ms. Dern, no offense taken. Linda's got a great aunt."

"Remember, you promised to tell me what this is all about."

"I remember. I'll be in touch."

I got through to Gloria Duchesne at her home. She had finished her work at the office but when I promised her that I'd pay her for her time and that May Dern and Linda Redmond would authorize us to take a look once she called May, she agreed to meet us there. I wanted to see more than just the Dern and Redmond files, but I decided to play that card when we were in the office. She'd have a tougher time refusing me to my face, given all that had happened. Duchesne told me she would tell Roger Vaneck what was happening and I hung up. Once again, we headed out to Meadowbrook.

We reached Wells's office at about 12:30 P.M., carrying in sandwiches and drinks we'd brought for lunch. Before we got started reviewing the files, I wanted to tell Gloria what had happened, in hopes it would shake things loose.

"Thanks for helping out," I said.

"Oh, no problem. My new job doesn't start for two weeks. By the way, I called Roger. He hasn't been in his office today. His secretary doesn't know where he's gone or when he'll be back."

"Okay, but we may want to look at other files besides the ones kept for May Dern and Linda Redmond. Gloria, you've heard about what happened to me out at the camp last week, right?" I said.

She nodded.

"What you don't know is that this morning, Al and I found a private investigator, Henry Werner, dead in his office. He'd been shot."

Her eyes widened, she let out a gasp, and put her hand over her mouth.

"Did you know Mr. Werner?" Al asked.

"Yes, not well, but he did some work for our office sometimes."

"Had he been in touch with Mr. Wells in the last few months?" Al asked.

"Not that I remember," Gloria whispered.

"Here's the deal," I said. "I believe your boss was involved in something illegal. I don't know what, but I think he and Werner were in it with another person. Maybe what he did is connected to all these killings, maybe not. What I can tell you is that in addition to the murders, a couple people have been blackmailed. For all I know, Wells was also blackmailed into doing something against his will. We'd just like to learn more."

Gloria looked down at the table, her face ashen. "I can't believe it," she said slowly.

"I know it must be hard to think about," Al said. "We don't know for sure that Wells was involved, and we'd be happy to discover he wasn't, but in the meantime we do need your help here, and right away. Things are moving real quick." His voice was quiet and low, and Gloria's face cleared a little as she looked up at him.

"It's just a lot to accept, that Chuck was doing things wrong," she said. "I had a hard enough time when he

was killed. If you're right, then I'll feel unbelievably
foolish and stupid."

"I understand," Al said, "but the best thing you can
do to feel better is to help us figure things out so the
violence stops. If we do something wrong, like look at
files we're not supposed to, it's our problem. You feel
free to tell anybody who asks what we did."

Gloria nodded. "Okay. What can I do to help?" She
assembled the files of May Dern and Linda Redmond
for us on a table. There were nine or ten red accordion
files full of manilla files that were, in turn, full of documents. The files were broken down into correspondence, client papers, notes and working papers, real
estate, and some with estate planning documents. Al
picked out a few things and didn't understand what they
were, but it didn't matter—all we wanted was anything
that referred to Werner.

In my first conversation with her, May Dern had said
that Wells had referred her to Werner and then she had
spoken alone to the private investigator. But I was hoping to find some kind of a report back to Wells, or correspondence that passed between Wells and Werner. I
thought that Wells might have written to Werner, possibly referring to the third person I was convinced was
involved.

Al and I went through most of the Dern-Redmond
files in an hour and came up with nothing. Everything
was straightforward. There was no mention of Werner
in any correspondence we looked at.

As I opened the second to last Dern-Redmond file,
one of the oldest files, which went back at least twenty
years, I shook my head. "Damn. I was certain these files
would give us something to go on," I said.

"Even though we didn't find anything, it doesn't mean

there's nothing," Al said. "These particular documents just aren't going to help us. There are plenty of files we haven't looked at. Plus maybe these guys were smart enough not to put anything on paper."

"I know, I'm just frustrated."

I skimmed through the documents, knowing they were too old for our purposes. I came to a file that contained trust documents and pulled them out. No surprise, the documents indicated that May Dern was the trust beneficiary. The trustee was Chuck Wells. And the lawyer drawing up the trust was none other than Roger Vaneck. Big surprise.

"Gloria," I asked, "did Roger Vaneck and Chuck Wells work together in the law firm?"

"Maybe eighteen or twenty years ago they did. Roger had started the firm, as I understand it, and Chuck joined him. After a few years, Roger went over to work at the bank and eventually became the president. He sold the firm to Chuck."

"You never worked for Roger?" I asked.

"No, that was well before my time."

"So Vaneck and Wells worked together, might have been partners," I said. "Damn, I never knew that."

Gloria reddened a little. "You never asked."

"I don't mean to give you a hard time," I said. "I'm mad at myself. So Vaneck might have known Werner."

"Oh, I know he did," Gloria said. Al and I stared at her.

"Well, I mean, sometimes we had office parties at the holidays and both of them always came. Roger always sent work to us and we used Mr. Werner sometimes. Roger and Mr. Werner certainly seemed to treat each other like old acquaintances."

"If it's Vaneck, then—" Al started.

"Hold it, Al, I've got to make a call," I said.

I grabbed the phone book and dialed a number I'd called earlier. This time, May Dern was in her room and I got her right away.

"Ms. Dern," I said, "it's Dan Kardon."

"Oh, you're a busy one, aren't you? I talked with Gloria—I hope everything's all right?"

"Yes, everything's gone nicely. But I have another question for you. I know that you used the Meadowbrook Savings Bank for the construction loan for the townhouses. Did you have other accounts with the bank?"

"Oh, yes, that was my family's bank for years and years."

"Roger Vaneck helped with the construction loan—was he your regular banker?"

"Yes, after Mr. Smith, the former president, left, Roger helped me with all our accounts until Linda came back, then she took over. But Roger was always looking out for me, very attentive."

"Before Linda came back, did he have you sign papers concerning your accounts at the bank?"

"Certainly. Seems like every year there were more papers to sign."

"Forgive me for prying, Ms. Dern, but were there family trust accounts administered by the bank for you?"

"Yes."

"And did Roger handle those?"

"Well, I assume so. But Chuck Wells was the trustee for those accounts. It was all too much for me. Chuck and Roger worked very well together, so I never had to worry about anything."

I bet they worked well together, I thought. "Did you—"

"Goodness, Mr. Kardon, I just got paged. I need to go."

"Okay, Ms. Dern, thanks, I've got what I need. I'll be in touch soon."

My mind was racing, trying to put things together. "Gloria," I said, "can you dig out the file for the Echo Pond Shores Realty Trust?" I asked. "I don't even need to see it. All I want you to do is confirm one thing for me. I'm guessing that the Echo Pond Shores Realty Trust is a nominee trust, that Chuck was the trustee, and that Roger and maybe somebody else are the beneficiaries. Can you check that for me?"

"Sure, let me look at our index of files. If we're lucky the file won't be in one of the boxes in back."

Gloria checked the computer, then went over to a number of boxes in a corner of the office. She located the box in a pile, pulled it out, opened it, and extracted a file. She then thumbed through documents in the file and finally grabbed what looked like a form and glanced at it quickly.

"You're right. Roger was the beneficiary. You can see it if you want."

Al and I looked at each other. "Bingo," I said. "Just hold on to it, Gloria. Other people may be interested later. But for now, please don't say anything to anyone about what we've talked about or what we've done, particularly Roger. We'll be talking to the police later today and I'm sure they'll be moving on it very quickly. I know this is hard on you, but you've been a big help. Thanks." As promised, I paid her for her time. We all walked outside and Al and I went over to my Blazer.

"You want to go to the local police or your buddy Blocker?" Al knew Blocker from his years as a police chief and from our previous case.

"I guess I'm more comfortable with Randy. I'm still not sure whether it stops with Roger Vaneck. Maybe Sheehan's in there somewhere, and if so, the locals may not want to hear what we have to say. You have a problem with going to Randy first?"

"No, but we probably ought to call right away."

We got in the car and headed east, back to Waltham to pick up Al's car. I let Al drive while I tried Randy's number. He wasn't in but was due back shortly, so I left a message to call me on my cell phone as soon as possible. Al and I agreed that if he didn't call while we were driving, I'd call and page him when we got back to Waltham. Neither one of us wanted to wait much longer. For a few minutes, we both stared straight ahead at the highway. I don't know what Al was seeing, but I saw the form of Werner lying as it had this morning. But on top of it I kept seeing other heads superimposed on the body.

CHAPTER

TWENTY-ONE

Finally I broke the silence in the car and shook my head. "Missed it. It was there all along," I said.

"You think he was taking money from Ms. Dern?"

"Yeah, I think Wells and Vaneck had a little scam going. Linda Redmond told me that when she came back to town, her aunt had less money than Linda anticipated, given all the family should have had. So if he was siphoning off money from Dern, he was probably doing it with other people, other accounts. Gloria Duchesne told me the last time I was there that whenever Wells was about to run out of money, he came up with something. So I'm sure Wells was in on it."

"How'd they work it?"

"Well, it's a small bank, so it almost certainly would have had conflict rules so that Vaneck himself couldn't be a trustee of May Dern's family trust. Instead, Vaneck and Wells set up Wells as the trustee. Vaneck controls things at the bank, Wells controls the information going to May Dern, and they bleed her, each taking something."

"What about the Echo Pond Shores Realty Trust you asked Gloria about?"

"That's a development out by the pond. A few homes are already built—that's where Jordan lives. Sheehan markets the property. There are ten, twelve more lots they're trying to sell with new homes. I thought Sheehan had the real interest in the development through the trust. But if Vaneck owns the property through the trust, then he's the one that's hurt if the prices go down. So he had an incentive to pressure Jerome. And Wells helped him with the trust."

"And if Vaneck's looking for some of the profits from the sale of the properties to cover up money he's taken from other accounts, he's getting nervous since the properties aren't selling."

"You got it. Plus, if he took loans from the bank itself for the development and covered up his involvement in it, he might be in deep shit with the bank. He might even face criminal charges for violating banking laws—insider loans, they're called.

"I feel like such an idiot," I continued. "Vaneck and Wells, a perfect combination. They could do real estate deals, defraud the bank, with Wells filing phony financial statements or other kinds of documents and Vaneck greasing the bank approvals. Wells could get exorbitant legal fees. The two could also refer to each other clients needing both estate planning and investment planning assistance."

"You said Redmond's blackmailer told her to send the payments to a bank account in the Cayman Islands, right? This guy wouldn't have had any problem setting that up."

"Yeah, and Vaneck's involvement in the Wells estate didn't make much sense, except that now I know he was either trying to stall for time or figured out a way to bury any evidence Wells might have kept of what they did together."

We were both quiet for a minute.

"Wells and Vaneck must have had a falling out, maybe over the camp, and Vaneck killed him," I said.

"I wonder what happened with Werner?" he said. "That's another guy who should have been on Vaneck's side. And what about blackmailing Daryl? Did Werner do that on his own or was Vaneck involved?"

"And how about Jerome?" I said. "How did Vaneck know he was at the golf course? I can't imagine Jerome would have arranged a meeting with him out there that late."

"Did anybody else know Jerome was going out there?"

"Only Linda—wait a minute." I banged her number into my cell phone. This time she answered.

"Linda, it's Dan Kardon."

"Hi, you sound upset. Is everything okay?"

"Things are getting a little crazy, I'll tell you about it later. Just one question, if you don't mind."

"Sure."

"The second time you scheduled a meeting with Jerome out at the golf course, did you tell anybody about it?"

"Wow, let me see if I can remember. I know I talked to him just after I missed the first appointment. I don't think I told anybody because I was nervous, and wasn't even sure the morning of that day whether I'd meet Jerome."

"Why were you planning to meet so late in the day? Was that Jerome's choice or yours?"

"I don't remember, but . . ." She paused for a minute.

"Whatever you can remember, please tell me. It's important."

"I had a meeting with Roger Vaneck late that afternoon. We wanted to increase the amount of our loan because of some more renovations we wanted to make. I have a vague memory I told Roger I wanted to meet at a certain time because I had to be at a meeting out by the pond afterward."

"Did you ever tell him you changed your mind, you weren't going to meet with Jerome?"

"No, it never came up in our loan meeting and I certainly never told him I was going to meet with Jerome."

"What did you do that day after meeting with Vaneck?"

There was silence for a minute. "I drove out to the golf course, pulled into the parking lot, then left and went home. I just couldn't do it. Dan, what's wrong? Why are you asking about what I did, and about Roger Vaneck?"

"Linda, I don't want to say anything out of turn here, but don't talk to Vaneck, okay? I'll get back to you soon."

She wasn't reassured but I didn't want to start spreading stories without nailing it further. I related what she'd told me to Al.

"By then, he was blackmailing her. Maybe he was nervous and followed her just to see what she was up to, then decided to confront Jerome."

"Yeah, or else he suspected she contacted Jerome either for help or to try to warn him off in some way."

We were both quiet, assimilating what we'd learned. I tried Daryl on the cell phone once more and again got a message.

For something to do while the miles flew by, I called

my office and I retrieved my messages off our voice mail system.

"Oh, shit," I said, playing back the last message.

"What?" Al said.

I listened to make sure I had it right, then put the phone down.

"Daryl called about three hours ago," I said. "Left a message that he wanted me to go to his house if I can for a meeting. He got a call and agreed to a meeting there scheduled for three-thirty." The car's clock read 3:07.

"What's the problem?"

"The meeting's with Vaneck."

Al nodded. "That's a problem. How far are we from Daryl's house?"

Thankfully, Weston was not far off our route. "Everything goes right, twenty to thirty minutes."

The car sped up. "Tell me the quickest way to get there."

I put in another call to Randy. He still wasn't back, so I left another message and also paged him. But since he wouldn't be familiar with my cell phone number on his pager, he might or might not get back to me quickly.

I directed Al off the highway, down a couple of major roads, and then to the back roads in Weston. As we drove, I described the house to Al and we talked about various ways to approach it.

"You have any kind of weapon with you?" Al asked.

"Nope. You?"

"No. But, son, I got to say, you call me again, I'll be packing."

We pulled up at Daryl's house. The gate was closed and we couldn't drive through without asking somebody on the intercom for the gate to be opened. We didn't want to give ourselves away yet, so we parked outside on the street and took a look inside. We could see two of the bigger cars there, though Wanetta's Porsche was missing. There was also a silver Mercedes sedan, presumably Vaneck's, parked in front.

Al and I walked around the house, going through the adjacent woods and in the back gate that Daryl left open and that Werner had used. Al and I worked out a plan. To get to the back of the house, we had to cross a stone patio that led up to some large windows and a back door. Apart from some metal patio furniture and a fancy gas grill, there was nothing to hide behind.

We took a quick look at each other, nodded, and moved across the patio, listening and looking for anything unusual. Nothing happened and we stopped at one of the back corners, next to the back door. Al gestured that he was going forward, then moved up along the side of the house toward the front. I followed. Every time we came to a window, one or both of us ducked low and peeked inside the house from a corner or side of the window. When we got to the front of the building, we had seen neither Daryl nor Vaneck.

At the front corner of the house, Al and I spoke in low voices.

"I'm guessing they're in the smaller den off the hall, to the right, or in the big recreation room at the end of the hall," I said. "Those are the most obvious rooms if Vaneck went in the front door."

"Let's cross the front, see if we can see anything on the other side."

We did that, seeing nothing in the windows of the formal living room. But on the far side, I was able to get a look in the corner of the window of the smaller den. Daryl sat in a large leather chair, his face partially facing the window and partially toward Vaneck, who sat with his back three-quarters to the window in a wooden armchair, holding a pistol loosely on Daryl.

I slid down next to Al and motioned him to move to the back. When we reached the patio, we stopped.

"They're in the small den and Vaneck has a gun," I said.

Al pulled the cell phone out of his pocket. "I'm calling the police. If I can't get Randy right away, I'll call the locals."

"I'm going in, if I can," I said. Al looked at me.

"They'll have people here in five minutes."

"You've seen what this guy did to Werner. We can't predict what he'll do. I can't give him another minute."

There was a pause. "Be careful," Al said. "Try to divert him, distract him till we get there. I'll tell them to come in without the sirens, keep from spooking him any further."

I walked over to the back door and pulled out the set of Jerome's keys that Daryl had given me. Daryl had said the set included a key to his house—I just didn't know which one it was. Even if I had a key to the house, it might not work on the back door, but I had to check it out as it was the only way to get in without raising a racket.

Another obstacle was stuck to a corner of the window of the door, a decal showing that the house had an alarm system. I couldn't do anything about it and had to hope the system had been disarmed.

The key chain had eight keys on it. The first six didn't work; the seventh did. I turned the key, opened the back door slightly, and stayed down on the ground, ready to roll in if necessary. I waited for a minute. The alarm didn't go off so I stepped inside.

I could hear Daryl's low voice but I couldn't make out what he was saying. Then I heard Vaneck's voice clearly.

"Screw that, Mann. I tried being reasonable. I've offered you all sorts of alternatives. Nothing satisfies you. Nothing made your cousin happy, either. You want it all but neither of you offered me a damn thing. No more deals." Vaneck gave a high-pitched cackle.

Again I heard Daryl respond. Even in the short time I listened, Vaneck's speech became louder, faster, more erratic. "Hitting you up for a little cash 'cause you're a fairy," he said. "Big fucking deal. That was Werner, always sleazy, looking for the quick hit. I just wanted the damn camp gone, the water back. But no, you had to turn your goddamn cousin into a martyr. Well, you're about to join him at the great campfire in the sky."

Al had suggested a diversion, but it didn't sound like I had much time. I opened the door to the large walk-in closet near the back door, the one where Daryl had said he kept his sporting gear. There were basketballs and footballs on the floor, softballs, golf clubs, tennis rackets, and baseball bats. For a moment I thought about picking up a softball, a baseball bat, or one of his larger golf clubs. Then I saw the gun.

It looked like a funky machine gun. About two and a half feet long, it was silver and black, with a large bore barrel and a chamber to hold the ammunition. I opened it up and saw it was loaded. So I took it down from the bracket holding it on the wall and held it in front of me, just like the guys with machine guns in every action movie I'd ever seen. Except this wasn't a movie.

As silently as I could, I walked out of the closet and moved down the hall quickly. I stopped when I stood next to the door of the small den.

"How you going to arrange it?" Daryl asked. "Make it look like a suicide?"

"No, too much work," Vaneck said. "Murder during a robbery. It worked for Wells and Werner, it's good enough for you."

I stepped into the doorway, gun held with both hands in front of me. Daryl still sat in the armchair, but Vaneck was standing in front of him, pointing the gun at him.

"Afternoon, Roger," I said. "Put the gun down and move over into the corner."

Vaneck was startled and took a step back. His gun hand wavered for an instant but then he steadied and kept the pistol trained on Daryl. Vaneck looked at me. Daryl gave me a slight nod then tilted his head toward Vaneck's legs.

"What the fuck is that, Kardon? You got an industrial size water pistol there? You gonna squirt the hell out of me and hope I melt away like the Wicked Witch of the North? Put that toy down or both you and the All-Star die."

"That happens, no getting away for you, Vaneck. The police know what I'm doing, where I am. And no, this isn't a water gun, real bullets come out of this." Vaneck kept looking at me while Daryl gave me a slight nod.

"Why not turn over the gun, end it here?" I said.

"What do I have to lose? You fuckers have already ruined me."

"You killed Wells. Why?"

"No harm telling you, I guess. He betrayed me, started doing deals with that asshole Sheehan. I'd gotten rid of Sheehan at the bank—I sure as hell didn't want Wells helping him compete with me on deals.

"He also started chickening out. We'd made money on a few bogus real estate projects, skimmed a little from a few clients together. I helped Wells, he helped me. Then he started screwing up—didn't tell me about the damn camp Jerome wanted until late—and he was soft on Linda Redmond. Plus a few of his other clients were starting to squawk, so he was trying to weasel out of things. That night, he was plastered, we argued. I hit him over the head with his own damn baseball bat, I got so pissed—he was going to ruin it all."

"How does Linda Redmond figure in?" The more Vaneck talked, the better the chances the police would show up.

"Bitch took her aunt's accounts away from me. We'd gotten steady money out of them over the years, till she came back to town. Then when they came in for a loan to do the mansion and filed financials, I realized Redmond had some cash herself. Werner helped me out on her background. All I wanted was some easy money out of her, but Wells and Werner turned out to be greedy, yellow skunks. Both sons of bitches tried to sell me out." No honor among thieves, imagine that.

"Why Jerome? What did he do to deserve to die?"

"I—hey, get back in the seat, Daryl." Daryl slid back in the seat he'd moved up on as I talked with Vaneck. Vaneck took another step back to maintain more distance. The gun stayed on Daryl, his eyes on me.

"Simple. I had all those properties on the pond to market. Jerome showed up with the damned camp. You think people would pay top dollar with gangbangers and graffiti artists right next door? Then Jerome dropped the water level. Made it even tougher to get good prices. I tried to reason with the man, but he wouldn't budge. I figured Mr. Basketball here would get rid of the property, I'd make my money, get out clean. Instead, he got sentimental and sloppy over his goddam cousin." Vaneck's voice was rising, he was breathing harder, and his eyes were narrow and fierce.

"And dumping me in the canteen? That was you and Werner?"

"Yeah, that was easy. You'd become too much of a pain in the ass. I don't know how you got out of there—we'd checked it beforehand."

"Well, you're not getting out of this one, Vaneck. Too many bodies, too much damage done, and you're making mistakes. Time to give it up."

"Not quite. Kardon, you almost messed things up royally. But now, it's nice, I get to wrap up two loose ends at once. And with you guys gone, I'll leave town for a while, follow some of the money I've shipped off-shore. A happy ending for me. But not for you. Say goodbye—" Vaneck turned his gun hand my way.

"Down," I yelled, dove forward on my knees and down to my left, and fired my gun. Vaneck brought his around and fired at where I'd been standing. His first shot went high, both because I had dropped and because the pellet I'd fired from the paintball gun had caught Vaneck flush in his stomach and knocked him back, splattering green paint as it did. My gun was an automatic. The second pellet hit him in the neck. My third shot splattered against the wall, sending paint everywhere, while Vaneck's next shot went into the ceiling, mostly because Daryl had hit the floor and thrown a rolling block into Vaneck's knee.

The block sent Vaneck backward and mangled his knee. Vaneck fell screaming to the floor, then tried to sit up and fire at me as I rushed in. Lying on the floor, Daryl reached over with a massive hand and grasped the gun, pushing Vaneck's arm away. Vaneck screamed something incomprehensible and grabbed at the gun with his other hand. There was a quick struggle over the gun and it went off.

Daryl rolled back on the floor with his eyes closed. Then he opened them and looked at me. "Got lucky," he said. I looked at Vaneck. The shot caught him square in the chest.

About then, Al Thompson and a number of Weston police came storming in the back door, guns drawn.

"We're okay," I said to Al. Daryl and I stood up. "Don't think Vaneck will make it."

"One of these days, maybe you'll leave something for me to do, Dan," Al said, scanning the room and seeing the paintball gun, "and next time we get you a real gun." I tried to laugh, but nothing came out.

A couple of the cops went over to Vaneck and checked him for a pulse. They didn't find one. Another cop got onto a radio.

Daryl stood up. The pistol he and Vaneck had fought over lay on the floor. Daryl looked around the room. There was paint all over the place, plus a few holes in the walls and ceilings. Daryl turned and looked at the cops.

"You don't mind," he said, "we'll wait in the kitchen." Al waved us away. We walked down the hall without saying anything, then we each grabbed a glass of water.

"Thanks," Daryl finally said. "Been around guns all my life, but never looked down the barrel of one. Kind of gives you a different view of things. That, plus Jerome getting killed."

"Yeah, I can see that," I said. "I'm just happy you're still around to have a view at all."

He shook his head, gave me a grin, and threw an arm around me. "You're one crazy dude. You jumped in that door with the paintball gun, I nearly pissed my pants."

"Sounded like Vaneck had just about lost it—seemed like a good idea at the time. And now that you mention it, how many of those four hundred bucks an hour suits you got on retainer would do that for you?"

"Those guys would have had the brains to hire somebody with a real gun."

"Yeah, but think how much more damage they would have done to the den."

Within minutes Randy was there with some state troopers. Then we were all shepherded to separate rooms while the police took statements. When that was done, they let Al and me go. Daryl's house was a crime scene but his life was no longer on the line.

In the next two days, I spent more time with the police while bank regulators went through the Meadowbrook Saving Bank's records. Ultimately, they determined that Vaneck had been dipping into a few accounts for a long time, with Vaneck benefiting far more than Wells. The regulators also found some phony real estate deals thrown in. The embezzlement grew much larger in the last few years, when the fortunes of the bank went down. Vaneck, in particular, saw his financial situation decline. The value of Vaneck's stockholdings fell dramatically even as his expenses—a big new house, kids starting college, lots of other bad stock purchases made on margin—piled up. Vaneck had apparently taken a big chunk of money to put together the Echo Pond Shores Realty development. He rushed it along as fast as he could, using Wells to help get the permits for the town and Jordan to build the houses. If the homes sold as he'd planned and at the prices he'd wanted, he would have covered most of the accounts he'd raided and made some money. But then Jerome came along.

We never found out for sure what happened between Vaneck and Werner. We speculated that Vaneck went ballistic when he found out that Werner had blackmailed Daryl on his own, jeopardizing what Vaneck was trying to do. But the truth of what happened, and Daryl's secret as well, died with them.

On the Thursday morning after Werner and Vaneck both died, I got on a plane to Johnson City, Tennessee. Jenny expected me the next day, but I couldn't wait. I touched down and drove out to her family's house, which was set below a hill just outside of town.

I arrived just before two on a hot, humid day. The fields on the way out to the house were a deep, gorgeous green. Some of the pastures contained cows, others had horses.

The house was a small ranch on a road with others like it. There were a couple of cars in the driveway, so I hoped to catch Jenny before she went off to visit her father, still in the hospital.

I rang the doorbell and heard her call out "Just a minute."

She opened the door, looking down to pick up a mop and bucket that had fallen as she arrived at the door. Her hair was tied in the back. She wore dirty cut-off jeans and a short-sleeve blue polo shirt frayed at the edges. Her face was sweaty and smudged with dirt. In her other hand, she held a dirty rag and a plastic bottle of cleaner. No matter how I looked at her, she was drop-dead gorgeous.

"Hi," I said, "can I interest you in a new cleaning product we have on the market?"

She looked up, yelled, threw down the cleaning stuff, and hugged me tight. I helped her clean the rest of the house, but not until the next day.

CHAPTER————

TWENTY-TWO

E arly in July, in the hot, unairconditioned gym in the town hall of Meadowbrook, a crowd gathered to attend a special meeting of the zoning board of appeals. Outside, a series of storms were coming through the area, periodically sending down sheets of rain as well as occasional flashes of lightning and peals of thunder. The only item on the agenda was whether the board should award a special permit to Daryl for the camp.

After the meeting was called to order, Brown, the chairman of the board, called Daryl up and gave him the floor. Sheehan was in the audience this time, not up with the board. Daryl turned his back on Brown and the board and squared away in front of the audience.

"I'm not a politician and I don't do speeches. What I can tell you is, I get the permit, we'll live up to the deal we've promised the town. And we'll run a great camp for kids. If I don't get the permit, I sell the land, with first dibs to Arthur Dennison, if he wants it back. If he doesn't, it goes to the highest bidder, and believe me, we've got some high bidders out there.

"Last time I was here," he continued, "Jerome was alive. Nobody had tried to fry Dan Kardon in a cabin. Roger Vaneck did these things, and he came close to killing me too. Some say that Vaneck was just a greedy man, not a racist, and nobody else has responsibility for what happened. But I'm guessing most of you know it isn't quite that simple.

"This town has good people in it. Some of you have been in touch with me, with Dan Kardon, as we've set up the golf course and camp. But this town also has some hateful people in it, people who live in fear of anybody different, who've used fear and corruption to get power. And they've used power to get what they want. I'm going to tell you about a couple of those men.

"George Sheehan pretends to care about this town. All he really cares about is lining his pocket and keeping control. Sheehan did everything he could to keep us out. He told the board what to do the first time around. Then when we offered to negotiate a deal that would have helped the town, Sheehan wouldn't even talk to us. Maybe you folks are intimidated by him, maybe he's done a lot of you favors, but to me, he's a little tyrant. He'll do anything to stay in power, including screw anybody who gets in his way. That means any of you, if he decides it'll help him." A number of people hissed and booed at Daryl, some waved their hands at him, but then a few clapped, and then a few more. It wasn't a large ovation, but it was a surprise nonetheless, and you could hear the buzz in the audience. Daryl kept looking out over the crowd, his face impassive, his voice dense and implacable.

"Also, the last time I was here," he continued, "another neighbor of yours, Tom Jordan, made a nice speech during the hearing. Thought you might like to hear it again." Daryl motioned to me. I turned on a tape recorder and played it over the public address system, as we had arranged. We played Jordan's full statement opposing the camp, including his "I'm not a racist" line. When that tape ended, Daryl spoke again.

"After Jerome lowered the water in the pond, he got a bunch of calls and phone messages from angry people in Meadowbrook. None of the people who left messages had the guts to leave their names, only their vile, disgraceful comments. I'm not going to tell you what most of those messages said. Don't want you going home tonight sick, angry, disgusted with your friends. But I'm going to play one message that was left on Jerome's tape. In fact, just to make sure you hear it, we'll play it twice."

I turned on the cassette player and the same voice we'd heard on the previous tape, the voice of Tom Jordan, one of the voices that had so sickened me when I played back the tape in Jerome's office, filled every corner of the large room.

"Get the water level back up before we plug the dam with your fat, black ass. Or maybe we'll cut off your dick and stick it in the eighteenth hole."

The room was silent. I rewound the tape in a few seconds and played the message over. Tom Jordan sat in the middle of the crowd, his arms folded tight across his chest, scowling. A few people hissed and gave low boos. People around him stared, pointed, and whispers began to build into a low hum. A few people called out to Jordan, reprimanding him. There were no hisses or boos directed at Daryl this time.

Daryl raised his arms, and the crowd slowly fell quiet.

"One last thing. Jerome Mann had a vision for the camp. He loved the pond. He believed in the people of this town. He thought that even if some people stood in the way of the camp, others would push for it. That's all I'm asking tonight. That the good people, the hard-working people of this town, the people who can still recognize the power of a dream to help a few kids see a better life, do the right thing and tell this board how to vote.

"But there's one thing I've done. I've done it because there's been too much bloodshed already. And because I believe you'll do the right thing. Two days ago, we closed the gate on the dam. The rain coming down to-night is raising the pond level back. We'll keep the gate closed until the pond is all the way up." The hall was absolutely still for a moment, then the murmurings and whispering began anew.

"The floor is yours," he said to Brown, the chairman. Daryl and I walked out the door of the hall, hearing the start of a small ovation.

Outside, he turned to me with a smile. "You know what I've always loved best? Not hitting the shot to win a game at home in the last seconds in front of a wild crowd. Silence, man, silence. I love to play in front of a crowd on the road, having 'em roar for their team and then, at the end, shut them up with a big shot. Feels so good to put people in their places." Later that night, after a long, raucous meeting, the board did the right thing. And a few days later, word came back to me through Lieutenant DeRosa that a couple of Jordan's workmen had admitted to helping Jordan beat me up outside the restaurant, apparently on directions from Sheehan.

Though it wasn't billed that way, a two-part memorial service for Jerome occurred in November. On the first Thursday of the month, Daryl put together a musical tribute to Jerome at Mann's Best Hope. A bunch of the bands who had played there when Jerome ran it came and played, all with stories about Jerome. It was a wonderful night, with friends from all the parts of Jerome's life in attendance—people from his real estate and business worlds, from high school and college, from the Shamrocks and basketball, and even a few from Meadowbrook, including Arthur Dennison, Linda Redmond, and Aunt May. I introduced Linda to Jenny and then got as far away from the two of them as I could for the rest of the night. I got Mike Steiner in the door for a little while so he could get a bunch of autographs.

At midnight, Whose Muddy Shoes came on to finish things. It was the band that Jenny and I had seen Jerome play with and the last band, it turned out, that Jerome sat in with. They played a couple of songs and then introduced "Bad Moon Rising." They talked about how well they'd played it with Jerome. They played it well again, with feeling, and the crowd responded, but to me, the band still needed a harmonica.

The next night, Friday night, the Shamrocks opened their season at home. Jenny and I attended with Mike Steiner, Al Thompson, and Randy. The Shamrocks were playing their long-time rivals, the Knicks. We had seats right behind the bench, and they'd had to jury-rig an area for Mike's wheelchair.

The Knicks won the opening tap. They worked the ball around the perimeter until Allan Houston took a jump shot from the right just inside the three-point line. The ball hit off the rim and Daryl came down with the rebound.

He made a beautiful outlet pass to the guard, then took off down the floor. He beat everybody else on the Shamrocks to the basket except for the man with the ball, who left it for him perfectly as Daryl trailed behind. Daryl dunked it and the crowd gave a roar.

After the first period, Daryl had fourteen points, at least six rebounds, and three steals. He was all over the place, moving with and without the ball, disrupting the Knicks on defense and then sprinting downcourt to key the offense.

In the second period, Daryl stayed inside, pounding the glass and working for lay-ups on the offensive end. The coach tried to substitute for him at one point and Daryl waved it off. The Shamrocks were leading by only eight at that point. According to another player quoted after a game, the exchange went:

"Daryl, take a break, we want you fresh later," the coach said.

"Coach, this one's for Jerome. Leave me in. I'm carrying these boys tonight, long as it takes."

On the Shamrocks' first offensive possession of the third period, Daryl ran down inside, where he'd been most of the second quarter, then circled back out to the wing. One of the guards hit him with a pass in the corner. Daryl turned and threw up a three-point shot. It was a shot he'd never have taken in earlier years and probably couldn't have made. But the summer in the gym paid off and the ball went in cleanly. The crowd, still returning from the break, started buzzing. By the end of the third quarter, Daryl had thrown in five more uncontested outside jump shots, simply because nobody expected him to take them. And the Shamrocks led by fourteen.

Another five minutes into the fourth quarter, with the lead up to twenty-three, the Knicks threw in the towel. They pulled their starters and sent in the second string. Daryl didn't care. He continued at a manic pace, rebounding inside, scoring from the outside, running the fast break.

With four minutes to go, one of his teammates was fouled and went to the free throw line. Daryl bent over and put his hands on his knees, breathing hard. He looked over to the bench and nodded. The coach sent in a substitute and Daryl walked slowly off the floor. The crowd rose to its feet and let out an enormous roar. The sound went on for at least two minutes. His teammates clapped and high-fived him; even a couple of the Knick players, perhaps mindful of Daryl's loss, nodded his way.

Daryl had asked me to come to the locker room after the game for a minute and gave me a pass to do so. I left the others waiting, with Al and Jenny listening to an ecstatic Mike Steiner recount the highlights.

I arrived in time to see Daryl head to his locker. But before I could approach him, and before he sat down, a group of fifteen or twenty sports writers, television and radio reporters, and cameramen besieged him. He stood up against the lockers, shaking his head at the commotion in front of him. They all questioned him at once, sticking microphones in his face.

"One at a time," he finally called out. He saw me and pointed his finger at me over the crowd.

A sportswriter called out, "Great game, Daryl, but your scoring was a big surprise, given the injury last year. You must feel pretty good about how you and the team played."

"Yeah. Good win, nice start to the season." Daryl pointed at a sportswriter for the *Boston Globe*. "Bob, put down that I dedicated the game to my cousin, Jerome Mann. He was a great player and a better guy. Wanted to do right by him, so this feels fine. 'Course, didn't plan on sending this shirt off to the Hall of Fame, but now I might have to," he said as he took off his kelly green jersey.

"What do you mean?" the *Globe* sportswriter asked.

"My new record. Expect I have the most points ever scored in an NBA game by a fairy."

Silence followed for a moment. A couple of his teammates, dressing at their lockers, looked up at Daryl, their eyes open wide. Then the tumult began. I smiled and caught Daryl's eye, giving him a wave. Daryl gave a wave back, told the reporters "no more tonight, boys" and walked through the crowd toward the shower.